The Other Guy's Bride

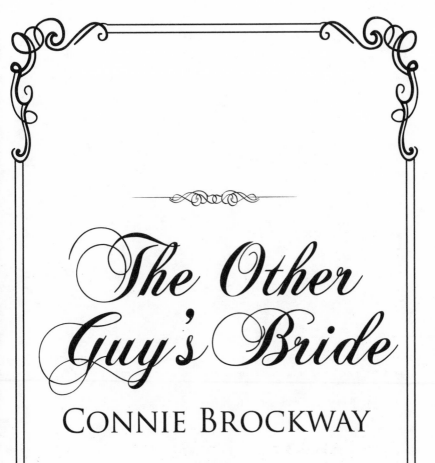

The Other Guy's Bride

CONNIE BROCKWAY

Montlake
Romance

Printed in the United States of America.

Photos from the Library of Congress

Cover design by Dana Ashton France

Published by Montlake Romance
PO Box 400818
Las Vegas, NV 89140

ISBN-13: 9781612181448
ISBN-10: 1612181449

Author's Foreword

In writing *As You Desire* (www.amzn.com/B004CFAWRU), the story of Desdemona Carlisle and Harry Braxton, I prefaced the initial chapter with the year 1890, when in fact, I'd meant to write 1880. Anyone who follows my posts on Facebook (www.facebook.com/ConnieBrockwayFans) or Twitter (www.twitter.com/ConnieBrockway) or who has had the misfortune of exchanging e-mail with me will hardly be surprised. Like Harry Braxton, I experience a mild degree of visual dyslexia. It has made me very fond of copy editors.

Somehow, I doubt the reverse is true.

If you would like to read excerpts from more of my stories, please visit my website at: www.conniebrockway.com.

Thank you!

Connie Brockway

This is for all those kind readers who asked,
"What happened to Harry and Dizzy?"

ACKNOWLEDGEMENTS

I have been wildly blessed in writing this book, and there are a slew of people to thank. First off, thank you Jeffrey Belle at Amazon for calling me up and saying, "I have something I'd like to discuss with you that I think you'll find interesting." It was pretty interesting. (That's Minnesotan for BOOYAH!)

Thank you also to the rest of the great team at Amazon. My thanks to my long-distance editor, Charlotte Herscher, for the kindness with which she identified the flabby parts.

I am one of those fortunate people whose friends are as talented as they are generous. Thank you to Eloisa James, who took the time she did not have to look over these pages; to Lisa Kleypas and Teresa Medeiros for singing "The Little Choo-Choo Train That Could" whenever I began to feel I couldn't; to Christina Dodd, for cackling gleefully from the sidelines; and most of all to my dear friend Susan Kay Law who has my back in so many, many ways. Love you, Suz!

Prologue

"Join the Foreign Legion," the dirt- and blood-stained young man muttered, jamming a cartridge into his rifle's magazine. "If you die, that'll make her sorry, by God." He dug another cartridge out from the bottom of his kit, ramming it alongside its fellow. "Only one problem: you'll be dead a lot longer than she'll be sorry, jackass."

He took a deep breath, counted to five, and stuck his head out from behind the boulder where he'd taken refuge, snapping off a couple of shots as he tried to locate the Mahdist tribesmen hidden amongst the rocks. A dozen reports answered in reply, peppering his face with shards of rock. He jerked back, breathing hard.

He'd counted five guns, but there could easily be ten. They'd been at it for two days now. As of last night he was the only one of his troop left. The rest were dead.

Sweat pouring down his back and soaking his shirt, he squinted up at the sun burning half a hand's span above the western horizon. His face was sunburned and blistered, and he had a hole in his left bicep that screamed bloody hell every time he shouldered his rifle and a broken collarbone that made the hole in his arm feel like an itch in comparison. He hadn't slept in forty-

1

eight hours. He was running low on ammunition and even lower on water. To his south, north, and east were at least five Mahdist gunmen intent on his death while to his west stretched a hundred miles of desert wasteland just as likely to kill him.

The situation did not look promising.

Inside a half hour it'd be dusk, and then, well, a bad situation would turn downright grim. The days were infernos, but at least there was some shade behind the boulder. The nights were worse, a frigid, bone-soaking cold that set your teeth chattering and your body shaking like a rag doll in the jaws of a pit dog. He didn't think he'd survive another night. If he was going to make a move, it had to be soon.

He didn't have much of a plan, more of a half-cocked idea, and since the last half-cocked idea he'd had was to join the French Foreign Legion—despite not being French—he didn't put much stock in it. Unfortunately, it was the only one he had.

He upended his kit, producing his remaining clips. Flicking open his pocketknife, he set to work prying off the tops of the cartridges, emptying the gunpowder into the well-worn folds of a letter he'd carried next to his heart over the past year. He watched the delicate signature disappear under the gunpowder, thinking he'd finally found a good use for the damn thing.

He tore the letter's second page into little squares, funneling a small bit of powder in the center of each and then twisting it into a plug.

"Join the Legion, see the world, die in glory!" he muttered as he worked. The only part of the world he'd seen had been the parched earth of one desert after another. As for glory...He looked around. There was no glory here, only sad, nameless corpses. That he wasn't one of them was a matter of pure chance.

"Too bad, Althea," he muttered, his thoughts turning from the letter's author, Charlotte, to the woman behind the letter—his nemesis, his warden, his guardian, his grandmother. Althea. The malevolent old woman had told Charlotte that Jim was a bastard and that as such he wouldn't inherit anything, not a name, not a place in society, not wealth. Charlotte had believed her because Althea did have a name, a position in society, and wealth.

When he'd confronted Althea, she'd coldly informed him that she would destroy, overturn, and prevent anything that ran counter to her will and it was her will to ennoble the family name, which meant Jim would marry only when and who she chose. The only way he would ever truly escape her influence, she'd said, would be to die.

He'd told her he would never bow to her will and that he would rather die than be her puppet. And then she'd looked him in the eye and told him yes, she would prefer if he died, too, since his younger half brother Jock was so better qualified to make the family proud.

So, he'd made a deal with the devil; he'd shed his name, go away, disappear forever, for all intents and purposes, die. The courts could declare him dead and give everything that should have been his to his half brother, Jock. In exchange, Althea would return the land that had been a bride's gift to her husband's family—and which Althea had inherited from her dead husband—to Jim's mother's family in the New Mexican Territory.

Althea had jumped at the offer.

And so, a little less than a year ago, the boy he'd been had died and James Owens had been born. The only thing he'd kept from his former life had been Charlotte's goodbye letter. Now even that would soon be gone.

"Bloody idiot," he muttered, looking sadly at the flyblown corpse of the horse that had been shot out from under him. "If you were so eager to die, you could have just jumped off Tower Bridge. At least you could have spared a good horse."

As soon as he'd finished twisting the last plug, he ripped a band of material off the bottom of his tattered shirt. He tore it into several thinner strips and tied the ends together, tucking a paper plug in at each knot. Then he rubbed cartridge grease up and down the length of the makeshift fuse.

When he was done, he took off his shirt, belt, and boots, shedding anything that might reflect the sunlight. His plan was simple. Come sunset, when the setting sun briefly blazed right in his enemies' eyes, he'd light the fuse and belly-crawl out to a shallow dip in the ground he'd spotted a hundred yards out. By the time he reached the depression, the linen would burn down to the gunpowder-filled plug, explode, then burn down to the next plug and so on. The Mahdists' eyes would stay on the boulder, thinking he was desperately wasting his last shots while in fact he'd be sneaking into their camp to take off on one of their horses.

That was the theory, anyway.

Because aside from not knowing if the setting sun would be bright enough to cover his scramble for that depression, he had no idea if the linen would burn or how fast it would if it did. And he didn't know if the gunpowder would sound anything like a rifle shot. And even if that all worked out, the rest of his plan depended on his being able to get up on a horse sans saddle but hopefully not sans bit, with a broken collarbone and a bum arm, take off, and stay ahead of his pursuers until he, well, got away.

No, sir, the situation did not look at all promising.

He was good with a horse. Damned good. As a kid, he'd been taken under the wings of his uncle's Comanche ranch hands, the best riders in the world. The question was, was he good enough?

He looked up. The sun had come to rest on the horizon now, spreading colors across the sky as bright yet as delicate as a *houri's* veil. Another minute and it would flare before disappearing. That was his chance, or as much of a chance as he was going to get. He tilted his head back, closing his eyes.

He was twenty years old and he did not want to die. "I swear, God, if I make it out of this in one piece, I'll never, ever do something stupid because of a woman again."

He opened his eyes, rolled over, and began crawling.

CHAPTER ONE

Within the ~~lovely~~ her intrepid young ~~heroine~~ heart awakened a feeling of gladness deeper and richer than anything it had ever before known!

—from the personal diary of Ginesse Braxton

*1905, THE BRITISH PASSENGER SHIP, THE LYDONIA,
BOUND FOR ALEXANDRIA, EGYPT*

"People don't die of seasickness, Miss Whimpelhall," Ginesse Braxton said. She wasn't absolutely certain of this, but she had long held the belief that a thing only counted as a lie if you knew it to be false. Unfortunately, rather than bolstering her patient's spirits, her words seemed to have the opposite effect.

"They should." An older woman dragged herself over the side of her bed and clutched the rails, her long, lank ropes of red hair swinging in time to the ship's pitch and toss. "It…would be…a mercy."

Ginesse patted her patient's hand. She'd spent the last four days listening to variations on this same theme, and while she felt a good deal of sympathy for poor Miss Whimpelhall, she could not really empathize—she had a disgustingly robust constitution.

She stuck her foot out, catching the china basin sliding past on the floor, picked it up, and held it out it invitingly. Miss Whimpelhall shook her head, closing her eyes tightly. After a few seconds, she sank back on the bed. "I am sorry to cause you so much trouble, Miss Braxton. Please, forgive me. I am a terrible nuisance."

"Not at all." Ginesse had never met so meek or apologetic a creature as Mildred Whimpelhall, and as neither Ginesse nor any member of her immediate family was overly familiar with either trait, she was understandably fascinated. Even more fascinating was Miss Whimpelhall's personal story; she was on her way to marry her fiancé, who commanded an English garrison in Egypt. Which made Miss Whimpelhall a bona fide heroine.

Ginesse knew all about heroines. As an only daughter, she'd escaped the unpalatable reality of life with six grubby little brothers into a world of books where men were identified by their gallantry and courage rather than by their farts and belches. Later, after she'd been banished from Egypt to England, she'd assuaged her homesickness by writing her own adventurous tales. Indeed, the penny press had even published one.

Not that she advertised her predilection. She kept it strictly to herself. People, especially men, found it so hard to reconcile a romantic disposition and intelligence. She didn't need any other strikes against her while trying to establish an academic reputation.

Miss Whimpelhall moaned again. "Maybe this is hell," she whimpered. "Maybe this is hell and I'm going to feel like this for the rest of etern...etern...et—" She didn't make it to the end of the sentence. Luckily, Ginesse still held the china basin.

"Well," Ginesse said, a few minutes later, "if this is hell, then I must be a demon, and *I am not a demon*." She chuckled to prove how silly such an idea was. "Oh, my, no. No, indeed."

She waved the air lightly with her hand. "Oh, perhaps comparisons may have been made when I was just a child and like many children given to acting imprudently." Her voice sounded less jovial than she'd have liked. "Nothing that would justify being stigmatized with an unsavory reputation."

She forced her voice to relax. "But as I said, that was when I was just a child. A long, *long* time ago."

A wan smile appeared on Miss Whimpelhall's lips. "So long ago? You are still very young."

"I am twenty-one," Ginesse replied. "And I hold a degree in ancient history and will soon hold another." And, if all went well, she'd soon win the esteem of the archaeological world.

And that of her family.

"Oh." Miss Whimpelhall sounded vaguely disapproving. "Regardless, you have been an angel of mercy to me ever since my faithless maid deserted me at the first port," she said. "How do you manage without one?"

"I've never had one." Her family had never been able to find an applicant who was both suitable and willing, for which frankly she was glad. She couldn't imagine always being shadowed by another person.

"Oh." Miss Whimpelhall nodded. "Well, thank God He put you in the cabin next to mine and gave you the divine inspiration to somehow intuit my distress."

There hadn't been anything divine about it; their adjoining cabins had thin walls.

A sudden wave crashed against the porthole, sending the ship pitching sideways. The door to the wardrobe swung open, flinging Miss Whimpelhall's possessions across the floor.

3

Miss Whimpelhall blanched and groped for a nearby towel, shoving it against her mouth. "I *want* to die. Please. Let me d—"

"Why don't you tell me more about your fiancé?" Ginesse suggested, lurching across the room to gather Miss Whimpelhall's scattered belongings. "You said you've been engaged to him for six years, during which time he has been entirely in Egypt."

"I did?"

"Yes. That must have been very difficult."

"It was. We did see each other occasionally." Miss Whimpelhall held out her hand, and Ginesse put a glass of water in it. She took a sip. "He was granted a four-month furlough two years ago when his father died."

"You must have missed him very much. And he, you. I cannot imagine being separated from a loved one for so long." At least she'd been allowed to return to Egypt for the holidays.

"Life is about making sacrifices, Miss Braxton," Miss Whimpelhall said. "Colonel Lord Pomfrey could not have advanced so quickly to so prominent a position had he remained in England."

"It's a wonder you didn't marry sooner. I'm sure you would have been a great asset to his advancement," Ginesse suggested carefully. She was being unconscionably forward. Her "unlady-like interest in other people's lives" was just one of her unfortunately many character flaws. She couldn't help it. People were a never-ending source of fascination to her.

Miss Whimpelhall didn't seem to take it amiss. "The army frowns on junior officers marrying. It distracts them from their duty in the field. But once they achieve a certain rank, marriage is very much encouraged as a steadying influence. Indeed, in the letter in which he proposed, Colonel Lord Pomfrey wrote that his general quite expected his senior staff to wed."

Ginesse smiled, albeit weakly. She wasn't certain she'd want to be proposed to in a letter, and she definitely wouldn't want someone asking for her hand in order to fulfill his superior's expectations. But then, she was hardly in a position to criticize.

"How *did* he advance so quickly? He must have proved his value in some notable way."

The seas had calmed down a good bit, and Miss Whimpelhall gratefully accepted the distraction, launching into a long and painstakingly detailed answer. Ginesse, who'd already heard most of her stories about Colonel Lord Pomfrey, continued picking up the room, her thoughts drifting to other matters.

This evening they would be arriving in Civitavecchia and from there begin the final leg of their journey to Egypt. Once in Cairo, she needed to find some way, any way, to hire men and porters to take her out to the dig site—generally an easy proposition if one had the necessary funds.

Her problems were twofold. First, she did not have the necessary funds, and second, the archaeological site where she planned to dig at was hundreds of miles out in the Sahara. Even if she did find the money, she stood little chance of convincing anyone in Cairo to guide her across the desert. No one in his right mind would risk endangering Harry Braxton's daughter on such a dangerous expedition no matter how much money she offered them. Of course, she could always claim that she had her father's blessing, but Egyptians were not generally gullible.

No, she would simply have to bide her time, trusting to Fate and her own ingenuity that a way would make itself known. After all, she could never have imagined that while working as a glorified clerk for Professor Lord Tynesborough and transcribing a boring bill of lading for some ancient caravan she'd stumble across a spectacular discovery. At first, she hadn't realized she'd found a clue as to the location of one of the Egypt's greatest legends: Zerzura. The White City. The Oasis of Little Birds. Home to a dead king and queen, guarded by black giants.

When she told Professor Tynesborough about it, he'd discounted it as wishful thinking and deemed it not worth further investigation. Then he'd invited her to dinner.

She'd been *vastly* disappointed. She'd rather liked Professor Tynesborough, the youngest distinguished professor in the history of Cambridge University, and she'd thought he'd respected her. But he'd simply proved to be another man who assumed she didn't know what she was doing.

So, she'd quit her job and begun researching on her own. It took months of laborious hunting and cross-checking, painstaking investigation, and informed guesswork to finally piece the puzzle together, but she had.

She didn't let anyone know what she'd discovered, not her fellow antiquarians or her professors. And most certainly not her family. As much as she loved them, she wanted, no, she *needed* to step out from behind her family's very long shadow and prove herself.

Her father was the most successful locator of tombs in Egypt, and her mother was a linguistic prodigy renowned worldwide for her translations of ancient Egyptian poetry. Her great-grandfather, Sir Robert Carlisle, was the world's leading expert on Egyptian papyri, and her oldest brother Thorne—though two years her junior—was already sought after for his expertise in ancient embalming techniques, an interest she personally thought rather disturbing though no one else seemed to find it so. And at only eighteen years of age, her brother Francis had recently been acclaimed for his uncanny genius in detecting forged artifacts—a talent that sprang, Ginesse suspected, from his skill at manufacturing them.

And she...?

The only thing she was known for was a series of unfortunate incidences in her childhood that had resulted in her being labeled a *djinn* and an *afreet*—Egyptian equivalents of imps and devils—and sent to a boarding school in England. Her parents had assured her it was for her own safety, but it had always felt like exile. She'd been an outsider there, a little too this, not enough that. Ever since she could remember, she'd been defined by her differences.

No more.

Henceforth her achievements would define her. And her first achievement would be discovering Zerzura. That is, if she could get there before Professor Tynesborough. A friend in the library had told her he'd been spending hours in the ancient manuscripts room, poring over the same materials she'd used in her investigation.

Then her great-grandfather had written from Cairo. Sir Robert had convinced the director of antiquities to interview her for an internship position at the Bulak Museum opening later that year. Obviously, Fate meant her to uncover the White City. Then, finally, she would put to rest all the nonsense about her being a jinx, and rather than being a source of amusement—and, yes, apprehension—she would inspire admiration and respect. She would earn her rightful place amongst her celebrated family.

"—a colonel after that, could they? And perhaps later than one would have expected. Though far be it from me to question their wisdom." Miss Whimpelhall's question recalled Ginesse from her daydream."Oh? Oh. Indeed, yes. You paint a most dashing picture."

"Dashing?" Miss Whimpelhall echoed. "That was not my intent. 'Dashing' is not a qualification one seeks in a husband. But I am sure you already know this."

Ginesse did not answer; she considered dashingness to be a definite asset in a husband.

"Oh, my," Miss Whimpelhall tsked lightly. "I can see you disagree. I am loath to take the part of advisor, my dear Miss Braxton, but," her unhappy voice dropped to a whisper, "I know of whence I speak. A beloved cousin opted for 'dashing' over 'dignified' with tragic consequences."

Ginesse was riveted. She leaned forward to catch every word. "Really?"

Miss Whimpelhall nodded. "She became engaged to a man who was not what he claimed to be. Luckily, all was revealed before they wed."

"And the tragic consequences?" Ginesse asked before she could stop herself.

Miss Whimpelhall looked at her askance. "Why, the scandal, of course. She did not even visit London the following Season."

That was the tragic consequences? *She stayed home?*

Miss Whimpelhall nodded sagely. "So, you see, my dear Miss Braxton, how important it is to be wary of 'dashing' gentlemen."

Ginesse had never met a dashing gentleman. In fact, she knew few gentlemen at all except for Professor Lord Tynesborough and her father, who, for unknown reasons, absolutely refused to be called a gentleman. Frankly, she would like to meet a man whose first thoughts in the morning weren't about dusty manuscripts, broken bits of ancient pottery, or desiccated limbs.

"Dashing or not," Ginesse said, "your fiancée is bound to be eager to see you. I imagine he will be waiting dockside, pacing impatiently, wringing his hands, his gaze fixed with expectant longing on every ship that enters the harbor." She sighed happily. "And when he sees you, he will sweep you up in his arms and—"

"Oh no, he will not," Miss Whimpelhall interjected. "He would never subject either of us to so vulgar a display. Colonel Lord Pomfrey is most dignified in all things. As, I hope, am I." Her momentary distress faded. "Besides, he won't be meeting me at all."

"Oh?"

"He cannot neglect his duty as commander and abandon the garrison simply to fetch me. It would be unseemly. And I would never ask it of him."

"Of course not."

"He has arranged for some fellow to escort me to him."

"Some fellow?"

Miss Whimpelhall gave a little shudder. "Yes. Colonel Lord Pomfrey says he is an unsavory character."

Ginesse frowned. "I don't understand. Why ever would your fiancée entrust your care to an unsavory character?"

Miss Whimpelhall flushed at the implied criticism. "Colonel Lord Pomfrey would never—That is, Colonel Lord Pomfrey has explained—Far be it from me to question—Here. Please, read for yourself. Colonel Lord Pomfrey is so much more eloquent than I." She reached behind her pillow and drew forth an obviously much-read letter, peeling off the final page and offering it to Ginesse.

"Oh…I could never…This is private correspondence…" But of course, she could. Even as she was demurring, she twitched the letter from Miss Whimpelhall's fingers and read:

> *After arriving in Alexandria, you will board*
> *the train for Cairo. There, you will be met by a*
> *man named James Owens who will guide you to*
> *the fort. He is a tall, yellow-haired American cow-*

boy with a most harsh aspect, but pray, my dear, do not be alarmed by his appearance. Though he is a ruffian of the highest order, he owes me his life and, rightfully, considers himself in my debt and has long been eager for the opportunity to repay it. He will be accompanied by a half dozen soldiers.

A cowboy! A *ruffian* cowboy! Fueled by dozens of dime novels, Ginesse's imagination immediately conjured up a hard-eyed, weather-beaten hombre in a black ten-gallon hat, a lariat draped around one of his shoulders and a saddle by his feet. Breathlessly, she read on:

I would send a full contingent of my men to escort you to my side were I not entirely certain that such a presence would only serve to provoke the attention of the lawless tribes that roam the desert. Of course, should you encounter them, my men will deal with them with decisive thoroughness, but for the time being, I have been instructed to maintain as peaceful a presence here as possible. Therefore, it is with regret but confidence that I have enlisted Owens, who is intimate with the scoundrels who roam the desert looking for easy prey. As they say, "The best ward against a jackal is a more vicious jackal."

He *was* a scoundrel! How thrilling! But how *dreadful* for Miss Whimpelhall.

You will be safe under Owens's care, though I must warn you to limit your interactions with him so that you are not offended by his rough manner or uncouth ways.

Now I must return to my duties. I most sincerely look forward to seeing you, Mildred. Pray do not wear anything yellow when we meet. I cannot abide the color. Perhaps a dark blue?

Your servant,
Colonel Lord Hilliard Pomfrey

It seemed a rather flat ending for a man to have written a woman he had not seen in two years. There ought to have been a bit more...*oomph*. But then, she was hardly in a position to judge, having never had a suitor, only some educational encounters with the library's would-be Lothario. She was simply not the sort that inspired *oomph*.

She was tall and frankly athletic. Being olive-complexioned, she tanned too easily, and though tow-headed as a child, her hair had turned an unremarkable brown. Though her mother staunchly declared her nose "Florentine" in size and shape, she knew it was simply large, just as she knew her mouth was too full-lipped and too wide. Her only attractive feature was the color of her eyes, an interesting shade of not-quite-blue, nor-yet-green.

Not that she regretted her looks. Her height and strong features made her look formidable, a fact she sometimes used to advantage when dealing with difficult people.

No one, she thought looking at her patient, would call Miss Whimpelhall formidable. Despite the red hair. She had soft, small features with pale skin and light blue eyes, now welling up with tears as the seas grew rougher again. A jar rolled out from under the bunk. Idly, Ginesse picked it up and read the label...

Oh, my. Apparently even the small glory of red hair wasn't Miss Whimpelhall's. Hurriedly, Ginesse tucked the jar of powdered henna into her pocket. The dear lady would be mortified to be caught employing cosmetics.

"So you see, I am to be quite adequately safeguarded," Miss Whimpelhall said. She added fretfully, "Though I do wish Mr. Owens sounded more prepossessing. I am a terrible coward. Not at all like you, Miss Braxton. You would deal much better with a man like Owens than I."

This was undoubtedly true.

"Just look at how you convinced the captain to make that unscheduled stop at Gibraltar. I wish I'd gotten off then."

"Have heart, Miss Whimpelhall. It won't be too much longer before we arrive in Italy. A few hours at most."

"Hours? I don't think I can last hours."

"Nonsense," Ginesse said bracingly. "Why, you haven't emptied your tummy in an—"

Miss Whimpelhall grabbed the basin. A long moment later she raised tragic eyes to Ginesse. Her lips trembled. "I can't do this anymore!"

"Of course you can, and I shall be by your side every mile of the way."

"Mile? *Mile.* Mile upon mile of...heaving...sea...Oh!" She gulped, sweat popping out on her forehead. "I cannot...be...on this ship. Any longer."

"Now, now—"

"I *cannot.* I *will* not," she said, sounding more determined than Ginesse had ever heard her. "I would rather die."

"But what can you do?"

"I will get off in Italy and proceed to Egypt by rail and whatever other means necessary. Will you help me?"

"Of course," Ginesse said. "But I don't really see how much help I can provide. You simply have a porter take your luggage from your room and walk off."

"Oh, Miss Braxton, you make everything seem so easy."

"That's because things generally are," she said with only a passing thought to the problem of Zerzura.

"But what if the captain should protest my decision to leave? I am not like you, Miss Braxton. I find it very difficult to ask men, even porters, to do things."

"You don't ask a man to do something; you tell him," Ginesse said. "Males do not do well with choices. They want direction."

"How ever do you come to know so much about gentlemen at so tender an age?" Miss Whimpelhall asked.

"Having six younger brothers has doubtless afforded me some insight into the workings of the male mind. Though honesty compels me to admit I don't find it a very deep or mysterious realm. What do you wish me to do?"

"After I leave the ship, deliver a letter to the captain. In it, I will explain all. And when you arrive in Cairo, if you would deliver a similar letter to Mr. Owens, I would be eternally in your debt."

"But what of Colonel Lord Pomfrey? How will you get word to him in…Where is he stationed?"

"Fort Gordon," Miss Whimpelhall said. "I shall send him a telegram—Miss Braxton, are you quite all right? You look most odd."

Fort Gordon was located far away in Egypt's western desert at a small oasis. A small oasis not thirty miles away from where she expected to find Zerzura.

It was meant to be. She had known it.

"Miss Braxton?" Miss Whimpelhall asked.

"Yes, yes. I'm fine," she replied. "Just a sudden bit of vertigo." Her thoughts raced wildly, arranging and discarding at lightning speed a dozen plots by which she could take advantage of this unique set of circumstances before quickly settling on one.

"Miss Whimpelhall," she said decisively, "you must let me arrange everything for you. I'll have your luggage removed, deliver your letters to both the captain and Mr. Owens, book your rail ticket to Egypt, and arrange for your transport to the train station. And please, you must not even think of venturing into an Italian telegraph station. Nasty places. Italian men have such... busy hands."

At this, Miss Whimpelhall gave a little whimper. Ginesse offered a silent apology to all Italian men.

"Besides, you don't speak Italian, do you? No? I thought not. I do. You must allow me to send a message ahead to Fort Gordon on your behalf."

"Oh, would you?" Miss Whimpelhall cried, clasping both of Ginesse's hands in hers. "I shall never be able to repay you. Never!"

"My dear Miss Whimpelhall," said Ginesse, smiling fondly. "You already have."

CHAPTER TWO

His stern face had been bronzed by the sun and carved by the wind and held an aloof stillness in his expression that came from years of silence and solitude.

—from the personal diary of Ginesse Braxton

Ginesse pressed her face to the train's window, her lips parting in a slight smile. Even though they'd entered the city through an unprepossessing and newer part of the city, it was still Cairo. It was home.

Minarets pointed heavenward like slender fingers, while beneath them the round domes of the mosques glowed as smooth and white as a concubine's breasts. To the south, the old city jumbled in fanciful confusion along twisting alleys and narrow, rutted lanes in direct contrast to the ponderous purposefulness of the European district with its orderly houses and wide, lebbeck-canopied avenues. The afternoon wind had begun churning dust from the streets and shaking it over Cairo's head like a manic cleaner woman beating a rug, enveloping the city in a shimmering shroud.

Ginesse threw up the window and craned her head out as the train slowed to enter the cavernous Misr Station. On the platform below crowded a mass of people: travelers waiting to board, porters vying for trade, guides shouting their credentials (mostly invented) and fees (mostly exorbitant), beggars pleading for *baksheesh*, and peddlers selling everything from iced lemonade to sticky buns.

James Owens was somewhere among them.

Her heart began to race. She had no cause to feel guilty about her impersonation, she told herself. She wasn't only helping herself, she was also saving Mildred Whimpelhall from a miserable two weeks in the company of an uncouth American cowboy.

It had been easy to assume Miss Whimpelhall's identity. After the gentle lady had disembarked in Italy, Ginesse had sent a message to the captain saying that Miss Ginesse Braxton would not be returning to the *Lydonia* but would instead continue her journey by rail. She'd then taken all of Miss Whimpelhall's luggage to her former cabin to switch them up, but before she could remove her own belongings, the porters had arrived to take all the luggage in the cabin to the dock. She'd only managed to snatch one of her valises. But aside from that small matter, things had gone perfectly.

No one had questioned whether the woman in Miss Whimpelhall's room was, in fact, Miss Whimpelhall. The poor woman had been sequestered in her room with seasickness from the very first day of their voyage. Even the attendants who'd brought Miss Whimpelhall's food and emptied the chamber pot hadn't had more than a glimpse of a prostrate figure with red hair lying on a bed behind a half-drawn curtain.

The red hair had been a matter of concern, of course. Ginesse hadn't been sure the powdered henna she'd liberated from Miss

Whimpelhall was up to the task of convincingly dying her own hair, but four days and eight applications of henna had indeed turned it an exuberant shade. The first thing she'd done in Alexandria was buy some darkened glasses, just in case Colonel Lord Pomfrey had mentioned Miss Whimpelhall's eye color to Mr. Owens. There was no possibility of anyone describing her eyes as light blue.

With that thought, she drew the glasses she'd purchased out of her jacket pocket and put them on. At once she felt more confident. Her impersonation was going to succeed, and once she got to Fort Gordon...? Well, something would occur to her. The Fates had led her this far, and she could not believe they would abandon her at the last minute.

The train squealed to a halt, releasing a cloud of hissing vapor. She stood up, hauled her valise from the rack, and peered out the window, searching for a rough-looking American. A handsome young Egyptian man in a European suit sauntered by below her window. She started, checked, and stared.

It couldn't be.

It was.

Haji Elkamal.

Haji had been the chief tormentor of her childhood. As a teenager, he had occasionally lived with his aunt Magi in Ginesse's great-grandfather's house. As Sir Robert's pet, he'd styled himself as a translator on a few of her great-grandfather's digs. Arrogant, dismissive, and maddeningly superior, he'd made light of her every effort to win approval. When she tried to speak the patois of the workers, he laughed hysterically; when she'd found a mummified cat, he'd disparaged it as common.

Her eyes narrowed. Haji had also been instrumental in her banishment from Egypt. It had been Haji who'd told everyone she'd set fire to that cache of ancient papyrus (which hadn't actually been all that old as far as ancient papyri went).

She tapped her fingers on the sill, thinking. This was no coincidence. Her great-grandfather must have sent Haji to collect her. Drat. Though she'd sent a telegram from Italy saying she'd be arriving in Cairo a few weeks late, she still should have foreseen this. Her great-grandfather had doubtless misplaced her message or, even more likely, never read it. Sir Robert Carlisle had no interest in forms of communication more modern than papyri. He decried the invention called "postcards" as the end of civilized interaction.

She would simply have to avoid Haji, she decided, plopping her hat atop her head. And if he did see her, he probably wouldn't recognize her. They hadn't met in six years, and she was no longer a little girl. She was at least three inches taller than him now, not to mention the fact that her once blonde hair was now very, very red.

Poor Haji. He would undoubtedly waste the rest of the day meeting every train, waiting for her to appear.

It served him right.

She leaned out of the window, watching with a smile as he wended his way through the crowds fruitlessly looking for her. So far, he didn't realize just how fruitlessly. She frowned as he stopped wending and hailed a tall, bare-headed, and disreputable-looking man with dark gold hair and three days' growth of beard.

Oh, no.

She peered more closely. The man certainly looked like a desperado: tall, whipcord lean, with broad shoulders and overlong, sun-streaked hair. His face was hard and still, his light colored eyes narrowed beneath dark brows. He looked stern and uncompromising.

And dirty.

Beneath a rumpled jacket, he wore a sweat-stained cotton shirt, his worn trousers held up by heavy leather suspenders and tucked into scarred, scuffed, knee-high leather boots. A black and white *khafiya*, the traditional desert scarf, was looped around his strong, tanned throat.

Desperately, she scanned the platform, searching for another "ruffian of the highest order." She didn't find any. He could only be James Owens.

As she watched, he pushed off the wall and went to meet Haji, moving with the easy, soft-footed grace of a large cat. A large *dangerous* cat.

Drat and blast. Why did all the scoundrels in Egypt have to know one another?

CHAPTER THREE

The possessor of a fine if slender figure, and ~~prettily~~
chiseled features, set off by starry eyes
and wavy hair.

—from the personal diary of Ginesse Braxton

"Bernie, is that you? It is! Are you mad?"

Only one person in all of Egypt called him Bernie, a curse Jim Owens called down upon himself when he'd instructed Haji Elkamal to send word of his death to a firm of London solicitors. Until that moment no one in Africa had known his real name; he'd enlisted in the Legion under a false one. He'd only given Haji the task because there hadn't been anyone else around when a viper had made a passing stab in his arm. He'd figured someone ought to give Jock confirmation of his death. It was too bad it would have also provided Althea with so much pleasure.

But despite Haji's knowledgeable—and gleefully fatalistic—assurances to the contrary, Jim had survived the viper's bite. Unfortunately, so had Haji's memory.

He turned around. "Don't call me Bernie again. Next time you do, it'll hurt."

"Fine. *James*, are you mad? The chief of police has sworn to have you arrested if you set foot inside the city."

"I've heard."

"LeBouef is looking for you, too, and his intentions are not pleasant. But you already knew that. Why would you risk coming here?"

Jim appreciated Haji's concern, though it was unnecessary. Somewhere during the course of the seven years since they'd met, Haji had turned from Jim's sometime accomplice into one of his few friends.

"Repayment of a debt."

Haji's eyes narrowed then widened. "Tell me it is not so! The repellent Colonel Pomfrey has finally called in his markers?"

"Colonel *Lord* Pomfrey, and yes," Jim said.

"This debt has chaffed you."

Jim didn't bother answering. Of all the people in world who might have stumbled across his half-dead carcass in the desert seven years ago it had to have been then Captain Lord Hilliard Pomfrey, as sanctimonious as he was sartorial and as conscientious as he was condescending. They'd loathed one another on sight, and all future contacts had only deepened their mutual antipathy. Even so, keeping Jim alive must have been some sort of spiritual test that Pomfrey would not allow himself to fail because even though they were deep in the desert, he had turned around and hauled Jim's carcass back to civilization.

He suspected Pomfrey spent every night on his knees annoying heaven with a tally of all the unreciprocated good deeds he'd done in his campaign for sainthood. Jim figured his name was near the top of the list. Over the years that idea had gone from irritating Jim to flaying him like sands whipped up by a windstorm.

"I have never understood why you feel so strongly about paying off this one particular debt," Haji said.

"A gentleman always pays his debts. No matter what the coin. No matter how long it takes." It was a lesson learned long ago, one of the few recalled from the life he'd abandoned.

"Gentleman," Haji scoffed lightly. "What the devil do you care if Pomfrey thinks you're a gentleman?"

"I don't," Jim said. "I care what I think."

"Aha! The iconic Wild West code of honor?" Haji brightened.

Jim didn't bother arguing. It wouldn't have done any good. Haji was a sucker for pulp fiction set in the American West.

"How is this debt of honor to be repaid? Are you to transport opium? Kill his rival?" Haji asked.

Jim raised an eyebrow. Either his reputation was a lot more interesting than he'd realized or Haji's concept of debt repayment was a lot more far-reaching. "Pomfrey? Ask me to do something illegal? Immoral?"

"Of course. A man could only be so ardently concerned about his immortal soul if there is cause."

Jim entertained the idea of Pomfrey as a secret vice lord for a few pleasant seconds before giving it up. "Sorry to disappoint you, but nothing as exciting as mummy stealing or drug running."

"But you are a mercenary," Haji pointed out.

"I prefer soldier of fortune," Jim said.

The Legion had listed him as dead along with the rest of his patrol. He decided to let the record stand. Since then he'd lived an eventful life in Egypt and North Africa, often crossing the line of what he knew to be ethical. Hell, he hadn't only crossed it; he'd left it so far behind he couldn't make it out anymore.

But no matter what he had done, he'd always remained grimly determined to repay his debt. He figured every man was entitled to a few illusions about himself, and one of his was that he still had some honor left. In a matter of two months, that is all he would have left of his former life. In two months Althea would appear before the courts and have him declared legally dead. Two months.

"So, what *has* Pomfrey demanded that you do to settle the account?"

"I'm to collect his fiancée off that train," Jim said. "Miss Mildred Whimpelhall."

"What? *You?* You are to play *terrassieur* to a lady?" Haji asked, choking on laughter at the thought of Jim in the role of paid male companion. "Where will you go first? The pyramids? The museum? Perhaps you can visit—"

"Shut up, Haji."

"I can't! It is too wonderful. Who would have thought Pomfrey capable of such subtle and adroit malice?" Haji asked. "I swear I am forced to reconsider my opinion of him. I wouldn't have credited him with so much imagination. To demand repayment for having saved your life in so banal a currency! There could be no more supreme declaration of how utterly inconsequential he considers you. It is sublime."

"I'm not her tour guide," Jim said. "I'm taking her to Pomfrey at Fort Gordon."

The hilarity faded from Haji's face. Fort Gordon was deep in the Sahara, near the Sudan border, a dangerous and hostile place. "I thought Pomfrey was in Luxor? When was he given the command of Fort Gordon?"

"Eight months ago. Really, Haji. You gotta keep up with the times. How are you going to know whether to duck or run if you don't know who's standing behind the gun?"

Haji ignored him. "Why didn't Pomfrey send soldiers to escort her?"

"He has. Half a dozen men. They're waiting for us upriver at Suhag. All I have to do is get her there. After that, I'm just the guide."

"Half a dozen men seems inadequate. Why not more?"

"Because what with his winning ways, Pomfrey has already managed to make enemies of all the local tribes. He's afraid that sending a slew of soldiers to fetch his fiancée would be advertising a hostage for the taking. I tend to agree. He thinks I'm his best chance of getting her to Fort Gordon without incident. I tend to agree with that, too."

Haji looked skeptical. "Really?"

"I might not speak the local dialect, but I haven't pissed anyone off, either. I figure two weeks or so and Pomfrey and I are quits."

Haji rubbed his cheek thoughtfully. "Whimpelhall. An interesting name. Is she pretty? I bet she is not. Pomfrey would never take a wife prettier than himself."

Jim disagreed. "Pomfrey would never take a wife other men didn't covet."

Haji considered this a second and then shook his head. "No. She will be ugly. I will bet you an English pound."

"Done."

"What else do you know about her?"

"She's a spinster, a redhead, and Pomfrey says I'm not to 'offend her delicate sensibilities' by attempting to converse with her, as she is a shy and genteel lady."

Haji grinned. "Oh, you'll offend her, all right. What are you thinking, James? Meeting an English lady in such squalid attire? You look like a drunk after a night on the docks."

Jim shrugged. "I didn't have a choice. I only arrived in Cairo last night. I woke up this morning to find my kit stolen." His kit held the few things he owned—a bedroll, a couple books, a hairbrush, and the deed of sale for his one extravagance, his Arabian mare and her foal. They were stabled in Luxor at the facility of a man who loved the breed as much as Jim did. "It took me until an hour ago to chase down the bloody bugger."

"Bloody bugger," Haji repeated thoughtfully, testing the words. "An odd choice of words for a cowboy."

Jim wasn't going to satisfy his curiosity. "What are you doing here, anyway?"

Haji sighed dramatically. "I have been sent here by my aunt, a terrifying woman who occasionally ferrets me out for some task or another."

"What's the task?"

"I, too, am to acquire a female passenger from the train."

"'Acquire a passenger'? It sounds as if you're taking custody of a wild animal."

"This is not far from wrong. I am here to meet Ginesse Braxton."

"Braxton?" Jim repeated. "Any relation to Harry Braxton?"

Though he'd never met Braxton himself—they hardly ran in the same circles—he'd had a few run-ins with Braxton's men in the Antiquities Service. None of them had been pleasant, and all of them had cost Jim in some coin or other. Usually gold coins. Braxton made it his business to interfere with the sale of questionably obtained artifacts. Which was sometimes Jim's business.

"His daughter."

"Why didn't Braxton come for her?"

"The whole family is in London awaiting the addition of yet another little Braxton before returning to Egypt. Apparently, Ginesse Braxton is being interviewed by Monsieur Maspero for a

position cataloguing Roman artifacts and had to come forthwith."
He snorted derisively. "Why would one not go to Rome if one
were interested in Romans?"

"Because there was an era when—"

"No. *Because*," Haji cut in severely, "she is a contrary, spoiled
demon of perversity. As a child she was a constant thorn in everyone's side, popping up at dig sites where she had no business, stealing off with bits of pottery and scraps of papyrus, always where
she was least wanted and most likely to cause trouble. A scrubby,
scrawny, yellow-haired imp. In fact, many were convinced Braxton hadn't named his daughter as much as identified her." At Jim's
querying look he elaborated. "Not Ginny, but *djinn*."

Jim grinned. According to legend, the *djinni* were minor spirits bent on mayhem and mischief.

"It was a happy day when she was sent off to England. But
now she is back, and I am to play nursemaid," Haji said, adding
under his breath, "Again."

"Maybe she's changed," Jim suggested, scanning the platform.
Where was the blasted woman?

"A *djinn* may change her appearance, but its nature stays
the same: meddlesome, disruptive, and dangerous. You will see.
Look for someone with a broken arm or in bloodstained clothing.
Ginesse Braxton is sure to be trailing right behind."

"You haven't seen her for years," Jim said. "You said she went
to school, probably boarding school. They press out dutiful young
ladies by the ream."

Haji grunted. "What do you know of English ladies, a desert
rat like you?"

"Nothing," Jim said amiably, his eyes on the train. The doors
were finally open, and the porters had unloaded the steps. Men,
children, and women were emerging into the hot, dimly lit sta-

tion to stand blinking uncertainly before the sudden onrush of beggars and vendors, pickpockets and porters.

He found Mildred Whimpelhall the moment she emerged. It would have been impossible to miss that magenta-colored head of hair, even half hidden under a hat.

Haji followed his gaze. "You owe me a pound," he said.

"Why?"

"Why?" Haji repeated incredulously. "Look at her. Too tall. Too thin. Her nose is too large, and her jawline is too strong. And that hair!"

Jim's gaze sharpened. The young lady's eyes were hidden behind a pair of lens-darkened spectacles, but the rest of her features, though decidedly bold, were symmetrical and faintly exotic... *Ugly?* Haji must be mad.

"She might be slender, but if you think she's too tall, that's pure unadulterated jealousy speaking."

Haji, who stood two inches below five and a half feet, huffed.

Jim wasn't paying him any attention. The girl turned to look over her shoulder, and for a second her face was silhouetted against the light coming from the tunnel opening behind her. Jim's breath caught in his chest. For a moment the ghost of the lad he'd been, ardent and receptive and easily moved by unexpected beauty, sprang into keen life once more.

"That profile, my friend," he murmured, "has graced many an ancient tomb."

"What?" Haji asked incredulously.

"Ankt and Isis, Diana and Artemis."

But those lips, he added silently, *are pure English.* Not the anemic, tight lips of an English matron, but the lush, come-hither lips of a mischievous English lass. Something tightened in his chest.

"But what about her nose?"

He cocked his head. "I'd call it...Florentine."

Chapter Four

She considered that he might be the possessor of a great deal of brute strength and audacity, for he was a rough individual, wearing a stubble of beard and long, unkempt matted hair.

—from the personal diary of Ginesse Braxton

"You'd say an elephant was dainty in order to win a bet," Haji protested.

"I'm gonna give you the hair," Jim admitted. Mildred Whimpelhall's hair was more than simply ugly; it was astonishingly ugly, a hideous broiled color that existed nowhere in the natural world.

But the rest of her…The rest of her, though dusty, sweaty, rumpled, and travel-stained, was definitely not ugly. And also not demure. While the other female passengers were milling around awaiting masculine companions to escort them, Mildred Whimpelhall had waded into the sea of pressing bodies, her dark skirts swishing, the carpetbag she carried bouncing against her leg, her dispirited-looking hat bobbing atop her incredible hair.

Sweat beaded above her crisply chiseled upper lip and her nose, requiring her to constantly push her darkened spectacles back up with a shove of her forefinger. Dust lay on her shoulders and dragged at the hem of the heavy, navy blue jacket and skirt that seemed to be the uniform of traveling females. Despite it all, she managed to convey a freshness that belied her bedraggled appearance.

She was younger than he'd expected, too. From what little Pomfrey had written in his letter of instruction, Jim had assumed the fiancée would be well past the first blush of youth. This girl's skin was silky and fine-grained, her bosom high, and her hips... It wasn't his heart that tightened this time.

"Miss Whimpelhall," he said, stepping forward. She was taller even than he'd first thought, the top of her head on a level with his eyes. "I am—"

"Mr. Owens," she said, stopping and looking him over in a most frank manner. "Yes. I have your description. You are exactly as I imagined. I would have known you anywhere."

She looked at Haji, tensing. The Egyptian made her visibly nervous.

"Welcome to my country, Miss Whimpelhall," Haji said, trotting out his most unctuous smile. "Haji Elkamal, at your service."

She didn't answer straightaway. She just stared at Haji from behind her dark glasses before abruptly thrusting her carpetbag into his chest. "Excellent. You may carry this. There's a good fellow."

Haji stumbled backward, grabbing the valise before it fell to the ground.

"Do be careful of that," she chided him. "There'll be no tip for you should you drop it."

Haji, in his European jacket and trousers, his black hair gleaming with pomade, simply gaped at her.

"Mr. Elkamal isn't a porter," Jim said, wryly amused. For a few seconds there, he'd felt something unfamiliar, dimly recalled, like thread sewn fast to some organ deep within had been pulled taut...But she was simply another xenophobic English tourist, after all. "He's an associate of mine."

"Really?" she asked. Eying Haji, she beckoned Jim forward with a single, calfskin-encased finger. He leaned in and caught the scent of travel on her but also something sweet, soft, and feminine.

"Do you think that wise?" she whispered loudly. "He looks downright villainous to me." She straightened. "But then I'm told you're an American cowboy. I expect you're familiar with his sort."

He had to give her credit. In less than three minutes, she'd managed to insult him, Haji, and America. She'd out-Pomfreyed Pomfrey. She beamed at him, as unconscious of giving offense as the sun was of shining. That beautiful siren's mouth was ripe with secret humor.

"Though I must say, your accent doesn't sound very much like a cowboy's." She seemed disappointed.

"Just trying to improve myself, miss," Jim replied. "If you'll wait here a minute, I'll fetch the rest of your luggage and have it sent on to the hotel."

"That won't be necessary. My luggage was lost during a storm at sea. That," she said, pointing at the carpetbag Haji cradled in his arms like a fat baby, "is all I have."

"Do not worry, honored *sitt*," Haji said, fumbling with the valise. "There're a number of places on El-Muski Street where you can buy clothes. European establishments. They'll have you—"

He trailed off as she held up that single finger again, silencing him.

"I was not worried, my good fellow. You have misunderstood." She spoke to him in the distinct syllables one used with the mentally challenged. She turned toward Jim. "I only meant that there is no luggage forthcoming, and as such we can proceed to Fort Gordon at first light tomorrow."

"Tomorrow?" Jim echoed, thinking. The sooner he fulfilled his promise to Pomfrey, the better. But then he looked down at her travel-stained dress, with its heavy material and layers of petticoats. "You can't cross the desert in those things. You'll roast."

She scowled as she followed his gaze. "I suppose you are right. I shall have to buy some new clothes. But I must do so at once. I don't want to dilly-dally in Cairo when I ought to be making my way to Colonel Lord Pomfrey."

"If *sitt* will allow me?" Haji had recovered his aplomb and was once again smiling. "Perhaps I can be of assistance?"

She turned her head in his direction, her brows climbing above the upper rims of her dark glasses. "*You?*"

He bowed. "If you please. My cousin is a dressmaker of considerable talent who creates beautiful gowns at a most reasonable price. English-styled gowns. His clothing is much sought after by the European ladies of the city, and his shop is but a few minutes from here."

"First a tyrannical aunt and now a dressmaking cousin. You're full of all sorts of surprises today, Haji," Jim said in Arabic, his tone bland.

Haji smiled sunnily. "You know very well that I have no such cousin," he replied in the same language. "But I know a man who will sell this terrible woman a made-over cast-off for an exorbitant price of which I will receive ten percent. If she continues to stare down her long nose at me, I shall tell him to make sure it has fleas."

"What is he saying?" Mildred Whimpelhall demanded.

"That it will be a great honor for his cousin to clothe Colonel Pomfrey's fiancée," Jim answered.

She nodded, apparently satisfied. "Very well, you may show me to your cousin's shop. It had better be clean. No lice or fleas," she said, drawing Haji's startled glance. She continued, "And no more speaking that foreign language in my presence. It is rude and unnecessary. Especially given that you speak English." Haji, who was immensely conceited about his public school British accent, preened. "At least passably enough to make yourself understood."

Startled, Jim almost broke into laughter.

"Oh, there will be fleas. Many fleas, you female dog," Haji muttered under his breath.

"What are you saying now?" She turned to Jim. "What is he saying?"

"He's begging your pardon for being rude," Jim said.

"Yes," Haji said. "I am sorry that my vocabulary is inadequate to express my feelings for you. But it is. I simply have no words."

"*To* you, not *for* you," Mildred corrected graciously.

Haji's face registered feigned surprise. "Thank you for the kind instruction. Unfortunately, I am not free to accompany you at this moment," he said. "Perhaps this afternoon?"

"What is wrong with right now?"

"I am to meet a young lady," Haji explained.

"Oh? Is it a *harem* girl?" she asked in shocked tones. Jim should have probably pulled her away, but this exchange was the most amusing thing he'd seen in months.

"No. *She* is a Miss Braxton," Haji replied, his sangfroid finally growing thin.

Mildred's gloved hand flew to her heart. "Miss Braxton, you say? But Miss Braxton was aboard the same ship as I! A lovely girl. Utterly charming."

Haji peered at her disbelievingly. "Miss Ginesse Braxton?"

"Yes, yes. Ginesse. A pretty, petite blonde *angel* of a girl. So sweet. Delightful company," she said. "I am sorry to be the bearer of such sad news, but Miss Braxton was afflicted with a terrible case of seasickness. Indeed, there were times she was so violently ill I feared for her life. She left the ship in Italy with the intention of continuing her journey by overland routes once she'd recuperated."

"She left the ship early?" Haji asked.

"That is correct." When Haji continued to stare at her in seeming incomprehension, she sighed in exasperation and said in a very loud voice, "*Missy. Braxton. Not. On. Ship.*"

Haji blinked.

"I believe she left a letter with the captain—" Mildred broke off, gazed at Haji's still-dazed expression, sighed again, and continued. "*She. Leavie. Letter,*" she made a scrawling motion in the air, "*with El Captain.*"

"This is terrible," Haji muttered in Arabic. "I knew that *afreet's* return would be a plague on me! Magi will kill me if I do not return with the brat. Mark my words, my aunt will find a way to blame me for this."

"You're speaking that mumbly-humbly again," Mildred placidly pointed out.

In a clear sign of his distress, Haji barely noted the insult. "I must go." Without another word, he dropped the carpetbag to the ground and hurried off into the crowd.

Jim turned to Mildred Whimpelhall. She was biting her lower lip, and oddly enough, it looked as if she was trying to hold back laughter. She caught his eye and cleared her throat. "What appalling behavior. Quite unconscionable."

"He's usually better mannered," Jim said, scooping her bag up. "Let's see about getting you to your hotel." He waved her ahead of him, and when she obliged, he fell in step behind her.

Outside the station, he caught the eye of a carriage driver parked on the far side of the street and raised his hand. The man snapped his reins over his horses' rumps. "We'll take a—"

"No," she interrupted him. "No, thank you. I believe I'd rather ride one of those little donkeys." She pointed to a clutch of tourists being hoisted aboard some long-suffering beasts.

"A donkey?" Jim asked dubiously. The donkey boys of Cairo were ubiquitous, the Egyptian counterpart of London's hackneyed cabs. For pennies, you could clamber aboard a donkey and be taken wherever you might want to go. It was the tourists' favorite way of visiting the bazaars. But it was also dusty and malodorous. "Are you sure you wouldn't rather take a carriage?"

"Yes." She bit her lip, looking uncomfortable. "I…Well, to be frank, the idea of being in closed quarters with you…That is, I'm reluctant to…" She trailed off, blushing profusely.

Jim looked at her, at a loss. He couldn't think of any reason why she wouldn't wish to share a carriage with him unless—Good God. She couldn't seriously think that she was in any danger from him? She was Pomfrey's bride-to-be. Even if he were the sort of scum who took advantage of closed quarters to impose himself on a woman, there was no one on earth he'd be less likely to do so to than her.

He muttered an Arabic curse, appalled.

"Is something wrong, Mr. Owens?" she asked stiffly.

"Listen, Miss Whimpelhall," he said. "We're going to be traveling a long way together through some pretty harsh land. And while we won't be traveling alone, we will be in close quarters. You are going to have to believe me when I say your reputation and, er, your virtue are as safe with me as if you were my own sister." His couldn't help glancing at her hair. "Safer."

"*Oh!*"

Apparently he shouldn't have said that. "May I help you into a carriage now?"

"I *prefer* the donkey," she replied coldly.

"Suit yourself." He shouted a few words in Arabic, and within seconds three donkey boys had surrounded them, vying for the fare. He picked a likely looking mount, giving directions and a *piaster* to its owner. Then without really giving it much consideration, he turned around and, putting his hands around her waist, hefted her up.

It took less hefting than he'd expected. She didn't weigh much under all that material, and the impetus threw her above his head, catching her off guard. She pitched forward, flinging out her hands to clutch his shoulders and brace herself awkwardly above him. His hands closed more tightly around her waist.

It had been a long time since he'd touched a woman, and then it had been more a matter of expedience than desire, a brief physical union that had left him feeling empty rather than sated.

That woman had been round and pillowy. Mildred Whimpelhall was not. She was taut and supple. Even through layers of thick gabardine, he could feel where her small waist flared gently into a sweet hip. A ripple of pure desire shot through him, stealing beneath his awareness and quickening his blood.

"Oh. Oh, my." She sounded breathless. He'd probably offended the hell out of her again. Small wonder, he'd been holding her aloft longer than necessary by half.

He dropped her atop the donkey as if his hands were scalded. He'd planned to accompany her to the hotel, but decided he'd better keep his distance from for now.

Pomfrey's bride, for God's sake. "I'll be at the hotel later tonight. Seven o'clock."

"I shall expect you," she said, her chin lifted to a haughty angle. She may have a delectable body, but it looked as if she had a temper to match that violent red hair.

The boy tapped the donkey on its rump, and the animal moved forward, Mildred Whimpelhall perched like an oddly elegant crane on its back. They had only gone a few steps before she turned round to look back at him.

"Just so we understand one another, Mr. Owens," she said, "I wasn't worried about my virtue being assailed. I was worried about my nose."

"Pardon me?" he asked.

"You, Mr. Owens, smell." And with that parting salvo, Mildred Whimpelhall bounced off into the crowds.

CHAPTER FIVE

True, he moved like a wild creature panther, light-footed and graceful, but he spoke in educated accents of a Swedish Hungarian prince.

—from the personal diary of Ginesse Braxton

Well, he *had* smelled, Ginesse thought as she jounced along on the back of the donkey through the winding alleys and narrow streets of Cairo. She pictured with satisfaction the startled look on Mr. Owens's face when she'd delivered her *coup de grâce* and refused to feel guilty.

How *could* James Owens believe she thought she was in danger of attracting his grimy—and thoroughly unwanted—attentions? It was embarrassing. She would *never* imagine he would... that she was the sort of woman he'd...Oh! She understood perfectly well she was not the sort of woman who inspired men's animal passion. And she did *not* want him thinking she had any misconceptions about herself in that regard.

She could still hear the horror—yes, *horror!*—in his voice as he'd breathed the Arabic equivalent of "Holy Mother of God." It was mortifying.

Not to mention disappointing. She had been so pleased with her initial impression of Mr. Owens. He'd looked like the exemplar cowboy: a lone wolf with the soul of a poet...She frowned. That sounded awkward. She would have to work on a better metaphor.

But his face had seemed intelligent; his manners, circumspect; his bearing self-possessed but without a trace of arrogance. She'd even glimpsed a touch of humor in his light gray eyes when she'd been taunting Haji.

And she refused to feel a twinge of guilt about that, either. As a girl, she'd suffered far worse at Haji's hands. He'd been a telltale and a bully, the first to catch her in some minor transgression and then tell others about it. He'd even been the originator of that nasty nickname, *Afreet*. It had felt good to get a bit of her own back.

And Mr. Owens *had* nearly laughed, she thought with a slight smile. She would bet her last pound on it. His wide mouth had curled up at one corner, and he had had to look away to recover his gravitas. All cowboys, she decided, ought to have humor as well as gravitas.

If he was a cowboy. There had been a slight but definite English public school flavor to his deep, soft voice. She sighed. More likely, he was some clerk from Liverpool. He'd probably never even held a six-shooter. That would account for his tasteless comment about her virtue being as safe with him as his own sister's. The cowboys in the books she'd read would never be so familiar. They had a deeply embedded respect for womanhood. Even the dastardly ones. On the other hand, it was hard to imagine an Englishman throwing her on a donkey and sending her off alone to a hotel. So perhaps he *was* an American.

By the time she arrived at Shepheard's Hotel, it was just past four o'clock and the streets were quiet. Few people ventured out into the oppressive afternoon heat, but there were some intrepid souls on the balcony. An elderly Copt with a trained monkey was entertaining them from the street below, the poor dispirited beast doffing his little fez and holding his paw out for *baksheesh*. A gentleman laughed and leaned over the rail. Ginesse glanced up and promptly blanched.

Of the half dozen people on the balcony, she knew three. Or rather, they knew her. An idly chatting couple, Baron and Baroness Heissman, had once found her after she'd wandered away from her family into a less-than-salubrious *suk*. The gentleman sharing their table, Dr. Younterville, had set her arm—both times it had been broken.

Why hadn't she thought about how small the expatriate community was in Cairo? She should have realized she might encounter people she knew. Though the food was notoriously bad, Shepheard's still maintained its reputation as the premiere meeting place for Cairo's luminaries—archaeological and otherwise. It was bound to be full of family friends and acquaintances.

"We are here, *sitt.*"

Ginesse slid off the donkey's back, keeping her face carefully averted from the balcony, opened her purse, and pressed a couple of coins in the donkey boy's palm. True to form, the boy immediately began to harangue her for more until a turbaned and uniformed doorman well into his middle years came racing down the hotel steps. She even recognized him; his name was Riyad, and he'd been a doorman at Shepheard's since she could remember. He shooed the raggedy lad and his donkey away at the same time as he secured her carpetbag and offered her an obsequious welcome in at least a half dozen languages.

Praying he did not recognize her as well, she readjusted her dark glasses and schooled her face to an impassive expression.

"May I inquire as to your name, *sitt*?" he said.

"Mildred Whimpelhall," she answered, half expecting him to cry out that she was an imposter.

But he only smiled warmly and said, "Ah, yes. Miss Whimpelhall. You are expected."

He escorted her into the hotel's massive lobby. Her heart sank further. The lobby was full of people congregated in little clusters taking their afternoon tea. And once more, she was familiar with many of them. Lady Sukmore was ensconced on a divan with two of her cronies, Mrs. Paurbotten and Miss Dangleford. The three comprised the worst snobs in all of Egypt and had ruled the women's social scene at Cairo's legendary Turf Club for decades. She'd been banned from attending any of the club "socials" since she was six years old and found trying to set Countess Munter von Halwiener's leopard free on the golf course.

"I won't have it!" a shrill masculine voice declared, drawing her attention to the reception desk. "You *will* find room for me and my entourage!"

A group of tourists stood in front of the long desk making loud noises and gesticulating angrily at the harassed-looking clerk. Riyad shot the group a disheartened glance and then turned to her with an apologetic smile.

"It appears there may be some small delay in registering you, Miss Whimpelhall. In the meantime, if you would be so kind as to take refreshment here in the lobby, it will not be long," he said. He lowered his voice confidingly: "The lobby is most especially prized as a place for young ladies to see and be seen." He fairly twinkled as he said it, as sure of her enthusiastic acceptance as an adult would be offering a sweet to a child.

"Is there somewhere private where I might wait?" she asked.

It was one thing to deceive Haji, whom she hadn't seen in six years and who had never struck her as being particularly bright in the first place; it was another to fool someone with whom she may well have dined just last year at her parents' house in Cairo or even here, at Shepheard's.

Riyad shook his head regretfully. "I am afraid not. I assure you, it will only be a short while."

He extended his hand toward an open chair in the middle of the room, but she'd already spied another vacant seat in a less conspicuous location behind one of the towering vases filled with potted date palms that ringed the lobby. Lady Sukmore and her companions occupied the seats on the vase's other side, but they would not see her behind the massive urn.

She brushed past Riyad and hurried over before someone else could claim the semi-seclusion.

"—fear this year's season shall be quite boring. I *pray* not," she heard Mrs. Dangleford say in dramatic tones.

"Be careful what you wish for, dear," Lady Sukmore replied. "I hear that Ginesse Braxton is due to arrive back in Cairo any day now."

Good Lord. They were talking about *her*. She looked around, trying to find another chair where she could sit, but the only vacant ones were those next to people. People who looked distressingly familiar.

"Such a bold-faced little scrap of a thing." Mrs. Paurbotten sniffed. "Looked you dead in the eye in a way that was quite unnatural for a girl. Even the father recognized it if the mother did not. Why, he called her his 'little adventuress.'"

It had sounded much nicer coming from her father's lips. "*I'm afraid we've raised an adventuress,*" he would say, laughing. "*She's never more alive than when something's at risk.*"

"Best thing they did was to send her off." Lady Sukmore again. "She made poor Mrs. Braxton's life a trial, you know."

Yes. I know, Ginesse thought, her mood darkening.

She hadn't gotten into trouble on purpose. Her intentions were always blameless. There just always seemed to be something irresistible beckoning her from some tawdry show window, down the meanest street corner, atop the highest minaret, or through the narrowest crevasse. Afterwards she'd always swear to be more careful next time, more prudent, less impetuous. And she'd meant it, every time.

"Should have sent her off far sooner than they did."

"Too fond of the girl," Mrs. Paurbotten said with a sniff. "Nothing good comes of a fond parent, and give a child *two* fond parents and...just look what happened."

"I shudder to think of the high cost to our archaeological community she might have caused had she stayed," Lady Sukmore said.

Sanctimonious old biddy. She'd no more interest in the "archaeological community" than she did the Muslim community.

"I suppose in the end The Fire was a godsend."

That *damn* fire. She hadn't intended to set the blasted papyri ablaze. It had been an experiment with a magnifying glass gone horribly awry.

"How's that?"

"At least it finally convinced Mrs. Braxton to send the chit away somewhere she could be managed."

The memory of The Fire was usurped by another of her mother, eyes unnaturally bright, standing in the foyer of the Misses Timwells' School of Edification and Improvements.

"Egypt is too dangerous a place for a girl as inquisitive as you. There are too many opportunities for disaster, and you seem bent on taking them all."

Ginesse had pleaded with her parents, insisting she would be more careful, more prudent, that it would never happen again. No one, including herself, had believed her. The two broken arms, a head contusion, sprained ankles, and more bruises and scrapes than she could recall weighed heavily against her.

"They didn't even attempt to get her into any of the more selective finishing schools but settled for an establishment known for indulging willful children."

And even there, Ginesse had never been able to completely tame her magpie curiosity, her thrill-seeking heart. It wasn't that she didn't want to study; she wanted to study *everything*. Her mind was like a sieve at the end of a fish trap, catching anything that came within its vicinity, a jumble of facts and curiosities, anecdotes and histories, nothing more valued than the next, nothing less interesting for being less weighty.

But ultimately determination had won out. She was here, wasn't she? She sat straighter, refusing to be cowed. How she loathed them.

"I don't wonder that she's come back. London society is far more excusive than we allow ourselves to be. She might be husband hunting…"

How *dare* they use her embarrassment, her exile, and *her life* as a way to pass the time between scones and flounder? She was on her feet, heading around the vase before she even realized it. Luckily, Riyad intercepted her before she could act.

"Ah, Miss Whimpelhall," he said. "If you will follow me?"

He escorted her to the front desk and left her to register, after which she was handed off to a young bellhop. The lad took her valise and led her into the Great Moorish Hall, where she finally felt free to remove the dark glasses. They started toward the grand staircase at the far end, its bottom steps flanked by a pair of life-sized Nubian maidens. Along with Mr. Runyan and Mr. Bradley, bankers who were great favorites of her mother's.

"Hassan," Mr. Runyan hailed the bellhop. "Good lad. We were just requiring an impartial judge to settle a dispute—Oh! What ho? I do apologize. I didn't see you there. Thought old Hassan was quite alone." He smiled politely, eying her with evident interest. Especially her hair.

She stopped walking, forcing the bellhop to pause as well. They were a good twenty feet away from the bankers, and the lighting in the hall was dim, the window shutters having been drawn against the late afternoon sun. She could only hope it was enough to disguise her.

They waited for her to say something, and when she didn't, Mr. Bradley stepped forward, smiling graciously if with a touch of perplexity. She had to figure out some way past them and quickly.

"By jingo, it doesn't look as if there's anyone about to introduce us properly," he said and chuckled. "But seeing as we're in a foreign country, I don't suppose there's any reason to stand on ceremony."

She took a deep breath and headed briskly toward them, the bellhop falling into confused step behind her.

"I'm Donald Bradley, and this is—"

"I am afraid I must disagree, sir. There is *always* reason to abide by the niceties of social convention, and I, for one, intend to do so." She swept past them. "What are we, sir, savages?"

Somehow, she refrained from turning to see their expressions, certain their mouths would be hanging open. They were both such nice gentlemen. And she had been so vile. But it had been necessary. Neither gentleman was likely to recall a thing about her other than that she was red-headed and a first-rate... Lady Sukmore.

Chapter Six

"Get up and fight like a man, you despicable varmint," he said to the snarling adversary at his feet, "for I'll not strike a man, even one as no-good as you, while he's down!"

—from the personal diary of Ginesse Braxton

"Find me some clean clothes by the time I'm done here and there'll be another *piaster* in it for you. Here." Jim flipped the kid some coins to make the purchase. He caught them in midair before bowing his way backward out the door, leaving Jim alone in the public bath's private room.

It was growing late, and the small window high in the tiled wall had darkened over, leaving the room in a misty semidarkness illuminated only by the sconce over the door. Wisps of steam rose from the raised pool in the room's center to collect on the ancient tiled ceiling and drip back to the slick stone floor. The room was hot and sour-smelling.

But then, Jim thought, that could be him.

He raised his arm and sniffed. Fine. Pomfrey's future bride had a point; he did smell. Though why she'd informed him of it in that insulted, haughty manner was a mystery. She couldn't have taken exception to his saying she was safe with him? Most unmarried ladies would be only too grateful to be so reassured that their guide would be conscientious with their reputations, reputations being stock and currency in the English marriage mart.

But then, she was not your standard-issue English miss.

Oh, without a doubt she was a young lady. The mellifluous upper-class accent, the haughty wing-shaped brows, the imperious angle of her chin: they were all the products of a first-rate finishing school. As was her unquestioned superiority to all other people and cultures. Which meant she wasn't different at all.

But how had she escaped with so much intensity intact? Her stride was too long and too purposeful, unseemly in a member of the leisured class. And no headmistress would have tolerated that open-mouthed smile. And the lithe, tensile waist he'd held was not the product of sitting in drawing rooms pouring tea. She was an enigma…

Why was he wasting time wondering about her? She was Pomfrey's enigma, not his.

He peeled off his shirt, wadded it up, and tossed it with more force than necessary onto one of the stone benches. Then, hopping first on one foot and then the other, he stripped off his boots. He'd just unbuckled his belt and had it halfway drawn from the loops when he saw the wisps of steam above the pool shiver. He ducked as a wooden club whistled by his face.

He spun to face his assailant and instantly recognized a swarthy, well-muscled man with thin lips and a scarred chin: Vincent LeBouef.

He glanced around for a potential weapon. There was nothing. LeBouef leapt forward and Jim twisted, jerking back, but the club caught his shoulder. Pain lanced down his arm; his fingers went numb. He pitched sideways, slipping on the slick tiles and crashing to his knees. He caught himself with his good hand and looked up. LeBouef sauntered forward.

"You know, James" the Frenchman mused, "I find myself wondering just how many times a man would need to be attacked to make him so adept at avoiding being struck from behind? It must be a great number."

Jim struggled to his feet. "You'd be surprised."

LeBouef shook his head. "On the contrary. If the man is you, then no, I don't think I would be."

"That hurts, Vincent," Jim said, making a show of grabbing at his back and wincing. With numb fingers, he managed to tug his belt free of another loop.

"You do not make yourself popular with your confederates, Jim. They do not like you."

"Maybe I oughta stand a few more rounds at the local pub?"

LeBouef laughed. It was a pleasant, amused laugh, a drawing room laugh. That was the frightening thing about LeBouef. He seemed so reasonable. So civil.

He wasn't.

"How did you know I was here?" Jim asked, buying time.

LeBouef shrugged, seeing no reason not to answer. "The boy that folds towels."

Jim nodded, unsurprised. LeBouef mined information from a huge population of "little birds": snitches, eavesdroppers, and rumormongers. He would have paid especially well for information regarding James Owens.

LeBouef's smile stretched. "You can imagine my surprise when I heard you were back in Cairo. It is so rash, and you, James, are not a man one would call rash. Do you have some sort of perverse death wish?"

"No," Jim said. "I am profoundly interested in remaining alive."

"Are you? I wonder," LeBouef mused, regarding him as though he were a puzzle for which he'd not been given the proper pieces. "You have nothing. No family. No home. You belong nowhere. N'est-ce pas? We are not so unalike in that, are we?"

Jim didn't answer. The longer LeBouef waxed philosophical, the more time Jim had to regain the use of his hand.

"I," LeBouef pointed the club at his chest, "was hounded from France by a tragically corrupt government. And you were hounded from...?" He raised a brow invitingly.

"Name a country. Chances are, I've been thrown out of it."

LeBouef laughed again, shaking his head with something approaching affection. "I do not understand. You could have been a rich man had you joined me when I asked. Yet you refused. It is as if you do not want wealth. But then, one must ask oneself, what other reason besides the acquisition of wealth would you have to be here?"

Jim didn't answer.

"You are something of a mystery, James. And I, to my great sorrow, am a romantic. What is your story? Tell me."

"I'm flattered, Vincent, and I hate to disabuse you of this little fiction you've built up around me, but look around. Egypt is full of men without countries, names, or families."

For a long moment LeBouef regarded him, the steely intelligence evident in his dark gaze. Finally he sighed. "It is as you say," he said, sounding mildly disappointed. "So. Where is my collar?"

Jim glimpsed a sliver of hope: LeBouef didn't know he'd already sold the pharaoh's ancient jeweled collar to another buyer. "Oh, I wouldn't look so relieved, James. I really wouldn't. Where is it?"

"Look," Jim said. "I'm not going insult you by saying there's been some sort of misunderstanding or that things aren't what they appear to be because we both know they're exactly what they appear to be. I came into possession of a certain item—"

"You 'came into possession of it' because I alerted you as to its whereabouts," LeBouef cut in, his voice chill.

"*Whereabouts* you were unable to access but I was," James said, bringing his hands up in a placating gesture. As he did so, his finger caught his belt and dragged it clear of another loop. "I know I promised it to you for a certain sum, but another buyer appeared."

"He undoubtedly *appeared* because you informed him of what you had in your possession."

"True."

The corner of LeBouef's lips curled.

"I'm a businessman. You're a businessman," Jim said in his most reasonable tone. "What would you have me do?"

"Do as you promised and deliver it to me."

"Promised?" James repeated. "For the love of God, Vincent, we're thieves," he said, and seizing the end of his belt, he jerked it free of the last loop and whipped the buckle straight at LeBouef's face. It caught him across the forehead.

Blood erupted from a deep gouge, spilling down LeBouef's face. He gasped, but he was too seasoned a fighter to drop his weapon. He swung hard, catching Jim full in the ribs. Jim doubled up, grimacing, but he bulled his way closer in, robbing LeBouef's next blows of some of their power. The Frenchman battered at him, raising his club to hammer it down on Jim's head, but Jim lashed his belt around LeBouef's arm, catching the free end and twisting it in a tourniquet around his wrist. He jerked hard, and the club dropped from LeBouef's hand.

Jim reared back on his heels, letting his feet slide out from under him on the slick tiles, causing LeBouef to lurch forward. He seized LeBouef's shirt collar, dug a foot into his gut, and pitched LeBouef over his head and straight into the stone bench behind.

LeBouef's head hit the marble with a sickening crack, and he collapsed like a marionette whose string had been cut.

Grimacing, Jim rolled over and climbed to his feet. He probed the corner of his lip with his tongue and tasted blood. LeBouef had gotten in more than a few good licks. His side ached, his shoulder throbbed, and his left eye was already swelling shut. He limped over to where the Frenchman lay and prodded him with a toe. Satisfied he wasn't feigning unconsciousness, Jim stripped off LeBouef's shirt and shrugged into it because he was betting the kid he'd sent to buy him clothes wouldn't be coming back.

With any luck, if he stowed him somewhere out of the way, LeBouef wouldn't be found until morning. By which time Jim should be far away.

He jerked LeBouef's wrists behind his back and lashed them together with strips he ripped from one of the towels. He should light out east, maybe head for India. The only reason he was still alive was because LeBouef didn't know the heavy gold and gem-encrusted collar was already out of the country, probably gracing the neck of the wealthy Austrian count's bullmastiff. The count had seemed inordinately fond of that dog.

LeBouef was going to wake up with murder in mind. Jim's painful murder. And he was going to hunt for Jim until he found him. The only way Egypt would be safe for him was if LeBouef was dead, a happy but unlikely occurrence unless...Jim gazed down at the unconscious man for a moment before sighing. Nope. He couldn't do it. He'd just have to write Egypt out of any future plans.

Resigned, he looped LeBouef's feet together and then hogtied them to his wrists. He stood up. His only problem was Mildred Whimpelhall. If he didn't take Mildred Whimpelhall to Pomfrey, he doubted Pomfrey would ever give him another chance to repay his debt. And that meant he'd die beholden to Colonel Lord Pomfrey.

And that ate at him.

He shouldn't care, but he did. The question was did he care enough to risk his life by taking the time to deliver Mildred Whimpelhall to Fort Gordon? It was stupid to even consider.

Someone else could take her to her fiancé. Someone else could see to it that nothing bad happened to her out there where "bad" was one's daily companion. He wasn't the only man capable of guiding her to Fort Gordon. He was just the best.

At his feet, LeBouef moaned. Jim deliberated a few seconds, shrugged, and clipped him across the jaw, knocking him unconscious again.

So what if he failed some test that only he cared if he passed? It wouldn't be the first time he'd failed, and it wouldn't be the last. Maybe he'd head to Asia or go north to the Baltics. There were still a few places left in the world where a man could lose himself. And if just the thought of that exhausted him down in a place far deeper than muscle and bone, well, at least he'd be alive.

Seven years ago he'd promised himself he'd never do anything stupid because of a woman again.

Taking Mildred Whimpelhall to her fiancée definitely fell under that category.

CHAPTER SEVEN

A frightened thrill coursed through her, and she knew without a doubt that the man before her had never wielded an accountant's pen, but only the Cold Hard Steel of a Six-shooter!

—from the personal diary of Ginesse Braxton

"Time to get up, Miss Whimpelhall."

Ginesse struggled out from the depths of an uncomfortable dream featuring a tall, disreputable-looking outlaw and blinked, her eyes adjusting to the darkened hotel room. She shook her head. She must still be dreaming because there was no other explanation for why James Owens would be sitting on the side of her hotel bed.

"What are you doing here?" she mumbled, looking around. Her window stood wide open to the terrace.

"We have to go. Now."

"What are you doing here?" she repeated. She gathered the bedsheets high under her chin, scrambling back on her heels until she banged into the bed's elaborately carved headboard. She could barely make him out. Just enough to see that he'd changed his shirt for a *zaboot*, the native tunic of the lower classes. It was not much of an improvement.

The garment stank of tobacco. And liquor, too. She sniffed. Yes, he *definitely* smelled of liquor. She peered at him over the linen's laced edge. She'd read that some men became capable of terrible things while under the influence of liquor.

"*What are you doing here?*" Her voice rose an octave.

"I'm taking you to your fiancé."

His tone was definitely not lecherous. She relaxed slightly. "To my fiancé?"

"Yes," he said. "We have to go. Now."

"I'm not going anywhere with you," she said. "Please remove yourself from my room at once, Mr. Owens."

"Miss Whimpelhall, I'm not asking—"

"Good. Because I'm not going." Good heavens. Did he really think she would go tromping off with him in the dead of night? She hoped she was made of sterner stuff than that.

"Listen, miss." He set one large fist beside her thigh and leaned forward. The white *zaboot* fell open nearly to his waist revealing a chest heavy with muscle, hard and contoured, the dark hair covering it glinting in the chance light. Quickly, she looked away, heat flooding her face. This was ridiculous. She'd read some extremely provocative Egyptian love poems without a blush. *Dry words about dead lovers,* an inner voice mocked. Nothing at all like this. He was real, so close that if she lifted her hand she could touch that wide, sculpted chest—

"No," she said. "I will not listen. Now, must I ring for an attendant or will you leave?"

"You're not calling anyone. Not until you listen," he said. He shifted, bringing his face into the light.

She forgot her apprehension and embarrassment. "Good heavens! What happened to you?"

He looked awful. His left eye was swollen, his lip was split, and a bruise darkened the already beard-stubbled angle of his jaw.

Enlightenment dawned on her. "You've been in a brawl! A *saloon* brawl," she breathed, recalling countless vivid descriptions of similarly battered men from her Western dime novels. She leaned forward to get a better look, the sheet slipping unheeded from her shoulder. "You have, haven't you?" A tantalizing, horrifying thought occurred to her. "Was it over a woman?"

"What?" He jerked back, a brief expression of bewilderment appearing on his stern countenance. She was having none of it.

"*It was!*" she declared. "You got into a barroom brawl over some..." she scrambled for the right word, "some *floozy!* Don't deny it."

Whatever had Colonel Lord Pomfrey been thinking to send such a man to escort as delicate and timid a lady as Miss Whimpelhall? It was unconscionable. James Owens would have terrified Miss Whimpelhall. Luckily, Ginesse was neither delicate nor timid.

With an impatient gesture, he reached out and flicked the sheet back over her shoulder. "There are no saloons in Cairo," he said.

"You know perfectly well what I mean. Some squalid establishment that caters to men's lowest impulses."

"*Lowest impulses?*"

"You...you should be ashamed of yourself," she said. Something deep within him would surely respond with innate decency to a gently bred lady. It always did in her novels. "You didn't start out as a desperado. You should...try to be a better man. I am sure you have it in you." She hoped she sounded more confident than she felt. "Somewhere."

For a moment he just stared at her and then abruptly stood up, looming over her, his eyes glittering in the dim room.

"You seen through me, miss," he growled, in a rich Western drawl.

It was *delicious.*

"I was in a saloon brawl," he admitted. "I ain't proud if it, but when demon liquor has his way with a feller, there's no telling what he might do."

"I knew it!" Ginesse breathed.

"You were right. And now that I'm coming clean, I reckon it's only fair to warn you, miss. I ain't one of your English lapdogs."

No, she thought, twining the sheets more tightly around her shoulders, he most definitely was not. She blinked up at him, uncertain what he meant, her heart racing wildly in her throat.

"*Comprende?*"

She frowned. "Pardon me?"

"You understand?"

"Yes."

"So, when I say we're going, we're going. I'm the ramrod, got it?"

Ramrod...ramrod...Oh! The *boss!* She nodded.

"And whatever else I tell you to do in regards to our trek, you're gonna do it and you ain't gonna argue."

"I would never argue. It's unladylike."

"You're arguing now."

She opened her mouth to—She closed it, swallowing hard. He sounded quite ruthless, and she felt a little frightened.

"Don't look at me like that," he said. "You ain't got nothin' to fear from me as long as you do as you're told. I got one aim, and that's to get you safe to your sweetheart's arms. He entrusted me with your care, and I," he looked away, his lips trembling ever so slightly, obviously moved by some great emotion, "and I live by the Code of the West. I aim to get you to him even if I have to carry you kicking and screaming the whole way."

Oh. My.

"Got that?"

"Yes." She caught herself on the brink of telling him she wasn't Mildred Whimpelhall and that she wasn't going anywhere with him. James Owens was far more than she'd bargained for when she'd begun this impersonation. Miss Whimpelhall had been right to be apprehensive.

But then she reminded herself that Colonel Lord Pomfrey had entrusted Mildred to Mr. Owens's care and Colonel Lord Pomfrey was a man whose opinion could be counted on. He would never risk Miss Whimpelhall's virtue, not to mention her very life, to a man who couldn't be trusted.

More importantly, Ginesse was growing ever nearer to her own goal, her future, her triumph. She must remember that. She must remember why she was here and what success would mean. She rallied her spirits, lifting her chin.

"You must promise me you'll resist all future temptation to imbibe spirits."

He regarded her bleakly. "I'll do what I can."

"Promise me."

"I don't make promises I can't keep. But I'll promise you I'll give it my best effort."

"I should not like to have to report your behavior to Colonel Lord Pomfrey," she said, hoping the threat might carry some weight, but fearing it didn't.

His mouth tensed, but he only said, "Neither would I. Which is why it's important we leave now. Before I succumb once more to the lure of liquor and a fancy lady."

"Now?"

He nodded.

"It is the dead of night."

"You're arguing again."

"But it *is* the dead of night."

"Miss Whimpelhall," he finally said, "we're set to cross a very hot, very big desert." The slight English accent had returned. His Western drawl probably only appeared when he was intoxicated or under duress from great emotion. Which was rather a shame. Bettering himself or not, she much preferred the Western drawl. "Which means we'll be doing most of our traveling before sunrise and after dusk," he continued. "Which means we start now. Within the hour."

She didn't want to argue with him. Leaving sooner rather than later served her purposes except…"But I haven't had time to refurbish my wardrobe."

"I've taken care of it."

"You?"

"I meant Pomfrey. I forgot that he'd made arrangements to have suitable clothing packed and waiting for you with the rest of our provisions."

She studied him. The feeling that there was something he wasn't telling her gnawed at her.

"You won't be too uncomfortable for the present," he went on when she remained mute. "We'll be on the river for most of the first two days, and it's cooler on the water."

"I see." She shifted to the side of the bed and stood up, drawing the sheets around her. As tall as she was, he was a good five inches taller. "Please leave."

He moved closer to her, looking down at her, his face shadowed and still. "I am sorry, miss, but we're leaving here now," he said softly. Dangerously. "You can go over my shoulder or on your own two feet."

This was not a callow younger brother or fond father, but a hard-faced stranger with a dubious reputation. She was out of her depth.

This is dangerous. He's dangerous, she thought. But if she wanted to get to Fort Gordon, she didn't have any choice but to go with him.

"I am not disagreeing," she said. "I only meant for you to leave in order that I can get dressed and pack what few things I have."

As abruptly as it had arrived, the tension evaporated. "Oh. Well, then you shoulda said something."

He moved to the open window and paused, silhouetted against the subtly lightening sky outside. "We'll meet in half an hour at the bottom of the garden rather than the lobby. There's no need to excite comment."

He didn't wait for her to answer but put a booted foot over the sill and silently disappeared into the night, leaving Ginesse to wonder: She knew why she didn't want to attract anyone's attention, but why didn't he?

Chapter Eight

"Clearly, you have not thought this through," Haji said. He tossed Jim the package he'd brought and then leaped into the *felucca*'s bow to join him.

Jim ignored the comment, handing off the package to one of the sailors to stow. "Did you get everything?"

Haji made a sour face. "By everything do you mean did I get clothing for that red-haired she-cat? Yes. Will it meet with her approval? No. Unsurprisingly, there were not many establishments catering to European women open at four o'clock in the morning. I had to resort to visiting a lady friend of mine who was not pleased to be asked to share her garments with an unknown female. I have no idea what she packed in that bundle. It could be rags. By the way, you owe me ten pounds for that." He looked around. "Where is Pomfrey's bride-to-be?"

Jim nodded toward the stern of the small sailing vessel where Mildred Whimpelhall sat, her hands braced on the gunwale as she looked toward the sunrise. The first thin light of day outlined her profile in a rosy glow, following the straight, sculpted length of her regal nose to the clean angle of her jaw and down her long, slender neck.

"Why is she still wearing those dark glasses?" Haji asked in disgust. "It is barely first light."

Jim didn't have an answer. He'd wondered about that, too, and in particular what color her eyes were. It had been impossible to tell their exact color in her hotel room, but far from being pale and weak looking, they'd appeared dark and brilliant, framed by long, curling lashes.

He'd noticed a few other things last night, too, because when the sheets had fallen down around her waist he'd have to have been blind not to take note of the full thrust of her breasts beneath her sheer cotton nightdress. He wished he hadn't. He didn't want to think of her as anything but the means to repay a debt. But she'd looked…He shook his head, refusing to follow his imagination any further. She'd looked like trouble, plain and simple.

He would have expected Pomfrey's bride to be a prim sanctimonious woman who lived her life along very narrow, very clearly defined lines. Someone with the imagination of a carp and about the same blood temperature. The last sort of woman Jim would have expected Pomfrey to marry would be a vivacious, feminine, full-blown romantic. And Mildred Whimpelhall was definitely that.

With no help from him, she'd cast him into the role of some sort of cowboy-outlaw. When he'd realized that nothing he could say was going to dissuade her of that opinion, he'd decided he might as well take advantage of it. He sure as hell hadn't been getting anywhere *asking* for her cooperation. If she wanted to believe he was a bad man, then a bad man he'd be, reasoning that if she didn't know what he was capable of doing, she might not risk finding out by flouting him. She looked like a world-class flouter to him.

His mouth curved into an involuntary smile. She'd looked like a new-fledged owl, staring up at him from her nest of bedclothes round-eyed with wonder, a little frightened, a little excited—

"I did the best I could."

Jim looked up, jerked out of his reverie by Haji's voice.

"The crew," Haji explained, nodding toward the quartet of men moving back and forth along the dock loading provisions and readying the boat. "They're Nubians. I know you don't speak Nubian, but they were the best I could do on short notice. The captain speaks some English."

Jim nodded. English may well have been the captain's only asset. He'd arrived drunk half an hour ago and had been trying to sober up ever since. As he watched, the barrel-chested Nubian belched and shouted an order to a boy. The lad hurried to the stern and began hauling the mainsail up the mast, making a mess of the process and earning bellows of rage.

"Good Lord. If we make it across the river without drowning it will be a miracle," Jim muttered. "Just how much am I paying them?"

"Twenty *piasters* a day each. Fifty extra for the captain."

"By all that's holy, Haji."

"Come, James. It's not as if you were paying them; Colonel Lord Pomfrey is. All you need to do is hand him a bill. Were I you, I should make certain it was considerably padded." He glanced at Mildred Whimpelhall and grinned. "Battle wages, I believe it's called."

His smiled faded. "But no amount of money is worth risking your life. This is madness, *habib*. LeBouef might not come after you himself, but he will set a price on you. Every wretch within fifty miles will be looking for you."

"Doubt anyone's going to be sneaking up on me in the desert," Jim said, though in truth Haji wasn't saying anything Jim hadn't already thought.

"You aren't doing Miss Whimpelhall any favors, either, James. You're setting her up as a target right alongside of you."

He'd thought of that, too. "LeBouef would have Mrs. Walcott and the British army on his head if he caused her any harm and he knows it."

"Bah!" Haji said, thwarted. "She is Pomfrey's bride. Let Pomfrey find another to guide her. Better yet, let him come for her himself."

Jim hesitated. Haji was right, and looking at the inexperienced crew and the drunken captain to whose dubious skills he was entrusting her made him reconsider. She was so young and vulnerable, and while he knew LeBouef was too savvy a businessman to waste money by sending men chasing across a vast, uncharted desert after him, that didn't mean some ambitious self-starter might not have a go at it.

"Listen to me," Haji pressed. "So, she is forced to stay in an elegant hotel for a week or so. Is this so great a burden?"

No. It wasn't.

"Yes! Yes, it is!"

At the sound of the frantic female voice, both men swung around to find Mildred Whimpelhall clambering over the crates toward them. The girl must have ears like a bat.

"Ah, Miss Whimpelhall," Haji said, his face smoothing. "I am sure if you understood what was at stake here, you would be happy to free Mr. Owens from his obligation."

"I do understand!" she protested, stopping atop a crate next to the boy still working industriously and unsuccessfully to haul the halyard to its topmost position. "I know *exactly* what is at stake, and I can assure you your problems are paltry next to my need."

Haji's gaze hardened. "Even if it's a man's li—"

Jim grabbed his arm, giving the smallest shake of his head. "Look, miss," he said. "I'm real sorry, but something came up that I hadn't anticipated. It seems like it would be best for everyone if someone else took you to Fort Gordon. Haji here'll set you up with a real good guide."

"I don't *want* another guide," she said, paling. "I want you."

Her adamancy startled him. "That's real flattering, but there's bound to be someone nearly as—"

"Oh, for heaven's sake," she sputtered. "I don't give a fig whether you're a good scout or bad guide or an indifferent whatever it is you want to call yourself. All that matters to me is that you are here *now*. It could be days before another guide can be found. I don't *have* days."

He couldn't imagine Pomfrey inspiring that sort of fervor, but he nonetheless said, "I understand your eagerness to join your fiancé, but there are matters involved that are out of my control."

"They are not! *You* are here. *I* am here. The *crew* is here. You were prepared to embark before *he* showed up." She stabbed Haji with a dagger-like glare.

"I am most sorry to have been the instrument of your disappointment, *sitt*," Haji said with pronounced irony.

She stomped her foot, and the crate she stood upon wobbled precariously. She didn't notice. She'd set her hand on her hips, her chest rising and falling in agitation. "Listen to me. I intend to leave for Fort Gordon today. At once. With or without you, Mr. Owens."

"Now, Miss. Whimpelhall. You're upset," Jim said, uncertain how to continue.

"With or without you," she repeated. She pivoted and pointed an imperious finger at the captain, who'd taken time off from barking orders at his lackluster crew to watch the proceedings with growing interest. "You, Captain. Do you speak English?"

"Yes," he admitted.

"Do you know someone who would be willing to act as my guide to Fort Gordon?"

"No." He shook his head in disgust. "It is far away across a very bad land. No."

Jim relaxed. He hadn't been aware that every muscle in his body had tensed.

"Could you find me someone willing to do so for, say, fifty English pounds?"

The captain abruptly ceased shaking his head. He squinted up at her. "My cousin's daughter is married to a Bedouin. He might—"

"No," Jim clipped out. "No. You can't just hire someone you don't know to take you on a trip like this."

"I don't know anything about you other than what Colonel Lord Pomfrey wrote," she said. "Apparently he didn't know much either. Certainly he didn't know you were a welsher." Her gaze racked him from head to toe. "I suspect he should have."

He'd been called worse, and he wasn't the sort of man to be goaded into doing something because of a few words. Still, it stung. "I guess he should have at that."

"Oh!" She stomped again. "Fine. Captain, as soon as these men disembark, you can start across the river."

"I'll need to be paid first."

"Of course. I have the money right—What are you doing, Mr. Owens? Unhand that man at once!"

He'd reached across the transom, grabbed a fistful of the captain's *galabeeyah*, and dragged him forward until the man hung face to face before him. Dammit. Now the captain knew she was carrying money on her. She'd just put herself in peril and she didn't even realize it. How the hell had she made it all the way to Egypt unscathed?

Had he thought he'd be putting her at risk by staying with her? She was already in danger, and it would only grow worse by the day, because that was the sort of woman she was, set on having her own way regardless of the consequences to anyone. Including herself.

"You're not taking her across the river alone," he explained to the captain. "Not for fifty pounds or a hundred pounds. Understood?"

The captain lifted his hands, squirming. "Of course not, *effendi*. I was not thinking clear."

"No!" Mildred Whimpelhall howled from atop her crate. "That's not fair. You can't just tell people to ignore me!"

Jim glanced over at her. "It's for your own good."

"Oh, how I *loathe* that phrase," she spat out. Her hat had fallen off during her scramble, and the terrible red hair was starting to come unbound, falling in Medusa-like ropes around her face.

"You may stop this man from taking me across the river, Mr. Owens," she declared, "but you can't accost every captain along this shore, and that's what you'll have to do to keep me from crossing this river. I'll go up and down the banks and ask every man with a *dahabiya* or *felucca* or a raft to ferry me across. Sooner or later, one of them is bound to agree, and there is nothing you can do to stop me, unless, that is, you plan spend your days shadowing me. And since you seem to be in a great hurry to be rid of me, I can't imagine you will do so. So you may as well go now, Mr. Owens, and leave me to my search."

He stared at her. She stared at him.

Shit.

"Allah be praised!" the boy beside her suddenly cried, leaping up and pumping the air with both fists as the mainsail caught the breeze and billowed out.

His triumph was short-lived. He hadn't tied down the mainsheet on the boom, and as soon as the wind filled the sail, the big wooden spar swept across the deck, knocking aside everything in its path.

Including Miss Whimpelhall. One minute she was standing there, glaring at him; the next, she was gone.

He leapt to the side of the boat just in time to see her sink beneath the water, her enormous dark skirts ballooning around her like a giant jellyfish, a jellyfish that was going to drown her.

"Leave Egypt now, James," Haji said calmly. "I will see that she is safe."

But it was too late. Jim had already dived in.

* * *

Ginesse plummeted toward the bottom of the Nile, weighed down by the heavy gabardine skirt. She opened her eyes in a thick stew of brown murk and felt a thread of panic take hold: she couldn't tell top from bottom. Disoriented and frightened, she forced herself not to struggle. She knew how to swim, but in these skirts it would be impossible. She had to shed them.

She began to work feverishly at the ties and buttons. Her chest ached, and her lungs felt close to bursting, but she knew to exhale meant she had only seconds to replace the air. Carefully, she let a thin stream of bubbles escape her lips as she yanked at the skirt. She was growing light-headed, her fingers fumbling...

And then suddenly two strong hands seized her and she was being propelled up through the muddy waters, the water breaking over her head as she was pushed up through the surface and into the air, choking and gasping for breath. Strong arms raised her up the side of the *felucca* where other hands accepted her, hauling her aboard like a net full of fish and dropping her on the deck.

She coughed, spitting water all over the deck, and then she was being lifted against a hard, broad chest and her head fell in the lee between a warm neck and muscled shoulder.

"Are you all right?" His voice was harsh, unsympathetic. He gave her a little shake. "*Are you?*"

"Yes."

She opened her eyes, blinking through the muddy water still streaming down her face, and found Jim Owens looking down at her. Of course. She'd known it was him the moment he'd touched her. His face was a mask, inscrutable and stony, his gray eyes roving over her face, touching on her hair, her mouth, and finally meeting her eyes.

"You dove in after me," she said, her voice faint and wondering.

He seemed to find this amusing, for his mouth curled at the corner again and she took that for a smile. "Did you think I wouldn't?"

She answered before she had time to consider. "I didn't expect you."

"I didn't expect you, either." His voice seemed odd, somehow nonplussed.

"Will you me take to Fort Gordon?" she asked without much hope. Of course he wouldn't. All her plans were for naught, all her dreams whisked away with the swing of a spar.

"Yes," he said in a resigned voice. "I suppose I will."

CHAPTER NINE

She was with him every day, a slender girlish shape, a bright ~~inquisitive~~ feminine spirit, reminding him of how lonesome was the life he'd led.

—from the personal diary of Ginesse Braxton

Jim kept his eyes on his oar and avoided looking at Mildred Whimpelhall perched on the gunwale ahead of him, dangling her bare feet over the edge. He wished she wouldn't. She made him nervous sitting there, as if tempting the river gods to have another go at drowning her. She seemed oblivious to any risk and to have completely forgotten yesterday's misadventure, as if falling into the Nile was an everyday occurrence.

Except for her bare feet, she was back in the hot-looking gabardine travel kit, having spent most of yesterday twined in a long piece of sailcloth while her clothing dried on the mast, the package Haji had delivered having been buried under piles of other provisions by the inept crew. That hadn't seemed to bother her, either. She'd been in high spirits ever since he'd agreed to take her to Fort Gordon.

He didn't have much choice. It was clear that she was going to attempt to find her way with or without him. Someone was going to have to take responsibility for getting her across the desert, and since he'd agreed to Pomfrey's request, that someone was him. For good or bad, she was his…until he turned her over to her fiancé.

A light breeze riffled the water, and he looked up at the mainsail. It luffed briefly before going slack again. The wind that could almost always be counted on to propel small sailing vessels against the Nile's current had failed, and now he and the Nubian sailors— if he dared insult sailors everywhere by calling them that—had been forced to lend their backs to the work of moving the boat upstream. It was hard, sweaty labor.

"Did you ever rob a stagecoach?" The question came out of nowhere.

He looked at her, startled, though he shouldn't have been. She'd been lobbing these sorts of questions at him all day. Do you own a six-shooter? Have you ever rustled cattle? What did whiskey taste like, and had he ever seen a buffalo herd?

"Or a train?" She was regarding him with unblinking concentration.

What sort of proper young lady asked the sort of questions she did? What sort of proper young lady was even interested in the kinds of things she was?

His own limited experience with well-bred misses had ill-prepared him for the likes of Miss Mildred Whimpelhall. They had been modest, genteel, and reserved creatures, all downcast eyes and faint curving smiles. Charlotte, for example, would have been just as likely to run naked in the streets as to ask a stranger such personal questions.

Mildred Whimpelhall, on the other hand, had more questions, more opinions, more...*talk* than any three people put together. Whatever English finishing school she'd been sent to, if he'd been her parent, he'd have demanded his money back.

"You don't have to answer if you don't want to," she amended.

"That's awfully decent of you," he said dryly.

"But I wish that you would." She peeked at him from under the sweep of spiky lashes. Her eyes—

Lord save him, those eyes. She had lost her spectacles in the river, which had proved a double-edged sword. When he'd scooped her up off the *felucca's* deck yesterday and her eyelids had fluttered open, he'd lost his breath. She had the most extraordinary eyes he'd ever seen, a true cerulean, the irises a soft, greenish blue shot with copper sparks and ringed by darker blue. They were the sort of eyes that made a man stupid and sent him to his knees.

Some men—not him.

Then Haji had come to see how she fared, and she'd swooned. She'd rallied soon after Haji left, disgruntled that Jim still intended to go through with his plan.

"Well?" She'd taken out a folded square of foolscap and the stub of a pencil. What was she writing, anyway? It seemed she was always scribbling away at something. "Have you ever robbed a train?"

"Just what sort of man do you take me for, Miss Whimpelhall?" he asked.

"I don't know. That's what I'm trying to find out," she answered. "But it's deuced hard when you only answer in monosyllables."

"Maybe the reason I don't reply is because I don't think you'd like the answers."

She considered this, stretching out a long leg to dip her toes in the water, affording him a glimpse of neat ankle, a high, elegantly arched instep, and pretty pink toes. His body grew hard at the sight, unnerving him. How could something as serviceable as a foot be so arousing?

"I might not," she finally admitted. "But don't you think I deserve to know the manner of man to whom Lord Colonel Pomfrey has entrusted my safety?"

"Shouldn't it be enough for you that he did?" he countered.

"No," she answered without hesitation. "It's my safety at stake, not his."

Another mark against the supposed finishing school. "Supposed" because he was beginning to think she'd never set foot in such a school. Young ladies did not go about insisting on autonomy. Older ladies might be forgiven for being strong-minded and independent, but she was far too young to have developed a taste for independence. And she was very independent.

She was also right. She did deserve to know the sort of man guiding her, whether he would prove faithful to the task or abandon her if trouble arose. He would want to know if he were in her position.

But he also wanted to answer because he wanted someone, *her*, to know him, to be something more than a ghost for a few short days, though he didn't examine why too closely.

"No, I've never robbed a stagecoach. Or a train. Or, before you ask, a bank."

"But you've robbed *something*," she said, watching him intently. "From someone."

"Yes. The dead." At her shocked expression, he gave a humorless chuckle. "I meant from tombs. I wasn't stripping the boots off cattle rustlers."

"Some people call that archaeology," she said stiffly.

"What's the difference?" he asked. "What I do is no less thievery, just less immediate."

She stiffened even more. He'd nicked a nerve. Interesting. "It's archaeology if the public benefits from it; it's thievery if it gratifies personal greed."

"Is your father an archaeologist by chance? Because you seem more than a little partisan," he said, amused. A lot of upper-class gents styled themselves amateur archaeologists. He'd sold quite a few things to them.

"No! I mean, yes." She flushed. "He is a gifted enthusiast. But he's *not* a thief."

That helped explain the bits of historical trivia punctuating her conversation and the idle observations she would make when they passed some ancient site or ruins.

"I'm sure your father abides by every rule involving the acquisition of antiquities," he said.

She only flushed brighter and cleared her throat. "Just so," she said. "But we weren't discussing my family, we were talking about yours."

"Actually, we weren't and we won't," he replied evenly, winning a peeved glance. She was worse than Haji and even more transparent.

"Well then, we were talking about your life on the wild frontiers of America."

"No. You were talking about it. I was rowing."

"But if you *would* talk about it," she said, "it would keep your mind off how hot it is and how hard the rowing is and how far we have to go yet before you can quit." Her words were doing little to hearten him, which, he suspected, was her intent. "Or how inefficient your crew is."

She cast a pointed look at Nubians lolling at the oars on either side of the *felucca*. "I daresay not one of them has ever rowed in unison. Do you think I should call out a rowing song? You know, to get you all synchronized and pulling as one?" she suggested.

"No," he said hastily. The captain had told him the men were uncomfortable having an unmarried woman in their midst. They thought her plunge into the river followed by the unusual absence of the wind was a bad omen. "I'm, ah, enjoying our conversation."

She smiled broadly, and he realized he'd just been black-mailed. "Do you have a mustang pony?"

Here at last was something he could talk about without reservation.

"I did. A tough little buckskin."

"Was he handsome?" she asked hopefully.

"Hardly. He looked like a gargoyle, had a trot that could break your back, but never stumbled on open ground and knew his way around a steer."

"But you're an adept rider, I'd imagine."

"Yes."

"Do you still own him?"

"No." Like everything, it had been sold after his father had died and he'd suddenly found himself an heir. Althea had swooped down like some malevolent angel, wresting Jim from his uncle's ranch and taking him away to her mausoleum-like house—he could not call that place a home. She had allowed him to bring nothing with him.

"Is it impossible for you to offer *any* bit of conversation without me having to pry it from you?" she burst out, surprising him. He couldn't imagine why she'd be so interested. "I appreciate your whole enigmatic, solitary wanderer identity, but you have achieved new heights of reticence. The Sphinx is more forthcoming than you!"

Enigmatic solitary wanderer? Is that how she saw him? He started to smile.

"Don't smile that way. You are purposely enigmatic, and it's obviously nothing more than a ploy devised to enhance your mysterious aura."

Great God. His half smile turned into a full-out grin. She was so unexpected. So amusing. "I have a mysterious aura?"

"You only wish," she refuted her earlier words with a *humph*.

"I'm sorry," he said, still grinning. She had crossed her arms over her chest. And lifted her nose in the air, turning from him. "There didn't seem to be any more to say on the subject. What would you like to know?"

"Do you have any siblings?"

"Yes. A half brother four years younger than me. Jock." It had been a long time since he'd said his name. It felt odd. Bittersweet. "He was a sweet-natured boy, studious and shy, always disappearing between the pages of a book. His mother died in childbirth." He'd been the only bit of warmth Jim had experienced in Althea's great cold house.

She beamed at him. "See? Was that so hard?"

"Yes."

She gave an unladylike snort.

"And do you have any siblings, Miss Whimpelhall?" he asked. "I don't know anything about you, either, other than that you're Pomfrey's intended bride."

"Oh," she said easily, "scads. Six younger brothers and one on the way. My turn. Where are your parents?"

This was *not* a memory he wished resurrected. "Both dead," he answered in a short, clipped voice. And then he found, oddly enough, that he wanted to say more. "My mother died when I was four. We lived on my uncle's ranch—it' d been in the family for generations, and after she died my uncle just took over raising me. Must have been hard for him. He wasn't married, and I imagine I was a handful."

"What of your father?"

"My parents stopped living together before I was even born. I never met my father. He remarried after my mother died. Then, when I was fourteen, he died and I inherited his…" This hadn't hurt him in a long time. There was no reason he should allow it to do so now.

"His?" Miss Whimpelhall prompted gently.

"His everything. Which wasn't all that much," he said. "Not to me. His mother decided I shouldn't be allowed to run wild like a savage, so she came to the ranch and took me away with her." He released a long breath, surprised to find he' d been holding it.

"I'm sorry," she said. "I…I know what it's like to be taken away from a place you love."

She looked so sad and forlorn. "It was a long time ago, Miss Whimpelhall. Things happen, you adapt. It's what living is all about."

She eyed him curiously at that, her expression slowly turning from sadness to approval.

"Now, before my voice gives out because this is a sight more talking than I'm generally used to doing, any more questions?"

She pondered a minute before her next question. "Do you like horses?"

"Like them? I respect them. I value them. I admire their grace and speed. I appreciate their willingness and spirit, but I don't know as one *likes* a horse."

"Of course you do," she burst out again. "You just as much as said so."

He couldn't help but smile at her insistence. "All right. I like horses."

"A fine cowboy you'd be if you didn't," she said in vindicated tones, smoothing her skirt with her fingers. "Do you have a horse now? Here?"

"Yes." He was going to leave it at that, but he could see the clouds gathering again in her incredible eyes and decided to forestall another squall. "An Arab mare and her foal."

She frowned. "Arabian mares are rare in Egypt since the epidemic."

How did she know that?

"Except amongst the Bedouins," she casually added.

"She belonged to a Bedouin," Jim said. "She cost me every penny I'd managed to save over a three-year stint. Not that it mattered. As soon as I saw her and she whickered a greeting, I had to have her."

"Oh!" Miss Whimpelhall sighed happily, nesting her chin in her palm. "That is so romantic!"

Jim snorted. "It was stupid. She costs me a small fortune to keep her stabled. I didn't give a thought to the future, of how I would care for her, of what I would even do with her."

Or maybe he had, more fool he. Maybe that's why he'd had her bred. Because somewhere deep inside he thought someday he might be the silent partner in a stable of such fine animals. An idle dream, perhaps, but since he had nothing else to spend his money on, he could afford to throw it away on an idle dream or two.

He forced himself to smile. "Is the interrogation done for the day?"

She blushed at that but nodded, a wounded look in her eyes, and he felt as though he'd just kicked a kitten. "Of course."

He ignored the impulse to apologize. There was a reason he'd kept to himself. There was a reason that few people knew about him and fewer still knew where to find him. A reason that he did not mingle with the other expats. Any of the things that would have attracted too much attention.

He was a ghost. Ghosts didn't own houses, take lovers, have friends, earn reputations, or own stables of horses. Years ago he'd made a pact, but it would last only as long as the rest of the world thought he was dead, and a dead man doesn't speak of his past. Except, he had.

He considered how much he risked and decided it wasn't much. Playing into Ginesse's cowboy fantasy was an innocent enough diversion, and if he slipped in a bit of truth every now and then, what matter? Just as long as it didn't get to be a habit.

As long as she didn't get to be a habit.

She was quiet for a while after that. But she wasn't the sort to let anything dampen her spirits. When she spoke again, it was easily and without self-consciousness. "Did you know that Cleopatra soaked her barge's sails in perfume so that when she went down the Nile her presence was announced by the wind?"

"No."

"They were purple."

"Oh."

"And when Marc Antony came to visit her, she carpeted her chambers with rose petals a foot thick."

"Why?"

"Why?" she echoed. "Because it was romantic."

He grunted, hauling back on the oars.

"You don't believe in romance?"

Uh-oh. She'd pivoted around on her seat, all curiosity again. "Romance is a fine when you're a kid, I suppose."

"You think that romance is for *children*?"

"Pretty much."

"That's terrible. Haven't you ever been in love?"

"Once. But like I said, I was a boy. It passed. Like ague." He considered. "Which I also had as a boy."

She stared at him in consternation, her brow furrowed. Then, abruptly, her forehead smoothed. "Ah," she said knowingly. "Your heart was broken."

"Not in the least."

She lowered her voice, regarding him sympathetically. "Is she the reason you are here?" She inhaled on a soft whistle of discovery. "Oh! I can see that she is!"

He waited, fascinated to see what she'd say next.

"The entire country of America was not big enough to contain your disappointment and your heartbreak, and so you fled to Egypt where you would never need to gaze upon her lovely, unattainable face again. Oh." She touched her fingertips to her heart.

He burst out laughing.

The dreamy expression vanished from her face, replaced by disgruntlement. "Say what you will, I *know* I am right. You were wildly in love and it ended tragically."

"Well, you're partially correct: it ended," he drawled, surprised he was amused. There'd been a time when all he'd felt was bitterness.

"How did it end?"

"She wrote me a letter breaking off our engagement." He could already tell by the look in her eyes that this was never going to satisfy her, and he resigned himself to answering before she asked. "She was warned off me."

"Because you were a gunslinger?" she asked hopefully.

She confounded him at every turn. One would think she *wanted* him to be a gunslinger. She didn't. He'd seen a few gunslingers.

"No, because she was told I didn't have the prospects that she had assumed I'd had."

Her nose wrinkled, as if she smelled something unpleasant. "She must not have really loved you, and you are well shut of her. A woman in love stands by her beloved regardless of his position or his prospects."

"You're being romantic again and far too hard on her. She was just a girl, barely eighteen, and her family had certain expectations of her." In her final letter to him, Charlotte had written that she could not marry outside of her family's wishes and that the lies he'd told her had served to erase her former feelings. He had never lied to her, but he'd been too proud to tell her so.

"She should have thrown their expectations in their teeth," she said with such feeling he wondered what her family had demanded of her. "Was she pretty?"

"Oh, yes. Very pretty." Pretty in the accepted sense of the word, with dewy skin and a rosebud mouth, neat hands and a rounded little figure. He'd met her at a party. He'd arrived late, brought along by a group of young men who'd wanted the diversion his presence would cause more than his company. He hadn't cared. He'd have done anything to escape Althea's house, even if only for an evening.

Charlotte had been an outsider, too, despite the obvious costliness of her dress and the fact that she'd attended one of England's most expensive, if not selective, finishing schools. She, his "friends" informed him with nudges and winks, smelt of the shop.

And he stank of cows.

He figured they were well matched, and before the night was through she'd let him steal a kiss. He'd never kissed a girl before.

That was all it took, he imagined, for a great many lads to fall in love. But she'd been sweet, too, and admiring. She made him feel like a gentleman and not some half-feral interloper whose demeanor and accent Althea and her "tutors" spent days disciplining out of him.

"Oh." Miss Whimpelhall looked away from him, a small downward cast to her lips. "Do you still…" She broke off. Apparently there were some things even Miss Mildred Whimpelhall considered too bold to ask.

"I don't suppose I do," he answered the half-voiced question.

Her head snapped back around. "Don't *suppose*?"

He shrugged. "Yes. I can't say that I've given it much thought. So, I don't suppose."

"But you don't know for sure."

"I guess." He couldn't understand why she was looking so put out.

"If you still loved her, you would surely know," she insisted.

"Would I?"

"Yes," she said. "At least, I should hope so, because it would be a very sad, pale approximation of love if you didn't know it for a certainty."

"You're an expert on romance, miss?"

"Well," she lifted a shoulder and left her answer at that.

"Do you speak from the experience of your own deep and abiding love for Pomfrey?" In a thousand years, he would never have imagined himself asking something so intimate of a young lady whom he'd known only a few short days. There were certain lines a gentleman did not cross. Whatever deficiencies had been tolerated in Miss Whimpelhall's education, Althea hadn't tolerated the same in his—often to his great physical discomfort.

She blushed profusely. "That's hardly your concern."

He wasn't having it. She'd more or less erased those lines herself.

"Ah. I see," he said. "You have carte blanche to ask me any questions you like, fully expecting them to be answered, but you deny me that same privilege. You don't play a square hand, Miss Whimpelhall."

She drew herself up at that, insulted. "I do too."

"So then," he said. "Do you love him?"

"Of course." He didn't believe her for a second.

"Really," he said. "Why?" Why was he pressing her? She looked thoroughly flustered, and he was not the sort of man to enjoy making a girl uneasy.

"What a ridiculous question," she sputtered.

And yet, he kept on. "Not at all. You claimed the role of authority; I'm just interested in your credentials. I'm looking for some advice. As you discerned, my past efforts have not met with great success. You might help ensure that my future prospects are brighter."

"Really?" she asked, looking both intrigued and flattered in spite of herself.

He nodded. "*If* you're the expert you say you are. I have to wonder. You won't say a word about your own heart. Maybe you don't love Pomfrey at all." He ignored the spark of pleasure ignited by that thought. "Maybe you've never even been in love. Maybe you know nothing about love except what you've read in a book about Cleopatra."

She looked cornered. "I do. I am, and I do too."

He regarded her closely. "What do you love about Pomfrey?"

"Well, he's...he's dashing."

Pomfrey? Perhaps he had a misunderstanding of the word.

"Dashing. Go on."

"And he is a dedicated, loyal commander."

Jim said nothing. Whatever his faults, Pomfrey was a good officer.

"He is conscientious, hardworking, and diligent."

"He sounds like he has the makings of a good plow horse."

She scowled at him, looking more annoyed than offended. "He's also noble and honorable. *And* romantic," she finished, looking him dead in the eye. "I would never marry a man who did not feel romantically towards me. A woman, even a woman who is not beautiful, likes to think that she inspires those sorts of finer, loftier, more beautiful impulses in a man."

She might not love Pomfrey, but he did not doubt for an instant that she'd just listed the attributes she most valued. For her sake, he hoped Pomfrey had some of them. Jim knew he didn't. Between Althea and the life he'd led in Egypt since, pretty much every last vestige of romance had been beaten out of him. And looking at Miss Whimpelhall, Jim was glad. Because she was too tempting, too much what he wanted—if he'd allowed himself to want.

"Are those reasons enough?" she asked.

"More than enough. You've half convinced me I'm in love with him myself," he said, and when she looked away to hide her smile, he told himself making her smile hadn't been his intent.

And knew himself to be a liar in more ways than one.

CHAPTER TEN

In the dark, direct depths of his terrible eyes she witnessed his slow awakening to the ~~wonderfulness~~ sweet, dauntless courage of the girl he'd been charged with protecting.

—from the personal diary of Ginesse Braxton

"Are you sure you wouldn't like me to take a look?" Ginesse asked James Owens. "I am well acquainted with bumps and bruises."

"I'm sure you are, and no," Mr. Owens replied from where he sat with his back against the mast, reading something. It was just coming on daybreak, light enough to make out his expression, which remained even more uncommunicative than usual. "Thank you."

She wondered what he was reading but didn't think she ought to ask. He seemed out of sorts with her, which was a shame because it was going to be a lovely day. The air felt fresh, the wind was steady, and even the gloomy Nubian crew seemed cheerful.

But then, why shouldn't they? They'd taken yesterday off.

The day had begun badly. The captain had gotten thoroughly drunk the previous night and by morning was passed out in his squalid little cabin, making it impossible for him to give the crew orders. That had left Mr. Owens, who didn't know a word of Nubian, to pantomime commands. As she couldn't very well sit by while the miscreants took advantage of the situation by pretending not to understand his directions, she had suggested Mr. Owens draw pictures.

The suggestion had not been well received.

So, she had taken it upon herself to draw very specific images of what was required and show them to the crew. Rather than carry out her illustrated orders, the despicable dogs had pretended to think she'd instructed them to run the *felucca* aground. She knew this because they'd done their plotting right in front of her, not realizing that she could understand—*and speak*—Nubian.

Of course, she couldn't report this to Mr. Owens. Instead, she'd been forced to make loud and, as it turned out, ineffectual statements about "feeling" that the crew was "up to no good," which Mr. Owens had dismissed as rampant racism even after they ran the boat onto the sandbank and spent the rest of the day lolling about, drinking and eating and making infrequent, perfunctory attempts to dislodge the boat. She had retired to the far end of the sandbar feeling most ill-used and put upon.

It had been late in the day before the captain had finally sobered up. When he'd seen what had become of his boat, he'd started shouting. Ginesse, never one to back down from a fight, had shouted back. And then Mr. Owens had entered the fray, and while he was trying to pacify her, the captain had taken a swing at Jim—or so the captain later claimed. Frankly, she suspected the captain been swinging at her—and had hit Jim purely by mistake.

Since then, the pleasant camaraderie they'd enjoyed the first day had disappeared. When she caught his eye, Mr. Owens's gaze held the same uncertainty one sees in the eyes of a man watching the approach of a feral dog.

She rose and wandered to the side of the boat to watch the landscape emerge from the predawn darkness. A silvery papyrus marsh materialized along the river's west bank. On the river itself, scores of boats appeared, pushing out of the thick mist rolling over the water: graceful *feluccas* and long, luxurious *dahabiyas*; *dhows* and serviceable little dories; and an occasional steamer belching smoke as it carried its passengers upriver to Luxor.

She wondered what those passengers thought when they saw an English girl standing at the bow of a ship under the watchful eye of a tall, stern man. They might think they were sweethearts, or newlyweds, or eloping. She might be anyone.

That was the one real unexpected joy she'd found in her masquerade: she'd shed her name and past and all the assumptions and expectations that went along with them. She'd never realized before how oppressive a family's belief in one could be, how much of a burden their confidence.

James Owens had no expectations of her. He didn't think of her as one of the female oddities at a male educational institution, or Harry Braxton's trouble-causing daughter, or Dizzy Braxton's changeling, or Sir Carlisle's awkward great-granddaughter, or a *djinn*, or an *afreet*.

It was liberating.

Without thinking much of it, she stepped atop the gunwale and grabbed hold of a shroud line for balance. Closing her eyes, she arched back, swinging lightly from the taut line, luxuriating in the sensation of not being Ginesse Braxton. She lifted her face for the first warm kiss of sunlight. The sound of wings, whispered and rushed, drew her gaze up as a flock of snowy egrets passed overhead, their wings gleaming like bleached bone against the opal sky.

She heard the captain give a command to let out the sails, driving them more swiftly over the water. She smiled as the breeze rushed across her face, teasing her hair from its confinement to fly behind—

"*Ukak!*" Stop!

It all happened in a matter of seconds. She looked around to see a *dahabiya* racing straight at them. The captain shouted again and ran forward, grabbing the mainsheet and jerking back, sending the boat lurching sideways. She clutched hold of the shroud line with both hands as the sudden motion knocked her off her feet and sent her swinging out over the water.

Panicked, she scrabbled wildly with her feet, trying to reach the deck. Below, the water rushed hungrily by, and before her the *dahabiya* came straight on. For a moment, time froze. She saw the striped sails against the creamy morning sky, felt the bite of the line against her palm, smelled the brackish brine of the river, and thought, *I am going to die. I am going to die, and I've never made love. I wish Mr. Owens had made love to me.*

And then, suddenly, a long arm looped around her waist. She clung to the shroud line, afraid to release it.

"Let go." She looked around. James Owens had hooked a leg around the stanchion, bracing his free foot against the outer hull, and was leaning out over the water, holding on to her. "Before that boat slams into us both," he suggested.

She let go. He swept her up out of the way just as the *dahabiya* passed, scraping against the *felucca's* side. For a second, he stood holding her, his chest moving like a bellows against her cheek, his heart thundering beneath her ear.

"Are you all right?" he demanded fiercely. "*Are you hurt?*"

"I'm fine," she said. She could not recall ever feeling so safe…

"Bloody, bloody *hell!* What the devil is wrong with you?"

She was stunned.

Until that moment, Mr. Owens had never raised his voice. Even when provoked by the drunkenness of the captain or the indolence of the crew, he'd remained soft-spoken and utterly self-possessed. Even when swearing in Arabic he'd done so in a quiet, businesslike manner.

She pulled away from him, and he let her go. "I don't know what you mean."

"Are you just flat-out determined to jinx this trip?" he shouted even louder.

The hideous word that had haunted her childhood ignited a flame in Ginesse's belly. Valiantly, she struggled to keep her anger in check. Even if he was not a gentleman, she should remain a lady. She'd worked hard to gain that distinction, to master her quick-fire temper and tendency toward precipitous words and actions.

"I am *sure* I don't know what you mean," she managed. He loomed over her. She straightened her back and tried to loom back.

"*Today,*" he shouted, "you nearly caused us to ram another ship; *yesterday,* you ran our boat aground; and *the day before that,* I had to dive into a filthy river after you!"

It proved too much.

"Well, at least you *finally got a bath!*" she shouted back. "Likely the first one you've had this year!"

And while they were shouting at each other another *dahabiya* appeared out of nowhere and clipped the bowsprit clean off their *felucca.* The impact pitched her into the stacked crates. She folded like an accordion, stunned and horrified. It wasn't possible. What was the likelihood of a boat hitting them twice in one day? Maybe she *was* a jinx.

The spirit in her fled. Tears welled up in her eyes. She curled into a ball, hid her head in her arms, and cried.

"Are you all right?" she heard Mr. Owens say, as large hands clasped her shoulders and pulled her upright. "Mildred, are you all right?"

She snuffled miserably again, wondering who Mildred was until she realized he meant her. She peeked up. He was on his knees, his brow furrowed with concern.

It was her undoing. She didn't deserve his concern. She'd lied to him, used him, made him dive into a river and risk his life for her, shouted at him, and now he was taking care of her.

She turned around, flung her arms around his neck, buried her face against his throat, and sobbed. She bawled in a way she hadn't since she'd been banished from Egypt: loud, heartrending sobs of undiluted wretchedness. And he let her. He just put his arms around her and let her cry.

"Now, now," he said finally, his voice awkward and self-conscious. "There now. You're all right. You're fine." He patted her head with one hand while his other arm tightened around her.

"No, I'm not," she wailed. "I'm *not* fine. I'm a disaster."

"No, you're not," he said. He didn't sound very convincing.

"I'm a disaster and you despise me!" she wailed. "You wish we had never met. You…you rue the day!"

"No, I don't," he said, using the hem of his shirt to dab at her eyes. "No ruing. I promise."

"You do," she said, sniffling. "And I don't blame you. I should, too, if I were you."

"No, I don't. Really," he said.

"You're just saying that to be kind. Everything I do turns out badly."

"It does seem that way, doesn't it?" he said, again with that odd, lost tone to his voice, still dabbing assiduously away at her tears. "It's not your fault."

She blinked away her remaining tears. "It's not?"

"No. You're…I don't know." It wasn't exactly a vindication, but it was enough. She smiled at him, suddenly happy, and thought she heard him catch his breath.

"And you really don't rue the day we met?" she asked.

"I really don't."

"That's awfully decent of you."

"Is it?"

"Yes. And I promise, I will not cause a moment's more trouble."

"That's nice." He sounded like he didn't have the least hope she'd keep her promise. She wasn't too sure herself, if it came down to it, but she was going to try her hardest.

She pushed herself to an upright position, and he rose to his feet, effortlessly pulling her up. She smiled sunnily up at him. He stared down into her face, looking a little strange. Then he turned around and without a word headed toward the back of the *felucca.* She watched him go, befuddled.

"Where are you going?" she asked.

"To my kit," he said.

"Why?"

He stopped, turned around, and looked at her. "Because I need a drink."

"Now, Mr. Owens," she said worriedly. "I know these last few minutes have been harrowing, but spirits, as we all know, only provide false courage."

"That's good enough for me."

She frowned. "You must try to resist."

He turned back around. "That's what I keep telling myself," she heard him mutter.

But he kept on walking.

Chapter Eleven

She might lack the lush upper embellishments of luckier ladies, but her delicate hands and feet, glorious luminous eyes, and tremulous lips more than established her sex.

—from the personal diary of Ginesse Braxton

"Look, Miss Whimpelhall. I'm going to talk to the police officer over there and find out the whereabouts of Pomfrey's soldiers."

Ginesse looked dubiously at the old man in an Egyptian uniform sitting outside a very small whitewashed building at the end of the wharf. He seemed to be asleep.

"I want you to just sit right there on that crate. Right where you are. Don't move, don't talk to anyone, and *don't touch anything.*"

She frowned at his inference.

"Do you think you can do that?"

"What a ridiculous question."

"Yes," he said evenly. "It's a ridiculous question. But, *do* you think you can do that? For five minutes?"

She gave a haughty sniff, turned her head away, and nodded. "Good."

She looked back around, but he'd already started down the pier. He glanced back at her. Thinking he'd changed his mind, she started to rise, but he shook his head, staring sternly at her until she sank dolefully back down on one of crates the crew had unloaded before dispersing.

She watched him appreciatively as he greeted the old man and the two of them fell into conversation. He looked wonderfully fit and virile. He'd bathed in the river the night before while they'd been moored offshore and she'd been trying to sleep in the improvised tent he had the sailors erect each night in the *felucca's* bow.

She knew she shouldn't have gazed out in the direction of the splashes. But she'd never been very good at resisting temptation, and in all honesty she hadn't tried very hard. She was really quite content to deal with the resultant guilt and shame because he really was spectacular. He'd been standing waist deep in the inky water, soaping up a broad chest and long, smoothly muscled arms. He'd plunged beneath the surface and then stood up, raking his wet hair back from his face as water ran in sparkling rivulets down his big body.

He was sleeker than she'd imagined—and yes, it shamed her to admit she'd wondered what he would look like unclad, but she was dealing in shame today—broad shoulders tapering to a flat waist and trim hips that disappeared into the water. The moonlight had glinted in the light dusting of golden hairs covering his chest and forearms, catching and releasing the shifting sinews in his arms and the corrugated muscles of his belly as he twisted, soaping up again, the rich lather gliding off his slick body...

Abruptly, Ginesse straightened, hunting for something with which to fan her cheeks. It was hot out here in the sun. She was still looking when Mr. Owens returned.

"My word, Miss Whimpelhall, I'm impressed. You've managed to stay put without getting into trouble for a whole five minutes. That has to be some sort of record."

"Not at all," she said haughtily. "Last year I went an entire fourteen minutes."

He hadn't expected that. His dark brows rose in surprise, and he laughed. It was the first time she'd heard him laugh outright. It made him look younger and far less severe, his teeth flashing in a broad smile, his eyes crinkling up at the corners, long dimples appearing in each lean cheek. She'd thought he was well in his thirties, but now she reconsidered. He might not be all that much older than herself.

She smiled back sunnily. She liked that she'd made him laugh. He should do so more often.

"The officer has sent a boy to find Pomfrey's men. It's a small town. It shouldn't take too long."

"And then what?" she asked.

"Then?" he echoed. "Then I hand you over to them. All I am to do from here on out is guide." She was certain she read relief in his expression. Had he found the task of escorting her that onerous? There'd only been three incidents. At least, major incidents. That wasn't so great a number.

"Do you have my money?"

At the sound of the captain's voice, she and Mr. Owens turned. The squat man was stomping toward them, a bulldog look of determination on his face. He stopped ten feet away, eying her warily as he addressed Mr. Owens. "You owe me my fee."

"Yup," Mr. Owens said, reaching into his shirt pocket and withdrawing a sheath of bills. He peeled off a number and offered them to the captain.

The captain swiped the money from his hand, counting them quickly and looking up. "This will not buy the repairs to my boat caused by this...this..." He looked straight at her.

"I would be real careful of what I said next," Mr. Owens advised softly.

"This person," the captain finished between clenched teeth. "You owe me another hundred *piasters*."

"You're lucky to get what we agreed on. You don't have a crew; you have a burlesque show."

The captain might not have known what a burlesque show was, but he understood the implication well enough. He flushed angrily. "Who is going to pay for a new spar? You are. Because *she* is to blame."

Mr. Owens smiled. It didn't look anything like the smile he'd given her. It did not reach his eyes. Ginesse felt suddenly sure she would tread softly were she the captain. "I looked at the broken end of that spar," he said. "It was rotting long before we boarded your boat."

"It does not matter. She pulled the boat into the *dahabiya*'s path and broke it!" croaked the captain, pointing at her.

"It's not really possible to pull..." Ginesse started to say, then reconsidered offering her insights as Mr. Owens shot her a quick, hard glance.

"Your boat isn't worth the nails holding it together," Mr. Owens said. "You know it; I know it." He peeled off one more bill and shoved it into the captain's chest. "Consider this charity. Now we're done. If I find anything missing from my cargo, I'll be paying you a visit."

The captain gasped with indignation, snatching the bill from Mr. Owens's hand and tucking it away. "I am no thief, Mr. Owens. I may be a drunk. I may own a humble—and now far humbler—boat," he shot a malevolent glare at her, "and at times I may be forced to employ undesirables and thieves, but *I* am not one. Your things are all here." As he turned and stalked away, Ginesse heard him mutter in Nubian, "I hope."

"May I get up now?" she asked as soon as he'd gone.

"No."

She rose to her feet anyway. "I would like to change into one of the gowns Colonel Lord Pomfrey sent. You have been putting me off for days."

At first there'd been no time or place to change on the *felucca*. The captain had offered her the use of the only cabin, a small, cramped area beneath the mainsail, but after a quick tour of the rat's nest, she'd decided she'd rather sleep on deck. After Mr. Owens had the crew construct a sort of shelter in the bow, she'd asked for the clothing. They couldn't be found.

After a cursory look, Mr. Owens had concluded that they were probably somewhere amongst the provisions he'd also been charged with bringing to the fort, but he didn't know where and trying to find them by unpacking everything would be a chaotic undertaking. She wasn't an unreasonable woman, so she'd agreed to wait. As such, she'd spent the last three days in Mildred Whimpelhall's traveling suit, which now sported several tears and was coming apart at the seams.

Looking at Mr. Owens in his fresh—relatively fresh—shirt and trousers, the leather suspenders hitched over each broad shoulder, a simple *khafiya* loosely knotted around his throat, she felt grubby. And hot. Incredibly hot.

It hadn't been so bad while they were on the water, but sitting on the dock under the blazing sun, she could feel the sweat trickling down her back and soaking into the close-fitting jacket. She'd rid herself of her petticoat, but that had only made the skirt grab her damp legs when she walked. She could not wait to rid herself of the malodorous, wretched rags.

Self-consciously she touched her hair. It hadn't been washed since Cairo, and it was a little, well, stiff. She feared there were still bits of the river entangled in it from her misadventure.

"Could you perhaps find the package with my dresses?"

In answer, he started unstacking boxes and crates, spreading them along the entire dock until he finally found one particular bundle and handed it to her.

"Thank you." She stood up and started down the dock. He fell into step beside her. "Would you ask the officer if I could use his office to change?"

At the end of the dock, Jim spoke to the officer, who graciously complied with her request. She slipped past the men into the tiny, one-room office and closed the door, putting the bundle on the table and pulling open the oilcloth wrapping. She frowned, poked her finger at the clothing, and lifted up the top layer. Her frown deepened. She peeled back another layer. Then she ripped the rest of the clothing from the bundle, searching for something, anything, she could reasonably be expected to wear.

There was nothing.

* * *

"I don't think I should come out," Mildred Whimpelhall called through the building's small shuttered window.

"Why?"

"Someone sent the wrong package of clothing. It's entirely inappropriate," she said in an odd voice. "I have no idea what sort of woman would wear these things. If it was a woman."

What was wrong? Maybe Haji's girlfriend hadn't owned any European clothing and had only packed a caftan. Quite possibly Miss Whimpelhall didn't like the idea of appearing in public in Egyptian clothing.

He was disappointed. But then, why should he presume to feel *anything* about Miss Whimpelhall's actions or attitudes?

Because when she cried and put her arms around your neck so tightly, you knew you should have untangled them because it wasn't your place to comfort or to hold or to touch or anything... and you knew you could no more have let her go than you could have wrested the sun from the sky.

"I'm sure it's fine," he said, angry with himself. "You're going to have to come out sooner or later, so it might as well be now. We don't have all day, Miss Whimpelhall. Especially if we want to leave come dusk."

"All right," she said in a tone clearly designed to act as a warning. She emerged from the officer's building, and Jim's mouth went dry. He blamed the trousers.

Where had Haji's lady friend gotten a pair of boy's trousers such as might have been worn by a military cadet? They left nothing to imagination, hugging her well-rounded buttocks and delineating the juncture at the apex of her thighs with peace-stealing effect. Half of him hoped she'd never put on skirts again and half of him wanted to rip the turban off the Egyptian officer's head and cover her up before anyone else saw her.

The *farasia* she wore over it was no better, the tantalizingly filmy cotton shirt revealing as much as covering her golden skin.

Beneath that, she wore an *antaree*, a short, tightly molded silk vest that pushed the tops of her soft bosom above its low décolletage.

"See?" she asked irritably, making a sweeping gesture at her attire.

He swallowed hard.

"Cover her before she is seen!" The elderly police officer had bolted up from his chair and was standing in front of her, trying to shield her from the street view. "She is indecent!"

Jim looked around for something with which to cover her.

"I'm not putting on that skirt and jacket again," she warned him, looking a little frayed, a little frantic. "If you or him wants to find some native clothing for me, I am more than willing to wear it, but I am *not* putting on that wretched costume again. Ever."

She meant it.

Jim turned to the poor officer who was looking around as anxiously as a Christmas goose for an axe blade. "Where can I find some suitable clothing?"

"Make her go inside. Do something!"

Dammit. She was going to cause an incident. Jim took up a place next to the officer, adding his bulk to the human shield he was trying to make. "Look," he told her, "you can't be seen here like that. You have to go back inside and wait while I find something to cover your...your..." He gestured toward her legs.

"I told you I didn't want to come out."

"And you were right," he said. "Get inside. Please."

Without another word of argument, she turned and marched back into the building, leaving him staring at a trim backside whose pert jounce had the blood thundering through his body.

With a silent groan, he went in search of something, anything to cover her up. If she didn't get him killed outright during this trip, the sight of her in those damned trousers just might do the job.

CHAPTER TWELVE

> *His edifice of hopes, dreams, aspirations, and struggles fell in ruins about him. It had been built upon false sands.*
>
> —from the personal diary of Ginesse Braxton

SIR ROBERT CARLISLE'S RESIDENCE, CAIRO
FIVE DAYS LATER

The boy knelt beneath the *mashrabiya*, the projected window's intricately carved screen, making a desultory show of hawking his sister's rice cakes to the infrequent foot traffic on the narrow, residential road. It didn't matter if he sold any. He'd come here with another purpose in mind. His sharp ears were tuned to what was happening in the room above.

* * *

"Her name does not appear on any of the passenger lists for those trains leaving Rome," Haji's aunt Magi said. Her gaze burned a hole in him where he stood fidgeting in front of Sir Robert's cluttered desk.

It had been years since he had been in this study. It looked exactly the same, wonderfully familiar with its shelves of books, the tattered oriental carpet, the scarred and ink-stained old mahogany desk, the carefully rolled papyri and small clay figurines. And even though the reason for his being here was unpleasant, he could not help the feeling of, well, homecoming it inspired.

"It is time to send a telegram to Mr. Braxton," Magi said.

He'd *known* he would somehow be held accountable for the *afreet*'s absence that now looked like it was becoming a disappearance. "Aunt Magi, I am sure—"

"*You* are sure of nothing." Magi, a slight, dark-haired woman whose smooth face belied her age, swung toward him. "If anything happens to that girl—"

"Now, Magi, I am sure Ginesse is capable of navigating the foreign rail systems without incident," Sir Robert said soothingly from behind the great desk. Though his white hair was a bit thinner and his brows a bit bushier, and the hands folded on the ink blotter wore more liver spots, at eighty-five he looked much as he had at seventy. "It is too soon to worry her parents. Perhaps she took a tender to Greece? It would have—"

"And *perhaps* she did not," Magi cut in. "Why did she get off the ship in the first place? She does not say. This does not say." She slapped the telegram she held with an angry hand. "We know nothing except she is not here and we do not know where she is."

"She will doubtless tell us when she arrives." Sir Robert tried again. "You ought to have more faith in the girl, Magi. She has always reminded me of her mother, an extremely prudent, conscientious young woman."

Magi and Haji stared at Sir Robert, Haji because no one who knew her had ever considered Ginesse Braxton either prudent or conscientious, and Magi, if he read her expression correctly, because she was thinking the same about her one-time charge, Desdemona. Haji would have ascribed this opinion to the fading faculties of advanced age, but Sir Robert had always believed the unsubstantiated best about everyone of whom he was fond. He thought Magi was a paragon of serenity.

They were still staring at him, unsure how to respond, when Hasima, the household's lone maid, appeared in the library door. "There's a lady and gentleman here to see Miss Braxton."

All three of them turned and stared at Hasima.

"I didn't know what else to do," she said defensively. "Always in the past when Miss Ginny does something and the authorities came you said I should act like I didn't know anything. So that's what I did. Should I tell them to go away?"

The three of them looked at one another.

"No, bring them here," Magi finally said.

Hasima disappeared and returned a few minutes later leading an English lady and gentleman. She waved them into the library ahead of her and then backed out again, closing the doors.

Haji studied them as the gentleman came forward and offered his hand to Sir Robert. He was a slender young fellow in his early twenties, fair-skinned with light hair and eyes, and an intelligent, mobile face. His companion was an unremarkable brown-haired woman with sloped shoulders and a diffident manner.

"Sir Carlisle," the gentleman said, reaching across the table to shake Sir Robert's hand. "This is indeed an honor, sir. I read your monogram on wine production and its relation to population surges in the third dynasty with great interest."

"You did?" Sir Robert said, brightening.

"Yes, indeed," the man said, straightening. "An inspired piece, sir."

Sir Robert puffed out his chest and preened a bit, stroking his luxuriant white moustache. "Good of you to say so." He frowned. "Who are you, if you don't mind my asking?"

"Excuse me. Allow me to introduce myself," the man said, bowing. "I am Geoffrey Tynesborough, professor of ancient history at Hart's College, Cambridge."

Haji frowned. That was the college where Ginesse had been studying. He looked over at Sir Robert, but he was not paying attention, rifling through the over-heaped contents of his desktop, muttering. "I have the original somewhere around here. Suppose you'd like to see it. Let me see…"

After waiting a moment, Professor Tynesborough cleared his throat and extended his hand in the direction of his companion. "And this lady is Miss Mildred Whimpelhall of Paxton-on-Tyne, Somer—"

"*What?*"

The Englishman looked around, startled by Haji's outburst.

"Did you say this is Miss Whimpelhall?" Haji asked.

The lady blushed profusely.

"Yes," Professor Tynesborough answered. "Miss Whimpelhall."

"But…but she can't be," Haji stammered.

"Excuse me?" the gentleman asked, his perplexity deepening.

"I was introduced to Miss Whimpelhall five days ago at the Misr train station by James Owens, a friend of mine who had been charged with guiding her across the desert to her fiancé, Colonel Pomfrey."

Miss Whimpelhall's eyes grew round, her mouth formed a little "o" of distress, and with a soft moan she pitched forward in a dead faint. Professor Tynesborough caught her before she hit the ground. Beneath the window one of LeBouef's little birds took flight, heading straight to his master's hand.

* * *

"But whatever reason would Miss Braxton have for impersonating me?" Miss Whimpelhall asked some time later from where she rested on the battered old settee in Sir Robert's library. He'd never been one to exchange old comforts for new ones just because he could afford them. Though Sir Robert was a very wealthy man, the only time he ever used any of that great wealth was when he was entertaining, something he did infrequently but enjoyed immensely.

"Because she is a demon," Haji answered through clenched teeth. "And that is what demons do. Make one's life a living," he glanced at Miss Whimpelhall, "inferno."

"But it makes no sense. I am loath to admit it, but yes, Miss Braxton did seem taken with my descriptions of Colonel Lord Pomfrey. But not to the point where one would suspect some sort of mania had taken hold of her." She looked slightly repelled by the notion.

"I should hope not. The Braxton women are known for their levelheadedness," Sir Robert said.

At this Magi gave a small snort. Sir Robert looked at her, brows raised. She looked back, brows lowered. Some silent form of communication was exchanged until, finally, Sir Robert sighed. "Fine. We'll send Harry a telegram."

It took a while, but they strung together a chronology of the events prefacing the professor and Miss Whimpelhall's arrival:

The lady, the real Miss Whimpelhall, had disembarked due to seasickness in Italy just as Ginesse Braxton was supposed to have done. But after a single day of recuperation, she had decided she could not allow herself to succumb to what she considered a character weakness and so had boarded the next ship bound for Alexandria. In the interim, she had discovered that through what she took to be a clerical error, Miss Braxton's luggage had been removed alongside hers from the *Lydonia* and delivered to her.

En route, Miss Whimpelhall had made the acquaintance of Professor Tynesborough, who was also on his way to Cairo. During the course of their conversations they had discovered a mutual friend in Miss Braxton, whom he was hoping to visit. He had been delighted to escort Miss Whimpelhall, along with Miss Braxton's luggage, to Sir Robert's house, where Miss Whimpelhall remembered Miss Braxton had been bound. And thus here they were.

"But why would she do such a thing?" Miss Whimpelhall asked again. "I thought we'd become friends. I was looking forward to thanking her again for her tender care of me."

"Perhaps I can shed some light on that," Professor Tynesborough said. He had been quiet during Miss Whimpelhall's recitation, but now he stood up from the chair he'd taken, clasping his hands behind his back. "Miss Braxton is one of my students." This caused Sir Robert's brows to climb.

"I met her during her first year at college. She wasn't like the other students, certainly not like the other women. I suspected her reasons for pursuing her degree were not entirely founded in her fascination with the subject. Mind you, she was a very good student. But no matter how well she did, she was always unsatisfied and looking for some other way to excel. There was a sort of desperation about her ambition that awoke my sympathy. So, I asked her to aid me in some of my research."

Why would Ginesse Braxton be desperate? Haji wondered, frowning. If she did not want to study Egyptology, she could have gone off and done whatever she wanted. Spoiled brat.

"About six months ago, she came to me with something she'd found that she claimed to be a transposed map. I discounted it as wishful thinking. Shortly thereafter, she resigned from my employ. I believe," he said gravely, "that at that point Miss Braxton felt that she'd fulfilled any obligation she had towards me and decided to continue her research alone."

"I'm not sure I understand what you're getting at, sir," Sir Robert said.

"A few months ago, troubled by our estrangement, I began to follow her research trail. I was amazed by what I—or rather, she— had discovered. I think she has identified the location of the lost city of Zerzura and that she has impersonated Miss Whimpelhall in order to gain access to the vicinity where she believes the city to be found: near Fort Gordon."

"But why would she do such a thing? Why wouldn't she tell her father or me so that we might help her?" Sir Robert asked.

Tynesborough hesitated before answering, and when he did so, his expression was gentle. "I believe she wishes to earn through her own endeavors a place in the annals of archaeology alongside the rest of her exalted family."

"What?" Sir Robert asked, bewildered. "That's ridiculous. She doesn't have to earn a place. She has one by merit of her birth."

"Perhaps it is not something you asked of her, but something she has asked of herself." Tynesborough's smile was sympathetic.

Blessed Allah, Haji thought, *the man is in love with the* afreet.

"I don't believe it," Sir Robert said.

"Can you come up with any more plausible explanation of why she would assume Miss Whimpelhall's identity? Ask yourself this: would she have been able to arrange to get to Fort Gordon by herself?"

"Bah!" Magi, who had been quiet during all of this, suddenly said. "That Ginesse has headed to Fort Gordon under another lady's name seems incontestable. Why she has done so will only be answered once she has returned." She pointed a finger at Haji. "You will fetch her."

Haji recoiled, horrified. "But, Aunt Magi, I have businesses to run. I cannot simply leave."

"Yes, you can. You were given a charge to bring Ginesse Braxton here. You have not fulfilled that charge."

He ground his teeth in frustration. Hard experience had taught him that his life would be intolerable if he refused. "As you wish."

"How wonderful!" The soft cry of delight came from Miss Whimpelhall. "Perhaps...that is, I am loath to suggest it, but I would be most grateful if I might join your expedition, Mr. Elkamal."

"No," Haji said. The last thing he wanted was to add another burden to an already onerous one. This fainting, waxy-faced woman was the worst sort of traveler.

"*Yes*," said Sir Carlisle. "If Ginesse has inconvenienced this lady, we owe it to her to do what we can to see that she is reunited with her fiancée as soon as possible. And I shall go, too."

"What?" both Magi and Haji exclaimed.

"She's my great-granddaughter, and if she needs rescuing, I daresay I should be the one doing it. Besides, if the girl finds Zerzura, I want to see it." He smiled suddenly as an idea occurred to him. "Why, we'll make a party of it!"

Once Sir Robert had set his mind on a thing, he did not change it. The years had only amplified this trait. It would do no good arguing.

"I will go, too," Magi announced, and when Sir Robert opened his mouth to protest, the look she gave him had it snapping shut again. Silently, Haji ran through a litany of Jim Owens's more colorful expletives.

"And I," the professor declared, then quickly amended, "That is, if I might impose upon you?"

Sir Robert peered at the professor suspiciously.

"No, sir," the professor said with commendable dignity. "I would never attempt to commandeer Miss Braxton's discovery. I wish to go for personal reasons."

"Those being?" Magi asked, haughtily.

The professor looked uncomfortable. "I feel responsible. Had I listened to her, this entire situation might have been circumvented. Now, if I may make a suggestion?"

"Go on," Sir Robert prompted.

"We should leave as soon as humanly possible."

"And why is that?" Magi asked, frowning. "From what you say she is well tended."

"Do you know Miss Braxton well?"

Everyone except Miss Whimpelhall nodded with varying degrees of enthusiasm.

"Then can you imagine the sort of trouble she will get into without someone who is aware of her, um, proclivities to protect her?"

CHAPTER THIRTEEN

"If I watch her much longer, it will end by my being madly in love with her," he mused. "I never could withstand a pretty face or winsome spirit."

—from the personal diary of Ginesse Braxton

THE EGYPTIAN DESERT, TEN DAYS LATER

The pistol shot rang out across the desert floor, and Pomfrey's soldiers dove for cover, including Neely, their grizzled lieutenant.

On the far side of the camp, Miss Whimpelhall started and looked down at the newly minted hole in the sand beside her and at what remained of the large, yellowish scorpion that had been sitting in it a second earlier. Then she looked at the rock in her hand, the one she'd just lifted from that same place.

"I fear I am once more in your debt, Mr. Owens," she said, her voice shaking just a bit.

"Think nothing of it," Jim said, calmly replacing his pistol in its shoulder holster and leaning back on his bedroll. He no longer got rattled at having to shoot things, climb things, chase things, or dive into things to snatch her back from the precipices she seemed always to be leaning over. It was all in the day's work. "Please. Continue with what you were saying."

"Are you really interested?" She sounded both doubtful and hopeful, and the combination was incredibly winsome. Added to which, he really was interested. She was an encyclopedia of the obscure and unusual. The theoretical finishing school she'd attended might not have tamed her vivacity, but it had definitely honed her intellect.

"I am."

She replaced the rock over what was left of the scorpion and edged away. "Where was I?"

"You were explaining how Akhenaten's name was expunged from the historic record. That rock you were holding was going to illustrate the expunging, I believe."

"Oh, yes," she said and began again. He listened, but his mind drifted. He found Egyptian history interesting enough, but not half so interesting as her. Ten days under the desert sun had bleached most of the plum color from her hair, turning it a soft cinnamon, and toasted her skin a light golden brown so that her blue-green eyes shimmered like a turquoise oasis in a bed of warm sand.

She still wore those damnable trousers, but at least they were hidden under an enveloping white *tob*, a robe that he'd bartered off a trader in Suhag. For the most part, it had been an uneventful seven days. Oh, there'd been a bit of food poisoning, a tent had caught fire, here and there a runaway camel, and now the scorpion, but nothing wholly unexpected.

It wasn't her fault that trouble dogged her steps. Take, for instance, the scorpion. A hundred people could have picked up that rock and nothing would have been under it; yellow scorpions were as rare as they were lethal. But if Mildred Whimpel-hall picked up a rock, there would surely be a scorpion lurking beneath it.

But while she was seldom to blame, she wasn't entirely inculpable. She was impetuous and impulsive and headstrong. Somehow she always managed to tempt Fate, and Fate never managed to resist.

Most times, it wasn't too onerous a task keeping her safe, and most times she courted nothing more than a few bumps and bruises—not always her own. But there had been times his blood ran cold. Like when she'd been hanging out over the Nile straight in the path of that oncoming *dahabiya*.

She could have died.

He'd never been so terrified. Not even when he'd crawled into the Mahdist camp seven years ago, certain any second the side of his head would be exploded by a bullet. So afraid that when he got her back on deck, he'd lost every scrap of composure and shouted at her. He never lost his temper. And it was while he was shouting at her and she was shouting back that a strange, unwelcome notion had stolen into his imagination, and moments later, when she'd flung her arms around him, that notion had taken root, and no matter how much he wanted it to, it would not be dislodged: he was besotted.

He told himself it was just an infatuation. It had been years since he had spent time in the company of a young lady. He was susceptible. And what of it, really? Many men had fallen under the spell of a siren; the essence of their allure was the very fact of their unattainability. And if he had a hard time imagining this forthright, ingenuous, outspoken girl in the role of a siren, what other term better identified her? She was unattainable and he was besotted.

So, he watched her, and remarked all her many grace notes, hoarding up every impression, every detail without hesitation or guilt, storing them up for a long future without her.

Yes. It was harmless, a blameless way to mark time. Almost innocent. Almost…

"—and the really juicy part of this is," she leaned forward as if she were divulging the name of her neighbor's paramour rather than a scandalous bit about a king who'd been dead for three thousand years, "there is some evidence in the written record that indicates *he* may well have been a *she*." She straightened, her expression delightedly scandalized.

"You don't say."

"I do!" she replied, nonchalantly swishing her horsetail swatter around her face to chase away the battalion of flies that accompanied them. They didn't bother her as much as he would have expected. Though Pomfrey had made sure they were well provisioned, even sending a mattress and china, it still had to be a far cry from what she was used to.

Yet she devoured the fava beans and oil mash served up every night for dinner with an appreciative appetite. She never complained about the arid wind that wrung the moisture from eyes and mouth, or the heat, or the stench of the camels. She was unfailingly good-humored and adaptable and engaging. It was as if she had been born to this sort of life.

Pomfrey had chosen well. Damn him. Though it did strike Jim lately that Mildred seldom mentioned her fiancé…But then she might not feel comfortable discussing her lover with him. Thank God. Because Jim didn't know if he could quite handle being privy to her romantic confidences.

For the hundredth time, he reminded himself that he'd been put in charge of delivering her to Pomfrey and that is what he would do. And because he'd been entrusted with her welfare as well as her safety, if that meant keeping her safe from him, then that is what he would do, too.

"Mr. Owens?" she asked, dragging him back from his thoughts. "Are you alright? You look a bit strange."

"I'm fine," he said. "And I'd rather you called me Jim. Jim is a sight easier to yell than 'Mr. Owens.'"

His carefully bland suggestion garnered an unexpected reaction. Rather than looking affronted or uncomfortable, she smiled at him, as pleased as a colt in spring clover. "You would?"

"I would."

"Thank you, Jim." She hesitated and he waited, hoping she would offer him the same intimacy, but then, as if reading his mind, her gaze dropped away.

He hadn't really expected her to give him use of her Christian name. There were proprieties to be observed, a distance to be maintained, and it seemed she was willing to see to that even if he wouldn't.

She was squirming now, visibly uncomfortable, and that hadn't been his aim. "Go on," he said. "You were talking about a pharaoh who might have been a pharaohess...?"

"There is no such thing as a pharaohess. It's like the word 'ruler,' not gender specific." She seized on the distraction. "Well, as I was saying earlier, in order to correctly position his, or possibly her, pyramid, its engineer would have made use of two *merkhets*, aligning the first with the North Star and the second along a north-south meridian."

She continued on, adopting the slightly dry, professorial manner he'd noticed whenever she spoke about ancient Egypt. He watched her, enjoying the sound of her voice, his gaze drifting around their campsite every now and again, looking for danger, but always coming back to her and always lingering a little too long.

He realized she'd stopped talking and was waiting for him to reply.

"You sure know your ancient Egyptian history," he said. "I've been here seven years and I don't know half of the things you do."

She blushed. "Well, I've been affianced to Colonel Lord Pomfrey for…for six years, and I knew I would be living in Egypt, so it only makes sense that I'd try to learn everything I could about the country, doesn't it?" She sounded a little too pleased with this explanation.

"It's commendable, though I'm not sure many women would take the same attitude," he said. "Six years, you say?"

"Yes," she replied.

Bloody hell. She must have been betrothed while she was still in the schoolroom. There was no chance it had been a love match, then. Likely their marriage had been arranged between her family and Pomfrey.

His loathing of Pomfrey grew. What sort of man betrothed himself to a child? And what sort of family allowed it? Still, though she said very little about her family, what she had said revealed nothing but warm affection.

What incentive had they had to marry her off? Money? Land? Or were they simply eager to align themselves with a titled family? Did she wish a different future for herself, or was she content to dutifully fulfill the bargain now that it had been struck?

Like Charlotte.

There'd been a time when the memory of Charlotte's willing acceptance of Althea's lies would have summoned up a deep and bitter anger. But that time had long since passed, faded alongside the memory of a desperate puppy love. Poor Charlotte, she'd done nothing wrong. And if Charlotte had been a pawn in her family's ambitions, hadn't he been just as readily Althea's pawn?

He'd been willing to give up everything, his life, his name, his heritage, to defy her and in the end he'd only given Althea what she had wanted from the start: uncontested control. How much easier to throw something away than to stay and fight for it.

His gaze strayed back to Mildred. How long, how hard would he fight to keep her if she were his? *Forever.*

"Owens!"

At the sound of his name, Jim looked around. Lieutenant Neely, a skinny, middle-aged veteran with a mouthful of broken teeth and a Cockney accent, was approaching. Jim stood up. "What can I do for you, Lieutenant?"

"Since you've drawn the attention of every desert rat within twenty miles by taking that shot, I'm giving you double guard duty tonight."

He sounded more sullen than commanding, and his gaze kept fidgeting away from Jim's. He was not a good leader, too anxious and too belligerent. He'd probably made his way up the ranks through pure attrition.

"Sure thing," Jim said.

The man hesitated, gnawing at his lip.

"Anything else?" Jim asked.

"Yeah," Neely said, taking Jim's arm and pulling him a short distance away. "Here's the thing, Owens. I think we ought to go back to Suhag. Now listen," he said before Jim could speak. "Hear me out. When we were there I heard some of them trader chappies saying as how they'd heard that Mahdists were rising up again and planning to attack caravans. You and I both knows I ain't got the men or gun power to engage a raidin' party."

"Those rumors have been circulating for years, Neely. We'll be fine." Jim clapped the man on the shoulder. "Even if someone were out there, the chances they'd stumble on us are about as good as finding a seed in a sandstorm. We're in the middle of nowhere, at least seventy miles from the Forty Days' Road."

That was not by accident. Instead of traveling along the ancient trade route, he'd taken them purposefully on a course south of it. The old caravan trail was still widely traveled and as such the most likely place for bandits and outlaws to seek their victims. Their current route led to a lesser-known oasis some three or four days out.

Neely shook his head violently. "The bloke that just come off guard duty swears he saw a glint in the distance. And last night I seen a fire. The boys are scared shitless."

Jim didn't answer because Neely was right; they were being shadowed. Jim had seen the signs three days back and had ridden out at night to see if he could get closer to their elusive escorts. He hadn't had any luck. But whoever they were, if they'd wanted to do them ill, they'd have done so by now.

Likely as not, they were just traveling in the same direction and wanted nothing to do with them. But trying to convince Neely of that wouldn't be easy. Better not to say anything at all. The soldiers had already caught the contagion of Neely's alarm. Their eyes darted nervously and they stood in little clusters, talking in low undertones, clutching their rifles. Recent conscripts, Jim guessed, green and suggestible. Damn Neely, anyway.

"Mirages," Jim said. "If there were raiders, they would have come after us long before this. I had a look around yesterday night. If there was someone out there, I would have seen them."

"You're wrong, Owens. Thing is you may be *dead* wrong," Neely said, mopping at his forehead. "They weren't mirages." He shot Jim a haunted glance. "You ever seen what those savages do to a man?" He took a deep breath, closed his eyes, and released it. "You don't wanta. I wish to God I hadn't. I been in service twenty years. I have one more year left before I'm discharged with my pension. One year and I'm for England. I don't want to die before then. We should go back."

"Listen to yourself," Jim said. "You're not making sense. How is going back any better? Bandits can follow us back just as easily as forward."

"No," said Neely with dogged insistence. "They'll be waiting to ambush us at that oasis. We start back now, they'll never expect it. We get back to Suhag and then we wait there for Pomfrey to send more men. Six ain't enough."

For a moment, Jim considered it. But he didn't believe they were in any danger, and they were halfway to Fort Gordon. To turn back now would be ridiculous. And if they did turn back, he would be honor-bound to stay in Suhag with Mildred until Pomfrey's reinforcements arrived. Two weeks with her. Maybe more.

And that, he thought with brutal honesty, would be a mistake. Every day in her company put a greater and greater strain on his resolve to act honorably, to do his job and walk away. He was very afraid that if he spent too much time with her, he wouldn't be walking away. "No, Neely. We aren't going back."

Neely stiffened, lifting his rifle. "We do if I say we are. I'm the officer in charge here."

Jim didn't say a word. He just stood, meeting Neely's eyes and letting the other man take his measure. He didn't want to hurt Neely. The lieutenant had probably never thought he'd make it out of Egypt alive, and now that he could finally see an end to his time here, hope had come hand in hand with fear.

Jim pitied Neely. But they weren't going back.

For a long few seconds, Neely ground his teeth in frustration, one eyelid twitching as he stared at Jim. Finally, with a sound halfway between snarl and sob, he turned on his heel and left.

"What was that all about?" Mildred had risen and was standing nearby.

"Nothing," Jim said. "He wanted me to take late night watch, is all."

"Oh," she said. "Do you have to go right now?"

No. Yes. Right now. Before it's too late...if it isn't already.

"No."

She flashed him her gamine smile. "Then I suppose you want me to tell you about the building of the step pyramids?"

"I want nothing more," he answered.

She sank back down to the ground, laughing a little and picking up a feather some high-flying vulture had lost.

He tried to recall Charlotte's face but it was gone. All he could see was the girl in front of him, leaning forward to draw him a picture in the sand with her vulture feather. Her hair was coming undone, a single strand curling around her neck like a lover's palm—

The rifle butt caught him hard in the temple.

He felt his knees buckle, and his last thought was that Le-Bouef would have laughed himself sick that Jim Owens had finally been caught off guard because he was mooning over a woman drawing stick figures in the sand.

CHAPTER FOURTEEN

Though great peril menaced her, she had always been a brave lass. Some would call her valiant, and not ~~unused to accidents~~ danger.

—from the personal diary of Ginesse Braxton

"You're coming with us!" Neely shouted.

"I am not," Ginesse said. She knelt where Jim Owens lay unconscious on the ground, her fingers gently probing the gash in his head, uncertain she would know what a crack would feel like even if she found one.

"Get packed and get those camels loaded! *Now!*" Neely shouted at his men, and they leapt into action, taking down the camp with a speed they'd never shown setting it up.

He turned back to her, glowering. "Goddammit, lass. Do you *want* to die?"

"I'm not going to die," she said.

"Right. Because you're coming with us and that's that. Owens can rot out here, since that's what he wants. But I been charged with taking you to the colonel, and that's what I aim to do."

"But you aren't. You're taking me back to Suhag."

"Just until some more men can be sent. Now, get up."

"No," she said, her gaze on Jim. "I'm not leaving Mr. Owens." Though his breathing seemed unlabored, he looked pale.

"Look, Miss Whimpelhall," Neely said, obviously making some effort to speak in a reasonable tone. "You don't come with us, and you might as well take Owens's gun there and shoot yourself in the head. Because you're gonna die out here sure as there's a devil in hell."

He'd struck Jim from behind; she hated him.

"Mr. Neely," she said in a hard, uncompromising voice, "let me make myself clear. I am not going with you. If you attempt to make me go by force, I shall fight you every step of the way. If you sneak up behind me and knock me senseless," here Neely had the grace to flush with embarrassment, "I shall take the first opportunity to run away. Because, Mr. Neely, I have more confidence in an unconscious Mr. Owens than I do in an unprincipled scoundrel and his equally dishonorable soldiers." Her scornful gaze swept over Neely's men. Not one of them could meet her eye.

They'd finished taking down the camp. The tents were packed, and the camels carrying provisions were already loaded and tethered to a lead line.

Neely pulled himself up. "Owens gave me no choice," he said with as much dignity as he could muster.

"And *I'm* not giving you one. I am not leaving him here."

His lips curled back in a snarl, and he dropped to a squat beside her so they were eye to eye. "Ever seen what them savages do to a man?" he asked, in a low, throbbing voice.

"They make 'im so as he's not recognizable as man, is what. Sometimes they cut chunks off him, skinning him alive, or taking pieces out of his insides and draping 'em over him. Or sometimes they let the desert do their work. They stake him out in the sun so his skin peels off like the blistered hide of roast pig, slit his eyelids off so he goes blind staring into the sun, and let the ants eat him bit by bit..."

She felt the blood drain from her face though this was not the first time she'd heard such stories. She'd been awake during similar conversations at her father's camp when no one thought ears that needed protecting would be listening. She'd heard equally horrific stories eavesdropping in on the *fellahin's* gossip, too, only the barbarians in their tales wore uniforms.

"I'd hate to think what they might do to a woman," Neely finished intently.

She swallowed but did not look away. "I am not leaving Mr. Owens."

They stared at one another a full minute before he surged to his feet, spewing epithets and dashing his hat to the ground. She watched him, unmoved.

"If I show up in Suhag without Owens, no one cares," he shouted at her. "But how am I supposed to explain how I'm there and you're not?"

"That's your problem."

"Dammit, woman, I don't care if I have to tie you to the camel, you're—"

He stopped because she was on her feet with a gun pointing at his chest. Jim Owens's gun. "I am telling you for the last time, Mr. Neely," she said. "I am not going to leave Mr. Owens, and since you have already declared you are not taking him with you—"

"It'd be worth my hide if I tried," Neely said.

"Be that as it may, I am not going without him. And if you take one step closer to me, I will shoot you. I do not know if it will kill you, but at this distance, do you want to take that chance?"

The men shifted uneasily, muttering. The situation had taken an unexpected and unpleasant turn.

"Goddamn you, woman!" Neely exploded, but this time there was more helplessness than anger in his voice.

She kept the gun trained on him. "You'll leave us a camel and provisions," she said.

He swore again and made a sharp gesture to one of his soldiers. "Untie that last camel," he shouted. He turned back to Ginesse as the man hurried to the end of the line to comply.

"Listen. I don't want to leave you here. I'm a Christian man," Neely said. "Mostly. Truth is, I don't know how hard I hit Owens. Pretty hard, I guess. Fact is, he might not wake up, and then where'll you be?"

A bottomless pit seemed to open up at Ginesse's feet. She swallowed, refusing to let it suck her down into it. She wouldn't believe it. Her father had been coshed in the head a number of times and he'd always woken up. Jim would, too.

"I'll take that chance."

He regarded her soberly for one last long minute, miserable but resigned.

"All right, miss. You win. I did what I could to make you come. And if it's any consolation to you for what I done to Owens, you might know that me and my lads will have to take the French leave because if we don't, we're sure to be court-martialed." He regarded her reproachfully, as if she had willfully done him a great wrong.

"You don't *have* to leave us," she said.

Neely snorted. "First off, that man has a reputation for bein' a hard customer," he said, nodding toward Jim, "and I don't want to learn if it's warranted. Second, my man saw a fire in the distance no matter what Owens says. So I guess I'd rather flee Egypt with my head on my shoulders than stay and have it lopped off."

But Jim had said there was no cause for alarm, and if Jim said there was no one nearby, there was no one nearby. "Then there's nothing more to say," she said, wishing Neely would go so she could put down the gun and go back to doing what, if anything, she could for Jim.

"I guess not." The solider who'd untied the camel led it over and handed the rope to Neely. There'd been a reason that particular camel had been at the end of the line. She was old and evil-tempered with a patchy hide and only one eye. She spat, hitting Neely's trousers. Ginesse decided she liked her.

Neely shouted again and another soldier untied his water skin from his saddle and tossed it to him. He caught it and flung it at Ginesse's feet. She didn't look down to where it landed, expecting Neely would try to divert her attention so he could grab for her gun. Once more he swore.

"If I were you, I'd make sure I was gone before Mr. Owens wakes up."

Neely spun around and started stalking toward his waiting men. He'd gone about five steps before he turned around. In amazement, she saw that his lips were trembling and his eyes brimmed with tears.

"What now?" she asked, growing exasperated. The man was worse than a Dickens serial story. Just when you thought it might end, something else popped up.

"You're a brave lass, Miss Whimpelhall," he said, his voice thickening. "As thick as bricks, but courageous as I am not. I wish I could promise you I'd tell them where to find your sweet, valiant bones, but the truth is, I won't. I'll tell them Owens took off with you and bandits got the pair of you. And when the next ship sails out of Alexandria, I'll be on it no matter what the outcome. So goodbye, Miss Whimpelhall. Don't think too badly of me when you're dying."

As farewell speeches went, it wasn't very heartening.

He swung up onto the camel's saddle and with a final salute, kneed the great beast into a trot, his men following suit.

The heavy pistol slowly dropped against her thigh, and she sank down next to Jim's unconscious body, watching them go until they were just small figures dissolving into the shimmering horizon. In a very short time it would be dark and then the cold would come, quick and dangerous.

She brushed her hand across Jim's brow. It felt a little warm but not feverish. She didn't even know if one became feverish due to head trauma. She studied him, worrying her lower lip. Should she try to wake him up? She couldn't remember if her mother had ever roused her father after a similar injury. And if she had, how? Water? A slap? Jostling?

What if she hurt him even more than he already was? What if something she did loosened something already perilously close to breaking and she caused permanent damage? In the end, she decided Jim's body would best know when it ought to regain consciousness. Gingerly, she cradled his head in her lap and forced herself to wait. She was not very good at waiting.

The thought that maybe they would die kept whispering through her imagination. If she did, no one would ever know. Even Neely's lie wouldn't help anyone find her; they'd be looking for Mildred Whimpelhall, who eventually would appear in Cairo and turn Pomfrey's funeral preparations to matrimonial ones and his sorrow to joy.

Ginesse sighed. Maybe one day when the Pomfreys were toasting their anniversary, they would pause and cast a passing thought to the strange young woman who for some unknown reason had masqueraded as Mildred and wonder why she'd done so and who she was.

There would never ever be any reason to suppose that Ginesse Braxton, Miss Whimpelhall's shipboard acquaintance, was the impersonator, especially since her great-grandfather would eventually read the telegram she'd sent and then everyone would assume she'd been lost somewhere in Eastern Europe, stolen to become some Asian prince's consort or eloped with a Bulgarian count.

It was all very romantic, and she was feeling a mite better when her eye caught the sparkle of the emerald ring she wore. Her mother had given it to her on her sixteenth birthday. Her mother...

What have I done?

If she died, she would have condemned them to a life of fruitless searching because no matter how slight the chance, as long as there was even the faintest possibility of her being alive, her parents would never ever give up looking for her. Never. They would hunt until they found her bones, or they themselves died. Because they loved her. They loved her, and they would never find her bones because they would be looking in the wrong place.

The thought of them searching for her year after endless year filled her with horror and shame. She should have left a letter explaining her plans with some responsible person to be delivered if she never arrived. And if she ever got the opportunity to do anything as stupid as this again, she would remember to write down her plans. But...but she hadn't thought she might die. She hadn't planned on Neely, damn him!

She looked down at Jim's bronzed, handsome face. His lashes cast a fan-shaped shadow over his high cheekbones, his hair tumbling in damp curls over his brow. He looked so much younger now, so vulnerable, the hard gaze extinguished, his expression relaxed, the implacable lines softened. She brushed the hair from his temple. She couldn't have left him, and given the choice again, she wouldn't. *God*, she hated Neely.

Why wouldn't Jim wake up? It had been almost twenty minutes. A quarter moon was rising in an orchid-colored sky. Soon it would be night. Carefully, she slipped her hand beneath Jim's head and eased it to the ground. There were preparations she needed to make before the frigid desert night arrived—

—he moaned.

She scrambled back to his side on her knees, bracketing his face in her hands. "Mr. Owens. Jim." A tear fell on his cheek. "Are you all right?"

"No," he moaned. He squinted up at her through one eye, grimacing. "What happened?"

"Don't move. Neely hit you from behind with his rifle."

He rolled to his side and pushed himself to a seated position, groaning. "Where...?"

"Don't try to get up. They're gone," she said, wrapping an arm around his shoulders.

"Gone?" He looked around, his expression astonished. "They left you here *alone*?"

"No. You're here. Now, stop. Your head is bleeding again."

He put a hand to his forehead, breathing hard and wincing. "How long ago?"

"Quarter of an hour or—*No!* You're in no condition to do anything about it."

But he was already struggling to his feet. She wedged a shoulder under his arm, supporting his weight as best she could as he climbed painfully upright. He was heavy and unsteady, and she had to wrap her arms tightly around his waist just to keep him from falling.

"Please," she said. "There is nothing you can do. You're only going to make yourself worse. You need to—"

But her words fell on deaf ears, for as she was talking his legs gave out, and with her arms around him, he crumpled slowly to the ground, unconscious once more.

CHAPTER FIFTEEN

Alas for his long-spent dreams! For he had once been given a glimpse of a higher purpose than the acquisition of money and the carnal pleasures it could buy.

—from the personal diary of Ginesse Braxton

"Mm. This is delicious. Do try a slice of the duck breast, Professor Tynesborough," Sir Robert said, waving his fork invitingly at a piece of perfectly grilled meat enrobed in a rich pomegranate brandy reduction, little pearls of glistening couscous cozying up next to it.

The professor shook his head regretfully. "I dare not out of pity for my poor camel. I swear I've gained ten pounds since our trip began."

"Haji, then you must help me out here," Sir Robert said, turning to him. "I can't do the cook justice by myself, and while he's the most prickly, easily offended of chaps, he's a dashed good cook and I should hate for him to give notice."

Haji doubted whether this was likely; they were more than a hundred miles out in the desert. Nonetheless, he speared a piece of the fork-tender meat and transferred it to his plate. He admitted that the cook had extraordinary talents. Where Sir Robert had found him and how he'd convinced the Coptic chef to come along on their "rescue mission" was a mystery. But then, Haji conceded, maybe not so great a mystery: Sir Robert had probably offered him a salary he could not refuse.

Sir Robert had spared no expense on this trip. They were seated under a tented pavilion, the open sides covered with gauzy netting that kept the flies at bay and billowed prettily in the slight breeze. White linen covered the table, and crystal and silver sparkled in the slanting sunlight. Beneath silver domes, an array of exquisite dishes awaited their perusal, including traditional Arabian fare such as a refreshing salad of chopped tomatoes with coriander and mint, chickpeas stewed in garlic, lemon, and olive oil, and tiny grilled pigeons stuffed with grapes.

The indulgences didn't stop outside the dining pavilion, either. Each day in the early afternoon two dozen porters and attendants set up a small town's worth of tents, complete with mattresses and pillows, their striped awnings stretching out over the front and back flaps to capture any passing breeze and thus ameliorate their daily afternoon naps. Sir Robert dearly loved his afternoon naps.

Once the sun had sunk low enough, the *fellahin* packed it all up again and they'd mount their cantankerous camels and sally forth for another three to four hours before their *reis*, Zayed— another of Sir Robert's personal hires—called an end to the day's progress. Then the *fellahin* would once more pitch the tents and set up camp as the chef prepared a final light repast for their dinner. After that they retired to their tents only to be woken before dawn with coffee and croissants followed by a few hours of travel before Sir Robert deemed it too hot to travel.

Needless to say, they were not racing toward Fort Gordon.

Nor would they be. Sir Robert was holding up extraordinarily well, but he *was* eighty-five. Even given the luxury of their accommodations, the quality of the food, and their easy pace, it was a rigorous journey, and no one, most especially Sir Robert, was going to test the limits of his endurance.

Except, perhaps, their *reis*, a Bedouin who had scant patience with his aged client's insistence on so many lengthy intermissions.

Haji glanced out of the tent where Zayed stood, arms crossed, staring out at the desert, disapproval in every line of his body. Haji did not know where Sir Robert had found a Bedouin willing to guide them, but then, Sir Robert had a long history in this country, and over those years he had gained the respect and admiration of a diverse group of people, the nomadic Bedouins among them.

"Miss Whimpelhall?" Professor Tynesborough said. "Some claret, perhaps?"

"I don't think I ought to," she demurred.

"Why, there's nothing wrong is there, my dear?" Sir Robert asked, all solicitude. Though the years may have depleted his endurance, they had not affected his idea of himself as something of a ladies' man.

"No," she said. "It is just all this rich food. I am loath to admit it, but I find myself pining for a simple slice of cold shoulder and perhaps a piece of cheese. *Cow's* milk cheese."

"Your stomach is nasty again?" Magi asked from her seat beside Sir Robert's, where he was never out from beneath her ever-vigilant eye.

"A bit," Miss Whimpelhall said, blushing. Haji had never seen a woman so given to blushing. Often just a reference to bodily functions could make her face flame bright red right to the roots of her brown hair.

Haji had thought Miss Whimpelhall as portrayed by Ginesse Braxton had been bad enough, but the real Mildred Whimpelhall was worse. She arrived late to dine every night. As soon as she spotted Magi and him, for a few telling seconds her brows shot up. She could not have made it clearer that she thought they should have been serving rather than dining. And in part, she was right. His aunt and he came from a caste far below the pashas and nobles. Miss Whimpelhall was always gracious, but the sort of graciousness that was meant to remind others of her superiority.

Not that anyone else seemed to notice, even Magi. But then Magi's world revolved around Sir Robert. She would be no more likely to note Miss Whimpelhall's prejudice than she was to note Haji's discomfort with it. In other words, not at all.

"I am sure something can be arranged, Miss Whimpelhall," Magi said and beckoned to one of the attendants hovering silently in the background. There had been a time when Haji might have been one of them. If not for Magi and Sir Robert.

"Tell me, Professor, where did Ginesse find this clue as to the location of Zerzura?" Sir Robert asked as they continued their meal.

It wasn't the first time the subject of the lost city had been broached.

"*Supposed* clue, Sir Robert," the young professor corrected gently. "Oddly enough, it was in a scroll found in Pope Urban the Second's library."

"Someone wrote in Demotic to the pope? Absurd! The language was last employed five hundred years before he was even ordained."

"I didn't say they wrote to him. I said they sent it to him. By a squire he'd sent to North Africa during the First Crusade, I believe."

Fascinated, Haji sat forward in his chair. It had been a long time since he'd enjoyed a purely academic conversation, and both Sir Robert and Professor Tynesborough had filled a void he hadn't realized he'd had. It was bittersweet to imagine what life would have been like had he had the means for a proper education.

"What would he have been doing in North Africa?" Haji asked.

Professor Tynesborough lifted a hand in apology. "I can't say. The papyrus only came to me because of the language it was written in. I glanced at it and promptly forgot about it. It appeared to be nothing more than a bill of goods from a caravan written during Cleopatra's reign, so not my bailiwick. Not ancient enough," he added for Miss Whimpelhall's benefit. "About five thousand years too young. I gave it to Miss Braxton to catalogue."

The chef, a heavily bearded Copt named Timon with skin the color of teak and a big belly he carried straight in front of him like a pregnant woman, appeared in the entrance to the dining pavilion. He bore a domed serving plate before him.

"What fool asks for cheese?" he demanded. "How am I to transport cheese through a desert? There is no cheese."

Miss Whimpelhall took one look at the contemptuous man and shrank in her seat.

"Ah, Timon," Sir Robert hailed the cook. "Miss Whimpelhall here is having a bit of a tummy upset. Unused to such glorious food, I shouldn't wonder."

The cook's dark eyes latched on to Miss Whimpelhall. "No cheese and no meat without spice or sauces."

"Then what have you there, Timon?" Sir Robert asked.

"The ingredients for a dessert that will make you weep for joy," he announced. "A tender crepe, orange liqueur, butter and sugar. I will prepare *en table*." He did not wait for permission—he simply clapped his hands, and at once an attendant arrived with a small table.

"Good show! At least I know you like a sweet," Sir Robert said merrily with a pointed glance at Miss Whimpelhall's figure, "and you must admit, Cook is a dab hand with desserts, so at least in this you won't be disappointed." He chuckled, oblivious to Miss Whimpelhall's embarrassed glance.

Haji was impatient to return to their previous conversation. "Pardon my curiosity, Professor, but why would a crusader send such a list to a pope?"

"Ah," Professor Tynesborough gently waggled his finger, "because that caravan had come from Zerzura."

The chef's head snapped around. "Zerzura? Zerzura is nothing but a myth."

"Probably," Professor Tynesborough agreed, apparently finding nothing unusual about trading archaeological theories with a cook and an Egyptian con man. By heaven, Haji liked the man. In some ways, he reminded him of Jim. "Miss Braxton's research suggests the Oasis of Little Birds lies in a mountain range deep in the southwestern part of Egypt. But no one has ever even seen this mountain range, let alone the city."

"No European," Haji said excitedly. "And while I have not heard of mountains, some men I have traded with have in turn traded with others who say they have been to the shoulders of the desert, a great plateau."

The cook paused in the process of sautéing some citrus fruit in butter and sugar. He slid a thin crepe into the golden syrup, making a disdainful sound. "And I suppose the Ark of the Covenant is waiting there to be discovered?"

"Hardly," Sir Robert said. "The Judeo tradition keeps careful track of such things. No, that was lost in Alexandria. But if there is a city that deep in the desert, it only makes sense that it would have been a primary center for the caravan trade as well as a cultural crossroads for the ancient world. Oh, there would be treasure there, indeed." He smiled at the cook. "But no ark."

"Now here," Timon announced, "is a treasure." He set the plate in front of Miss Whimpelhall before serving the others. Then, with the slightest of bows, he left the pavilion.

For long, appreciative moments, no one spoke as they devoured the dessert. Finally, Sir Robert shoved himself back from the table. "I do enjoy roughing it now and again," he said, patting his stomach fondly. "Makes one appreciate the finer things in life, what? I say, I wonder how Ginesse is faring? Do you suppose they've arrived at Fort Gordon yet?"

"If not yet, very soon," Haji said, thinking of Jim. Haji would not like to be around when Jim discovered Ginesse's masquerade. He was not a man who took being made a fool of lightly. Ginesse had best pray Jim remembered who her father was and then pray that he cared enough to let it make a difference. Haji wasn't sure it would.

"Good. Good. I should hate to think she's not having as fine a time as we are." Sir Robert rolled his eyes toward Professor Tynesborough. "She was always a bully little camper, quite as at home in the desert as a Tuareg raider. Acted more like a son than a daughter."

"That's interesting," Professor Tynesborough said. "I wonder if she found it a reprieve to come to London and be treated with the gentle regard and tenderness young ladies are generally accorded there."

Sir Robert frowned as if this thought had never occurred to him. "I always thought she liked her life very much. Did she infer otherwise to you, Professor?" he asked.

"No," the professor hastily assured him. "I was only wondering. She seemed mostly eager to get another degree, yet she was never one of those students who lived and breathed their studies. I thought perhaps she sought an excuse to stay in England and not return…here," he finished weakly.

"Oh," Sir Robert said, his brow furrowing and his lip stuck out in a thoughtful manner. He looked sad, Haji realized. He damned Tynesborough for dispelling one of the old gentleman's fond illusions.

"I think she was quite happy in Egypt, Sir Robert," Haji put in, winning a grateful look from Sir Robert. "I knew her well, remember. You gave me the role of nanny to her when she was allowed to visit the concessions where Mr. Braxton worked."

"Nanny?" Sir Robert asked, perplexed. "Is that how you saw it?"

Haji made a slight, dismissive gesture and smiled to show he felt no rancor over it. "Well, wasn't I?"

"No." Sir Robert's noble old face creased with hurt. "I considered you more like a big brother to her and asked you to watch over her in that spirit, not as a duty or as an employee, but as a family member. I thought that was clear."

Haji froze. No. He hadn't known.

"But then, after the fire, after Ginny left, well…it was clear you did not think of us in the same way because you disappeared." Sir Robert regarded him with a mildly reproachful look. "I don't mind telling you it was quite…empty in the house with both

you and Ginesse gone. But then, I suppose young men must follow their own course. I do wish you had stayed in touch with us
though. Even if you didn't consider us your family, we consider
you ours. Why did you leave, Haji?"

*Because of my guilt. Because of my pride. Because I kept the
fire Ginesse started burning in order to blame her. I thought once
rid of her that the owners of those concessions where she'd been
allowed to run amok would notice me, would take me seriously,
would teach me.*

But they hadn't. Without Ginesse, there was no reason for
Haji to be at those digs. The only one who'd ever truly shown an
interest in his education had been Sir Robert, and he'd betrayed
him. Haji couldn't remain in Sir Robert's house, seeing how much
everyone missed Ginesse and knowing he was responsible. And
all for nothing. Over the years he'd assuaged that guilt by trans-
ferring much of the blame to Ginesse.

"I thought it best," Haji said and was saved from having to say
more by Miss Whimpelhall.

"How...democratic," she said and smiled brightly.

CHAPTER SIXTEEN

Shyly, she lifted her tremulous lips to his, and in this reverent gift of herself, he knew the sublime pleasure of her pure, sweet kiss.

—from the personal diary of Ginesse Braxton

"Please, Jim," Ginesse said. "I need just a few hours' rest before we set out."

It was a new tact, because the old one, where she tried to rationally explain that traveling so soon after a head injury was not advisable, had been getting her nowhere.

Jim, in the process of hunting through the saddlebag Neely had left, stopped and studied her closely. She contrived to look exhausted, which wasn't hard.

"Bloody Neely," he muttered under his breath. "All right, Miss Whimpelhall. A few hours, but I have to tell you, Neely didn't leave us much. There's no tent in here, no food, no coal. Pretty much all that's in here is a couple blankets and a change of uniform and tinderbox."

"That despicable worm—" Ginesse began.

"Gets worse," Jim said. "That water skin he left has less than a day's worth of water in it."

Ginesse stared at Jim, having a hard time comprehending the enormity of Neely's betrayal. She'd been confident that once Jim had roused, they would continue on more or less in the same vein, simply less a half dozen travel companions. But now she realized that Neely had never meant her to make it out of the desert. Oh, he'd left them an old, one-eyed camel all right, but that had been nothing more than a sop to his conscience. What good would a camel do them if they didn't have any food or water for days? The camel might survive, but they wouldn't.

But, Ginesse thought fiercely, Neely hadn't reckoned on Jim. A dozen Neelys weren't worth one of him.

"I can't understand why Neely didn't take you with him. The fool all but signed his own death warrant," Jim murmured for what had to be the fifth time. "Especially if I—" he finished in a dark murmur.

Ginesse didn't reply. Anything she said was bound to smack of fabrication, so she opted to stay mute. Because she sensed that he would be angry with her if she told him that she'd refused to leave with Neely. Very angry.

"The oasis we're heading for is not the same one you were leading Lieutenant Neely and his men to?" she asked to distract him.

"No. It's closer."

"Why weren't we heading there to begin with, then?"

"Because it's off the route we were taking by a good twenty miles, and we were carrying plenty of water to make it to the oasis where I'd initially planned to stop."

Ha! she thought triumphantly. Neely had not counted on there being another, closer oasis. So much for his dire predictions.

"But it's still a couple days' ride at best, so we don't want to waste precious time sleeping when we should be traveling, especially at night when we won't be sweating."

Yes, she thought. It made sense. But it made no sense if he ended up face-first in the sand with her unable to move him. "Just a few hours. Please," she said.

He met her eye and finally nodded. "Look," he said, "there's only the one blanket and the camel's blanket and the camel."

She frowned.

"That's pretty much all we have for warmth."

"And each other," she said reasonably.

He started. "Well, yes. I was going to suggest—"

"Of course you were. It would be silly not to cuddle together. My brothers and I used to do so all the time. My mum called it a puppy pile. So you lay next to the camel and I'll curl up into you, like a spoon."

"Ah. No," he said. She peered at him, wondering why he sounded so strange. "No, you press up next to the camel and I'll sandwich you in."

She shrugged. "All right."

Perfectly reasonable and innocent-seeming ideas had always been her *bête noire*, Ginesse realized some minutes later when she lay on her side wedged between the stinky, one-eyed camel and Jim Owens's taut, hard body. True, he was warm. No, he was hot. It emanated from his skin, seeping into hers. And she felt very safe and secure, but she didn't know what to do with her hands. She tried clasping her hands together in an attitude of prayer and nestling them between Jim's shoulder blades, but that created an unwelcome space between Jim and her, and since the whole object of sharing body heat was to share body heat, that rather defeated the purpose.

Besides, the *afreet* within her suggested, since all that masculine beauty was now on the table, so to speak, it seemed a shame not to take advantage—just a small advantage—of what circumstance had thrown her way and see whether he felt as good as he looked.

He did. That was the problem. He felt even better than he looked. She looped an arm around his waist, and at once his whole body went still and tight, like he'd received an electric shock. He was so…dense, so hard, like a living statue, like warm granite. She rested her hand on the corrugated planes of his belly that jumped into sharp relief. She laid her cheek against his back and heard him make some sound of discomfort.

"Are you okay?" she whispered worriedly.

"Yes. Yes." She felt more than saw him nodding vigorously. "I'm good. This is fine. It's fine. Go to sleep."

Sleep? How could she ever sleep? His virility flooded her senses, both arousing and soporific at the same time. Amazing. She'd never experienced anything so alien, so exotic, and so delicious. She resolved to stay awake and hoard every moment, catalogue each sensation, each shift of muscle and each heartbeat—

"Are you praying, Mr. Owens?" she asked, certain she'd misheard him.

"Yup," he said. "Now, if you don't mind I better get back to it."

* * *

It was, Ginesse found, uncomfortable to hold a conversation while sitting atop a camel. Particularly when both participants were sharing the same saddle. Even more particularly when one of the participants, who just happened to be thoroughly male, was sitting behind the other and his arms were looped casually around her waist, his broad chest bolstering her back and his long thighs bracketing her own. And when his breath stirred one's temple and one's head fell into a natural lee beneath his chin, well, conversation proved nearly impossible.

They'd been traveling since just before midnight, and it was now only a few hours until dawn, the coldest time of the night. Overhead the Southern Cross sparkled like ice chips against the sable sky. In front of them rose a huge, miles-long sand dune, its rim an undulating knife-edge limned in cool blue light.

"Is it large?"

"*What?*"

At his barked question, Ginesse started. "Is the oasis large?"

"No."

He shifted behind her, plainly uncomfortable.

"Will there be other travelers there?"

"I doubt it."

She frowned. He'd been taciturn ever since they'd climbed aboard the camel and was only growing more so. It was fine with her if he didn't want to talk. She was having a hard time concentrating on anything but the feel of being in his arms. Ever since she spent the night curled next to him, all she wanted was to return to that state or some state like it.

She was twenty-one, an independent, modern woman who'd been kissed enough times to realize that there were different types of kisses and different proficiencies of kissers, and she was eager to add to her list of life experiences. Specifically, she wanted the experience of kissing Jim Owens. There, she'd acknowledged it.

Of course, it was futile. He wasn't likely to make love to another man's intended. He had too much honor. Besides, even if he were receptive to the idea, she could not allow it. She was supposedly an engaged woman, so committed to another man she'd traveled across the world to be at his side. What would Jim think of Mildred Whimpelhall if she kissed him? For that matter, what would Miss Whimpelhall, the real Miss Whimpelhall, think of Jim Owens if he tried to kiss her? What sort of man kisses another man's bride?

A man who cannot resist that bride, a man overcome with desire. For whatever reasons.

Oh, hell and ruination and bother over what Mildred Whimpelhall would have thought. Ginesse Braxton *didn't care. She* wished Jim Owens would kiss her, and as sad a comment on her own moral probity as she knew it to be, Ginesse Braxton wouldn't think less of him for it.

Perhaps if she told him who she really was…But if she did, he'd likely just turn around and take her back. So, she might as well rest in his sheltering arms and enjoy it.

Time passed and she relaxed. The camel's gait was as lulling as a rocking chair, moving her gently against Jim with each step. His heat soaked through the layers of thin cotton into her back and spine and hips and lower. She snuggled deeper into his embrace and felt his thighs tense and…and something more, lower, pressed intimately against her.

She should have been mortified, horrified, aghast, at the very least embarrassed. She wasn't. Pure feminine empowerment leapt within her, startled out of dormancy by the meaning of that hard, masculine ridge. Jim Owens was as aware of her as a woman as she was of him as a man. She smiled triumphantly into the darkness. So, he had no more interest in her than his hypothetical sister, had he?

"Say something," he suddenly said. He sounded strained.

"Excuse me?"

"You haven't said a word in half an hour. Say something. Tell me about the history of saffron or how to make Chinese cricket cages or the ritual uses of obsidian. Something. Anything." More than strained, almost desperate.

She half turned to face him. His eyes glittered, catching the rebounding light off the dune. With a sound deep in his throat, he suddenly slipped a big hand beneath her knee, lifting her leg up and over the pommel, rotating her in the saddle so that she now rode sidesaddle, cradled sideways against him, her legs draped over his thigh.

He breathed out a low whistle of relief. "There. Now. Talk."

He was, she realized with a thrill, more than aware of her. He wanted her. And while part of her, that newly awoken feminine *djinn*, wanted to test her powers, the sensible academian knew better.

She cast about for something to say. "Napoleon Bonaparte estimated that should one use the materials in the Great Pyramids to build a wall around the country of France, the completed structure would be ten feet high."

"Hm." He stared fixedly in front of them.

"A fifteenth-century Florentine is responsible for making Cupid synonymous with love. During Carnival he visited his ladylove dressed as Cupid, wings and all, and brought with him a hundred and fifty men to serenade her, conveying before them a brilliantly festooned cart. At the end of their songs, he threw his wings atop the cart and the whole thing burst into flames, setting off devices that shot arrows into the air. One, so it's said, piercing his lady's heart and winning her favor. When the display was over, he coaxed his horse backwards all the way down the street until he was out of her sight, swearing he would never turn his back to her."

"Good Lord," Jim said at that, "the man sounds like a complete imbecile. How many people got hit with his arrows—besides his lady friend?"

"It was romantic. But then, I forgot I was addressing someone who thinks romance is juvenile," she said, aware it made her unhappy and she had no right be unhappy over Jim Owens's romantic inclinations or disinclinations. "Let me see, what would interest you...?" She furrowed her brow. "The Luxor Temple was begun by Amenhotep the Third, an Eighteenth Dynasty ruler, but enlarged by Ramses the Second when—"

"No," he said.

She blinked. "No, what?"

"Nothing more about Egypt's dead kings and pharaohs, their tombs or papyri. No more recitations. Tell me something *you* are interested in."

His words penetrated slowly. "I am interested in these things." Then why did she sound so doubtful? "I am." And so defensive?

He looked down at her. "No, you're not. You're trying to impress your...impress Pomfrey. As soon as you start talking about pharaohs your voice gets all tight and determined, like you're taking oral exams. It's not a prerequisite, you know."

"What's not a prerequisite?"

"You don't have to know every Egyptian ruler's name and burial site in order to live in Egypt."

"That's not it at all," she said stiffly, all thought of kisses and female power vanished. "I find it fascinating. The various dynasties and houses, the empires...Don't you?"

"No."

Her mouth fell open, stunned. The words he'd uttered were not only inconceivable, in her family they were tantamount to sacrilege. "You don't?"

He shrugged, the nonchalant gesture effectively consigning her world, her life, and her family to a negligible hobby. "Oh, I think it's interesting in small doses, but dynasties are built on graves. I prefer the living."

She refused to believe it. "But I was under the impression that you were…that you made your living due in a great part to your knowledge of ancient Egyptian history and artifacts. You've worked at the concessions!"

His mouth quirked up at the corner, and he looked down into her face with some amusement. "I know my way around a tomb site, but that's just my job, Mil—Miss Whimpelhall."

She didn't know how to react. Her entire life had been centered in one way or another around Egyptian archaeology. It was what defined her entire family: her great-grandfather, her father, her mother, her brothers…and, of course, herself. She frowned, looking away, and felt his chest rumble against her arm. He was *chuckling*, she realized.

Her scowl deepened. He had no right to laugh at her, to question her interest, her ardor, or commitment. Who was he to say what she found fascinating and what she didn't? He didn't know her. He thought she was Mildred Whimpelhall, a spinster from London.

Jim had never met Ginesse Braxton. How could he begin to understand how important this was to *her* that the name Ginesse Braxton be included in her family's illustrious ranks? He couldn't because he couldn't fathom what it was like to be the cuckoo in the nest. *Not* that she was a cuckoo. She wasn't! She'd proved that by earning a degree in ancient studies. She *was* proving that by discovering Zerzura, and it *was* fascinating!

She hadn't thought of the lost city in days, and now this reminder of what was at stake and the reason for her journey came racing back to her. She hadn't precisely forgotten, she'd just been caught up in their day-to-day travel and Mr. Owens's mysterious history, and her silly scribblings and their conversations and his grave-eyed charm and his warm embrace...Zerzura had simply slipped to the back of her mind. She had so completely immersed herself in her role as Mildred Whimpelhall, she'd forgotten who she was.

"I'm sorry you don't share my enthusiasm for the ancients, Mr. Owens," she said stiffly. "But you're quite, quite wrong. I am passionately interested in Egyptian history and archaeology."

"You know," he said, looking more puzzled than chastised, "if you think this will impress Pomfrey, you're wrong. He knows nothing about archaeology and cares less than nothing for tombs and pharaohs. You don't have to be anyone but yourself, Miss Whimpelhall. Believe me," he said, his voice softening, "that is enough."

"Sometimes it isn't," she said so softly she couldn't tell if he'd heard.

"All right," he said, with a touch of resignation. "Then tell me something I'll be interested in."

"I have a better idea," she said, unwilling to follow the path his questions had set her on. She did not want to examine too closely what had brought her to this point, to this masquerade, to deceiving Jim. "*You* tell *me* something."

There was a subtle change in his body. Not a stiffening precisely, more like an inner retreat, a distance developing between them as surely as if he'd set her on the ground.

"What would you like to know?" he asked.

"Colonel Lord Pomfrey wrote that you are a scoundrel."

"Did he?"

She slanted a glance from under her lashes and nodded. "Are you?"

"Define scoundrel."

"Someone of questionable integrity."

"Then he's right." He shifted her in his arms so that she was lying back in the crook of his elbow, looking up into his face. His mouth was relaxed, his voice composed, but there was a hard quality to the gaze fixed on the landscape ahead.

"Yes," she admitted then, "Colonel Lord Pomfrey said you are a ruffian, too."

"Right again." A small muscle leapt in his jaw.

"And Colonel Lord Pomfrey said you were rough and uncouth," she continued, adding before he could accept the fault for these sins, too, "but I do not find you either."

This won a startled glance from him.

"But he says you are in league with the bandits and," she demurred from using the word "jackal" as Pomfrey had in his letter, "outlaws."

"I'm flattered Pomfrey wasted so much ink on my foibles." He didn't sound like a cowboy now. He sounded like the haughtiest European aristocrat—bored, amused, but underneath coldly angry that someone would have the audacity to judge him.

"Colonel Lord Pomfrey says you're not to be trusted—"

"Do you even know his first name?"

The question, coming as it did out of nowhere, flustered her. "I…What do you mean?"

"Colonel Lord Pomfrey. You never use his given name." He was looking down into her upturned face, moonlight carving his into hard angles and cold planes.

"Of course I know it," she said, trying to sound convincing because in truth she did not remember Pomfrey's Christian name.

"Because if you were mine, I would want you to say it, even when I was not there." He was so close she felt his warm breath sluice over her lips, so close she could see the way his lashes tangled at the corners, so close she could see flecks of sand at the base of his throat. His gaze had turned smoky and brilliant all at once, with an intensity she'd never seen before. It made the breath catch in her throat and her heart race.

Fool that she was, even though she intuited that danger roved very near and that she ought to keep very still and very silent, she could not keep from whispering, "Why?"

"Because every time you said my name, it would touch your lips." His voice lost its hard edge, grew as dark and smoky as his gaze. "Like a kiss."

She could not look away though he gave her plenty of time to do so. Instead, her chin lifted, her body leading where her mind refused to go. He bent his golden head and lightly, gently, brushed his lips across hers.

She felt a tingle, her nerves galvanized into pleasured awareness. He gathered her closer, his mouth moving more firmly over hers. She did not resist the subtle insistence of his mouth. She melted against him. One hand supported her back while the other traced the length of her neck downward, brushing the thin cotton shirt off her shoulder to caress the top of her bosom where it swelled above the tight satin undergarment.

She arched into his touch, and something seemed to break within him, some deep restraint he'd imposed upon himself. He crushed her closer, his heart pounding against her breast, deepening his kiss, his mouth slanting sideways, his tongue sliding along the seam of her lips, and when she gasped at the unexpected contact, his tongue slipped deep within her mouth, intimate and erotic and thrilling.

He shifted her, breaking off their kiss, and she made a sound of protest but his lips did not leave her. They skated from the corner of her mouth down along her jaw and from there to follow the course of her neck, feathering warm, damp kisses along the way. He paused at the hollow at the base of her throat and licked, tasting her.

It was thrilling, so deeply intimate, and she shivered, her head falling back against his shoulder, allowing him easier access. His fingers brushed along her shoulder and down along the outer side of her breast, inciting an indescribable need to be touched more, to be handled more, to feel more. She wanted his hand on her breast; her nipple ached for some form of relief and at the same time, more of this sweet torment.

She twisted in agitation, and his palm rubbed her nipple. She gasped with the pleasurable feel of it and pushed her breast hard against his hand, abandoned to sensation and anticipation.

"Please. Please," she panted.

But he didn't please her. His hand slipped from her breast; he pulled his mouth slowly from hers. She stared up at him, lost and uncertain and unsatisfied. So unsatisfied.

Beneath the dark tan, he looked pale, but that might have been the moonlight. Only his eyes seemed alive, and they were flames. He did not look at her for a few seconds, he only muttered something under his breath. Then he lowered his gaze to her. The fires had been banked, and his expression was unreadable. Gently but resolutely, he pulled her *farasia* back into place before easing her upright in front of him.

When he spoke, his voice was cool and distant as a memory of winter. "As for your original question of whether I can be trusted," he said, "I guess that answers it."

CHAPTER SEVENTEEN

Though he had struggled desperately against it, it was a Higher Power than man's that directed where his heart should love.

—from the personal diary of Ginesse Braxton

The sun stood directly overhead by the time Jim spotted the outcrop of rocks that marked the oasis.

He looked down at the woman sleeping in his arms and congratulated himself on getting her here without ravishing her as she'd ravished him, utterly, thoroughly, entirely laying him and his supposed honor to waste. *Honor.* He'd spent the last seven years card-sharking, hustling, grave-robbing, and selling his fists and his gun to the highest bidder. It had been hubris to think he had any honor left to lose.

It wasn't enough that he'd fallen in love with Pomfrey's bride-to-be, but then he'd had to taste her, kiss her, know for himself what was meant for only Pomfrey to know. Any man with an ounce of integrity would have respected that no matter what the provocation. And small enough provocation she'd supplied, curled up against him, sweetly trusting, barely awake. His body hadn't cared.

Each moment he'd held her had extended itself into its own torturous eternity; each damn step the damned camel took that rocked her against his loins had chipped away at his brittle self-restraint. And when she'd called him on his many sins, he'd seized on it as an excuse to finally do what he wanted to do— or rather, he thought grimly, a portion of what he'd wanted to do because as soon his mouth had closed on hers and her hands had crept up to cling to him for support, he'd wanted more. He wanted all of her.

And if she'd been a whit more experienced, had evinced a degree more familiarity with passion…

But then he'd heard her plea, and though he thought it stemmed from excitement, he could not guarantee it to his heart, and that organ refused to allow what honor so easily ceded. He loved her and he would not frighten or hurt her, no matter how certain he was that whatever apprehension she felt would have soon given way to something exquisite. Her lithe body had arched into him, her hips lifting in unconscious appeal, her lips opening effortlessly beneath his, her breast thrusting into his palm. A shudder coursed through him at the memory, and he smiled grimly into the burning desert wasteland thinking it a fitting metaphor for his unquenched desire.

Thank God, after the long, terse, silent hours that followed, hours during which, no doubt, she'd prayed he wouldn't force himself on her again, she'd fallen asleep. It had provided an unexpected boon, allowing him to taste for scant moments what he couldn't have forever: the slide of her hair against his lips, the velvety texture of her cheek, the light, lithe form gathered against him. Though the arm supporting her drowsing head was knotted in agony for being so long in one position, it was a small price to pay to be able to look down at her, to mark the way the toasted color of her skin edged to apricot on her cheeks, how her lashes were tipped in gold, the distinct outline of her full lips, the haughty contour of her nose.

He looked up, forcing himself to keep his gaze fixed on the oasis as it slowly grew larger; it offered no respite. He felt each of her inhalations, the little beat of air against his neck, the relaxed curl of her fingers over his shoulder where her hand had crept in her sleep. For the long years of his self-imposed exile he hadn't wanted or needed anything or anyone, reconciled to his isolation, satisfied to be an observer looking in from the outskirts of what he'd concluded was a game with no winners.

But now this slip of a girl had rolled into his life like a feckless archaeologist, tunneling beneath his defenses, carelessly exposing his heart, piecing some things together—shattering others. He'd thought himself as empty and indifferent as a mummy, yet with the first sidelong look from her eyes he'd felt the excruciating kick of his heart coming back to life.

And the damn thing kept beating, refusing to heed the sage advice of experience and reason no matter how much it hurt. And *God*, how it hurt. Because she could never be his. Never.

His gaze drifted down to her, rebellion coiling in his heart. She was susceptible, romantic, and inexperienced. She thought he was some sort of cowboy-cum-villain-cum-tarnished knight. Given her nature and misconceptions, he might successfully seduce her. He had some skill; he had not lived a celibate life, and those ladies with whom he'd shared a bed had been eager and willing to instruct a devoted if infrequent pupil. He might seduce her.

He closed his eyes, fighting the taunting images his thoughts roused.

Then what? Then what?

He didn't have a thing to offer her, not even a name. Years ago he'd made a deal with the devil, and while he would have fought the devil for her, other innocent lives would be bruised if not broken in the battle.

Althea had expected Charlotte's betrayal to break him, so that he would finally learn the humbling lesson that no one cared who he was, only *what* he was, and that was only as much as Althea would allow him to be. But it hadn't broken him. Instead, it had imbued in him a steely resolve never to bend to her will. And in that last fateful meeting, she'd realized it.

"*Then I wish you dead,*" she'd said. "*Be dead. Go away and die so that Jock can inherit. Go away and die...or wait until I see that you do.*"

He'd been so young, so fierce and heedless. He'd looked into Althea's eyes and seen nothing but his own hatred mirrored back at him and known she would have him killed if she could.

And he hadn't cared.

But he had cared what would happen to his mother's brother, his uncle. He had cared what would become of the Youngblood ranch, the only home he'd ever known.

At the time, it had seemed a fair trade. Althea had never given him anything, not a smile, not a kind word, not a penny that wasn't already his. The only thing she'd given him were hard lessons in the harshest way possible. So, in receiving nothing, he'd learned to *want* nothing from her. He'd learned to disparage anything she valued, to despise what she withheld, to hold in contempt everything she exalted. It had been easy to walk away from the birthright she'd valued so much more than him.

He'd never had any regrets. Until Mildred.

Until her, he'd never considered the ramifications of his long-ago abdication. Until her, he'd never counted it a loss. He couldn't even offer her a real name. Or a home, a place of permanence with friends and associations, a life rich in all aspects.

He owned a couple of horses and what he carried with him in his kit.

For a few fateful moments he considered going back. His death had not been made official yet. There were still a few months left before Althea took the case to the courts. After that, it would be too late. He might reclaim his name, but everything else would be lost. Even if he wanted to sue to have his birthright returned to him, he had no money to pay for the litigation.

But he couldn't. He could not buy his happiness at the expense of another. Not at the expense of his half brother, Jock, who would have grown used to thinking of himself as their father's heir, or of his uncle who, with the reversion of the acreage, might return the Youngblood ranch to its former glory.

Besides, Mildred Whimpelhall belonged to another: a dashing, conscientious, hardworking, diligent, noble, and *romantic* man. Someone worthy of her love.

"Is that the oasis or is it a mirage?" she asked in a small voice.

He looked down. She did not meet his gaze. She must have awakened while he'd been lost in his inner struggle.

"It's the oasis."

It wasn't like the picturesque ones cited in poetry. It was nothing more than a jagged outcropping of rocks, a stony fist punched up from beneath the earth's crust, bringing with it a thin but steady stream of water that collected in a small, shallow pool. A fringe of grasses encircled the pond along with a pair of stunted doum palms.

Jim kneed the camel beneath the shade of the outcropping and dismounted. A snake slithered along the base of the rock and disappeared. Jim marked the hole he'd gone into and then turned and, without asking permission, scooped Ginesse out of the saddle and set her on her feet. The long hours aboard the camel had made her legs weak, and she swayed slightly. He caught her and felt her flinch. He cursed silently and snatched his hands back.

Without a word, he turned and untied the pack from the camel's back. He tossed it into the shade and then went about uncinching the saddle. He felt her eyes on him and without looking up from his task said, "The water will be warm and a little salty." His voice was calm, even, giving no hint to his turmoil. "There's a tin cup in my kit. Use the end of your robe to strain it."

He heard her move away and rummage in the satchel. A moment later there was a musical splash of water and a small gasp. He glanced around to find her standing calf-deep in the water, her robes bunched high in both hands. Sunlight shimmered in her hair. Though sweat had left pale tracks down her dust-caked cheeks and her nose was burnt, her lips were spread in an irrepressible grin. As he watched, she unwrapped the *tob* and tossed it to the shore. Then, without the slightest hesitation, she stripped the *farasia* over her head, leaving her in the snug, low-cut, ruby-colored *antaree* and the wretched boy's trousers. His body sprang to instant attention.

"Turn around," she commanded.

He did, as much in frustration as relief. Something sailed by the periphery of his vision and landed in a heap at the base of the outcropping. Her trousers. Followed shortly thereafter by the *antaree*. She laughed. She had to be giddy. Maybe she had heatstroke. Because she was stuck in the middle of nowhere with a man who'd recently mauled her, abandoned by her escorts, left to die—and he would not forget that, he vowed—and she was laughing.

No, he thought. It was not that she was oblivious to the danger or gravity of her situation. It was simply not in her nature to let fear extinguish pleasure. She lived in the moment, and this moment was joyful. He should be as wise.

"Drat!" she exclaimed. "Would you please toss me my clothing?" She sounded a little hesitant, but not wary. "In my enthusiasm to be rid of them, I'm afraid I just hurled them anywhere. I'd like to rinse them out."

He picked up her clothing and tossed them over his shoulder. He heard them land in the pool, and she giggled.

"Let me know when you're done," he said. "I'll throw your things over the rocks. They won't take long to dry."

After a few more minutes of splashing, she called out, "I'm done. You can come and get them. They're on the bank."

He turned around, keeping his gaze fixed on the edge of the pool, but he couldn't entirely avoid seeing her. She was crouched so low in the water that it covered her shoulders, her hair fanning out over the still surface like a bolt of caramel-colored satin. The water was cloudy, churned up by her movement, but he still had an impression of her arms crossed over her chest, of a brown, sylph-like form kneeling in the three-foot-deep waters, a desert naiad.

She watched him with an unwavering gaze, her beautiful eyes unblinking and direct, unreadable as the windswept desert, but also, thank God, without fear of him.

He collected her clothing and spread them out over the rocks. Then he went and slipped the nose peg bridle off the camel and slapped her on the rump. She didn't need any further invitation; a few seconds later he heard the water sloshing and a yelp of protest. He smiled. There'd scarcely be room in that pool for both the camel and Mildred.

"You shouldn't stay out in the sun," he called over his shoulder. "Wade over into the shadow of the rocks while you wait for your clothes to dry. You'll burn otherwise."

"Yes, sir." She sounded wry.

He went about setting up camp, forming a sort of shelter in the narrow lee between two of the standing rocks by stretching the camel's blanket above it and holding down each end with rocks. He then made quick work of digging a shallow fire pit over which, if they were lucky, he'd roast that snake. They wouldn't be able to use it for warmth, because the only fuel they had was some hard coal he'd found at the bottom of Neely's pack.

Bloody Neely. Bloody, stupid *dead* Neely. No one would give a damn that he'd left Jim to rot, but he'd pretty much signed up for the firing squad when he'd abandoned Pomfrey's future wife.

Except she wasn't going to die. He wasn't going to let her. *By God*, he wasn't going to let her die. He was going to take her to Pomfrey, and then he was going to walk away. She was going to live in comfort and contentment with a man she respected and admired. She would be happy, and knowing that would be enough for him.

And him? The first thing Jim was going to do after delivering her was find Neely. He doubted very much he'd be in a very conciliatory frame of mind when he did.

"Would you please go round to the other side while I get dressed?" she asked.

He did so, and a moment later she called for him to come back. When he did, the first thing he noted were the trousers and *antaree* still lying baking in the sun, which meant she had nothing on beneath the flowing white robes except the thin, thigh-length shirt. It shouldn't matter. The *tob* contained yards more cloth than most English dresses and was so loosely draped that it afforded no more than a suggestion of the figure beneath.

But suggest it did. Any move might reveal the outline of a lithe limb, a slender hip, or a high, rounded breast and the next movement conceal again. Inadvertently, with each graceful move, with each step, she was performing a peep show as stimulating and enticing as any seen in Cairo's red light district. The fact that she was completely oblivious to it only made it more agonizing.

He stood staring like a schoolboy for a few seconds, then he turned and strode straight into the water.

Chapter Eighteen

Shyly, she lifted her tremulous lips to his, and in this reverent gift of herself, he knew the sublime pleasure of her pure, sweet kiss.

—from the personal diary of Ginesse Braxton

Jim stood bare-chested in the pool, wringing the water from his shirt. He'd been dunking and twisting the shirt for the last ten minutes, and from the way he was going at it he might just wring it in two. But then, if he hadn't been so engrossed, he would have noticed her staring at him.

The corrugated muscles rippled in his flat stomach as he leaned over, his biceps and the long tendons in his forearms standing out in stark relief as he twisted the poor shirt with a violence all out of proportion to the task. The light furring of dark gold hairs that covered his arms and chest grew darker and thicker, as it narrowed low on his belly and disappeared beneath his waistband.

He would have looked like a selkie, all clean and unmarked, except for a puckered divot on his upper left arm; and the long, jagged rope of red scar tissue along the ladder of his ribs; and another thin sickle-shaped mark beneath his right shoulder blade; and a…Good Lord, the man was a morass of scars. Unexpected anger filled her that he'd so abused such a perfect body, that he'd so little regard for himself. But she didn't have any right to feel proprietary about Jim Owens.

She huddled, growing more disconsolate with each moment, the fleeting pleasure provided by her dunk in the water gone.

He must think her the worst sort of trollop, engaged to one man and swooning in the embraces of another. If only she *had* swooned. No, she'd been as fervent to touch as she had been to be touched, as eager to kiss as be kissed.

Evidently, despite his caustic self-denouncement, she'd repulsed him because he couldn't seem to bring himself to look at her, and when he did his face was tight with something she could not interpret but feared was censure. How could it be anything else? In Jim's eyes, she had betrayed Colonel Lord…Lord—What was the drat man's Christian name?! She'd acted dishonorably, and for a man as honorable as Jim, that would be anathema.

She deserved his censure. At least, Mildred Whimpelhall deserved it, the hussy.

However, might not Ginesse Braxton be judged more gently? After all, *she* was not promised to anyone else. She had not committed herself to another man. She was simply a young woman with a passionate nature, a little impulsive and sometimes reckless. But she hadn't betrayed anyone or anything, except perhaps a certain unnecessarily restrictive and really, when one considered it in the light of historic precedents, obsolete morality.

If only Jim could see it that way.

Her mouth twisted. If he *could* see it that way, then without a doubt she would be flat on her back beneath him. No, she could not tell Jim Owens who she was. Her masquerade was her best chastity belt. Possibly her only chastity belt, she thought dolefully, eying his broad, muscular back. But that didn't mean he had to think Mildred Whimpelhall was a completely fallen, or in this case fall*ing*, woman.

She stood up as he waded out of the pool. He glanced at her, then averted his eyes and headed into the shade at the far end of the outcropping. There he sat down and grabbed hold of his boot's heel, yanked the boot off, upended it, and dumped the water from it. He did the same to the other, then stripped off his socks and wrung them dry.

She took a deep breath and walked over to where he sat. He saw her approach and dug into the kit beside him for a shirt and hastily pulled it on. Then he simply sat there warily watching her approach, his knees bent, his feet flat on the earth, his hands curled into fists atop each knee. Tension radiated from him. She couldn't help glancing at the heavy ridge between his legs and remembering the feel of that male member pressed against her hip. Heat poured into her cheeks.

"I've come to apologize," she said.

He stared up at her, looking utterly confounded. And then, with what sounded like a long-suffering sigh, his hands uncurled, his arms relaxed, and his shoulders sagged. "You really mean it, don't you?" he asked.

She frowned. "Of course I do. My actions were unconscionable. I am engaged to be married. I should never—"

"Hold on. Stop right there," he said, climbing to his feet. "Did it ever occur to you that I ought to be the one apologizing?"

He raked a hand through his damp hair, shedding sparkles of water. "I was entrusted with taking another man's bride-to-be to him so they could wed. I can't think of a more inviolable charge than that. But I betrayed it. No honorable man would have done so."

He was taking the high road, absolving her of her part.

Her frown turned into a scowl.

She didn't *want* to be absolved. She wanted equal status in that embrace. People she cared for were always making excuses for her and finding some implausible explanation for the things she did that turned out wrong. She understood, she even appreciated the impulse, but those would-be champions failed to understand that by assuming her sins they relegated her to the role of child.

What she'd felt last night—what she felt now—was definitely not childish.

"Nor any honorable woman," she said with some heat. "I betrayed an even greater trust because I accepted Colonel Lord Pomfrey's proposal of marriage. I am supposed to love him."

"*Supposed?*" He seized on the word.

She cleared her throat. "I mean, I do love him."

"Do you?" He'd only come a step closer, but with that small movement he filled her vision. She could see the rise and fall of his chest beneath the linen shirt, the little jump of a muscle in his jaw, the deep indigo ring around the pale blue-gray irises.

"I'm marrying him, aren't I?"

"Are you?"

She stepped back; he followed her, his arms loose at his side, his pace slow yet somehow predatory.

"Are you?" he repeated.

She stopped her retreat and lifted her chin, feeling her lips quiver, on the cusp of telling him the truth. What would he do? Would he despise her? Of course he would; he was an honest man, and he would despise dishonesty in others. Her courage deserted her on the thought.

"Yes," she whispered.

The single word stopped him in his tracks, as though he'd taken an unexpected blow.

"I'm sorry," she whispered.

He looked tired. Beat. "You've already apologized," he said, half turning from her.

God knew what impulse drove her. She could have stayed mute, *should* have stayed mute. "You said you ought to apologize. But you haven't yet. Why not?"

He turned his head, impaling her with a piercing gaze. "Don't play with me, Miss Whimpelhall." His voice was a dusky vow, a promise and a threat, a warning and a temptation. "You might not like how the game turns out."

"Why didn't you apologize?"

He faced her. His gaze had gone dark and lambent, except for the spark deep within, a carnal awareness that made her knees go weak and her heart start racing. Nervously she wet her lips with the tip of her tongue. His gaze fell on the simple act with wolfish intensity. "Because I don't regret it."

Something had changed in him. His smile was lazy but his attention was sharp and focused, all his concentration bent on her, leaving room for nothing else. The desert dissolved around them, the heat, the pond, the sun, all of it disappeared, leaving only the two of them.

She couldn't look away from him, couldn't think of a word that might dispel the strange sensation. She bit her lip and too late realized she'd again drawn his narrowed gaze. She felt as though he were kissing her again. Her body tingled with sensual awareness, a slow, molten heat pool, low, between her legs.

"Don't do that," she said a little desperately. The cool, grave cowboy had been replaced by a predatory male. She wasn't sure she liked it; she was definitely sure she didn't know how to handle it.

"Do what?" he asked.

"That."

"I'm not doing anything."

"You're…importuning me."

Her word choice seemed to amuse him, but he backed away a few steps and leaned against the boulder, crossing his muscular arms over his chest. "No more than you're importuning me," he said.

"I'm not. I won't. I realize the danger now, and I won't…do anything that would require me to apologize again."

"Damn."

"Don't say that!"

"Why?"

His words vexed her, his gaze, his smile, the quality of his attention inciting a sort of deep itch in her. It tingled in her lips and fingertips, a light throbbing in her nipples. It was an itch she could not scratch. Only he could. She moved a step nearer to him, frowning at his self-containment, his amusement.

"Because you must never kiss me again, and I must never kiss you," she said breathlessly, knowing she was tempting him, knowing full well that she placed herself at risk, at risk of something dangerous and exciting, something she intuited she would only know from him.

"I know."

"We owe it to…to Colonel Lord Pomfrey."

"I know."

He was watching her approach, his pose relaxed, even indolent. She wasn't fooled. There was an underlying tension, a coiled quality lurking behind his cool gaze.

"I am a woman alone and dependent on you."

He did not say a word.

Emboldened, she took another step forward. "I am at your mercy."

"Miss Whimpelhall," he said in a low voice, "I doubt you have ever been at anyone's mercy."

"I am," she insisted. She took another step and had to tilt her head to look up at him.

"I could say the same thing to you."

Above a jaw roughened by a day's growth of beard, his skin was fine-grained and clear. His lashes shadowed the gray eyes, and the small lines at the corners deepened as they narrowed. She couldn't have stopped herself from cupping her palm against his cheek had she tried. With her touch, his eyes fell shut, and when they opened again, they blazed emotion.

"You're walking close to the fire, Miss Whimpelhall," he said.

It hadn't been her intent: she had always been a creature of impulse, following instincts both deep and inexorable. She followed them now, resting her hands lightly on his chest. It rose and fell heavily beneath her touch, his heart drumming thickly against her palms.

She angled her head and touched her lips lightly to the base of his throat. A shudder passed through his body, and suddenly, he came alive. His arm lashed around her waist, dragging her hard against him while the other cupped the back of her head, as he dipped her back so that she needed to cling to him to keep from falling.

"What is it you want? A primer course in seduction?" he growled down at her, his lip curling back over his strong white teeth, his eyes burning like embers in his dark face. She shivered. "Of course. What else would I be?" he said with a feral smile. "Well, I can do that. I can be that."

His mouth descended on her, hot and urgent and punishing, and she reveled in it, in his strength, his hunger, his want. Eagerly, her mouth opened to his, her tongue welcoming his. It swirled in her mouth, the heavy warm muscle simulating the sex act in her mouth. Little lights danced across the tapestry of her inner eyelids as she arched into him, her fingers digging deep into his shoulders.

Vaguely, she became aware that he was lowering her to the ground, of pebbles and rock shards sharp beneath her back and legs. He covered her, his leg between her thighs, one arm beneath her shoulders, the other clasping her jaw, holding it still for his sensual assault. She panted against his mouth, her hips rotating in an instinctive invitation against his leg.

He jerked his head away, closed his eyes, and sucked in a deep, agonized breath—

Which is why he didn't see the rifle barrel until it prodded him in the side.

CHAPTER NINETEEN

The cold eyes of this man sent a thrill of horror through her very being.

—from the personal diary of Ginesse Braxton

There were four men, all dressed in indigo robes, and that was about all Jim had time to notice.

He grabbed the rifle barrel and shoved, unbalancing the gunman, then yanked the rifle from his grip as Mildred scrambled for his kit and the pistol inside. He surged to his feet, swinging the rifle like a bat and catching his assailant in the side of the head. He collapsed, unconscious, as Jim spun to face the next man just as a rifle blast went off next to his face. He froze.

Somewhere behind him a man shouted at him in a language he didn't understand. Jim raised his hands in the universal sign of surrender. A man in inky blue robes and a turban, his face so heavily veiled only his eyes were visible, snatched the rifle from his upraised hands and clouted him sharply on the head. He rocked back, dazed, but managed to stay upright.

Another man grabbed Mildred by the arm and jerked her to her feet. He dragged her over to where Jim stood and shoved her at him, barking an order neither of them understood. He caught her arm and edged her behind him.

"We are English citizens," Jim said. "You will be punished if any harm comes to us."

"They're Tuaregs," Mildred said in a voice gauged for his ears alone, "not Egyptians, and they are a hundred miles from their homeland. They must be traders. They *could* be slave traders." She kept her voice low, her eyes averted. "If they are, they might speak Arabic."

Jim didn't question her. He'd heard of the Blue Men of the Sahara with their distinctive blue robes, but he'd never crossed their path before. They lived far west of the places he haunted. These must be the same riders who'd been shadowing them before Neely and his men had taken off. When they saw that Neely split apart, they'd evidently decided since the odds now favored them they might as well take the opportunity to rob them. Damn Neely.

Quickly, he assessed their situation. Besides the one lying unconscious at his feet, they faced three men: the one who'd spoken, the one with the rifle, and one holding the lead line of half a dozen heavily laden camels, at the end of which was tied a magnificent smoke-gray Arabian stallion.

Jim figured the one who'd fired the rifle to be their leader. Though he was not the one shouting orders, he was the only one with a firearm, currently trained on Jim. Jim addressed him.

"You will only bring ruin to yourself and your people if you harm us," he said in careful Arabic. "The English will find you." Though the man's face, like those of his confederates, was covered, Jim could almost feel his answering smile because the threat was hollow and they both knew it. The Tuaregs lived in lands occupied by the French, not the English.

"We do not *seek* trouble," the man replied in halting Arabic, but from the slight emphasis he placed on the word, Jim took it to mean that he wouldn't avoid trouble if it happened by.

"We came for water and found you here enjoying the woman." Jim felt himself tense at the flat statement and forced himself not to react.

"Didn't quite get there, no thanks to you," he said, winning an amused snort from a couple of the men.

The leader was on a fishing expedition, trying to gauge how much Mildred meant to him, possibly to determine how much he could ransom her for, possibly for some other reason altogether. He just didn't know. He had to play this right. Both their lives depended on it.

The man pulled the veil off from his face. Years of wearing the indigo-dyed material had stained his lower face so dark a blue he seemed to have an indigo beard. He was neither young nor old, but that indeterminate age between twenty-five and fifty which desert dwellers wear so similarly. His gaze slew toward Mildred. "Who is she?"

"Mine."

"Your wife?"

Jim thought quickly. The Tuareg might take her for ransom if they thought her valuable enough. Or they might just take her. "No. Just mine," he said coldly.

The man nodded thoughtfully, then said something in his native tongue to his subordinates. One of them came forward and dragged the unconscious man away; the other took the rifle and trained it on Jim. The leader came forward, stopping in front of Mildred. "She has red hair." He cocked his head. "At least, red enough."

"Yes," Jim agreed. He had no idea whether this was a good thing or a bad thing, and the man's face wasn't telling.

"A red-haired woman is good luck."

Something in the man's tone, coupled with the manner in which he was eying her, must have conveyed the man's meaning to Mildred, because she trembled ever so slightly and her skin blanched. She didn't say a word, however. She simply stood eyes downcast, meekly submissive. Wise girl.

"Is it?" Jim asked with a harsh laugh. "Take a look at the luck she's brought me." He waved a hand at the oasis and their inadequate shelter, the antique one-eyed camel.

The man smiled in return and moved to stand in front of Mildred. He cocked his head first one way and then the other, trying to get her to look him in the eye but she refused. He grinned at Jim.

"She is well trained. How long have you had her?"

The Tuareg thought she was his slave. He must be younger than he'd realized or far less experienced with outside cultures. Otherwise he would have known that Europeans didn't keep slaves.

"A while." Jim shrugged.

"How much did you pay for her?" he asked, his speculative gaze still on Mildred.

"Too much," Jim said.

"Hm."

From his position next to her, one of the Tuareg's subordinates reached out and cupped Mildred's breast, grinning. Mildred gasped. Quick as a striking snake, Jim's hand lashed out and seized the Tuareg by the throat. Choking, the man clawed at Jim's wrist; Jim barely felt it. He squeezed, his gaze narrowing on the twisting, struggling man.

"Enough!" thundered the leader, but a red haze had descended over Jim's vision, a primal need to destroy. He shook the man as a mongoose would a cobra, felt the other man's hands weaken, dimly heard Mildred shouting his name.

"I said 'mine,'" he whispered, through clenched teeth.

The Tuareg leader grabbed the rifle, shoving the end against Mildred's temple. "Stop!"

Jim stopped. He opened his hand, and the man slipped to his knees, retching in the sand at Jim's feet.

The Tuareg spoke sharply, and the man scrambled back, his head low to the ground. The Tuareg returned his gaze to Jim. He did not look happy, and Jim wondered if Mildred could ride, because right now her only hope looked to be if he could distract them long enough for her to get on top of that stallion—

"Forgive that one. He is a pig with the manners of a dog," the Tuareg said in a hard, angry voice.

Something had changed the situation in the last few minutes; the Tuareg leader's previous smiling and patently insincere geniality had vanished. He looked like a cat that had had his whiskers shorn. In other words, pissed off.

"He's disgraced," Mildred whispered from beside him. "I've… I've read about this. In his culture, it is forbidden to touch another's property without his prior consent, and the leader is responsible for the actions of his subordinates. So he has been shamed. He might feel the need to make amends. But be careful what you say; he will try to twist any careless comment into something at which he can take offense."

Jim gave her a small nod to let her know he had heard. Some of the more isolated tribes he'd come across were notoriously patriarchal, at least outwardly. If he seemed to be asking her counsel, his status would be lowered, which he couldn't afford right now. The information she'd whispered was invaluable, but he was too experienced to rely much on this man's sense of obligation. He might make use of it, but only to a very specific point. The tricky part was figuring out where that point was.

The man was a trader, and the first rule of bargaining was to let the other guy make the first offer. So he held his tongue.

For long, silent minutes, the men took each other's measure, and then, with an impatient gesture, the man began to speak. The words were a mixture of Arabic and his native language and more was left unsaid than said, but in a short few sentences Jim had the gist of it.

Apparently some time ago this group's chief had insulted another clan's chief, and as the other clan was substantially stronger, richer, and more powerful, their chief had rethought his initial stance and sent Juba, the man in front of him, to purchase an Arabian mare from Bedouins as a placatory gift. Disappointingly, the Bedouins had been unwilling to part with any of the more valued mares, and they had been forced to return with a stallion.

Jim listened to all this without remark, keeping his expression haughty.

It seemed to work. Juba gnawed on his lip. If Mildred was right, he would be hoping that Jim would make some comment he could purposefully misinterpret. Then he could salvage the situation by taking righteous offense, killing Jim, and taking off with Mildred. But Jim remained implacably silent. The Tuareg would assume he was awaiting an apology.

And once Juba apologized, he'd be forced to let them go unharmed. In every nomadic tribe Jim had encountered, a universal truth prevailed: as much as one might want to, one simply did not rob or murder someone to whom one has made a formal apology. In a twisted sort of way, Jim even understood the concept.

"I have this wondrous horse," Juba finally said, red-faced with ire. "He is a King of Stallions. See for yourself."

With apparent boredom, Jim glanced toward the gorgeous creature prancing restlessly at the end of the line. He looked back, his expression noncommittal.

The Tuareg clapped his hands and shouted. From out of the shadows limped the man Jim had cold-cocked with the rifle, leading the stallion. He stopped in front of Juba, warily eying Jim.

"Look," Juba said. "Every line perfect. Note his noble head, the small, neat ears and wide nostrils. Look how he stands with his neck so regally arched and legs so straight. He is first among stallions." The Tuareg beckoned him over. "Feel. See for yourself, how sound, how well-muscled."

With a shrug, Jim crossed over to the horse. The stallion's nostrils quivered at his approach. Catching scent of something alien, he backed up, pawing the earth, his ears twitching back and forth as he listened intently.

He truly was superb. His topline was level, his back short and broad. As Juba had pointed out, his neck was long and arched, with the clean throatlatch typical in the best of the breed. Unlike the stocky, heavily haunched little mustangs he'd ridden as a boy, this animal, though not appreciably taller, had the long, leaner muscles and smaller hooves of a creature suited to covering long distances.

Jim held out his hand, and the stallion stretched his neck, his large, luminous, dark eyes fixed on Jim. He took a tentative sniff, the warm, moist air brushing over Jim's knuckles, then withdrew his head and waited. Slowly, Jim ran his hands over the animal's croup up to his withers and down his legs. The stallion stood easily, every now and again flicking an ear in his direction.

"See? Is it not so?"

"He is a fine horse," Jim agreed carefully.

"Fine? He is unequaled in all of Egypt. A horse fit for an *amenokal*."

"Ah-huh."

Juba scowled, wheeled around, and paced back and forth in front of the stallion, finally coming to a stop right in front of Jim. His blue-stained face broke into a huge smile, displaying very white, very broken teeth. "I like you. You, too, are a son of the desert. You touch a horse knowledgably. Not as knowledgably as a Tuareg," he lifted his shoulder apologetically, "but as good as a Bedouin."

Jim didn't say a word, waiting for what would come next. He had a pretty good idea.

"Because I like you, I am thinking that I will make you a trade. There will be no bartering in this trade," he said, and from the lethal glint in the otherwise amiable face, Jim could well believe it. He appreciated the warning. "It is not even a trade, really. It is more a gift."

"Yes?"

"I will trade you this Prince of the Desert, this Brother to the Wind, for that camel."

Jim waited.

"Yes? I see. I understand. You are struck speechless with your good fortune. As would I be were I you. There. Is it done?"

"The one-eyed camel for the stallion?" he said. "That's it? That's the trade?"

"Yes!" Juba laughed, making an effusive gesture. "I amaze myself." He turned and began to untie the stallion from the end of the caravan, and then abruptly he stopped and turned back around, as if just remembering something, something of such little consequence he was embarrassed to even bring it up. "Oh. And the woman, too."

He heard Mildred make a small choked sound, but he didn't so much as glance at her.

"Do we have a deal?" Juba asked.

"You bet," Jim said.

* * *

Ginesse watched Jim secure his kit, emptied of his pistol, over his shoulder and accept the canteen Juba offered. Then he leapt lightly atop the stallion's bare back—a saddle was not part of the deal. He looked down at Juba. "The girl is a virgin. I believe your leader will set great store by that," he said in a loud, but otherwise inconsequential tone.

Ginesse thanked him for that. He'd just turned her virginity into part of the gift the Tuaregs were bringing to the chief, the *amenokal*. Juba would be much less prone to rape her now that his compatriots had been informed of her increased value. She hoped.

She stared at Jim, willing him to turn around and look at her and somehow relay that everything was going to be all right. Even dazed with fear and shock Ginesse could not help but admire his horsemanship. Her father was a good rider—no, a great rider— but he had nothing on Jim Owens. There was no violent kicking, no coarse whoops, or lashing of reins. Whatever he did was done noiselessly, undetectably. One instant the horse was standing perfectly still, the next the pair of them were flying silently out across the sand, past the reach of their fire's light, a centaur come to life.

He did not look back.

CHAPTER TWENTY

She steeled her nerves to do what she must, praying

she would not be required to make the

Ultimate Sacrifice.

—from the personal diary of Ginesse Braxton

"My father is Harry Braxton." Ginesse spoke in Arabic, keeping her voice carefully respectful as she followed the Tuareg leader through the camp. "He is an important man. A fierce chieftain. He will reward you well for my safe delivery to Fort Gordon."

Juba ignored her, as he'd ignored all her pleas and petitions for the last four days.

"Please, you must listen," she said urgently.

He looked around, as if surprised to see her still there. She stopped, holding her hands palm up in supplication. "Please, my father—"

"Sold you," Juba interrupted. "Enough. You are a slave, not my wife. You will make my ears bleed with your lies and pleas."

Whatever her father's reputation, it had not extended to Libya. Each day Juba stuck her on a camel in the middle of the caravan. Each night, he pitched his sumptuous tent and left her to huddle next to one of the camels for warmth. He let the desert be her warden; it proved a vigilant guard.

Where could she go? How far would she get on foot before succumbing to the elements? And if she did manage to steal off on one of the camels, even the swiftest one, eventually they would find her and bring her back.

But today was different. They had left the dunes behind and were heading into rockier terrain: a mixture of sand and gravel occasionally broken by low plateaus and shallow *wadis* where small stands of tough little acacias huddled. Juba called an early halt to their travels and had his tent pitched at the mouth of a small fissure.

The men exchanged wary glances but set about making camp, building a fire, and unloading and hobbling the camels. Ginesse felt Juba's eyes on her more than once. The harsh conditions, her ultimate destination as a gift for a powerful leader, and her virginity had so far kept her safe and well-fed. She feared that was coming to an end.

That first night she had been certain that Jim would come back for her, steal into the camp in the dead of night and take her out from under their noses. He hadn't come back.

And a good thing, too, because the Tuaregs had also expected him. They'd lain in wait, the rifles across their laps, their eyes alert to the smallest movement out in the desert. The next night, and the next, she'd remained awake straining to hear the sound of Jim's stealthy approach. But he hadn't come back then.

She was frightened. If she let herself think, she would edge to terrified. Each time Juba glanced her way, she trembled. Each time she thought of him lying over her in the way Jim had, her stomach rebelled and she had to knot her fist against her lips to keep from retching.

Time was running short. She should have stayed out of his sight, made herself as inconspicuous as possible. Now he was studying her thoughtfully, stroking a dirty, broken thumbnail up and down his cheek. She could almost see him consider his options. He had only Jim's word that she was a virgin, and if she proved not to be, well, Juba could always claim he'd been deceived by the slaver who'd sold her to him. True, he would be embarrassed, and that certainly weighed heavily with him, but how heavily? Not enough, she feared.

Damn that henna powder, for Ginesse had no misconceptions about her desirability; her value lay in her red hair and its ability to bestow good luck on whoever possessed her. It wasn't even that red anymore.

"Go into my tent. Wait for me there. We will discuss your father and your ransom."

He was lying. He wasn't even making any concerted effort to hide the fact. His tone was indolent, his gaze scornful.

"Please. We can talk out here—"

"We will talk in my tent," he cut in brusquely. "Later. You go there now and wait for me. Unless you wish to learn how a slave is punished amongst my people."

"No," she whispered.

"Good. Because you would end up in my tent either way." He pointed at the tent. "Go."

She had no choice. She bowed her head and did as he commanded. Inside, the tented was outfitted with accoutrements worthy of a sheikh. The sand had been covered with thick layers of Persian carpets, a half dozen pillows of gem-colored embroidered satin piled in the center. Silk tassels the size of gourds hung from the ceiling alongside a pair of ornately worked copper lanterns, as yet unlit.

A table of hammered brass that carried an enameled carafe and demitasse cups squatted near the center of the tent, and a low ottoman bed had been set up along one side. This, too, was piled with pillows and covered with a striped blanket. A water pipe stood near its head.

It all looked very civilized and comfortable, and Ginesse wheeled around and began hunting for something she could use as a weapon. Juba kept a curved dagger in a sheath at his waist, and she had seen knives strapped to the upper arms of the other men. Perhaps there was something…

Five minutes later she gave up her search. Except for some clothing, the tent was remarkably antiseptic. There was nothing she could use as a weapon except the spurs on a pair of boots. That would have to do.

Frantically, she set to prying off a spur, one ear tuned to the movements of the men outside. When she was done, she carefully set the boots back in their original position. Then she waited, her heart thudding dully in her chest.

She listened to the low back and forth of conversation between the men, the clang of cooking pots, the soft "*nurrr*" of the camels, and the crackle of firewood. The light grew murky inside the tent and the wind rose, sending sand hissing along the tent's sides. Then, as the last light faded from the tent and she'd struck the flint and lit the hanging lanterns, she heard Juba bark some peremptory commands. Men reluctant to comply answered in grumbling complaints, but a bit later she heard the groaning of camels being roused from their rest.

He was sending some, if not all of his men, away. Likely those he least trusted to keep a secret.

Her heartbeat kicked into a gallop, and she backed further into the tent, clenching the spur tightly behind her back. Her hand grew slick with sweat, and her knees felt watery.

It seemed like she stood like that, facing forward, forever. The camp had gone preternaturally quiet, the only sound the occasional moan of a camel or snap of the firewood breaking. She heard a man say something, a muttered reply, and then footsteps leaving.

Then, finally, horribly, she heard the sound she'd been dreading: the self-assured footfall of a man approaching the tent.

She lifted her chin, horrified to feel tears welling in her eyes. Furiously, she blinked them away. She was better than that. She was braver.

.She saw his silhouette looming large against the tent flap, his robes swirling around him on the quickening breeze, tall and ominous and infinitely threatening. A dark hand seized the flap and switched it violently aside. He ducked his head and entered.

Jim Owens.

CHAPTER TWENTY-ONE

It was ~~divine~~ ~~magnificent~~ ~~amazing~~ ~~incredible~~
~~transforming~~ beyond her
ability to convey.

—from the personal diary of Ginesse Braxton

She was a tall woman, but she looked heartbreakingly fragile standing at the back of the tent. She stared at him, rooted to where she stood, her whole body shivering uncontrollably.

"I never left. I was always out there. Watching. I couldn't come sooner because they were expecting it." He was speaking too fast, too urgently, the words tumbling out past the constriction in his throat.

God, she must have been terrified. She must have thought he'd abandoned her. But there'd been no way to tell her, no sign he could have given that wouldn't have been picked up by her captors. If they'd suspected for even a second what he was about, she would have ended up in Libya as a slave.

"But I wouldn't have let him—" He broke off, gazing at her beseechingly, willing her to understand.

He'd endured the torments of the damned these the last four days, knowing how she must be suffering. More than once he'd been on the verge of throwing caution to the wind and taking his chances. But while he would take chances with his life, he couldn't with hers. So he'd bided his time, waiting until the tribesmen were separated and their guard down, each moment extending into a hellish eternity. Then tonight, Juba had sent two of his men ahead; they wouldn't be returning anytime soon.

"You came." It was barely more than a whisper, and God help him, he couldn't read anything in it, couldn't tell if it was shock or disbelief or condemnation or something else that flavored her voice, and ultimately the only reply he could make was the simple truth, a promise as much as an assertion.

"Always," he said. "I'll always come for you."

With that, whatever paralysis had held her broke. She launched herself across the tent, flinging herself into his arms, wrapping her arms tightly around his neck. He staggered back a step under her momentum, clasping her high against his chest.

"I knew you would come," she sobbed against his throat. "I knew you would, I just didn't know when, and then when you didn't I was afraid something terrible had happened to you!"

He closed his eyes, fighting the wave of emotion that threatened to drive him to his knees. She'd known he was coming. She'd trusted him, had faith in him. She had never doubted him. Instead, she'd worried about him. *Him.* When she was the one in the hands of a slave trafficker.

"Never leave me like that again."

"Never."

She was crying in earnest now, her whole body racked with sobs, tears spilling from her eyes and streaming down her cheeks as she gazed up into his eyes. He was lost, incapable of thinking clearly, uncertain what to do, what to say, how to *fix* this. Always in his life when something went wrong, he acted, he *did* something; he sought, he tracked, he stole, he fought, he used fists and muscle and brain and cunning and he acted. But here, now, with her, he had no idea what to do.

"Are you all right?" he asked, turning her face up to his, searching her eyes, trying to see into her, to discover if he'd been too late after all. "*Are you all right?*"

"Tell me what to do," he said. "Tell me how to make this better. Should I kill him?" Now there was an idea with some real merit.

"No!"

"It would be a fair fight. Juba and the only other man left are tied up and unconscious right now, but I could rouse Juba, wait a while, and then use broadswords or guns. His choice. Or fists." He liked the idea of fists.

"No!" she said. She pushed back a little. "No. You...you..." Their eyes met. He watched in fascination as her pupils grew larger, her lips parted, full and rich and incredibly inviting. The tip of her tongue dabbed at the center of her upper lip. It utterly undid him.

A maelstrom of relief and lust awakened in him, turning his body rock-hard. He felt each point where she was pressed against him in excruciating detail, the soft weight of her breasts, her slender waist, her lithe thighs dangling against his, the slight mound at their apex riding above his brutally stiff erection.

He didn't dare move, didn't dare breathe. His control teetered on the brink of dissolving completely.

And then she was kissing him. Not a gentle, questing kiss, but a hot, searing, opened-mouthed kiss. Her hands were bracketing his face as she lifted her body up along his, her legs rising to wrap around his hips.

And his body reacted before his mind had time to engage.

He reached down and rucked up the robes that kept her from him, his tongue deep in her mouth, reveling in the taste of her, the heat, and the urgency of their kiss. His hands found her round, firm buttocks and lifted her higher, a rumble rising in his chest at the delicious torment of her rubbing against his cock. Abruptly, she tore her lips from his and unwrapped her arms, and before he could even curse himself for being too bold and too rough, her hands dove down between their bodies. Heedlessly, she ripped his shirt apart, scattering buttons across the red and gold Persian carpet, and yanked it from his shoulders.

She was intent on her work, her gaze fixed on his chest, her breath coming in little pants, her skin flushed. Her hands flowed down his chest, her palms riding the shift of muscle to his waistband. He felt the buckle coming undone. She jerked at his trousers' strained buttons, releasing him. Her fingertips brushed against the swollen head of his erection.

He closed his eyes, teeth clenched in an effort to force control over his overwhelming impetus. She was having none of it. He felt her knees hitch higher around his waist as she lifted herself on his chest, felt her rise up against him, rubbing into him, a sob of frustration deep in her throat.

Nothing he had ever experienced before compared. He felt his honor shredded on raw desire, felt his principles blasted away in the furnace of passion. He tried. He chanted an inner mantra: *She's not mine his. She's not—*

But she was. Damn his honor, damn Pomfrey, damn the world. *She was his.*

"Please," she whispered hoarsely. "I don't know…I can't…"

He did. He could.

He shifted his hands beneath her thighs, gripping her tightly, and lifted, seating himself at her slick opening. Slowly, he lowered her onto him, watching her face all the while, shuddering with the restraint he tried to exercise. She gasped with pleasure, and then the gasp turned to one of hurt surprise. Her gaze flew to meet his, a little betrayed, a little afraid. He moved once, breaking through the thin membrane, and held there. Her inner muscles clenched hard around him, instinctively trying to halt a deeper possession. Too late. He didn't say a word, God help him. It was all he could do to stay there, rock-hard and immobile, and let her accustom herself to the feel of him.

Her hands clamped down on his shoulders, her forehead pitched in a scowl, and beneath her robes her breasts moved in startled agitation. She started to rise up, to withdraw from this too intimate connection, and then he felt it, the slow release of her inner muscles, the gradual acceptance. Her eyes flickered wider by another degree, again surprised, but no longer betrayed.

He clasped her soft hips in his hands and rocked against her, into her. A small cry escaped her throat and wonder filled her face. Bracing herself with her hands on his shoulders, she pushed down, bringing him deeper inside of her, then lifted, slowly gaining rhythm as she worked his body to her own untried purposes.

He took it as long as he could, jaw clenched, eyes shut tight against the sight of her awakening desire lest it take him to crisis before she was ready. But in the end her unpracticed moves, her soft mews of frustration proved too much.

He lifted first one of her hands then the other to the cross-beam supporting the tent's roof and curled her fingers tightly over them.

"Hold on to this," he whispered against her damp neck. He thrust deep into her. She gasped and held tight to the tent beam, his thrusts into her sending the lanterns swinging gently, so that the golden glow touched and released her ardent face, painting her in instances of passion transfixed. Again he thrust and again, hard, deep, but it was all gone, all control, all thought, only the knowledge that she was his.

Dimly, he grew aware that she'd released the tent beam and her fingers were dug deeply into his shoulder muscles, that her legs were high and tight around his waist, and that she countered each of his thrusts with one of her own, awkward, exquisite little jerks, writhing against him, driving him mad in her quest for her own release. More than his own climax, he wanted to see her face when she found hers.

He gripped her hips and held her hard against him, rocking into that soft mound, dragging his flesh against the small, silky bead of pleasure buried there. Her head fell back, her hands clenched in fists against his chest, and an anguished sound rose to her lips, her face straining.

With a gasp, she came, suddenly, ravishingly. Her eyes flew open and locked with his, her expression amazed and confounded. His lust was rising to a crescendo, and he let go of it with one powerful thrust, his eyes never leaving hers, letting her see what she did to him, how she took him from himself, how she destroyed him.

With a muted roar, he spilled himself hot and urgent within her.

A part of him, the outlaw part, disreputable and covetous, exulted in what he'd done, while the shadow of the honorable man he'd meant to be recoiled.

Gently, he lifted her, tenderly unhooked her legs from around his waist, carefully set her down. With a sound like a sigh, the robes fell from around her waist to her feet, concealing her. She swayed a little, and he caught her by the elbows. Her gaze searched his face, but he could not interpret that questing expression.

It was too late for apologies, too late to be the sort of man she deserved. "It can be something more than that," he said. "Something…better. I promise."

She was gazing at him uncomprehendingly. "Better?"

The pools of golden light shed from the lantern still swayed overhead, revealing then concealing her face.

"I am not a good man, Mildred. I have done things you would despise, but I have never killed a man and I have never taken from a man anything he rightfully owned." He took a deep breath. "Until you."

She backed away a few steps. "Pomfrey *owns* me?"

He found a smile for her affronted tone. She would rail at being called any man's possession. "Not you. But the right to call you his bride."

The right to call her his bride and build her a house and buy her gowns and jewelry; the right to show her the world and see her eyes glow as she made some new discovery or learned some fascinating bit of minutiae; the privilege to introduce her to statesmen and officers and witness their admiration and her bemusement. All the things he would never be able to do. Because he was no one. A shadow. A living ghost.

He had nothing to bring to a marriage, nothing to offer her in Pomfrey's stead. *Nothing.*

He'd selfishly, forcefully, and thoroughly compromised her. There'd been no tenderness, no regard for her virginity, no softly murmured encouragement or slow building of anticipation. She'd been terrified for four days, uncertain of her future, and then, when she'd been waiting for her would-be rapist to appear, he'd arrived instead. It was so natural, so understandable. In her sudden liberation from fear, in gratitude and relief, she'd responded instinctively by celebrating life at the most primal level. He'd used her spontaneous reaction as an excuse to take what he'd wanted, what he'd wanted since the moment he'd first seen her.

She would be a fool to accept him, and Mildred Whimpelhall was no fool. But she *was* a lady. And he would be a gentleman. He would offer for her, and she would accept. What choice did she have? What choice had he left her?

He took a deep breath. "Miss Whimpelhall, I cannot undo the last minutes, but I can make them right. If you would do me the honor of marrying me, I promise you that I will do everything within my power to try to make you happy."

"Undo? *Make them right?*" The surprise in her voice took him aback. He supposed he deserved that.

"Yes," he said stiffly. "Did you think I was so lost to decency that I wouldn't ask?"

"I didn't *think* about it at all," she said, her eyes flashing. "*I* wasn't thinking."

She needn't remind him of his sins; he knew them all quite well. But again, he supposed he deserved that, too. "You should do so now."

"Should I?" She sounded uncertain and defensive. She crossed her arms in front of her chest, but rather than making her look imposing, the gesture only succeeded in making her look incredibly young and vulnerable. "*Why* should I marry you?"

"Why?" he repeated numbly.

"Yes. Tell me why you want to marry me."

Because I am a selfish bastard. Because the thought of you in another man's arms hurts deeper than a shank in my side. Because even if I never see you again and die sixty years hence, your image will be the last thing to fade from my mind's eye. Because I want you. I want you.

"I compromised you. I couldn't...I am not without honor, regardless of how my actions seem to disprove that claim. Please, you must believe that."

"Oh, I do," she said in an odd voice. The lantern had ceased its slow pendulum swing now, and her expression was lost in the dusky shadows. "I believe you are a *most* honorable man."

"Thank you." If she believed in him, anything was possible. Somehow they would make this work. Somehow he would make her happy.

"And while I am most cognizant of the *honor* you do me," she said in a flavorless, oh-so-careful voice, "I am afraid I must decline your offer."

"What?"

"I am not going to marry you," she said.

Her words made no sense. She wouldn't marry Pomfrey without telling him what had happened or at least informing him that she was not the virgin he would insist on his bride being. She was simply too honorable. And she could not be so naïve as to believe that if she told Pomfrey the truth he would still marry her.

Unless she did not know him at all.

That had to be it. She felt obliged to honor her commitment to Pomfrey, without realizing that he would not have her. Of course she didn't know him, how could she? She'd been a child when they'd been betrothed, and they'd been separated most of their engagement.

Jim raked a hand through his hair. "Miss Whimpelhall,"— what idiocy to speak so formally now—"Mildred. You must marry me. You must realize that what I did has changed everything for all of us. Pomfrey included."

She frowned as though she was having difficulty comprehending what he was saying. "Because I am a…fallen woman?"

He didn't know how to answer. She had never flinched from frank talk before, and there had never been a time that required frank, clear-headed talk like now. She must be made to realize that Pomfrey would not have her. "Yes. I would never have said it in so many words,"—in fact, he'd throttle anyone who did—"but, yes."

"I see."

"Listen to me. I would do anything if only circumstances could be otherwise, but they are not. I am not the husband you would choose. I wish to God I was some other man. Still, I am hopeful that we can make a marriage work. You cannot deny there is passion between us. That must count for something."

His words seemed to drive home the immutability of what they'd done, for as he finished speaking she swayed. Even in the sparse light he saw her face drain of color.

"Yes. Something. But no. I won't marry you." Her voice was shaky.

He frowned, a growing sense of desperation seizing him. He realized he'd assumed she would agree without hesitation and that deep within him he'd been *glad* it had come this, *pleased* the issue had been forced, certain of his victory—yes, *victory*—and with that realization came guilt and self-loathing. He'd compromised her if not consciously, purposefully.

And yet, she still refused him.

"Mildred. Marry me. I will do whatever I can to make you happy."

"I have no doubt." He could barely hear her.

"Then marry me." He reached across the distance dividing them and seized her upper arms and dragged her to him. She did not come voluntarily. That hurt him more than any words she could have said. He let her go and looked down into her face, willing her by the sheer dint of his resolve to consent to his proposal. "Please."

"No."

"Why? What if you are pregnant? What if you are with child?" he demanded, helpless and furious. "Have you thought of that? What will you do then?"

"Pomfrey will provide for him."

"You poor, misguided fool," he whispered. "Don't you see? Pomfrey will not have you. He most certainly will not have another man's bastard."

She met his gaze unblinking. "Pomfrey will not know," she said in a clear, empty voice. "There are many ways to lose one's virginity. I will claim one of them. And if I am pregnant, many children are born early."

He felt as if his heart stopped beating. He did not believe her. Her words ran contrary to everything he knew about her, everything he *thought* he knew about her. He shook his head slowly, negating her words, looking for some other explanation, some other reason for her refusal.

"What did you think?" she asked, her emotions raw in her voice. "Pomfrey is a colonel with a brilliant career ahead of him. He has power and prestige, the respect of his superiors and the admiration of his men."

Each word cut him like a razor blade. He flinched as if he felt the lash on his back.

"He is noble and honorable, though perhaps not so *honorable* as you, for as you have pointed out, he would refuse to marry me if he knew of this. Of us. But he has a venerable name, wealth, and status. You have…a horse." Her voice broke on a sob. "I'm not going to give up my future because of a lapse in judgment."

A lapse in judgment. She could not have found better words to destroy him. Her words threw up a mirror, showing him in excruciating detail how far he fell short of any hope he could ever aspire to her hand.

Of course. Of course she would choose to lie to Pomfrey rather than marry you. He would have done the same. He stood very still, very straight, like he had another time years before accepting a similar judgment: *Worthless. Inferior. Only good dead.*

"You've obviously a much clearer view of things than I," he said. "I commend you on your perception and, of course, your decision."

If possible, her face grew even paler, and he hated that, hated that he'd hurt her even now. He couldn't stand to look at her, and so he grabbed hold of her wrist and pulled her toward him, spinning around and pulling her after him as he stalked from the tent.

"What are you doing?" she asked, her voice rising in trepidation. "Where are you taking me?"

"Where you've been wanting to go since the day we met, Miss Whimpelhall," he ground out between his teeth. "To bloody Colonel Lord Pomfrey."

CHAPTER TWENTY-TWO

She would live out her days in a ~~convent~~ nunnery,

her battered spirit bruised and yearning, her

heart broken.

—from the personal diary of Ginesse Braxton

Though the newly discovered muscles deep within her ached and a sharp stab of pain occasionally lanced between her legs in protest, Ginesse mounted the one-eyed camel without any help. Silently, she waited as Jim set loose the remaining camels and sent them off with a smack on the rump into the desert. When he caught her eye, he explained shortly that he was no murderer and that the Tuaregs would eventually catch their camels.

"How *honorable*," she drawled furiously.

"Not really. Or I'd leave them the horse, too," he said, pitching additional water bags over the camel's back and jerking Ginesse's knee out of the way in order to cinch the saddle tighter. "But I figure everyone should pay for their stupidity, and he's the cost of theirs."

That had been the last time he'd spoken to her. Which was wise because ever since he had told her he wished to *God* he was *some other man*, that though he could not *undo* the preceding minutes, he would nonetheless still act honorably and *make it right*, she been toying with the idea of unloading the rifle packed in a scabbard behind her and shooting him.

What made it all so unendurable was that ten minutes before he'd made these comments he had been buried deep inside her and she had never felt anything more *right* in her life. Even now, she would not undo those moments. He'd taught her the most intimate pleasure imaginable, a pleasure so deep, so intense, so *shared* that she hadn't known where his body had ended and hers began. All that had existed had been a mounting anticipation, the narrowing spiral toward an exquisite crisis that had crashed over her, leaving her weak and vulnerable and clinging to him. Vulnerable because she loved him. The bastard.

In the last few weeks, she'd learned that what she wanted, what she had *always* wanted, more than respect or admiration or approval or a place alongside her brothers in archaeological history, was to be seen for who she was, unencumbered by her accident-ridden past or by scholastic expectations or by the glow of her family's illustrious careers. Jim Owens had only known her as a girl with a fertile imagination, an insatiable curiosity, and a romantic disposition—and some issues regarding impulse control. The girl who she was, not the girl she was trying to be.

Just as she saw him.

Cowboy, duke, store clerk, or Bedouin prince. Labels didn't matter anymore. She didn't see any of them. She saw a strong, stern-faced man; a man of rare laughter but great humor; a man thoughtful and deliberate, but capable of swift and bold action; a man well-read and well-seasoned; a gentleman and a scoundrel;

capable, devious, and, damn him, honorable. The man she loved. The man she wanted.

And now that she knew what she wanted, she would not be satisfied with anything less. If she couldn't have Jim Owens's heart, she wouldn't accept any piece of him. She would not be part of some sad story of unrequited love. She would not spend her days hoping he did not come to regret his "honorable" offer. She had already spent too many years trying to be what she thought others wanted her to be. She wouldn't spend her life trying to be Jim Owens's beloved. She either was or she wasn't.

In spite of it all, she'd *wanted* to say yes. She'd wanted to believe passion, as he'd said, 'must count for something.' She wanted to believe that regardless of what he said, or did not say, he cared for her in a way that could become love. And if she spent enough time willing it to be so, she knew herself well enough to recognize that she would make herself believe it. Just like she'd made herself believe that she had a passion for archaeology and Egyptology that equaled her father's or her brothers'.

How strange to realize that now, when she'd discovered that was not who she was, that might be all she had left.

So, she'd done the only thing she could think of to protect herself from making that disastrous leap of faith, from heeding the tempting call of his honorable intentions. She'd thrown up between them the only barrier she knew he would not try to breach: Pomfrey.

He'd looked so shocked, so *offended*, when she'd told him she had no intention of telling Pomfrey they'd...had a physical relationship. But the assertion had served its purpose. And just to drive home the point that he must not press her, must not pursue the subject, must not play havoc with her resolve, she'd added the fantasy that she wanted the things Pomfrey could give her and he could not. She had expected him to be disgusted; she had never anticipated that he'd turn into this hard, cold-eyed stranger.

It was for the best. It made it easy to remember that he'd offered her an honorable alternative to being a "fallen woman," not a passionate declaration of undying love.

Undying love. Perhaps she was a fool, but she knew such a thing existed. She'd been witness to one of the world's great love stories: her parents. Was it too much to want the same? Perhaps it was, but she could not settle for less.

They rode far into the night. Though his possession had left her increasingly hurt and aching, she refused to complain. He stayed well ahead of her, silhouetted against the desert moon, so seamlessly melded with his gray stallion that they might have been a single creature. Finally, sometime after midnight, they came upon a copse of low-growing thorn bushes and he circled back to her side.

"We'll rest here," he said, dropping lightly from the Arabian's bare back.

She tapped the camel with the riding stick, ordering it to kneel. For once, the cantankerous creature complied. Gingerly, Ginesse swung her leg over the saddle and slipped off. Her legs folded beneath her the minute her feet touched the earth, but she never fell. Jim was beside her, swinging her easily into his arms, his face set and angry once more.

How had she ever thought him enigmatic? She could read him so easily now. His frustration, his guilt, his concern. Surely there was love there? Why hadn't he said so then?

"Why didn't you say something?"

"Because it's none of your business," she said. Treacherous, unfaithful body, it melted against him.

His eyes glittered like hoarfrost. "Let's get this straight, Miss Whimpelhall. Until I deliver you to Pomfrey, everything about you, *everything* is my business."

He jounced her higher in his arms and she startled, flinging her arms around his neck to keep from falling. "Do you understand, Miss Whimpelhall?"

She swallowed, uncertain to how to deal with this cruel-seeming stranger. "Yes."

"Good." He carried her a short distance and eased her down, holding on to her arm as she sank gracelessly to the ground. He went back to the camel and unsaddled it, returning with the blanket from her back. He snapped it open. "Lie on this."

She didn't argue. She was sore, cold, and exhausted. She barely kept awake long enough to open the canteen he brought her and take a drink before she collapsed, asleep as soon as her head touched the blanket.

It was still dark when she came to and found herself once more in Jim's arms. A faint light was sifting in from the east and the moon had set.

"We're leaving? Let me down. I can walk."

"No, you can't," he muttered.

He must have saddled the camel while she slept, for it was ready and waiting, the gray stallion tied behind. He deposited her sideways in the saddle and then mounted, drawing her onto his lap.

"This isn't necessary," she said. "I am perfectly capable of riding alone. I did so all last night."

He closed his eyes briefly, as if to bring his temper under control. When he opened them, he sounded more composed. "I know that, and I regret it. I also know you must be in some pain and that last's night ride only made matters worse," he said. "You shouldn't be riding astride. Not for a while yet. But the fact of the matter is that as much as I'm sure you don't want to be anywhere near me, let alone in my arms, we don't have the luxury of waiting for you to heal. I'm sorry."

Heat rose in her cheeks. "How far are we from the garrison?"

He hesitated. "I'm not certain. The Tuaregs didn't follow a straight trajectory. In the course of tracking them, I lost my reference points. We could be three days or a week."

She heard a slight underlying tension in his voice. "Do we have enough water?"

He didn't equivocate. "Probably." He tilted his head. "You're quite the pragmatist, aren't you?"

She couldn't hear any mockery in his voice, but she stiffened nonetheless. "I like to know where I stand."

"Don't we all," he murmured and clucked lightly to get the camel moving. "Don't we all."

* * *

From his seat atop the stallion, Jim watched Ginesse swaying atop the one-eyed camel with some concern. She was ahead of him, and her head was bobbing a little too loosely. She looked like someone's dirty bag of laundry. The once pristine robes had long since ceased to be white, her hair was knotted and tangled with bits of twigs, and her face was streaked with dust and sweat. And still he thought her the most gorgeous creature on earth.

He was undeniably mad. And it was a madness he doubted he'd ever recover from. Because as much as he wanted to, he could not deny how much she meant to him. He could not look at her without feeling a deep sense of recognition, of homecoming, of a long journey well-ended. Which had to be the definition of insanity when one was referring to a woman who'd told you she did not want you, that she would abdicate her sense her honor—and regardless of what she might appear to be, he *knew* her to be honorable—in order to marry someone else.

"How much farther do you think?" she asked faintly, swaying lightly atop the one-eyed camel.

His concern deepened. They'd been traveling for four days since leaving the Tuareg camp. Whenever he asked her how she was faring, she answered that she was fine. He didn't believe her anymore. Because she would never have asked such a question unless she felt her strength waning. She never complained, never. She was as intrepid as she was stubborn.

Even though they'd spent the first day in terse silence, he should have realized it wouldn't last. Not with her. Before the second day's sunset, she was relating little anecdotes about dead kings and Tanzanian bipeds, Napoleon's hygienic practices and the best way to serve cactus.

But they'd run out of food yesterday morning and spent the day beneath a makeshift shelter, hiding from the sun. Their water rations were quickly being depleted. If they didn't make it to the fort by tomorrow, he'd have to kill the horse—a better fate than dying of thirst—so they could continue on.

"Soon." He'd never lied to her, but then he'd never needed to.

"Oh."

"Do you need some water?"

"No. It's just…the sun is so hot. Does it seem hotter to you?"

"We'll stop and rest." It was still morning, vestiges of last night's cold still keeping the heat at bay. If she found the sun overwhelming now, she would find it unbearable in a few hours.

"No. The longer we rest the longer it takes. We have to press on."

He shook his head. "I'll have to strap you to the camel in a few minutes."

She gave him a weak, crooked smile. "Well, you can't say you wouldn't enjoy that."

Good Lord, the girl was audacious. Audacious and gamine and utterly beguiling. He'd never met her like before. He never would again. He wouldn't spend a day searching. He would settle for a memory of a three-week trip across a blasted desert taking the only woman he would ever love to another man, a trip surely designed in Hades for sinners.

They had an unspoken agreement that they would not touch on any "too personal" subject, in particular what had happened in the Tuareg's tent. Now, she'd broken that unvoiced pact.

He should have expected it. She would never play by the rules.

"I might at that," he admitted wryly. "But you wouldn't. We'll just take a short break."

"No. No…I'm just really tired. Perhaps…if you would just… hold me in front of you? I could sleep."

This could be dangerous territory. Despite the slight formality with which she addressed him and her concentrated effort to avoid touching him, she could not hide her body's response to his. He'd carried her on the camel in front of him after he'd realized what discomfort she'd been in. He'd noted the way she melted against him for the briefest of moments when he first took her up in his arms, how her eyes grew luminous when he looked at her mouth, the way her breath skittered when he brushed the hair from her eyes.

Just as she would have noticed his reaction to her. She'd have to be wearing armor not to. So after two days she'd announced she was perfectly able to ride independently. It had proved a double-edged sword. His relief was patent, but he missed her body close to his even more.

"Of course." They reined in their respective mounts. He got off and tied the stallion behind the camel then climbed aboard the camel behind her. Without any hesitation, she relaxed back against him. Awkwardly, he looped his hand around her waist and took hold of the reins. She rolled her cheek into his chest. Her eyes were already closed, a faint wry smile playing about her cracked lips. "Don't worry, Jim. I promise not to take advantage," she murmured.

"More's the pity," he murmured.

He had taken advantage. And given any encouragement, he would again. But she hadn't heard. She was already asleep.

CHAPTER

TWENTY-THREE

"You thought to have your way with this poor darling girl didn't you, you infernal skunk, because she was alone and unprotected?"

—from the personal diary of Ginesse Braxton

Colonel Lord Hilliard Pomfrey stood in the garrison's lookout tower with his field glasses pressed to his eye. "I believe that there are *two* Arabs atop that camel, Jones."

The fresh-faced lieutenant beside him made some adjustments to the field scope mounted on the floor and peered into the lens at figures a mile out and closing slowly. "Indeed, you are correct, sir. One of the men is carrying the other before him. Perhaps he is injured and they are seeking medical aid?" he suggested.

"An Arab seeking medical attention from the King's Army? Not bloody likely. No, they'd seek help from their own people."

"Unless they were travelers set upon by bandits?"

"Hm," Pomfrey mused. "Perhaps. Though we are far enough from any of the main caravan routes that it would be surprising."

Fort Gordon had been built on the remains of an ancient Roman fortress at the westernmost edge of what Pomfrey thought could only be an ironically named "New Valley," an immensely long geographic ridge separating the northern sand dunes from the southern dunes. The site was significant only in that it was one of the few oases of any size that occurred before entering a virtual no-man's-land of rock and sand and wind, and because it guarded a border no one was likely to try to cross. But, by God, if they did, they'd have His Majesty's army to deal with.

Simply put, Colonel Lord Hilliard Pomfrey had the privilege of commanding England's most remote continually manned outpost. He took pride in that fact. Few men were up to the challenge of facing down such extreme isolation; he was one of them. Like himself, his men were handpicked by him for this duty. And while he was rightfully proud of that strength of character that enabled him to endure, he was not too proud to admit it would be nice to share his isolation with a helpmate to support him in a domestic capacity.

He withdrew the binoculars from his eyes, frowning. Even allowing for a leisurely pace, Mildred and her escorts should have arrived a week ago. Were something untoward to have happened, surely Neely would have sent a man ahead. Besides, that is precisely why he had pressed Owens into service; the man was a ruffian and a scoundrel, but his knowledge of the desert and its peoples was unparalleled by any man he knew, at least any white man. He was confident Owens would keep her safe.

"Should I have the men open the gates?" Jones asked.

"No. We'll wait and see what they have to say for themselves," Pomfrey said. "Pick two of your best riflemen and have them keep them in their sights until we discover what it is they want."

"Yes, sir," Jones said, snapping off a smart salute before leaving Pomfrey alone in the tower, his thoughts returning to Mildred and her unexplained delay.

Perhaps he should have sent a better grade of men to serve as her escort. He had a full complement of brave, seasoned soldiers to choose from, but he'd sent an old campaigner one year from being discharged and a bunch of fresh recruits.

At the time it had seemed the obvious decision. Neely was there just to provide escort. He didn't expect Neely and his men to engage in a battle. It was Owens's express job to keep them out of any dangerous situations. But even if there had been hostilities, surely Neely, a career veteran, and his boys were up to the task. And he *knew* Owens was. The man had an absolute knack for surviving the unsurvivable.

Pomfrey had been leading a squadron on a reconnaissance mission deep in the desert along the Sudanese border when they'd spotted Owens. He'd been limping along, leading an all-but-dead horse out of the Libyan desert, with what Pomfrey would later discover were two bullet holes in him, a couple broken bones, a severe case of dehydration, and mild starvation.

Ever cognizant of his duty as a Christian, he'd order his men to a halt so he could rescue the poor boy. Owens just stood there swaying as Pomfrey had swung from his camel, barking an order for his men to fashion a litter. They jumped to comply as he'd asked the boy his name. While awaiting a reply, he'd taken the opportunity to shoot the poor horse in the head.

What happened next still amazed him. Owens had started as the horse collapsed, and before Pomfrey realized what was happening, Owens's right fist had lashed out and caught him full in the face, knocking him to the ground.

"You bastard!" the young man had shouted. "You bloody bastard! I owed that horse my life."

A couple of his soldiers roughly seized the boy, causing him to gasp in agony. Pomfrey took the higher road.

"Treat him gently, lads," he'd said. "The sun and the wind must have driven him mad."

The boy threw himself forward, but his soldiers kept a fast hold of him. Pomfrey climbed to his feet, gingerly working his jaw.

"I owed that horse a debt!" the boy sobbed. "He carried me faithfully, and this is how he's repaid!"

Pomfrey had looked sadly his men. "See? What sane man could think himself indebted to a soulless animal?"

The boy's last bit of energy had by then been expended. He'd staggered on his feet, unable to hold up his own weight. "Let me go," he panted.

"You say you owed that animal a debt. What of the debt you owe me, young sir? Have I not saved your life? And yet you repay my conscious act of charity by striking me. Is that honorable? Is that *noble*?"

His words had the desired effect on the battered young man. He stopped fighting. He squinted as though having trouble focusing. "I'll repay you," he'd rasped. "I vow, I will repay you. I wouldn't be beholden to you for any reason."

And he'd fallen unconscious.

It was that episode which had convinced Pomfrey that he could trust Owens, who was, in his own primitive, heathenish way, an honorable man. If Owens felt so strongly about his obligation to a horse, he must feel ten times that to the man who'd saved his life. No, he had no qualms about sending Owens to protect Mildred. He just hoped he hadn't overestimated Owens's abilities.

He dragged his attention back to the two Arabs approaching the garrison. He wished they would just go away, but it looked as if they wouldn't.

"Open the gates!" the rider bellowed.

Good heavens. He was *English*.

"Sir?" his young lieutenant called up to him.

"This is Mildred Whimpelhall, blast you to hell!" the man on the camel shouted. "Now *open the bloody gates!*"

Mildred? "Open the gates! Open the gates at once!" Pomfrey called out, hurrying down the stairs. He arrived at the gates just as it swung open and Jim Owens rode in.

"Mildred? Good heavens, Owens, what happened?"

Owens carried her in front of him, bundled in filthy Egyptian rags, her face all but hidden by a swathing veil, only one long knotted rope of reddish hair falling over Owens's arm. What he could see of her face was just as filthy as her clothing, encrusted with dust and sweat. Her eyes were closed, and he could not tell if she was breathing.

"Is she all right?"

Owens nodded. He looked just as wretched as the woman he held, his skin burnt beneath the coating of dust and salt whitening his lips. "She's fainted. She needs water and food. And rest."

His eyes fixed on the unmoving bundle, Pomfrey gestured to two of the nearest soldiers. "Get her down from there, and for God's sake get her out of those rags," he ordered.

They hastened forward and lifted their hands to take her from Owens, who with an odd appearance of reluctance shifted her gently to their waiting arms.

"Careful," Owens barked. "Be careful. She has had a hard time of it."

Those enlisted men's wives "living on the strength" had arrived along with one of his junior officer's wives. They divided their fascinated stares equally between Mildred and James Owens.

"If you would be so kind as to see to Miss Whimpelhall, Mrs. Bly?" Pomfrey asked. "A bath and some new clothing?"

"Water first and then food," Owens counterordered. "Then you can worry about making her pretty."

Pomfrey flushed. "That goes without saying."

Owens slid from the camel's back as they took Mildred away. The man was near done for, Pomfrey realized. His legs could barely hold him, but when one of the soldiers put out a steadying hand, he shook him off.

Pomfrey offered him a thin smile. "As soon as you've eaten and cleaned up, you can report to my office and tell me where the rest of my men are," he said. He nodded to his young lieutenant, who, though standing at attention, was slack-jawed with wonder. "Jones here will see you to the men's barracks."

"Of course," Jones said. "If you'd follow me, Mr. Owens?"

Owens nodded tiredly and began following the eager young subordinate, but Pomfrey felt he owed the man something more. The trip had obviously tested Owens in unforeseen and unpleasant ways, and yet he'd arrived with Mildred. His faith in Owens had not been misplaced after all.

"Owens," he called out.

Owens stopped, his shoulders sagging with exhaustion, and looked around.

Pomfrey smiled. "Well, you always said you'd repay your debt to me. I guess you've done so at that," he said amicably. "I should say that makes us even."

An odd, wry smile curled Owens's cracked and bleeding lips. "Would you?"

"Why, yes," Pomfrey said. "Wouldn't you?"

"Not even a little bit, Colonel. In fact, not at all," he replied, and with that enigmatic statement, he turned and limped away.

* * *

An hour later Pomfrey was still pondering what Owens had meant when Owens appeared in the doorway to his office. He'd washed, shaved, and changed into the regiment's khaki drill clothing, his own being beyond salvaging. Nonetheless, he still looked awful. Dark circles underscored his eyes, and his cheeks looked hollowed out, his cheekbones jutting under peeling and raw skin.

"Ah, Owens. That's all right, Hobbins," he said to his assistant who had leapt up to dutifully guard the sanctity of his commander's office. "Come in, Owens. Have a seat."

He motioned for Owens to take the chair across the desk from him and waited while Owens was seated. "Would you like some tea?" he offered, picking up the pot Hobbins had recently brought in and pouring himself a cup.

Owens ignored the offer. "How is she?"

"She?" Pomfrey echoed.

"Mi—Miss Whimpelhall."

"Oh," Pomfrey nodded. "Fine, I should imagine, or I should have heard otherwise. Thank you for asking."

"You mean you haven't seen her yet?"

"Of course not," Pomfrey said in sincere surprise. "I can guarantee you, she would not thank me to visit her in her current state. She would be mortified. I shall see her in due course, when she is feeling more the thing. Perhaps tomorrow."

Owens's light-colored eyes glittered oddly.

"Now tell me about Neely and the rest of my men."

"They deserted us," Owens said flatly.

"*What?*"

"Neely got it into his head that we were being followed by some sort Mahdist raiders. He wanted to turn back halfway into the journey. I refused."

"Neely left Miss Whimpelhall with you and absconded?" Pomfrey asked incredulously.

"I don't know the particulars. He coshed me. When I came to, he and his men were gone and Miss Whimpelhall was still with me."

"Well, for God's sake man, what did she say?"

"She wouldn't say much." Something softened in his eyes for a second, and a half smile flickered briefly over his austere face.

"Why not?"

He shrugged. "She wouldn't say that either."

"But that's preposterous." Pomfrey drummed his fingers impatiently on the desk.

"That's Mi—Miss Whimpelhall."

Pomfrey stiffened, taking exception to Owens's familiarity. How dare Owens presume to instruct him on what his fiancée was like?

Owens was gazing steadily at a place in the center of the desk through half-closed eyes, either indolent or absorbed.

"Were you?" Pomfrey asked.

Owens pressed his lower lip in and bit it, as though keeping back a snarl. He looked up. "Were we what?"

"Being followed by raiders?"

"No. We were being shadowed by Tuaregs."

"Tuaregs?"

"Yup. They closed in on us about a week back. Caught us unawares."

"Good Lord," Pomfrey breathed, furious. "Then Neely was right and you needlessly endangered my fiancée!"

Dull red swept up Owens's neck into his lean face. "No," he said softly. "They were traveling parallel to us. They would never have dared approach us had Neely stayed. They had nothing but a couple of antique rifles, and there were only four of them."

As much as Pomfrey wanted to believe Neely wouldn't act in so craven a fashion, he didn't doubt Owens, not when he could so easily confirm his story with Mildred.

He sat back. "What happened?"

"I sold Miss Whimpelhall to them for that horse you saw, snuck into their camp four days later, and got her back. We've been making our way here ever since."

Pomfrey felt his blood grow cold. "*You what?*"

"There wasn't another way to ensure her safety. If I hadn't sold her, they would have killed me, and that would have been the end to it." Owens met his shocked gaze with a flinty one.

Pomfrey's hand flew to his mouth in horror. Mildred! She had spent four days as the captive of desert scoundrels. If they'd defiled her...If? His stomach twisted with anger and anguish that Mildred, an intensely virtuous woman, should have suffered so horribly.

And what of his command? He doubted he could keep quiet what had happened to her, and when it came out, they would forever after carry the stigma of her victimization. Horrible. Horrible...

"God help us," he whispered, not realizing he spoke aloud. "Her shame…How can I…?"

"How can you *what*?" Owens asked in a hard, cold voice.

Pomfrey's round-eyed gaze met Owens imploringly. "Tell me they didn't…? Is she…?"

"No," he clipped out. "They didn't touch her."

Relief so profound swept through him that he sagged back in the chair, his eyes shutting as he offered up a prayer of thanks. When he opened them, he found Owens watching him with barely contained contempt. He pulled himself together and straightened, angered anew. It would be easy for Owens to accept damaged goods; he was damaged himself. He couldn't understand the mortal wound such a…such a misadventure would cause a woman as sensitive as Mildred.

"No thanks to you, I take it," he said sharply.

A muscle jumped in Owens's jaw. "Nope."

"Well, then. We're finished here," he said, suddenly wanting nothing more than to be done with this conversation, uncomfortable with the notion that somehow Owens was interviewing him and that he was not faring well. He picked up a report he'd already read twice and pretended to study it.

"First, I have a request," Owens said.

Pomfrey looked up from the paper and raised a brow inquiringly.

"The stallion."

"What of him?"

"If you haven't shot him yet, I'd like to give him a chance to recover before I leave."

Pomfrey felt himself flush anew. "Take however many days you need," he replied coldly and went back to looking at the paper. He heard Owens climb painfully to his feet and start for the door.

He kept his eyes focused on the report, relieved. But then Owens stopped walking.

Irritated, Pomfrey looked up. Owens was standing a few feet from the door, half turned away, on the cusp of exiting. Why didn't he just go? "What now?"

"Treat her well."

Impatiently, Pomfrey set the paper down. *Now* what was the man talking about? "Treat who well?"

"Your fiancée."

Pomfrey stared. The man was beyond presumptuous, and he'd just about had enough of it. "I'm sure that's none of your concern, Mr. Owens."

"She's a brave girl, Pomfrey, with a spirit like a flame. Bright and ardent."

Mildred? Now he was dumfounded as well as affronted. Mildred was not ardent. She was calm and deferential, a refuge from the tempestuous, wicked world, not a part of it.

"Don't extinguish that flame."

"That sounds like a threat."

"It's meant as a suggestion."

"Thank you, Owens," Pomfrey said coldly, struggling to keep his composure. "I shall take it under advisement."

Owens started to turn again and once more checked. Pomfrey's lips compressed so tightly they began to go numb.

"And when she gets silent, and she's rarely silent," Owens said, "if you wait long enough she'll be back chattering like a magpie because she has too much joy in her to hold on to disappointment."

Chattering like a magpie? A tingle of alarm started in Pomfrey and grew. He'd never known Mildred to chatter. Her conversation was sedate and high-minded, and while she always maintained a pleasant demeanor, one would hardly call her joyful. In

225

fact, she was sounding more and more of a stranger, and as he realized this he realized, too, that he'd never spent any extended periods of time with Mildred. Some long weekends at house parties, a few holidays at her father's country estate, but mostly his courtship had taken place in letters.

Now he wondered if letters had been a poor substitute for personal experience. A person could mask certain less salubrious traits and edit out character flaws in the written word.

"And remember when something…unexpected happens, she will think she's to blame and you'll need to assure her she's not."

"Unexpected?" Pomfrey echoed.

"Yeah. You know. It's when you think everything is going along fine that you should start looking for meteor showers or stampeding wildebeests."

Meteor show—"What in God's name do you mean?"

"She's impulsive."

No. *No.* Mildred could not be impulsive. He *loathed* impulsiveness in all its shapes and forms. Lord deliver him, what sort of terrible mistake had he made?

"Impulsive people court trouble, and she," Owens looked past him to some inner vision and smiled, his voice dropping to a whisper, "she is a very ardent suitor."

And just that easily, Pomfrey understood.

He surged to his feet, the chair toppling back and crashing to the floor. "You've *had* her, haven't you?" he choked out in a hoarse voice. "You *bastard*. You sonofabitch! You took her, didn't you? *Didn't you?*"

Owens didn't answer; he didn't have to.

A red haze flooded Pomfrey's vision, and he charged from behind his desk, spinning Owens around and ramming his other fist into his belly. It was like hitting a bag of wet sand, hard and dense, but Owens, exhausted and weak, went down to his knees. Pomfrey didn't care. Dimly, he heard Hobbins shouting in the background, a woman's scream, and the sound of boot heels running. Owens had lost any claims he had to a fair fight.

Pomfrey raised his fist and slammed it down into Owens's face. He fell forward under the force of the blow, bracing himself on the floor with one hand. Pomfrey kicked him hard in the side, his lips curled back over his teeth, a sob coming from deep in his throat, "Bastard. You've ruined her! *Ruined* her!"

He stepped back, curling his fist to deliver another blow, but then Owens's head slowly rotated and the silvery eyes marked him, gleaming with some hot inner fire, and he felt a cold shiver run up his spine even though he had righteousness on his side.

"Don't you *ever* say that about her again," Owens ground out in a low voice.

"Don't you tell me what to do with regards to Mildred! You *polluted* her." He raised his fist again and swung it as hard as he could down at Owens's face. It never touched him.

Owens surged to his feet like a coiled spring abruptly released, catching Pomfrey's fist in his bare hand and jerking him forward straight into an upper cut that came out of nowhere. Light exploded across Pomfrey's vision, and he staggered back.

Owens came after him, catching hold of his shirtfront and straight-arming him backwards. Pomfrey's head hit the wall hard, dazing him. Frantically, Pomfrey delivered a series of blows to Owens's midsection, but the bastard didn't even appear to feel it. He kept Pomfrey pinned to the wall with one hand and drew the other back to deliver a finishing blow.

"Let him go!" a woman cried out. "Jim! No!"

A disheveled woman in an oversized dress appeared, grabbing hold of Owens's arm. "Jim!"

Owens looked over at her, his lips twitching back in a snarl. "Back away, Mildred."

Pomfrey's bleary gaze slew to the woman, narrowed in confusion, then widened in recognition. "Mildred?" he rasped. "That's not Mildred!"

Owens's gaze snapped from the woman back to him. "*What?*"

He should have known the woman Owens described couldn't have been Mildred. He should have known it would be someone like *her*.

"That's Harry Braxton's brat."

CHAPTER

TWENTY-FOUR

His stern face was awful to behold, and she quailed before the Terrible Knowledge of what her pride and vanity had done to this Prince of the Prairie.

—from the personal diary of Ginesse Braxton

A half dozen soldiers flooded into the office, knocking Ginesse aside and launching themselves at Jim. They wrestled him back against the wall with an audible thud. It was excessive. An eight-year-old boy could have done as much because all the fight had gone out of Jim. He didn't resist, he simply looked at her over their heads, his gaze betrayed and wondering.

Colonel Lord Pomfrey, a trim, sandy-colored man with a receding hairline and a lush moustache, snapped a linen kerchief from his uniform jacket pocket and dabbed the blood from his mouth while looking with loathing first at her and then at Owens.

She and several others had witnessed that he'd been first to strike a blow. Perhaps with this in mind, he made a sharply dismissive gesture to his men. "That won't be necessary," he said. "Let him go and leave. Now."

Reluctantly, the soldiers released Jim, and with backwards glances, they filed out of the room.

"Hobbins, shut the door behind you," Pomfrey ground out.

"You're her. The *afreet*," Jim said tonelessly, still watching her.

This wasn't how she imagined telling him. No. Coward that she was, she hadn't imagined it at all. She'd been too afraid to, and now looking at his face, she realized her instinct had been right.

"All that time. All that time knowing how I…and you were never…" he whispered, his head shaking like a dazed man.

"I'm sorry."

He'd looked away from her, his gaze fixed on a place near the floor, his brow furrowed in concentration.

"What the hell are you doing here pretending to be Mildred?" Pomfrey demanded.

Her gaze slew to Pomfrey, to Jim, back to Pomfrey. "It's…it's complicated."

"*Where's Mildred?*"

"She's fine. Really," she said hastily. "I met her aboard the *Lydonia*. She was horribly seasick and got off the ship in Rome." Her gaze flickered back to Jim. He was still staring fixedly at nothing. "She was going to finish her journey by rail. I…I took her place."

"For God's sake, why?" Pomfrey asked.

"I needed to get here, to find the lost city of Zerzura—"

"Jesus," Jim whispered.

She turned toward him pleadingly. He looked straight through her. "No one would guide me if they knew who my father

230

was. No one would dare to risk my safety by bringing me here. I thought if I told you my real name, you'd take me back."

Pomfrey's face grew red. "Do you mean to tell me you think I am any less responsible or that I care less about my fiancée's welfare than your father does about yours?" he stormed.

Ginesse looked at him with loathing. She had his measure now. Pomfrey was the sort of man who thought himself the center of the universe, who considered everything that happened, anything anyone said, somehow related to him.

"*Of course* nothing would have happened to you. I would never have sent for Miss Whimpelhall if there was any danger."

"But something *did* happen to me," she said, unable to stem her anger. "Miss Whimpelhall *was* in danger. Because the men you sent to protect your fiancée were inadequate to the task. Had I been Mildred, you would be responsible for exposing her to a trauma from which she would not easily recover."

"Impertinent girl!" Pomfrey shouted. "I suppose I am to thank you now? What hubris! But then hubris is rather your bailiwick, isn't it, *Miss* Braxton?"

She went cold under the venomous lash of his voice. She wanted to plug her ears and flee from what he would say next. She didn't. She wasn't ten years old anymore. There was nowhere to hide from her actions. No one to whom she could run. Desperately, she glanced at Jim, but he was not looking at her. His jawline was tight, his brow furrowed as he stared at some inner demon. Or *afreet*.

"Everyone in Egypt knows your reputation as an overindulged brat incapable of the least modesty or self-restraint, a miscreant and a nuisance," Pomfrey said in a thick, harsh voice. "You're an object of ridicule and derision amongst the expat community. A calamity."

She closed her eyes. He could have not have found sharper words with which to stab her or a more tender place to cut. Everything she'd thought to do by coming here fell apart, shredded by his accusations. The brilliant discovery with which she'd hoped to bury her past, the feeling of never being good enough, her failure to live up to everyone's expectations, to make good on the promise of her famous name, mocked her in Pomfrey's relentless voice. She was a jinx, an irritation, a meddler. *A disappointment.*

"How could you mistake this…this *person* for my fiancée, Owens?" he demanded. Jim started and looked over at her.

"Look at her. A brazen, walking compendium of misfortune, irritation, and mishap. Sent away in shame. And now she's returned," he finished, "a full-blown adventuress and a profligate."

She wanted to cry a denial, but the words couldn't get past the constriction in her throat.

"And still in shame," Pomfrey said meaningfully.

"That's enough, Pomfrey," Jim finally spoke.

Pomfrey's gaze swung to Jim. "You are willing, I assume, to do the right thing by her?"

The right thing? Please, say no. Don't think of me that way. Please.

"Yes." He sounded numb. "Of course."

A small sob escaped her lips.

"For your sake, I hope you mean that," Pomfrey said. "You do know who her father is?"

"I know."

Pomfrey gave a small snort of laughter. "Of course. How could you not?" he shook his head.

Jim didn't speak. He didn't look at her. He didn't defend her. Not a sound to refute Pomfrey's denunciation or to protest Pomfrey's defamation. Certainly he said nothing about loving her. He was all dutiful resolve, stiff and erect, like a man facing a firing squad, she thought bitterly.

Well, she wasn't going to be his bullet.

"No," she whispered so quietly no one heard.

"You poor bastard. There'll be no escaping the consequences this time."

"That's enough, Pomfrey," Jim repeated. "This is no longer any of your concern."

"No," she repeated.

"I beg to differ, Owens. As the person inadvertently responsible for throwing her in your way and you in hers," Pomfrey said, "it is indeed my responsibility to see that—"

"*No.*"

Both men looked over at her. She stood trembling, wounded and uncertain except for one vital thing: she would not marry Jim Owens. She would not marry him to placate society's expectations, not to please her parents, not to satisfy Pomfrey's moral code, not to be Jim's act of contrition or to give him a forum to demonstrate how much honor he had. She would not marry him even to please her own heart. Because it would be a temporary thing, a preface to its breaking—if it hadn't broken already.

If he'd cared for her, if he'd loved her at all, he would have championed her. He hadn't. He'd stood silently by and let Pomfrey tear her to bits.

"I am *not* marrying Mr. Owens," she said, "and nothing you can say, nothing anyone can say, can make me do so."

And before either could speak, before her tears began falling unchecked down her cheeks, before she heeded an inner voice shouting, "*Fool! You love him! Marry him!*" she ran from the room.

* * *

233

Pomfrey turned to Owens with a sniff. "You have more luck than a pistol at a swordfight, Owens," he said. "The girl is lost to all decency, obviously a complete wanton, a wh—"

Jim's fist shot out.

Pomfrey collapsed to the ground unconscious.

CHAPTER

TWENTY-FIVE

Little wonder, then, that bitter grief had now returned to torture him.

—from the personal diary of Ginesse Braxton

They locked him in the stockade for four days. No other prisoners occupied the other cells that ran the length of the room. He was alone, and that was fine with him. He needed to think, and that was best done in a place where he wouldn't see Ginesse Braxton—Ginesse, not Mildred—because she did things to his thought processes, such as dammed them up completely.

She acted and he reacted: viscerally, irrepressibly, and ruinously.

She fell in the water; he dove in after her. She laughed; he smiled. She mentioned the beauty of the sunset; he saw colors in it he hadn't ever noticed. She peeked at him from under her gold-tipped lashes; he grew hard as Damascus steel. Pomfrey said something derogatory; he wanted to kill the sonofabitch with his bare hands.

Things like that.

He was not a reactive sort of man. His life had often depended on him taking measured, deliberate action after careful, rational consideration.

He should have known she couldn't be who she said she was because if he wasn't relying on objectivity to survive, he was relying on his attention to detail, the hunter's eye for anything out of place or unexpected, and the details about "Mildred Whimpelhall" didn't add up.

There'd been any number of clues: that hideous red hair dye for starters—Pomfrey would consider a woman who dyed her hair a floozy; her youth; the hundreds of ancient Egyptian facts and anecdotes she knew; her familiarity with how to mount a camel. Jesus. As Harry Braxton's kid, she almost certainly knew Arabic. She'd probably spent her days as the Tuaregs' captive giving them history lessons.

She'd appeared and laid to waste the foundations he'd survived on, and that unnerved him. She'd come into his life like a sandstorm, eroding his self-control, uncovering dreams he'd thought buried, and stripping away his indifference.

It was just as well they kept her away from him because he was hoping that if he sat here long enough, out of her proximity, he'd be able to regain some of his perspective and figure what the hell was going on. He stood up and stared out the barred window at the parade grounds where a platoon of men were going through an arms drill.

Across the grounds, he could see the married men's barracks where the few women in the fort resided with their families. Some children played a game in the dust beneath the raised walkway.

That's where Ginesse would be quartered. He moved to the other side of the cell and dropped down to the floor, sitting with his back against the bars. He didn't need to be watching for her. He needed to think. What did he know? Not assume, *know*.

He knew that she'd manipulated him, lied to him, and pretended to be someone she wasn't. And apparently, she'd done so to chase after some pipe dream involving Zerzura, which any treasure hunter worth his salt would be able to tell you was nothing but a myth told by some Arab traders in the fifteenth century to keep the European adventurers busy in Libya and out of Egypt.

Then, halfway through their journey, she'd given herself to him with the sweetest abandon and afterward claimed she would rather deceive her supposed fiancée Pomfrey than lead the life he offered her. Which, if not the most honorable act, at least made a sort of practical sense *if* she'd been Mildred Whimpelhall. But she wasn't Mildred Whimpelhall. She was Ginesse Braxton and as far as he knew not promised to anyone...

He stiffened. Maybe she was promised to someone else. He knew nothing about her. Maybe when she'd been rhapsodizing about Pomfrey she'd actually been describing another man, someone she knew. She was an impetuous, ardent woman. The circumstances had been extraordinary. In a moment of impulse—and God knew she was impulsive—she'd surrendered to a combination of unprecedented relief and undeniable physical attraction. But as soon as reality reinserted itself, she'd remembered that other man. It was the only thing that made sense—

Except...

Why hadn't she told him then who she was? Why continue to pretend to be Mildred Whimpelhall, who would not give up a life of prestige and relative comfort because of a "lapse in judgment"?

He got up again, pacing the ten-foot length of the cell back and forth, thinking back to his interview with Pomfrey, before Ginesse arrived, when he still thought she was Mildred Whimpelhall.

How long had he involuntarily held Colonel Lord Pomfrey up as the bar against which he measured himself? What a fool he'd been, how naïve and credulous. During those few brief moments when Pomfrey thought his fiancée had been raped, his first thoughts had not been for her pain and terror, it had been on how her "shame" would reflect on him.

And Jim had been glad, savagely, unworthily exultant that Pomfrey had revealed himself to be so little, so self-absorbed. Because in those moments he'd realized that Pomfrey was no contender for Mil—Ginesse's heart. She couldn't love him. She might trade passion for privilege, but she would never wed so slight a man. He had absolute faith in that, faith in her. He only needed to wait for her to discover what Pomfrey was for herself.

But he had no capacity for patience or guile where she was concerned. He hadn't been able to leave without provoking Pomfrey. Then she'd appeared, her hair flying about her face, a dress two sizes too large swirling about her feet. He could still see the look of shock on Pomfrey's face, shock and relief and exultance because she wasn't his fiancée.

And in the space of a few seconds everything had changed.

Once he'd been in a boxing match in some seedy town he'd forgotten the name of. His opponent was a big German with ham-like fists and a head like a cannonball. At the end of the fifth round, the German had decided the round bell didn't mean anything and as Jim had turned to go to his corner, the bastard had sucker-punched him. Somehow Jim had remained upright though barely sentient, only dimly aware of the crowd shouting at him, dazed and disoriented.

He'd felt exactly the same way when he'd heard Pomfrey identify Ginesse Braxton. A dozen conflicting emotions vied for precedence: anger, relief, confusion, acrimony, elation. A hundred memories from the past three weeks flashed through his mind, each taking on new, but no clearer, meanings.

She'd lied to him, used him, made love to him, and then, when Pomfrey's words had finally penetrated, when he'd once more offered her his name and his protection, she'd refused him. Again.

With a sudden growl, he grabbed hold of the cell bars and banged his forehead against the iron rods, willing himself to accept that there could very well be another man, some Oxford scholar or one of her father's protégées. Or it could be simpler. She might want something more than he could offer—and how could he fault her for that? She might have seen him as a brief, intense infatuation but not a man with whom she could share her life. Not a man worth giving up the lifestyle, the community, the cachet of being a Braxton. And again, how could he fault her for that?

"Owens! Move back from the door," a guard ordered him, as he entered the room.

Jim pushed himself back from the bars as the guard came forward and unlocked his cell. "Colonel said to let you out," he said.

Jim raised his brows. He didn't see Pomfrey as a compassionate commander, but then he couldn't see a lot of things.

The guard smiled thinly. "Jurisdiction's a bit dodgy. You're lucky you're not a soldier, Owens, or you'd be living in that cell for the rest of your life like as not."

"Yup," he answered. "Where's my horse?"

"In the stables. The rest of your things are in the quartermaster's office, but I wouldn't count on seeing that pistol of yours until you leave."

"Thanks." He left the stockade and headed straight for the stables, where a wiry, red-haired man in a leather apron met him at the door.

"Nice bit of horseflesh," the man said in a thick Scottish accent. "Poorly used though, sir. Poorly used." He shook his head disapprovingly.

"How long before I can ride him out of here?"

The man blew out his cheeks in disgust. "Tomorrow at the earliest. Day after would be more to me likin'."

A couple days. If he stayed out of her way, if he just kept his head low, stuck to the barracks…Who was he fooling? He couldn't keep away from her unless they kept him in a cage.

"I'll be back tomorrow."

CHAPTER TWENTY-SIX

The fateful day had arrived when All Would Be Revealed!

—from the personal diary of Ginesse Braxton

Pomfrey had apologized to Ginesse Braxton. He'd lost his composure. His near giddy relief that the woman Owens had described—an intemperate, loquacious, and impulsive woman who'd been held captive for four days and *nights* by savages—was not Mildred had given way to giddy scorn. He felt he'd behaved badly, and he blamed the girl, again, not without cause. She was definitely at fault. But he was a gentleman and a gentleman's code demanded he apologize.

Besides which she was the daughter of Harry Braxton, a man renowned for his protective instincts, hot temper, and far-ranging influence in Egypt. And apparently she also meant something to James Owens, a man with an even more dangerous reputation, if less well-known.

So he had asked her into his office and apologized. The bold creature had simply said, "Fine," and then she asked him to send her with a full escort out forty miles into the desert so she could dig for a lost city.

Well, he had made it clear in no uncertain terms that he was not the sort of man to reward duplicity and deceit. Even if she had arrived with the proper letters of introduction and credentials he wouldn't have granted her request. His men had far better and more important ways to occupy their time.

Nonetheless, he resolved never again to be involved in so distasteful a scene as the one that had played out in his office. He was so much better than that. And to prove it, he was dining with them both that very night.

Which is why he was standing in front of his dressing table mirror making sure his tie was knotted to perfection, not a strand of his gleaming pomaded hair was out of place, the ends of his moustache were trimmed within a degree of one another, and his nails were buffed to a high sheen. He would be a living example of gentlemanliness at its highest order. He had just made a last, small adjustment to the lay of his tie and allowed himself a small smile at his reflection when his batman knocked on the door.

"Come."

A soldier popped his head around the door. "Sir, an Arab scout has just arrived with news that a caravan is approaching the fort and should be here within the hour."

"A caravan? What sort of caravan?"

"Dunno, beggin' your pardon, sir. The scout said it was belonging to an old English gent, some sort of archaeological bloke, but I couldn't make out the name given by the Arab scout what come with the news. But I did make out that there were other English folk with 'im. Big caravan. Twenty-five men and as many camels."

Pomfrey smoothed his hair back one last time. It wasn't unheard of for expeditions to arrive at Fort Gordon, but it was an infrequent event and put undue stress on the garrison's provisions. "Probably some old fool looking for...for Zerzura, whatever that is. We'll doubtless be inundated with more of the idiots by the end of the year."

Unhappily, he blew out his cheeks. "Tell Jones to have quarters prepared for them and to tell them I'll meet with them come morning..." A thought occurred to him, a way to curtail the punishing ordeal of dinner without surrendering an iota of good manners. "Wait. Instead, tell Jones to show them to my dining room as soon as they've had a chance to clean up."

"As you will, sir."

Well satisfied, he flicked a piece of lint from his jacket sleeve and went to dine.

He arrived to find Ginesse Braxton and James Owens already seated, she at the far end of the table and Owens at the side. Owens was studying a glass of red wine as though it could tell him the answers to the universe, and Ginesse Braxton was similarly involved with the pattern on his personal china.

At least Miss Braxton had made an attempt to look presentable, Pomfrey thought and at once commended himself on his generosity of spirit. Sergeant Dodd's wife, closest to Miss Braxton in form if not height, had given her several dresses. This one was a modest-fitting gown of apple green lawn with a high lace collar and cuffs. She'd gathered her nutmeg-colored hair into a tidy chignon, and though she was no beauty, she did have about her a sensualist's allure, a certain haughtiness in the set of her brow, the fullness of her lips, and her large, exotically tilted eyes. Added to which was the remarkable color of her eyes. Garish, one was tempted to say.

"I am sorry to be delayed," he said, taking his chair at the near end of the table. "I've just received word that we are to be joined shortly by more guests."

"Really? Who are they?"

"I'm afraid I was unable to ascertain that. These Arab scouts we employ are categorically incapable of learning proper English, so we are forced to try and decipher their Pidgin English," he said in an amused tone.

"Why don't you learn Arabic?" she asked.

"Excuse me?"

"If you come into a country and employ its denizens, I would think the onus of communicating with them falls on you."

"You would think wrong," he said. "I believe I have a right to expect those in the army's service to be able to adequately express themselves."

"If the man you'd employed claimed that he knew 'proper English,' I would agree with you. But by your own words, you hired him knowing full well that he did not," she persisted pleasantly. "Which leaves the burden of communication to you."

Her expression grew pensive. "I shouldn't be at all surprised to learn that he has made the same assumptions about why you do not learn Arabic that you have made about why he hasn't learned better English. Only in his case he can tell himself that while he was able to learn *some* English, you have not the faculties to learn *any* Arabic, which makes him the more intelligent man."

"No scout of mine would *dare* make such an assumption."

At which point Owens, who until now had remained silent, burst into laughter.

Pomfrey's mouth pleated with anger as he glared at Owens. But the tall, young American was concentrating on twirling the stem of the wineglass between his fingers, watching its rotation while smiling in open amusement.

"I could learn the blasted language if I wanted to," Pomfrey said and at once regretted the statement because—

"Then why don't you?"

—because of *that*. Her. *She.*

"I have more important things with which to occupy myself. Such as the running of this entire garrison."

"That sounds like an excuse," she said without rancor, and somehow that made it worse.

Who did she think she was to reprimand him? She hadn't even had the decency to try to expiate her disgrace by marrying her seducer. "You, Miss Braxton, are in no position to—"

Owens caught his eye. "I wouldn't," he said in a voice so soft he might have imagined it, a voice so low that Miss Braxton, still regarding him expectantly, would not have heard.

No trace of his previous humor remained in Owens's pale gray eyes. He looked like a great tawny predator, all alert watchfulness. He was a frightening man, Pomfrey conceded in the privacy of his own thoughts.

"Colonel?" Miss Braxton prompted. "I am in no position to what?"

Pomfrey flushed, pretending he hadn't heard Owens, that his warning had not been necessary. And it hadn't been; he was a gentleman.

He waited while the Arab attendant cleared away the soup bowls and brought in a second course of roast mutton before turning a haughty gaze on the girl. He had himself well in hand now.

"You are in no position to lecture those who have actively served their country for longer than you have been alive."

He derived, he feared, unworthy satisfaction in watching her skin grow red with embarrassment. He glanced at Owens. Though the American had no cause to take umbrage, Owens might not see it the same way. He watched over the Braxton girl like some preternaturally vigilant warrior guard, which would have been touching if the girl showed one whit of regard for him. But she didn't.

As far as Pomfrey could see, she wanted nothing more to do with him. Doubtless her initial experience with the carnal embrace had been disappointing and unpleasant. He had little sympathy for her. What had she expected, coupling like an animal out in the wilderness with a ruffian like Owens? Solicitude? Gentleness? Even the most treasured bride would be bound to find the initial introduction to her wifely duties disturbing, perhaps onerous. He could well imagine with Owens they had bordered on brutal. Perhaps that is why she had refused to marry him.

He couldn't be rid of the pair soon enough for his liking. And while he was stuck with Ginesse Braxton for the near future, he could at least look forward to ridding himself of her watchdog.

"Owens," he said, slicing off a piece of meat, "the stable master says your horse has made a remarkable recovery and is ready to ride again. When do you expect to be leaving?"

"I was hoping to leave tomorrow," he said.

Miss Braxton, in the process of raising her water glass to her lips, checked. "So soon?" she whispered.

Owens turned to her at once, his gaze sharply compelling. "Is there any reason I should stay longer?"

With a peculiar show of defiance, she lifted her chin. "I can think of no reason if you can't."

"You have already dismissed the most persuasive reason."

"I do not consider it a reason, but a nostrum."

Dolefully, Pomfrey chewed his meat. Lord, but they were an exhausting pair. Just being in the room with them sapped his energy and soured his mood. They were both too elemental, too intense, their emotions too raw and their pride too great. It was like dining with feuding emissaries, neither of whose language you understood.

"Nostrum?" Owens pushed back his chair and slowly rose from his seat. His gaze locked with Ginesse Braxton's. The water in the glass she held shivered. Pomfrey froze, his forkful of meat arrested halfway to his mouth, half expecting Owens to toss the chit over his shoulder and carry her off for a good drubbing. *Then* what was he supposed to do?

What Owens would have done or said next, Pomfrey would never know because at that moment, Lieutenant Jones arrived, shepherding in Fort Gordon's newest visitors.

With a sigh of relief, Pomfrey looked around and then started in amazement. A nicely plumpish redheaded woman was being escorted in on the arm of a somewhat stout, elderly gentleman in a white linen suit. Trailing close behind came a second, slender, well-groomed young man, obviously a gentleman.

"Mildred!" Pomfrey breathed.

"Hilliard!" Miss Whimpelhall said, then, "I mean, Colonel Lord Pomfrey. How…how nice to see you again."

"Miss Braxton!" said the young man, his rather somber young face breaking into a pleased smile.

"Ginny!" the old man piped in.

"Great-Grand!" Miss Braxton cried, shoving back her chair with so much force it nearly fell over, rushing to the old man's side and flinging her arms around his neck.

"Jock," whispered Jim Owens.

And the young man, who'd been fondly witnessing the happy reunion between the older gentleman and Miss Braxton, looked at Owens. His gaze slowly sharpened, and his expression went from polite interest to incredulity to astonishment and then, finally, undisguised pleasure.

"Good Lord. I came to Egypt to uncover the dead, and it looks like I have already had my first success," he said wonderingly. "How are you, Your Grace?"

CHAPTER

TWENTY-SEVEN

All the bitterness of his strange, young life, the reason for his self-imposed exile, his long and lonely vigils in the desert, had proved for naught.

—from the personal diary of Ginesse Braxton

"Did you call that young man 'Your Grace'?" the old gentleman asked as Jock strode forward and seized Jim in a warm embrace.

"Say nothing," Jim murmured and gently pushed Jock away. "The man's making some sort of jest," he said with forced heartiness, willing his half brother to say nothing, to do nothing more to endanger what Jim had spent years trying to ensure: that Jock inherit the dukedom.

In the past few minutes it had grown even more important to him to do so. Because he'd witnessed that first moment when

Jock's gaze had found Ginny. He'd seen the spark of elation, the brightness that had entered his face, and he knew without a trace of doubt that Jock was in love with her.

Jock, he'd realized, must be the paragon Ginny had been describing all those days ago. An honorable, even noble young man. Dashing? Jim was no judge, nor could he say if Jock qualified as romantic. But "conscientious, hardworking, and diligent"? God, Jock had possessed those qualities as a boy; as a man he would be exemplary.

Jock must be the reason she'd refused him, and if Jock would just keep his mouth shut, he could have both Ginny and the dukedom, and Ginny could have the man she loved and the life that he would have liked to have offered her.

But his half brother was either oblivious to his warning or didn't care, for he turned to face the company. "It's no jest, I assure you. I have been looking for Bernard for nearly two years."

"Bernard?" Pomfrey echoed. "Well, there you have it. Your mistake after all. This man's name is James. James Owens."

"That's right," Jim said desperately. "A case of mistaken identity. Sorry to disappoint you, Mr.—"

Jock clapped Jim's shoulder. "There's no mistake, Colonel. Allow me to present my half brother, Bernard James Owens Tynesborough, Duke of Avandale." He turned to Jim. "Trust me. I'll explain everything later."

Jim barely noted the astonished expressions of the others. He regarded Jock numbly. All his years of endless roaming, all the years of living on the edges of society, of being nameless, of being careful never to succeed too well at anything lest he drew attention to himself, of refusing to work the premium concessions because some aristocratic dilettante might recognize him…All of it for nothing, because of a chance meeting with his half brother.

Oh, there was a good chance that the news of his being alive would not reach England in time to keep Althea from having him declared legally dead. But the world would soon know it was untrue, and even if the Avandale inheritance stayed with Jock, he could never wear the title. There were too many witnesses that Bernard, Duke of Tynesborough, long presumed dead, was alive. And it made too delicious a story. Poor Jock. With just a few words, he'd given away a dukedom that in just a matter of months would have been his.

And what of Jim's Uncle Youngblood? When Althea heard he was alive, there was no possibility she would ever return the land that had been part of the Youngblood ranch for a hundred years. She would probably sell it to a rival ranch for no other reason than spite.

He wanted to weep.

His weary gaze found Ginesse, stranding motionless next to the old man. Strangely, he wanted to explain it all to her, to apologize to her. He wanted to tell her he'd wanted to do the right thing, that his intentions had been honorable, that he'd tried— God knows, he tried.

"That's preposterous," sputtered Pomfrey. "He's an American. Or is this one of those convoluted matters of progeniture where some eighteenth cousin five times removed finds himself suddenly a titled lord?"

"Half American," Jock corrected. "And not at all. His mother was my father's first wife. She returned to her father's ranch in America when Bernard was still in leaders. When she died a few years later, Bernard stayed on in America with his uncle. Avandale remarried and I am the result of that union, but later, after my father died, Bernard returned to England and inherited the title. And me, eh, Bernard?" he finished with a smile.

Such a simple recitation of something that had always seemed to Jim so tragically Greek in its heartless exploitations, betrayals, and perfidy.

Jim's mother, Alva Youngblood, had been one of what the English press had termed "Buccaneers," a bevy of nouveau-riche American heiresses who had invaded England to trade well-filled coffers for coronets. Alva had simply been more naïve than others. She had believed the destitute, charming, and facile future duke of Avandale when, at his father's command and in spite of his mother's countercommand, he had declared his undying love. She'd accepted his proposal.

She had remained naïve until she'd discovered that her enormous dowry, a gift from her cattle baron father, had been used not only to make repairs to the future duke's much-neglected estate, but to provide houses, servants, and gifts for both of that same future duke's mistresses, one residing in London, the other in Paris.

Brokenhearted, she'd forthwith taken her infant son and decamped, returning to her father's ranch to find that the price of her coronet had cost her family dearly and that drought, bad investments, and poor timing had conspired to all but bankrupt the once prosperous empire.

The recently made duke saw no advantage in reuniting with a wife who would only cost him money to maintain and had nothing more to offer. Via a politely worded letter, he applauded her decision as the best for all parties concerned and suggested that she, and entirely incidentally his infant son, stay in America. And so she had.

After Alva's death, the duke had dutifully complied with his mother's wishes—his father no longer standing in the way of her sovereignty—and wed another rich lady. The difference being that this time, the lady came ready-made with a title, an impeccable lineage, and a thorough understanding of what was required of her. Jock's mother.

Jim had never known her. She'd died years before the duke. After Avandale had died of a heart attack in some whore's bed in Cannes, Althea had arrived at his uncle's ranch with a battery of lawyers and documents granting her sole custody of the duke's heir and snatched him away from his home to "try and salvage something useful out of the sordid misalliance."

Jim closed his eyes for a second against that final memory, surprised it still had the power to hurt him.

"Why is he here?" Miss Whimpelhall, a smallish rounded woman asked. "Why have you been looking for him for two years, Lord Tynesborough?"

"It's rather a long story," Jock answered.

"We have time," Ginny said, breaking her unnatural silence.

"Later, perhaps," Jock told her gently. "If Bernard—or should I call you Jim now?—wishes. I fear I have already over-stepped myself and said more than I have a right to. I will only add this," his eyes found Pomfrey, "he has broken no laws of man or God."

"Perhaps not in England..." Pomfrey muttered under his breath, but Jim heard him.

Before Jim left the garrison for good, Pomfrey and he would have to have a little discussion about how he was to comport himself regarding Miss Braxton. And he would be leaving the garrison and it would be soon. He had endured any number of ordeals since he'd arrived in Egypt: bullet wounds, knife gashes, sandstorms, thirst, thugs, unfriendly tribesmen, rival thieves, and murderers hired to eliminate him, but he did not think he could endure witnessing Jock courting Ginesse.

"Well," Sir Robert said jovially, "just think, Ginny. You have been led across the desert by a real duke. Not many young ladies can say that, what?"

But Ginny did not look gratified. She looked stricken, and damned if he could imagine why.

"Well, if you aren't going to tell us what you are doing traipsing about in Egypt, Avandale, we might as well eat," Sir Robert said, oblivious to the tense undercurrents in the room. He waddled toward the dining table, looking over the various dishes with interest. "Hm. I don't suppose you have a bit of Stilton about, eh? Miss Whimpelhall here has been positively pining for a bit of cheese, haven't you, m' dear?"

Miss Whimpelhall, whose long-awaited reunion with her fiancée had been overshadowed by Jock's announcement, made some demure sounds.

Pomfrey, finally seeming to realize his neglect of his future bride, hastened forward to pull out a chair for her. She settled like a small brooding hen as Pomfrey bellowed for the staff to bring out more place settings.

"Excellent," Sir Robert said. "Ginny, sit down. You look a mite peaked. You'll want some red wine."

Ginesse returned to her chair, taking a seat and taking hold of her wineglass almost simultaneously. She took a long draught, emptying the glass.

"That's my girl," Sir Robert said approvingly. He dropped into a chair and looked up at the rest of them. "Professor, you're hovering. Do sit down. And you, young man," he turned his leonine head in Jim's direction, "sit by me. You can regale me with all the splendid adventures you had with my great-granddaughter!"

Dear God.

Ginesse blanched visibly, and Pomfrey blew out his moustache, shifting uncomfortably on his feet.

"I am sorry to have to disappoint you, Sir Robert," Jim said, "but I am sure you will forgive us if my brother and I continue our reunion in private. There is, as you can imagine, much to be discussed." He inclined his head, waiting attentively.

Though visibly disappointed, Sir Robert had no choice but to give his permission. "If you must," he said.

"I must," Jim answered. "Perhaps another time."

Sir Robert brightened. "I shall hold you to that, m'boy. Now Pomfrey, about that cheese…"

Jim clasped Jock's arm and half pulled him from the room and from there out through a door leading into the small yard where they wouldn't be disturbed. Only then did he stop and face his brother. For a long moment neither spoke, Jim looking in vain for some trace of the solemn, bespectacled little boy who'd shadowed him through that great, cold house, and Jock, he assumed, was doing likewise.

"You look much the same," Jock finally said, shaking his head. "I might say bigger, but you always seemed inordinately big to me. Certainly harder. You never did wear your heart on your sleeve, but one could mostly read you. Now…You might be made of adamantine, Jim." He smiled. "I shall have a hard time getting used to calling you that."

"You look entirely different," Jim said. "You were such a quiet lad, studious and unassuming."

"Survival tactics," he answered. "You defied her; I faded from her."

"I never meant to abandon you."

"I never considered that you did. We both did what was necessary to survive," Jock said. "I was better equipped than you to live under her dominion, but you, you could never manage it. How many times did she have you beaten?"

"It doesn't matter."

"If you say so."

"I wanted you to inherit, you know. I meant you to have it all," he said sadly, knowing it was too late.

"I know."

He looked so pleased; Jim didn't have it in him to tell him of the other lives he'd ruined with his announcement. Besides, it would serve no purpose.

"I also know that Althea threatened that if you ever returned she'd sell your mother's land in America."

Jim started and stared. "How?"

"I was there that day, in the library. I'd fallen asleep in one of the alcoves, and when I awoke I heard you and Althea. If I'd made myself known she would have punished me for eavesdropping, so I stayed hidden. I heard it all, including the bargain you struck."

"Jock, it had nothing to do with you."

"I beg to differ. It had everything to do with me. I was only twelve, but I already knew I wanted no part of her plans. I never wanted to be the duke, Jim. That was your role and one I did not envy you. You were better suited to it than I."

Jim looked at him in surprise.

"I only wanted to be left to my studies. Even though I knew I could do nothing about it at the time, I resolved never to let her make me Duke of Tynesborough in your stead."

Jock must have read something of Jim's astonishment. "Why are you surprised? I didn't want a purloined title and a life built on some else's sacrifice. Would you?"

"No," Jim said, shamed by his younger brother's integrity. He had never thought of Jock's feelings in the matter. He had arrogantly and unjustly assumed the quiet boy would fit into whatever mold Althea prepared for him. How humbling to discover that at twelve years of age Jock had shown a strength of character lacking in many grown men.

"I am sorry, Jock. I meant no harm. I sincerely thought you would want to be the duke. Had you not heard us in the library, you might have been content to inherit, and you would have made a fine duke. Far better than me. I wish you had never heard."

Jock snorted derisively. "You do not play the humble role well, brother. But I'll enjoy your accolades until you've a learned a few of my many faults and rescind them." Jock smiled. "And as for hearing you and Althea, be glad I did. I kept silent knowing full well the pressure Althea was capable of bringing to bear if opposed. I waited until I came of age two years ago and arranged for us to meet at the offices of the family's solicitors where I begged the private use of one of their rooms.

"Once we were sequestered, I informed Althea that I knew all about her plan to make me duke and how she'd blackmailed you with the lands your mother had brought to the marriage and over which she had full control until I reached twenty-five. I told her I would not stand by and allow it and that if she ever attempted to have you declared dead I would go before the House of Lords and reveal everything I had heard."

"Brave lad."

"Terrified lad. My limbs were so unsteady I had to remain seated throughout the interview. I am sure she thought me beyond cavalier."

"Good man."

Jock smiled, looking pleased. "And then I told her that in addition, unless she was willing to sign over your mother's lands to your uncle, I would reveal her as a perjurer and an extortionist."

Jim laughed. He couldn't help himself. Blackmailing the blackmailer. There was a certain attractive symmetry to it. "What did she say?"

"Althea is nothing if not predictable. Nothing means more to her than the Tynesborough name, even though she only wears it through marriage. She signed the papers then and there. We have not spoken since."

"You mean—"

"Yes. For the last two years your uncle has been sole owner of the Youngblood ranch," Jock said. "And I have been making inquiries to find you."

Jim dragged a hand through his hair, uncertain of what he ought to feel, how he ought to react. For nearly seven years his life had been a desert, a vast emptiness stretching into a featureless future, and now he'd been given a way out. He should be overjoyed to regain his birthright without sacrificing anyone or anything to do so. He should be elated that Althea had not won, not over him and not over Jock. He should be ecstatic to finally be able to find his way back home.

Home.

Unwillingly, his gaze flickered toward the dining room window. The drapes obscured his view of her, but he could feel her presence inside, like a flame drawing him.

"Don't you have anything to say?" Jock asked, amused.

"It all seems unreal," he said. "I never thought to go back to England."

"You don't have to, you know," Jock said. "In all truth, there's not that much to go back to and what's left is adequately managed by the bankers. The house has fallen into disrepair, but the farm is still there. The only other property of any value is the Mayfair property, and Althea has use of that until she dies. Which by all accounts could be any moment."

"I should see her."

"Why?" Jock asked, for the first time a deep bitterness entering his voice. "She made your life hell. She hated and despised your mother, and she hated you for being her son. She wouldn't thank you for visiting her." He tipped his head. "But if you should want to go to spit in her face, well, I could understand that."

He didn't. Not at all. He frowned, examining this unexpected reaction. He supposed he ought to want to confront his grandmother, to stand before her healthy and able, to flaunt his triumph in her face. But he didn't. Both Althea and the boy he'd been were parts of a past so distant, he could hardly imagine them. Both seemed like characters in a book, one he didn't care to visit again.

"No, I don't suppose I do," he murmured, feeling the last vestiges of his fury dissolve.

Jock nodded. "I can understand not wanting to leave," he said, taking a deep breath and turning his face to the sky and the millions of pinpricks of light spread like a veil across a dark river. "I can see why you would want to stay here. This land is spectacular. And Sir Robert has been regaling me with stories about your exploits. He says you had a hand in locating Thutmosis the First's tomb," he said, adding with just the slightest proprietary pride, "Miss Braxton wrote a monograph on it, you know."

"No, I didn't."

Jock was everything a young aristocrat should be, the very best example of his kind: decent, intelligent, and compassionate. Jim was everything a survivor needed to be: duplicitous, cunning, and ruthless.

"Isn't it odd?" Jock mused. "Here we are parted for years and yet somehow our paths have led us both here, to the same place."

And, Jim thought hollowly, to the same woman.

CHAPTER
TWENTY-EIGHT

But she could still dream of what had been, of what might have been, of the beauty and mystery and passion of something she would hold secretly in her woman's heart as a sacred treasure!

—from the personal diary of Ginesse Braxton

"I am glad to see you looking so well, Ginesse. The newly found duke said you were exposed to quite an ordeal during your journey. He seemed quite concerned for you, but you look fine to me," Sir Robert said, beaming at Ginesse. "What an adventure you have had! You must take after you mother. She never looked so well as when she was in some sort of trouble."

Ginesse regarded her great-grandsire with great affection as Sir Robert tucked her hand more securely into the crook of his

261

arm to lead her on a postprandial stroll. So many men of his generation, and her own, were stodgy and moralistic. Sir Robert saw everything through a prism of optimism.

"Mind you, I never doubted you would prevail for a minute, though Magi lacked my faith." Magi was the pragmatist to Sir Robert's optimist due, no doubt, to having enough experience both with Ginesse's mother and Ginesse herself to refute any wholesale confidence in happy outcomes.

"I'm sorry to have caused her concern." The sun had set and a three-quarter moon hung against the velvety sky like an earring in the lobe of a Nubian goddess. From the barracks drifted the homely sound of male conversation and desultory work being done. The scent of a cheroot's smoke wafted down to them from the guard tower nearby. For a second she wondered if it was Jim, smoking. But Jim didn't smoke. At least, as far as she knew. But then, there were many things she hadn't known about James Owens Tynesborough.

"I shall prostrate myself as soon as I return to Cairo."

"Oh, you won't have to wait so long as that. She insisted in coming along."

"She did?" Ginesse asked, delighted. "Where is she?"

Her great-grandfather made a slight face. "That colonel has segregated her. She is dining with the rest of his Arab staff tonight. I would have protested had I not been sure she would have been treated a great deal better there than at Pomfrey's table."

"But I will see her later?"

"You might want to wait until the morrow. It's been a long trip."

"Of course," Ginesse agreed. "I shall seek her out first thing in the morning."

"Haji came, too."

"Haji?" Ginesse said, surprised and not pleasantly. "Why?"

"He insisted," Sir Robert said with such open-eyed candor that Ginesse immediately suspected Haji had not been the one doing the insisting. She didn't say so, however. If Sir Robert wanted to cast Haji in a noble light, far be it from her to spoil his fun.

"What's wrong, Ginesse? You are not holding on to your youthful prejudice against the lad, are you?"

Her prejudice against *him*? Only great strength of character kept her from blurting out a sharp retort.

"Haji has turned into a very fine scholar," Sir Robert continued, "all the more remarkable for having been largely self-taught. He has some very insightful theories about the reason your lost city was, well, lost."

"Hm."

"He might prove an invaluable colleague in your search for Zerzura," Sir Robert suggested as if the idea had only now occurred to him, though she didn't believe it for a moment.

"Zerzura," she murmured, for the first time in days her thoughts turning to the lost city and the reason for her being here. Thank heaven she still had Zerzura; it was all she had left.

"Yes. Professor Tynesborough told us all about your discovery and how he followed your trail in the libraries and how he came to the realization that you had indeed made a magnificent discovery and how badly he feels for having rejected your research without first hearing you out."

"No matter."

"You seem to have left a trail of men owing you apologies for bad behavior," he said with a little twinkle.

The only man whose bad behavior interested her was James Owens. She had to stop thinking about him, had to stop referring everything that happened somehow back to him. He was not the center of her life. He was not even part of her life anymore.

"Fancy this, Ginny. Haji is convinced you dislike him and confesses he feels your antipathy might be warranted."

"How good of him," she replied dryly. Leave it to Haji to pre-empt any complaints she might voice about his backstabbing tendencies with a saintly confession.

"I shouldn't be surprised if he didn't offer to help you find Zerzura to help make things right between you."

Make it right. Jim's words. She blew out a thin, unsteady stream of air.

Her great-grandfather suddenly stopped walking, scowling. "Something is wrong."

"No," she denied, "everything is fine."

"No, something is definitely wrong," he insisted. "You are pulling the same face I vividly recall from your childhood. The one you made behind your mother's back whenever you felt you'd been ill-used. Now, out with it."

"It's nothing, I just don't need anyone else to 'make things right' with me, that's all."

Sir Robert's bushy white brows shot up. "Anyone else?" he echoed.

"Yes," she said tersely. "I am not a child. I am not piece of luggage. I am not a donkey. Haji's only sin was that he didn't put out the papyri I set on fire. I suspect so that he could get me permanently banned from the dig sites. I doubt he meant to get me banished to England.

"I could have gone back and put out that fire myself, but I didn't dare because I was afraid of being punished. A fear that, as it turns out, was well founded since it was that little experiment that got me shipped off to England."

"Oh, I can assure you, my dear," her great-grandfather said with deliberate irony, "that decision was not made on the strength of one such act alone. I believe the list went several pages long."

There would have been a time, and not that long ago, when the reminder of her many and varied transgressions would have aroused a panicked need to address and refute each charge. It all seemed a great waste of energy now. The truth was, she liked who she was, she understood her strengths and acknowledged her weaknesses, and she no longer felt the need to apologize for herself to anyone, including herself.

The woman was the product of the child, and as a child Ginesse had been inquisitive, mercurial, and unruly. The woman Ginesse had become was still inquisitive and still prone to act first and think later, but as anyone who insists on skating on thin ice knows, she had also learned to be quick-thinking and resourceful in order to survive. She'd not only survived; she'd thrived.

"All I meant is that I don't blame Haji, and I think his insistence that he was somehow the defining moment of my life is beyond arrogant. I have designed my own fate, thank you very much. I alone initiated whatever has happened to me before and since London. It was my choice to impersonate Miss Whimpelhall, to search for Zerzura, to deceive Mr. Owens, and," she swallowed, "everything else."

"'I am the master of my own ship,' and that sort of thing, eh?" Sir Robert asked gently.

"Precisely."

"And what Carlisle woman worth her salt wouldn't feel exactly so?" he said brightly—Sir Robert ascribed to ancient Egyptian chronological practices that followed one's family tree through its matriarchal branch. They'd strolled a short ways farther before he spoke again.

"Poor Miss Whimpelhall," he said. "I do hope she has not wasted her time in coming here."

"Why would you say that, Great-Grand? You must know she has come to finally marry Pomfrey after a long engagement."

"She doesn't act much like a woman who's just been reunited with her beloved after years of separation. I think she anticipated a warmer reception."

"No," Ginesse said slowly, her concern for Miss Whimpelhall temporarily distracting her from thoughts about Jim. "She didn't. On board the *Lydonia*, I once asked her if Colonel Lord Pomfrey would sweep her off her feet when they met. She was horrified by the suggestion and quite adamant that she considered any such overt demonstrations of affection beneath both her and Colonel Lord Pomfrey's dignity."

Sir Robert shook his head. "Oh, Ginny. And you actually believed her?"

"Of course. Why wouldn't I? She's a very restrained, very temperate lady."

Sir Robert smiled oddly. "She's a lady who dyes her hair red."

"So did I," Ginesse pointed out, uncertain what this had to do with Miss Whimpelhall's character.

"Exactly."

She couldn't decide if his oblique comment was complimentary or critical and so opted to ignore it entirely.

"But enough of Haji and Miss Whimpelhall and Colonel Lord Pomfrey," Sir Robert said. "We are far enough away from any open windows for us to get down to the matter at hand. Tell me what is really going on."

"Going on?"

"With you and Tynesborough."

Tynesborough? she thought in some confusion before it dawned on her that her great-grandfather must be referring to James Owens. Never having known Jim as, well, Jim, understandably Sir Robert called him by his surname.

Ginesse hesitated. She wasn't certain hers was the sort of confidence one shared with one's great-grandparent. On the other hand, she knew no one whose judgment she trusted more. Her parents were too close, too fond, and too apt to champion whatever side of an argument benefitted her. Oddly, her brothers tended toward an opposite reaction.

"I'm not sure what you mean," she finally said, knowing it to be a feeble response.

"That young man," Sir Robert said briskly, "is in love with you. What do you intend to do about it?"

Her heart fell, and she sighed gustily. Until now, she hadn't realized how much she'd been counting on Sir Robert's advice. But how much use would it be if he had already so greatly misread the situation? He used to be such a perceptive man. Ah, well, she supposed age had finally caught up with him.

"You're mistaken, Great-Grand. Mr. Owens doesn't love me," she said, then added in the interest of full disclosure, "though he has asked me to marry him. Twice."

"Mr. Owens has?" Sir Robert said, eyes widening with interest.

"Yes, but it has nothing to do with love."

"Really? And how do you know this?"

"Because both times he proposed, he did not posit affection or, for that matter, *any* sentiment as a reason he wanted to marry me. He certainly did not say he loved me. And when Colonel Lord Pomfrey made those—" She broke off. She could not repeat Pomfrey's cruel words; it would only force her great-grandfather to take some precipitous action. But Jim's failure to champion her cut as deeply as his obligatory proposal.

"Made what?" Sir Robert asked.

"Nothing," she said. "He just did little to advance Mr. Owens's suit."

"And why would he?" Sir Robert asked, bewildered. "Come now, Ginesse. Admittedly, you were never the most sensible member of the family, but being as familiar with the masculine nature as only the sister of six brothers can be, you must realize that men, particularly men like Mr. Owens, have a hard time expressing what is in their hearts."

"Mr. Owens presented several well-considered explanations for why he wanted to marry me, and none of them had anything do with what is or, in this case, is *not* in his heart."

"And what were those explanations?"

To her great mortification, Ginesse felt the heat rising in her cheeks and prayed her great-grandfather would not notice in the dark. Unfortunately, he had horrifyingly good night vision.

"Oh," he said, blushing himself. "I see." He cleared his throat. "Mr. Owens feels that having been so long in his company unchaperoned, your reputation is at stake."

Bless him. "Yes," she said, breathing more easily. "That's it exactly."

"And you are certain his offer stems from a gentlemanly sense of responsibility and nothing more."

"*Culpability,* not responsibility," Ginesse corrected. "He feels…*guilty!*"

"Oh, dear." Sir Robert chewed on his lip, a habit he fell into when he was troubled.

"You must believe me when I tell you Mr. Owens is fully aware that I consider mutually romantic feelings essential in a marriage. Knowing that, if he did care for me, he would have said as much, wouldn't he?"

"What exactly did he say?"

She released his arm and worried her fingers together at her waist, looking down at the ground, not wanting her great-grandfather to see her tears. "He said he wished he was *someone else*."

Sir Robert winced.

She sniffed, nodding in agreement. "Then he said that since he wasn't we would just have to accept it and that he was not lost to all decency. And he said that though he could not undo what had happened," she blushed again, "he would 'make it right' and that he would try to make me happy."

Sure enough, she could feel her tears starting to fall, and she couldn't say whether they were angry ones or miserable ones. Probably both.

"Oh, dear," Sir Robert said again, looking at her very closely and very earnestly. "He seems so in command of himself, one forgets he still is very young."

Now she wanted to stomp her feet in frustration. Whatever did Jim's youth have to do with anything?

"It makes no difference. I refused him. And now I do not wish to discuss Mr. Owens any longer."

For a moment, she thought her great-grandfather was about to say something more, but then he regained her arm and drew her forward once again.

"All right," he said after a while, "if you don't want to discuss Mr. Owens, though I suppose we ought to call him Avandale now—"

"And that's another thing," she burst out.

Her great-grandfather stopped and waited patiently.

"He never told me *anything* about being a duke. Why would a man ask a woman to marry him without first mentioning he happens to be a duke?"

"I'm not sure—"

"I am. He does so to *test* her. To discover her priorities and her character. And if not knowing he is a duke that woman should say no to his initial proposal, then there is no possible way she can reverse that decision and say yes to any subsequent proposals. Not that there's the least likelihood of there being any future proposals, especially if she…if she…" She'd started blubbering.

"If she what, m' dear?" her great-grandfather asked gently.

"If she told him she wouldn't marry him in the first place because all he had was a…"

"A what?"

"A horse!" she bawled, and turned on her heel and fled.

* * *

Sir Robert Carlisle stared after his bolting great-granddaughter. For a moment, he considered calling her back and explaining to her that he hadn't been speaking of James Owens when he'd made his initial query about what she intended to do about the man who loved her, but of Geoffrey Tynesborough.

But then, good sense prevailed. Why muddy already considerably clouded waters?

So, he thought, the newly discovered Duke of Avandale had proposed to Ginesse not once, but twice. Now, that *had* been a surprise. Though, he supposed it shouldn't have been; after all, she had her mother's charisma and her father's eyes.

And her wonderfully Florentine nose.

CHAPTER

TWENTY-NINE

She was miserable.

—from the personal diary of Ginesse Braxton

The following morning Ginesse left her room in Pomfrey's house early and waited outside the building where Magi had been housed, prepared for the tongue-lashing she richly deserved for failing to leave any clue as to her whereabouts with anyone. But after one look at Ginesse, Magi, not known for her demonstrative nature, flung her arms around her and held her tight for a long moment. It was a much more effective rebuke than anything Magi could have ever said. Never again, Ginesse swore, would she cause those she loved to worry unnecessarily and vowed as much to Magi as they walked across the parade grounds.

Whether Magi believed her was another matter entirely.

"What a gorgeous animal," Magi said as they neared the stable's corral.

A small group had gathered at the rails including Lord Tynes-borough to watch Jim's gray stallion being led out of the stables by an uneasy-looking lad. The gray was pawing the earth and making feints at the poor boy, who darted back from his lunges.

"Miss Braxton, Miss Elkamal," Lord Tynesborough hailed them. "A fine morning for some choice entertainment."

"What might that be?" Magi asked.

"The stable master has declared Jim's horse intractable and ordered Jim to remove him from the stables unless he can prove otherwise. Jim is a magnificent horseman," Lord Tynesborough said admiringly. "He learned the art from his grandfather's Comanche cowboys."

"It sounds most interesting," Magi said, "but I am afraid I must see to Sir Robert's morning tisane. I will see you later, Ginesse." And with a slight inclination of her head, she left them as Jim emerged from the stable.

He was gloriously handsome with his rumpled gold hair, his shirtsleeves rolled up over his strong, tanned forearms, his collar open at the throat. He glanced in their direction and frowned—apparently no one told him he'd be providing the entertainment for the day—before his gaze found hers and pulled her in. They might have been alone. She imagined she could hear his heartbeat and feel the warm buffeting of his breath, though his gaze was so cold it seemed to frost the very air between them.

"You'll have a better view if you sit up on the top rail," Lord Tynesborough suggested, blithely unaware of any tension. She looked around. A few of the women had perched themselves on the topmost rail of the corral. "It's entirely safe," he assured her. "The horse is on a lunging line."

As long as the other ladies were up there, Ginesse could see no reason why she shouldn't join them. She accepted Lord Tynesborough's hand and climbed up the rails, settling sideways on the top.

Lord Tynesborough smiled up at her with an unusual degree of warmth, confusing her a bit until she realized he probably hoped to join her on her search for Zerzura.

Sure enough, his first words confirmed her suspicion. "I owe you an apology, Miss Braxton. After you left my employ, I could not shake the feeling that I had been rudely dismissive, so I followed your research, or as much of it as I could, and came to the inescapable conclusion that you were right and that there is a city waiting to be discovered out here."

She should have felt a leap of exultation, validation, at least some sort of unworthy triumph, but all she felt was a sort of temperate gratification. *Damn* Jim Owens.

"Do you forgive me?"

"Yes. Of course," she said, wishing he would stop regarding her so soulfully, like a puppy who knows she is holding a bone behind her back. In this case, the bone being Zerzura.

"How long did Mr. Owens live in America?" she asked, looking for another topic of conversation.

"Fourteen years," he said. "Ten of those without a mother. From what I gather, he had few female influences growing up. He was probably ill-prepared for the change his life would take when our grandmother fetched him from his uncle's ranch after our father died."

"I imagine it was a rather wild young man who arrived at your doorstep," she said, half smiling in spite of herself at the thought of an unruly young Jim terrorizing the staid old retainers of some moldy manor house. "A right barbarian," she said, her eyes on Jim.

He held the lunge line slack, waiting patiently for the gray Arabian to approach him. He bided his time, casually swiping the line's frayed end on the ground, giving the horse no excuse to bolt at an unanticipated movement.

"Hardly. Not inside the house, at any rate," Tynesborough said. "Though anyone testing him at the school where he was sent would earn a fair demonstration of what he was capable of—and there were, I am sad to say, many eager to try to intimidate an outsider, mistaking a difference in accent or manners for ignorance and," he glanced at her, "barbarism."

She flushed.

He reached out and briefly touched her hand where it rested on the corral's top rail, regarding her sympathetically. "I know you didn't mean it that way, but there were many who used far crueler terms who meant it precisely that way. The Duke of Manure and Lord Yokel were some of the less offensive titles they called him, though rarely more than once in his presence. He was a strong, athletic lad even then.

"But at Avandale Hall, in our grandmother's and my mother's presence, he was entirely circumspect, even courtly, as odd as that word might seem. Unfortunately, he suffered there as well."

His words painted a depressing picture of an orphaned boy thrown upon the shoals of English society. She knew firsthand how unkind children could be. She could all too well imagine the cruelty of those rough schoolyard encounters: the jeers and mocking laughter, the hot blood rising in one's face, the hopeless sense of powerlessness, the tears that choked off the ability to speak and could not, *must* not fall because then the taunts would become howls of ridicule.

She'd endured her fair share of epithets. Luckily, the Misses Timwell quickly weeded out the most bullying students. But those dear ladies could not be omnipresent, and Ginesse had been a prime candidate for mockery, being skinny and big-nosed and easily provoked. But at least she'd had parents and siblings who'd loved her.

Where had Jim's sanctuary been?

"Surely your mother or grandmother did what they could to prevent others from abusing him?" she asked.

Tynesborough did not answer right away. He looked uncomfortable, clearly trying to find a politic answer. In the corral, the stallion had finally been overcome with curiosity and was approaching Jim cautiously.

"Jim was completely unfamiliar with women. He regarded the fair sex with something approaching awe. Certainly with reverence." Tynesborough smiled sadly. "He learned that duplicity and cruelty are not gender-specific traits."

Ginesse frowned, unsettled by Tynesborough's suggestion. Had his mother been the hackneyed version of the wicked stepmother? Had she treated Jim unkindly, resentful that her son was not the duke's heir?

"What do you mean?" she asked.

"I ought not to say, but your relationship with my brother seems strained. I understand. He can appear very cold and remote and stern. He had to be."

She frowned.

"Our grandmother strongly resisted her son marrying Jim's mother. It offended her that the Avandale bloodline should be polluted."

"Why did they marry then?"

"The old duke was as strong-willed as his wife. Avandale was falling into financial ruin. Jim's mother's family was, at the time, immensely rich. She brought that wealth to the family, quite saved the old manse from going under, truth be told. In addition, she gave a huge parcel of land to the old duke."

"Why would she do that?"

"Who can say? Perhaps she really thought my father loved her? Perhaps her father liked the idea of his daughter being a duchess?" He shrugged sadly. "It doesn't matter. What does matter is that Althea, our grandmother, never reconciled herself to the idea of a half-American inheriting the dukedom, and when Jim did, she made it her mission to do everything within her power to eradicate from him any traces of his American manner, attitudes, accents, memories. He was not allowed to speak of his family in America or his life on the ranch. Ever. Some of her methods were...brutal."

Dear God. She shuddered, wrapping her arms around herself and holding tight against the picture Tynesborough painted. And if this was her reaction to a secondhand recounting, how much more horrific had the reality been for Jim?

"Jim learned to hide behind a mask of indifference. It's not who he is. Not really," Lord Tynesborough said. "Indeed, he had planned to forfeit his title in order to guarantee that others whom he cared for deeply would not suffer."

"Is someone suffering?" a feminine voice asked.

Ginesse look around. Miss Whimpelhall was toddling toward them under the shade of a lacy parasol, her hands encased in little lace mittens, her long skirts sending up little puffs of dust. "Not the poor horse, I hope?"

For a moment, Ginesse sat frozen, unable to segue from the story she'd heard to the banal pleasantries expected of her. Luckily, Lord Tynesborough was better at such things than she.

"No, indeed, Miss Whimpelhall," Professor Tynesborough greeted her, his expression smoothing to polite interest. "The horse is in fine fettle. That seems to be the problem. He's raising havoc with the stable lads, so they've elected to call in the heavy reinforcements—my brother. I hope you're prepared to witness a master horseman in action?"

Amazingly, Miss Whimpelhall produced a dimple. "I am always interested in adding to my education, Professor." She looked up at Ginesse, showing not a bit of surprise at where she was sitting. Apparently, her recent travels had loosened her strict sense of decorum. "Hello, Miss Braxton."

"Good morning, Miss Whimpelhall," Ginesse said, finding her voice. "Would you care to join me for the exhibition?" Ginesse asked, indicating the rail.

"Good heavens. I mean, no, thank you."

"Will Colonel Lord Pomfrey be joining us?" Lord Tynesborough asked.

"No, I am afraid not. He is otherwise engaged," she said, her eyes on Jim and the stallion.

The gray was finally standing quietly. Jim moved to his side, placing his hand on his withers. A shiver ran through the stallion's glossy hide as in one smooth, unhurried movement, Jim slipped the hackamore over his fine-boned head. Then just as smoothly, he took hold of a handful of mane and vaulted onto his back.

The stallion danced, sidling backwards and away. Jim leaned forward, shifting his legs, and at once the horse quieted. Then, at some unseen signal, the horse flowed forward into an easy gait. Jim moved with him, more like an extension of the horse than a passenger.

"Magnificent, isn't he?" Lord Tynesborough whispered with undisguised admiration as, in his excitement, he once more covered her hand with his.

Jim looked over at them. The stallion shied, tossing his head.

"He ought to have a proper bridle," Miss Whimpelhall said.

"He doesn't need one," Tynesborough said. "Watch."

But Jim was done. He swung a leg over the gray's back and while it was still cantering, slipped off, landing neatly on his feet.

"But…aren't you going to ride him some more?" one of the enlisted men asked. "I got a pound said you'd stick on his back for five minutes."

"Sorry," Jim answered, his gaze briefly touching hers, then her hand, still covered by Lord Tynesborough's, and passing on. "I've seen everything I need to see. You shouldn't have any trouble getting him into a stall now. Just be careful about touching his sides. He's been trained to the leg, not the mouth."

The crowd began to disperse, and Ginesse was about to climb down from the rail when she saw Haji Elkamal. He noticed her as well. He looked away, his lips pleated, and then with the air of a man set on doing an onerous task, he came over to them. He bowed to Lord Tynesborough and Miss Whimpelhall, then nodded to Ginesse.

"Hello, Ginesse," he said. "I have not had the opportunity to welcome you back to Egypt."

"Hello, Haji," she said without enthusiasm. Magi's silence had been an unexpected kindness, but she did not fool herself into thinking Haji would be as forgiving. He had never been shy about criticizing her. Mentally she resigned herself to listening to him harangue her for impersonating Miss Whimpelhall and whatever trouble, real or imaginary, great or small, perceived or tangible, she had subsequently gotten into because of it. It was an old, old pattern.

"You call Miss Braxton by her Christian name?" Miss Whimpelhall asked, looking confused.

Haji turned a baleful eye on her. "Yes. I did. Is there a problem, Miss Whimpelhall?"

Haji had always been oversensitive and prickly, looking for slights and rebuffs where none were given and triumphantly pointing out those that were. He'd been a tiresome boy, and he looked to have turned into a tiresome man.

"Oh, for heaven's sake, leave off, Haji," she said irritably as the stable boy lost control of the end of the lunge line and the stallion began prancing around the enclosure looking like it was all great fun. "Miss Whimpelhall is unaware of the lengthy history between us. She would have been just as surprised to hear Professor Tynesborough call her 'Mildred.' Isn't that right, Miss Whimpelhall?"

The little woman's glance flickered between Haji, looking stiffly imperious; Professor Tynesborough, looking uncomfortable; and Ginesse.

"Yes. I suppose. I didn't mean to offend you, Mr. Elkamal," she said, blushing so profusely that had Ginesse a more suspicious mind, she might have termed "guiltily."

"Of course it is," Ginesse said. "Haji's familiarity is due to our long-standing..." She hesitated. "I was going to say 'friendship,' but that would have implied a regard on Haji's part that is largely missing. So let us say instead, Haji's familiarity is due to the fact that he was my unwilling companion during childhood."

Miss Whimpelhall looked ill at ease. Lord Tynesborough looked disconcerted. And Haji looked petulant. "I believed I was tolerated only inasmuch as I was useful in keeping an eye on you," he said with stiff formality. "I may have been wrong. If I was, I am sorry."

"Is that supposed to be an apology?" Ginesse asked. "Because if so, it's a poor excuse for one." Where had Jim gone? The stallion was galloping around the corral now, making a game of evading the enlisted men's attempts to catch him.

"Colonel Lord Pomfrey intends to hold a small dinner party this evening to welcome me to the garrison," Miss Whimpelhall said with forced brightness, striving valiantly to deflect the terse course of the conversation.

"We shall all look forward to it, I'm sure," Lord Tynesborough put in, doing his best to aid her. They'd both wasted their breath.

Haji's face had darkened with anger. "I am sorry if my apology does not meet with your approval. I did not have the advantages of a refined finishing school or college education where I could polish my deportment. Though it appears not to have done much for your manners."

"Oh, please," she said. "You could have had an education to rival the finest available anywhere, at any institution. You were handpicked to be mentored by one of the most prominent Egyptologists alive, my great-grandfather, singled out from heaven knows how many, and yet you shunted it all aside out of pure, unmitigated *jealousy*."

Haji gasped. She didn't care. She was tired, heartbroken, and suddenly angry. Yes, she had made mistakes, but she was tired of her past chasing her down.

"I have been given free rein to plan the dinner menu," Miss Whimpelhall said desperately. "Sir Robert has offered the services of his chef. Isn't that kind of him?"

"Most kind," Lord Tynesborough said as the stallion suddenly erupted into a series of violent bucks. Men began shouting something about wasps; women scrambled from their perches. Ginesse barely noticed.

Neither did Haji.

"If I was jealous, who could blame me?" he said, glaring up at her. "You were born to your position. Everything was handed to you: the tutors, the entrée, the name. I had to work to be noticed, excel to be praised. You only had to be Ginesse Braxton."

"And you don't think that I was aware of that every *bloody* moment?" she asked furiously.

This time Miss Whimpelhall gasped.

"Disappointment. Pest. *Afreet*," Ginesse said. "Do you imagine I didn't realize that even though I had every opportunity at my disposal, every advantage, how far below the mark I fell? But at least I stuck it out. I fought to be worthy of what I'd been given. You just ran away."

Haji turned ashen at her last words.

"I've achieved something," she said, feeling the tears begin to form. "I *will* achieve something. Something that will make people proud of me, that will make their efforts toward me worthwhile. What are *you* doing?"

He didn't have a reply. He simply stood staring at her. She refused to give him the satisfaction of breaking off their glaring contest.

Suddenly someone was shouting a warning and the stallion charged the fence, swerving at the last moment but not fast enough. His hindquarters struck the rails with such force it knocked Ginesse clean off, pitching her into the corral.

She landed hard on her shoulder, her head striking the soft dirt with enough force to stun her. Dimly, she heard Haji shouting in Arabic, Miss Whimpelhall's alarmed cry, a horse whinnying in pain. Inches away from her swimming vision clots of earth sprayed up like sea foam, churned by enormous hooves striking close to her face.

And then, just as quickly as she'd fallen, strong arms scooped her up against a broad chest. A thundering heartbeat pounded against her cheek. She tilted her head back and saw the unmistakable chiseled outline of Jim's jaw as he carried her out of the corral. She closed her eyes again, feeling secure and safe in Jim's arms as she never would in another's.

Then, he stopped and she opened her eyes and found Jim's gaze to be grimly averted from her. But Lord Tynesborough stood close by, his expression filled with concern.

"Are you all right, Miss Braxton? Should we get the doctor? Someone fetch the doctor," Lord Tynesborough shouted.

"No. No, please. I'm fine. I just had the wind knocked out of me," she said, wishing against all pride and all hope that Jim would just keep walking, just carry her away.

Instead, he dumped her in Tynesborough's arms.

"You'll have to learn to act quicker around her," he said, and without another word, stalked away.

CHAPTER THIRTY

The cruel and insurmountable truth was that the one

upon whom she had bestowed her sweet, undying love did

not love her in return.

—from the personal diary of Ginesse Braxton

The food had been excellent—apparently Sir Robert had lent the use of his chef to Pomfrey—the wine free-flowing. Sir Robert must have insisted on inviting Haji and Magi to the party, and Pomfrey hadn't dared decline. With Haji, Jock, and Sir Robert leading the discourse, the conversation had proved lively and amusing. Pomfrey's junior staff and the few wives took advantage of the impromptu party to break out their dance shoes and put on their finery. Everyone was having a grand old time.

Except for Jim.

He leaned a shoulder against the wall, nursing his third tumbler of the excellent scotch whiskey Sir Robert had brought with him and watched her. He tried not to. He tried to abide by all the lessons of decorum and self-restraint he'd learned in the various classrooms life had enrolled him in. He'd finally concluded that nothing had prepared him for her. He simply had no self-control where she was concerned.

She wore a gown of thin, petal-colored material that molded close to her hips and swirled about her feet. The color made her eyes look teal blue and turned her hair to a rich tawny. Short, puffed sleeves hung from the very points of her shoulders, the neckline dipping in a low vee over her bosom, exposing a thought-challenging amount of skin. It curved even lower in the back. He could see the tender channel of her spine disappear under a thin black velvet ribbon cinching her waist.

He could no more keep from watching her than he could keep from breathing. He watched her smiling at Jock, laughing at something he said, and spent the whole dinner reminding himself that he'd literally handed her over to him. Jock was deserving of her, he kept reminding himself. Jock had refused to take what Jim had offered him on a silver platter. That's the sort of superior, principled man he was. And he was rich, too. Though as second son Jock hadn't been bequeathed much from their father, he'd inherited a small fortune from his mother's side of the family.

In short, Jock could give Ginesse everything she'd ever wanted.

And now they were dancing, Ginesse clasped lightly in Jock's arms as the ragtag orchestra Pomfrey had installed at one end of the mess hall managed a lively cakewalk. Her skirts swirled around his feet, and her head was tipped back…Jim flashed on another image of her with her head thrown back, her eyes half shut, her lips parted in ecstasy.

He finished off the rest of the scotch.

"Lord Avandale." He looked around to find Haji's aunt at his side, a handsome woman of indeterminate age. She also looked every bit as formidable as Haji claimed her to be.

"Jim."

She inclined her head inquiringly and stopped at his side, obliging him to push off the wall he'd been holding up.

"Just call me Jim."

"As you wish," she said and fell silent, watching the dancers. He puzzled over what she wanted.

"Do you know how to dance?" she asked after a bit.

"Yes," he answered. It had been a compulsory part of his education.

"Why do you not dance then?"

He essayed a tight smile. "There are few ladies present and many far more worthy gentlemen than I queuing up for that privilege."

She made a dismissive sound. "A convenient excuse."

Startled, he looked at her, and she gave a light laugh. "I have been employed for a very long time by an opinionated and loquacious family," she said. "I fear they have had more of an influence on me than I on them."

"I'm sure it was mutual."

"I hope so. I am very fond of them. Though over the years they have tested my serenity in various ways. Take for example Ginesse's mother, Desdemona. There were times when I had to physically restrain myself from trying to shake some sense into her. She could be so blind to the obvious."

"I imagine Ginesse must remind you of her," he said.

"Ginesse? Not at all. If anything, Ginesse has always seen things too clearly. She sees every imperfection she owns, knows all her shortcomings, and she finds them very hard to forgive. And she cannot quite accept that others might be able to do so."

"I'm not sure I understand," he said.

"I know." She smiled inscrutably. "Which is why I find myself desperately wanting to shake you."

And with that last enigmatic statement, she glided away.

* * *

Ginesse danced a waltz with Lord Tynesborough, performed the Military Two-Step with several junior officers, took a half turn around the room with her great-grandfather, and was amazed, and disconcerted, when Lord Pomfrey requested her to partner him in a schottische. She found him a surprisingly good dancer.

She did not dance with James Owens.

She caught occasional glimpses of him talking to some of the officers or Haji. He looked remarkably handsome, and she noted the other ladies in the room casting openly admiring glances at him. Hussies.

She was bowing to her partner at the end of the last dance when Jim caught her looking at him. He raised his glass a few inches and gave her his crooked smile, toasting her from across the room. Heat swept up her throat. Hastily, she looked away, hurrying off the dance floor in the opposite direction from him. She took refuge at the refreshment table, where she found Miss Whimpelhall pouring herself a glass of punch.

"Miss Braxton, you are the belle of my ball," Miss Whimpelhall said in greeting. She spoke without a whit of envy.

"Only because of my fine borrowed feathers," Ginesse replied. "Thank you again."

Miss Whimpelhall smiled. "It suits you far better than it ever would me. I bought it on a whim shortly before we sailed from London, I don't know why. I should never have felt comfortable in it. It's a good thing I didn't have time to have it properly hemmed."

"I am sure it would look even better on you," Ginesse said.

"Thank you. But I don't believe Colonel Lord Pomfrey would approve."

Her great-grandfather's suggestion that Miss Whimpelhall had secret romantic longings came back to Ginesse. "Is it so important that he do so?"

Miss Whimpelhall looked at her in surprise. "Of course. He is going to be my husband."

Ginesse had never been good at masking her emotions. She did, however, manage not to speak and congratulated herself on her control.

"I do not think you have a high regard for my fiancé," Miss Whimpelhall said carefully. "I did warn you he was not dashing."

"Yes, but…" Ginesse hesitated, then plunged ahead—so much for self-control. "But you deserve 'dashing,' Miss Whimpelhall. And warmth instead of coolness. And romance rather than duty. You should have them."

"Oh, my," Miss Whimpelhall said, looking a little helpless and a great deal moved. "I am touched by your concern. Truly I am. But I know Hilliard very well, and he is precisely the man I want."

Ginesse regarded her with poorly masked skepticism.

With a small sound of exasperation, Miss Whimpelhall linked her arm though Ginesse's and led her to the far end of the mess where they could enjoy some privacy.

"Miss Braxton," she said, turning to her. "Ginesse. You and I are very different creatures. I know you think Pomfrey phlegmatic and straitlaced, perhaps a little boring. And judgmental."

Her apologetic gaze said what she could never bring herself to say, that she disapproved of Pomfrey's attitude toward Ginesse.

"Perhaps he is," Miss Whimpelhall continued. "But for all that, he has the makings of a fine officer. He can be a good man given the right circumstances and under the right influence. More importantly, he is someone I understand because he is very like me."

"Hardly, Miss Whimpelhall—" Ginesse began in protest.

"No, don't deny it. I know my faults, and recently I have been made even more aware of them. Pomfrey and I suit one another."

"But what about passion, my dear Miss Whimpelhall?" Ginesse asked, unconvinced.

"Passion," Miss Whimpelhall repeated. "Deliver me from passion." At Ginesse's stunned expression she continued on a little dryly, "I look at you and Mr. Elkamal and your great-grandfather and Mr. Owens and even, to some extent, Lord Tynesborough, and I am unnerved by your intensity. Your passion unsettles me. You burn so brightly, Miss Braxton, you feel things so deeply.

"I dislike standing so close to the fire. Like that dress, it is far too uncomfortable." She softened the comment with a smile. "For myself, I much prefer tranquility and harmony to..." she shook her head, "whatever it is you own in such abundance. For all that you can never understand my choices, I assure you I would be equally as mystified by yours."

For a long moment, Ginesse studied her and saw in her gaze nothing but sincerity and affection. How rare to find a person who understood what they needed before deciding what they wanted. Ginesse nodded. "You're a wise woman, Miss Whimpelhall."

"Someone has to be," she said, and Ginesse laughed at her unexpected candor. "Now, wish me well and give me your blessing."

"I do and I do," Ginesse said, feeling every inch the fool for having so underestimated this small, meek woman.

"Good. Ah, I see Pomfrey is looking concerned that we have been standing here so long in deep conversation. He considers you a very bad influence, you know," she said with a twinkle. "I best go reassure him."

Miss Whimpelhall had no sooner left than Ginesse spied Haji Elkamal heading toward her, a determined set to his jaw.

"Hello, Haji," Ginesse said tiredly. She was in no mood for another emotional scene with him. Since the afternoon when Lord Tynesborough had told her Jim's history, she had been struggling to find an excuse there for his failure to champion her to Pomfrey. Perhaps his tragic past had rendered him incapable of feeling the sort of love for her that she wanted?

"I would like a word, Ginesse," Haji said.

"Please. Miss Whimpelhall is right. We *are* exhausting. Let's declare a truce if only to make my great-grandfather happy."

"I'm not sure exactly what you mean by that, but don't worry, I've only come to apologize. Sincerely apologize, I mean," he said. He looked contrite. Very unlike Haji. "Several things have made me reconsider my attitudes."

"Oh?" she replied. "My little speech got through to you, did it?"

"Hardly," he said, flashing the wicked grin she remembered so well. "Miss Whimpelhall did."

"Miss Whimpelhall gave you a dressing down?" Ginesse asked in astonishment. She was willing to believe that Mildred had unexpected strength, but she wouldn't have credited her with quite that much assertiveness.

"No." Haji laughed. "She didn't speak to me at all. She spoke to Colonel Lord Pomfrey. She was responsible for Magi and me being invited tonight."

"She was?" she asked in surprise.

"Yes. It was so unexpected. It…" He blushed. "It quite humbled me."

She made a derisive sound.

"It did," he insisted. "You see, I have spent the last three weeks thinking Miss Whimpelhall was the very worst sort of bigot. But putting aside my own prejudices, I realized how willing I was to misinterpret certain of her gestures—a chance expression, or a casual aside. And that made me reconsider what I thought I knew about our relationship, and realize I may have been seeing it through a similarly clouded lens."

"Well," Ginesse allowed, "it wasn't entirely cloudy. I am sure you were saddled with me more often than was fair to you."

"No more than any convenient nanny would have been. And what is wrong with that?" he asked in the manner of one making a startling realization. "Many families use their older children to watch after the younger. Regardless, I wish to make amends. I offer you my services in your search for Zerzura. I have already spoken to the *fellahin* from the caravan, and they have agreed to work as your diggers. I will act as your foreman."

"But my great-grandfather…"

"Has already declared that he intends to remain at Fort George for as long it takes for his great-granddaughter to make her spectacular discovery."

Ginesse's thoughts whirled. The dream she'd longed to realize hovered just out of reach; all the pieces that would make it possible were coming together as if drawn by some unseen hand. She could find Zerzura. She would gain immediate international fame. She would be recognized as an authority on par with her father.

She could leave Jim.

Right now that seemed like the best reason of all. She was heartsick, and she didn't know how she'd be able to recover if she was forced to see Jim Owens every day.

"When could we begin?" she asked.

Haji smiled, and now she could see the excitement kindling his eyes, and she realized that this was more than simply a way to make reparations. He had the Egyptologist's fire in his eyes, the same one she'd seen in her father's and great-grandfather's eyes but had never felt in her own heart. "We could leave tomorrow if you so desired. It will only take a short while to load the provisions."

She was about to say more when Lord Tynesborough appeared, weaving his way through the crowd. He smiled as he made their side. "Mr. Elkamal, if you aren't going to take advantage of so lovely a potential dance partner, might I?"

Haji bowed. "As the lady wishes."

"Miss Braxton?"

She accepted. It would distract her from thinking about Jim. Gently placing his hand on her waist and taking her free hand in his, Lord Tynesborough moved her gracefully out onto the dance floor. He had excellent form, guiding her expertly through the steps, his face alight with pleasure, his conversation light and amusing but not so garrulous it interfered with the music. She could almost forget he wasn't Jim…

* * *

Jim glowered down at his empty glass; it was better than glowering at Jock, who was grinning like a Cheshire cat, his hand on Ginesse's ribcage, his fingertips grazing her bare back. They were waltzing, and apparently in this as in all else, his half brother excelled. She certainly seemed to appreciate his expertise.

Her head was tipped back, her slender throat impossibly tempting. Her skin glowed beneath the lantern light like the plushest velvet. Her wide mouth curved in a slight smile with lips that would be as pliable as warm candle wax and taste like forbidden fruit.

Which she was. Forbidden to him. Because Jock was in love with her and Jock was a good man and a decent man, not the sort of man who would have taken a lady's maidenhead. And definitely, most definitely, not the sort of man who would have taken the maidenhead of a bride he'd been entrusted to bring to her groom. And Jim was...

Jim was.

Because that particular pilfered bride was his.

Principles and decency be damned. He'd go mad if he stood there any longer watching another man make love to her. He was not willing to trade his sanity for whatever chimeral satisfaction he might garner by being able to tell himself he'd done the right thing. He didn't give a damn about the right thing. He cared about Ginesse. He couldn't let her go without doing everything in his power to keep her.

He banged down his empty glass and strode onto the dance floor, putting his hand on his half brother's shoulder with a shade too much force. "May I cut in?" he asked in a voice as soft and dangerous as steel on stone.

He didn't hear Jock's reply. It didn't matter anyway. She already was in his arms. He rested his hand on her slight ribcage, and the heat from her exertions permeated his palm. He felt the press of each long finger as it settled on his shoulder, and he enveloped her free hand in his.

He swept her into the dance, twirling her a little too quickly in the turns, forcing her to cling to him. They did not speak. He looked down, wanting to kiss her until she kissed him back, until she wrapped her arms around his neck and whispered his name against his throat. Her body felt as supple and lithe as a reed in his arms. A strand of wild honey-colored hair came loose and fell along her collarbone, gold filigree on an ivory field.

She tried to avert her eyes, and he pulled her closer, too close, improperly close, until she lifted a resentful gaze to his.

"Stop that," she breathed, her bosom rising and falling above the delicate lace in an agitation that had nothing to do with the dance.

"Stop what?"

"Stop looking at me like that," she said in a hoarse whisper.

"I can't help it," he said.

"Then let me go."

"Never."

Her eyes widened, shot with alarm, something more. "You're drunk."

"Unhappily, no. Though not for lack of trying."

"You must be. You're making a scene."

He looked around and found she'd spoken no less than the truth. Several men were watching them, their gazes sliding quickly away when he caught their eyes. The ladies looked openly alarmed.

God. As if he would ever hurt her. As if he could. He stopped dancing, took her hand, and hauled her off to the side of the dance floor to where a pair of junior officers stood watching the dancers. One look at Jim and they beat a hasty retreat.

He moved nearer, turning her so her back was to the wall, using his breadth to shield her from curious gazes. She was frowning, her head turned. By every criteria they belonged together. He understood her better than any knight errant ever would, her moods and temper, her humor and intelligence. He stared at her helplessly. He didn't know what to say, how to convince her to marry him.

He could please her physically, but she already knew that. They were both wanderers, but if she wanted a home, he could give her that now. If she wanted a venerable name, wealth, and status, he understood that. He could even appreciate it. It was a reasonable ambition. Far more reasonable than marrying a penniless nomad. And he could fulfill that desire.

But he didn't know where to begin, how to press his suit to a girl who'd already refused him twice. And so, in the end, he didn't press his suit at all. He simply caught her chin between his forefinger and thumb, tipping her face up to his.

"Marry me," he said, searching her eyes for some sign, some indication of how to proceed.

Her gaze held his. His heart beat in his chest like a drum.

"Why should I?" she asked, her voice hushed and oddly hopeful and terribly vulnerable.

He swallowed, feeling lost and uncertain. "Well," he said, trying to sound reasonable, "I've got a few more horses now."

She stared up at him, the blood draining from her face.

Then she slugged him.

* * *

Ginesse pushed her way through the buzzing crowds, her eyes stinging with furious, wretched tears.

"Good heavens!" someone said.

"Haven't seen a roundhouse blow like that since Peddler Palmer took out Billy Plimmer in '95."

"Braxton's gel, you know."

She finally found the door and Haji standing openmouthed beside it.

"We leave for Zerzura as soon as possible tomorrow," she said, whisking past him into the night.

* * *

Jim worked his jaw gingerly, touching his fingertips to his lip. They came away bloody. Apparently, that had been the wrong tack to take. But damned if he knew what the right one was. He glanced up to find people staring at him. He could imagine what they were thinking. He didn't give a damn. He'd shouldered his way through most of the crowd when his path was blocked by Jock.

"Jim," he said, his face set and angry. "What did you—"

"I wouldn't, Jock," Jim cut in. "I wouldn't say another word if I were you. I wouldn't…I didn't…Not a single thing she could have taken exception to…" The words just quit. He brushed past his brother, shoved through the door, and took a long, deep breath.

He needed to think, and it was becoming pretty bloody obvious that wasn't going to happen anywhere in her vicinity.

CHAPTER THIRTY-ONE

The raw, untamed beauty of her majestic surroundings only filled her bruised and battered heart with melancholy.

—from the personal diary of Ginesse Braxton

"Amazing," Lord Tynesborough said.

They were facing a long, rocky escarpment that seemed to knuckle out of the sand from nowhere. Composed primarily of black dolorite, it stretched for miles to their west, ending in a dun-colored horizon. For the last three days, they'd been traveling a line due north in a broad grid pattern. Their persistence had finally paid off.

Because they now stood at the terminus of an enormous, as yet uncharted geological feature, at the entrance to a broad *wadi* that cut north into the escarpment a hundred yards before splitting in two, one side angling west, the other continuing north, possibly through to the other side. It was impossible to tell how wide the escarpment was at this point, but she estimated at least a mile.

"Does anyone know this ridge exists?" Lord Tynesborough asked.

Haji, never one to publically declare his ignorance, contrived to look mysterious while being noncommittal.

"Then we may be the first Europeans to ever see this part of the desert," Lord Tynesborough breathed, entranced.

Ginesse had asked him to come for no other reason than it would have been churlish not to, especially since by the time Ginesse had found Haji the morning they'd started their journey, he'd already informed Lord Tynesborough where they were heading. His disappointment would have been too much to bear. They'd left before noon, Sir Robert cheerfully sending them off with the caravan's *fellahin* and his cook joining them for good measure. By mutual, unspoken agreement no one mentioned her hitting Jim. Except for Haji that first day.

"You have ruined a good man," Haji had said shortly after they'd left Fort Gordon. He'd prodded his camel to draw parallel to hers.

"Pardon me?" Ginesse said coldly.

"Jim Owens." Haji nodded. "He used to be a good man. A model of reticence. Calm, self-possessed, and coolly deliberate in the most harrowing circumstances. I quite looked up to him. But you have reduced him to a madman."

She stared at him, rendered speechless.

"You should be ashamed of yourself, Ginesse. Especially if you have no intention of putting the man out of his misery."

"Why, of all the obnoxious, unsolicited—" she began.

"Enough," he broke in, closing his eyes and pressing his fingertips to his lips. "We will say no more," he intoned with unassailable finality. And they hadn't.

Ruined a good man, indeed, Ginesse fumed. There was nothing good about him.

Jim's *proposal* should have ended her infatuation; he might as well have offered to buy her, for clearly he thought he knew her price. "*I have a few more horses now.*" He couldn't have made it any clearer that he considered her an avaricious little gold-digger. The only mystery was why he wanted her at all. But what he *wanted* and what he felt he should do could be very different things. He'd compromised her, and for him that constituted a good enough reason to marry. Her pity for what he'd endured at his grandmother's hands had remained, but it didn't excuse his cavalier treatment of her.

Well, it wasn't for her. And maybe now he'd finally realize that. Just to make sure, she'd left a letter for him. He'd probably already left Fort Gordon. He was probably halfway to Cairo now. Good. From now on she would concentrate on what was important: her career. She had taken a short detour, but now she was back on track, more determined than ever to make a name for herself.

No, Jim Owens wouldn't be bothering her again.

At least not in the flesh.

Because while anger sustained her through the day, at night her dreams betrayed her. Each night he had waited for her with heated kisses and strong arms that lifted her against a rock-hard body, a slow grind of his hips—

"How did you manage to puzzle out that this topography existed out here?" Lord Tynesborough asked.

"Oh. I didn't," Ginesse said, clambering atop a nearby rock and looking around. "In the papyrus he sent with the caravan to the pharaoh, the merchant included an exacting account of the provisions they carried to sustain them. The pharaoh was something of a pinch-penny. He demanded a full accounting of every drop of wine and grain of rice. In addition, the merchant kept a record of how many slaves accompanied them and their daily allotment of provisions. So I knew how long the journey was and made a rough estimate based on the bill of goods as to how far they traveled each day."

She pivoted slowly, looking for some clue as to where the entrance to the city could be. "Later sources added bits and pieces to the puzzle," she continued, only half paying attention. "There was a place name mentioned that I identified as being similar to those occurring in this region's dialect and a written observation of a constellation that would have appeared at the described location only in this sky. They all led here. But I had no idea *that* was waiting for us." She pointed at the escarpment.

"You've done magnificently well," Lord Tynesborough said, his gaze warm with admiration. "You must be most pleased. Most pleased, indeed."

"Thank you," Ginesse murmured, hands on her hips as she surveyed the *wadi*. They'd already made camp at the *wadi*'s entrance, which was protected from the west winds and had easy access to several small caverns where they could take shelter alongside the camels if the need arose. It shouldn't; it was still early winter, the weather predictably hot and dry, the wind insistent during the days but quiet at night.

"Where would you like to begin?" Lord Tynesborough asked. Just the fact that he'd given her complete province of the dig was proof of how far she'd already come in establishing herself as an expert.

"The stories all mention the city as being guarded by twin black giants, but this whole end seems to be one large black rock. I suppose the twins could be metaphors for two local tribes." She sighed. "We might find something farther up the valley floor."

"What of the little birds?" Haji asked, referencing the White City's other name, the Oasis of Little Birds. "We should look for a source of water that would draw migrating flocks."

"Yes," Ginesse agreed. "We'll split up into three different groups. Haji will head along the edge of the escarpment and look for any signs of water, though if there was water it might no longer exist.

"Lord Tynesborough, if you would take a group on the west branch of the valley, I'll lead another straight ahead as long as it leads. Mark as far as you are able to explore in the next four hours and then return. We'll meet back here to relate our findings."

Unfortunately, Haji was not as enlightened a man as Lord Tynesborough. "I think we should divide into two groups and explore this valley first. Later, if we find nothing, we can move the entire camp west."

Ginesse shook her head. "I disagree. We need to accomplish as much as possible as quickly as possible. The season is half over already. The weather may change at any time."

"Bah. It is still a month early for the *al-khamasin*," Haji said, naming the infernal wind that could drive across the desert with the force of a hurricane, whipping up sandstorms of epic scale. "We should not divide ourselves so thin. Many eyes are better than fewer."

"It is Miss Braxton's decision," Lord Tynesborough said.

Haji capitulated by throwing up his hands. "Yes. Of course. As you will. *Yalla! Yalla!*" he called to the workers, motioning for some of the men to follow him. When he spied the cook, he took his temper out on the poor, overweight man by calling, "You can come with me, too, Timon. No one will be eating for hours yet."

"Thank you, Professor," Ginesse said. She had no doubt she would have prevailed, but she appreciated not having to argue with Haji.

"You're welcome," he said.

She turned to gather her own little group, but he caught her hand in his. She looked around to see what he wanted, thinking he had another suggestion about where to look for Zerzura, and instead she found his gaze fastened on her face with limpet-like dedication.

Oh, dear.

"Miss Braxton, Ginesse," he said, drawing her closer. "You must know how very much I admire you."

"Thank you."

"But my feelings far surpass mere admiration."

Oh, no.

"Indeed, I have fallen in love with you." Lord Tynesborough smiled wryly, and for the first time she noted a resemblance between him and Jim. "Though 'fallen in love' sounds so precipitous and thoughtless and there is nothing rash or careless in my feelings for you. They are deep and constant and true.

"So let me say instead that I love you," he continued, his gaze alight with tenderness, "and that each moment I spend with you only makes me love you more. You are bright and courageous and funny and wise, and I wish most ardently, most hopefully, that you feel to some degree the same and that if you do, please, Ginesse, *please* do me the immeasurable honor of becoming my wife."

It was the most romantic proposal she could have imagined. Everything she wished to hear—far, *far* better than "I have a few more horses." If Lord Tynesborough had made such a lovely declaration a year ago, before she had met Jim, would she have answered yes? She didn't know. She had never thought of him that way. She had never realized he thought of her that way.

He was that much of a nice gentleman. He was intelligent and earnest, handsome and well respected. He was easy to converse with and valued her opinions. He loved her; she had no doubt about it. He was, in short, perfect.

Except he wasn't Jim.

Damn Jim, anyway.

"Professor—"

"Geoffrey. Jock, if you like."

"Geoffrey," she said gently, remembering all the times she hadn't measured up, all the ways words could hurt. "I cannot imagine any woman who would not be honored to be your wife."

He waited.

"But a man as remarkable as you is entitled to far more than honor from his wife."

He flinched, a subtle movement but she saw. It hurt her. She didn't want him to feel the pain she was experiencing.

"As tempting as it would be to say yes if only to know the continued pleasure of your companionship, I like you far too well to let you settle for less than you merit, less than I so profoundly know you to deserve. So with regret, I must decline."

"But, Ginesse," he said, a shade of desperation in his voice, "might not you learn to love me?"

"I would never chance hurting you with hope for love when knowing you already are loved is the only possible answer you should accept."

He took a deep, unsteady breath, nodding as graciously as she would have expected him to. "Is there—"

"Geoffrey," she forestalled the inevitable question. She couldn't lie, but she would not answer. "I shall devote myself to my career. If we find Zerzura, there will be years of work ahead of us. And I do mean 'us,' for I consider you my collaborator in this, as I do Haji."

He managed a smile. "Well then, I shall have even more reason to hope for our success. Who knows? Perhaps after five years digging at my side, you might eventually succumb to my charm."

She didn't answer, and with one last, crooked smile, he touched his fingers to his forehead and moved past her, calling out for half of the remaining workers to follow him.

She gathered together a small knapsack with the tools of her trade, a flask of water, and an electric torch, then found the stout staff she'd been using as a cane and prod. Downcast and disheartened, she nonetheless led the last group of men into the *wadi*.

This wasn't how she'd imagined these moments to be. She'd envisioned herself filled with a zealot's anticipation. Instead, the old, all-too-familiar feeling of emptiness filled her. She rallied her spirits, told herself it was simply fear standing in the way of triumph. She was poised on the brink of a magnificent discovery, and she would revel in every moment of it.

She instructed the workers to spread out and move up and down either side of the narrowing valley, looking for an ancient path, some broad flat area, the entrance to a cave. Most references called Zerzura a city, but some simply termed it an oasis and a few called it a "home to a dead king and queen."

It might be that Zerzura was a mountain temple built into the sides of the cliffs, or a small palace tucked away in some valley. At times it was described as golden, at others "white as a dove," so she admonished the workers to keep a sharper eye out for any areas that looked different in color from their surroundings. They worked slowly for the next three hours, the men picking their way amongst the rock litter up and down the sides of the shallow gorge.

Ginesse had been staying mostly on the *wadi*'s floor, but the farther in they traveled the more littered it grew, forcing her to pick her way around piles of rocks and loose shale. She poked every nook and cranny with the end of the staff on her ascent, climbing about halfway up the side when she noted an oddly shaped boulder near the top of the rift. If one squinted, one might say it resembled a great big…duck.

She squinted harder. Definitely a duck, not a dove. On the other hand, ancient Egyptians were known for taking poetic license when it suited them. She couldn't leave it without investigating. It took her lot longer to climb to the top of the rift than she'd thought it would, and when she finally made it, it was only to find that the duck was just a duck. No secret chute opened at its base, its bill wasn't pointing toward the entrance to a vast temple. It was just an oddly shaped boulder.

What *was* interesting was that standing next to the duck she could see the desert on both sides of the escarpment. It was far narrower than she'd assumed. To the south she could see their camp and to the north a vast emptiness interrupted by the dark outline of a tall, solitary hill a quarter mile away. In between, the sand plain stretched in one long, flat expanse.

She tipped her head. She frowned. She looked down at the black rock she stood on and she wondered. If she had approached the escarpment from the north rather than the south, she would have seen that sentinel hill standing right before the black, craggy terminus of the ridge. Two black giants?

Perhaps Zerzura only revealed itself from a northerly approach. There was only one way to find out.

She looked down the *wadi*, but the workers had disappeared from sight. She didn't doubt they were nearby. They were moving slowly. She could call out and wait the hour it would take for them to climb up to her and then lead them in a few hundred yards to the base of the escarpment, or she could just satisfy her curiosity by going herself and be back in twenty minutes or so. She had already spied an easy route down the ridge to the desert floor.

Using her staff for balance, she carefully picked her way down the side of the escarpment. For once, things proved as easy as she'd hoped, and ten minutes later she stood on the sand, a rising wind buffeting her robes. She peered up at the ridge, looking for some sign of a city, and she saw nothing, though to the west the dun-colored horizon seemed to have risen higher.

With a disconsolate huff, she trudged farther away from the base until she stood roughly halfway between the cone-shaped hill and the escarpment. She turned around, leaning heavily on the staff. The end of it sank deep and then deeper, far too deeply.

For a terrified moment, she thought she had stumbled across a rare desert trap, where the sand acted like fluid, sucking down anything not broad enough to stay afloat. Frantically, she threw herself lengthwise onto the sucking sand—

—and promptly fell through the earth.

CHAPTER THIRTY-TWO

There arose in his warrior's heart a strength of purpose, a holy resolve to brave the battlements of his darling girl's too-guarded heart and make her his own!

—from the personal diary of Ginesse Braxton

Dear Mr. Owens—

Jim, standing just outside the stable, swore under his breath. *Mr. Owens?* By God, if she thought she could get away with calling him "Mr. Owens" after all they'd been to each other, she was sadly deluded. He went back to reading the letter some kid had handed him as he'd been leading the gray into the stables.

He'd spent two nights in the freezing desert trying to decide what his next move should be. He'd returned when it had become glaringly obvious he didn't have any idea. How do you court a woman who answered your last proposal by giving you a black eye?

Marshaling his composure, he started the letter again.

Dear Mr. Owens,

I am writing you this letter in the off chance that when we meet again—or perhaps I ought to say 'should' we meet again because if I had my druthers we wouldn't—you have the gall to resubmit your marriage proposal. I advise you not to waste your time or mine.

He had to look up at this point and take a few deep, calming breaths before he could read on. The witch! If he was known for anything it was his self-possession, his coolness under fire, but then he had never been so embattled before. And it was all her fault. *Her.* The girl. The inimitable *she.* The authoress of all his misery. The thief who'd stolen his peace of mind.

His heart.

Dammit!

I do not care a fig (she'd underlined this so heavily that the pencil lead had broken through the paper) how many horses you have, and I have no desire whatsoever (again the thick underscore) to marry a duke. I would not marry you now if the future of humankind depended on it.

I trust I have made my position clear.

Sincerely,

Ginesse Roberta Braxton

"Then what the hell does the woman want?" he shouted out loud, drawing the startled glances of the soldiers sitting outside the barracks cleaning their guns before drill practice. He looked at them, waving the piece of paper in the air.

"Can someone *please* tell me what the woman wants? First, she won't marry me because I don't have anything to offer her," he told the alarmed-looking men. "Fine. So be it. Did I wish she'd have said yes, she'd marry me in spite of the fact that I couldn't offer her a bloody thing? Well, yes. I did. But I understood. I even applauded the decision. It made sense."

The alarm was fading from the enlisted men's faces. A few even nodded in sober agreement.

"*This* makes no sense." He stabbed the paper with his finger. "Because now that I have something to offer her, now that I can guarantee her a life of comfort, now that I have a name worth wearing, now that I'm a *bleeding duke*, I've ask her again and she *still* won't marry me.

"Can someone explain this to me? Does anyone have an answer? And if you do, would you please tell me?" He looked up at the sky. "Would *You* please tell me? Send me a sign. Set a bush on fire. Just give me some bloody clue about what I'm supposed to do to get this woman to say yes."

"Well, son," said an old-timer, resting his rifle across his knees, "the way I sees it, you musta done something wrong."

"Yes. Yes. I admit it. I did something wrong," Jim shouted. "But I'm trying my damnedest to make it right."

The old-timer squinted up at him. "You, ah, you didn't put it to her that way, did you?"

"What way?" Jim said.

"You did, didn't you, you damn fool?"

"Did what?" Jim demanded frantically.

The grizzled veteran rose stiffly and shouldered his rifle. He looked at Jim a moment, shook his head sadly, then disappeared inside the barracks.

"What did he mean?" Jim demanded of the rest of the men. "What was that about?"

"I believe old Pyke there thinks the lady might love you," another man ventured from where he sat.

Jim strode over, leaned down, and pointed at his eye. "Does that look like love to you?" he asked. "Because it sure as hell doesn't feel like it."

"Love can hurt," said another man, calmly polishing his barrel.

"If I were you, I'd find the lady and ask her, not us," said a youngster so wet behind the ears he'd yet to be introduced to a razor.

Jim stared at him. Ginesse had told him in no uncertain terms she didn't want to see or talk to him, wanted nothing to do with him whatsoever. Seven years ago Charlotte had written him a similar letter, though she hadn't said she never wanted to lay eyes on him again, and in fact, the whole letter had been couched in much gentler words. Jim had never seen her again. He hadn't ever tried.

He could have gone to Charlotte or written her and rectified her misconception, exposed Althea as the lying conniver she'd been. But his pride wouldn't let him. Where was his pride now?

Vanished without a trace. That's what Ginesse Braxton did to him.

"You know," he said grimly, "I think I might just do that."

He strode across the parade grounds, heading for Pomfrey's house and where he assumed Ginesse would be. When he reached the house, he pounded on the door, girding himself for a confrontation, half prepared to throw her over his shoulder and carry her off.

Colonel Pomfrey opened the door. "Oh, Owens. It's you," he said. "I was just heading for my office. I can see you have something to say. Say it while we're walking."

"Where's Miss Braxton?" he asked.

Pomfrey brushed by Jim. "She's not here."

"Fine," Jim said, falling into step beside him. "Where is she?"

Impatiently, Pomfrey swept a hand out in a general westerly direction. "Out there somewhere, I should imagine."

"*What?*"

Pomfrey didn't slow his pace. "She left two days ago, the day after she did," he glanced sharply at Jim's eye, "that. Went looking for that infernal lost city of hers."

"What?"

Pomfrey shot him an unfriendly look. "Good heavens, man, are you hard of hearing? I said she's out hunting for Zaboza, or Zerbata, or whatever it's called."

"You let her go off in the desert alone?"

At this, Pomfrey drew to a halt. "Of course not. I know you have little respect for me, Owens, but at least credit me with being responsible. I would never have let her go off by herself. She took Sir Robert's porters and attendants and is accompanied by Professor Tynesborough."

Jim tensed. Jock? Jock wouldn't have any idea what sort of dangers awaited her, what sort of disasters lurked. He wouldn't stand a chance of keeping her safe. And they'd already been out there together for two days?

"Where exactly did they go?"

Pomfrey started walking again. "How should I know?"

Jim seized his arm, stopping him. Pomfrey glared down at the hand holding his forearm and coldly back up into Jim's eyes. "You must have really liked the accommodations in the stockade."

Jim bit back his frustration. He wouldn't do Ginesse any good sitting in a cell. "I need to know, Pomfrey," he said. "You don't understand. She's like a lodestone for natural catastrophe. I have to find her."

For a moment, he thought Pomfrey was going to refuse to say more. Then, he shook off Jim's hand. "Sir Robert said they were thirty-five miles west on the twenty-fourth degree, somewhere between twenty and thirty minutes."

"I'll need to borrow another horse to pack water."

"Blast you, Owens, you better bring it back healthy," Pomfrey said.

"I will. Thank you."

Jim headed back to the stable, tucking the letter inside his shirt.

Against his heart.

CHAPTER
THIRTY-THREE

He was swarthy and ugly of countenance, wearing a stubble of beard and long, matted hair, while his brows were shaggy and his eyes evil and bloodshot.

—from the personal diary of Ginesse Braxton

Haji and his men searched three miles of the south-facing ridgeline. They climbed up and down, investigating every cave and crevasse and looking beneath every ledge before he decided to turn back and go over the same area again. He'd learned the necessity of being thorough from Sir Robert, and he had no intention of being the man who walked past Zerzura. Besides, he owed Ginesse Braxton his best effort.

The workmen were happy to oblige. Compared to their usual workloads, this was a stroll. Even the cook, Timon, made a surprisingly scrupulous searcher, especially for someone so seemingly sedentary. Haji felt a little sheepish about insisting the fat Copt join the search. He worked hard enough as the camp cook.

They were about a quarter mile from the camp when Timon's strength began to flag. He'd disappeared beneath a ledge of rock for long minutes before reemerging, breathing heavily, his face above his thick beard slick with sweat. He moved slowly, bent over slightly at the waist as he waddled tiredly down the steep side of the *wadi*, his hands pressed to his belly.

Haji studied him curiously. Somehow the fat Copt had managed to gain weight on their trip.

"You look ill, Copt," one of the other workers said. "Perhaps you are too old or too fat for this sort of work."

Timon grunted and flashed a tired smile. "I am afraid you are right, my friend," he said. "It is my back."

Haji's head had snapped around. He stared at the cook, studying him closely, only now seeing hands that were a shade lighter than the skin on his face, a beard too black for his brows, cheekbones too pronounced for the weight he carried on his body. Until this moment, Haji realized, he'd never heard Timon speak Arabic; he'd always spoken in English to Sir Robert and the rest of the party. And now he knew why: this man spoke Arabic with a French accent.

LeBouef.

Why hadn't he seen it before? But then, who would ever imagine one of Cairo's most notorious criminals being so exceptional a cook? Added to which, Haji knew the man only by reputation and vague descriptions. He had probably come to kill Jim but, ever the opportunist, had been sidetracked by the promise of treasure.

And now another inspiration occurred to Haji which made sense of the increased size of Timon's belly.

Haji thought quickly. LeBouef had a reputation for being as amoral as a jackal and just as vicious, especially when cornered. Haji couldn't risk putting one of the *fellahin* into his hands as a hostage.

"You do look in considerable discomfort, Timon," he said, contriving to sound worried. He turned to the rest of the workers. "You men continue on here. I'll see that the cook gets back to camp, and then I'll return."

"You are most kind," Timon said in English, "but I can go back myself."

"Nonsense. You are too important to risk your health. Who would cook if you cannot? Lord Tynesborough? No, no. I have medicines in my tent for every occasion." It was a patent lie, but LeBouef couldn't know that. "I will find one for what ails you."

LeBouef could hardly refuse, nor did he. It didn't take more than twenty minutes for them to reach the camp. There, Haji bade LeBouef sit by the cold fire pit and, after a quick inquiry about LeBouef's "symptoms," hurried to his tent. He found a length of rope and his pistol and returned to where he'd left LeBouef.

He was still sitting, but as Haji watched, he shifted his "belly," muttering as he did so.

"Why don't you just take it off?"

LeBouef looked around, smiling. "Take what off?"

"The stomach. I imagine it's hot. Or is that where you've hidden whatever it is you found?"

"I don't know what you mean. I found nothing." His eyes were wide with feigned fear, but there was nothing fearful in their depths. They were cold and assessing.

"You disappeared into a hole; when you reappeared your belly was bigger than when you went in. Now, hold out your hands. If you do not, I will shoot you."

LeBouef hesitated a second and then held out his hands straight in front of him.

"Thank you, Monsieur LeBouef."

The dark man's eyes flickered with appreciation. "Bravo, Mr. Elkamal. Now what?"

"I am trying to decide whether to shoot you or not. You're far too dangerous for me to try to search you for weapons. However, if I shoot you in your hand, I think that might level the playing field."

"That won't be necessary," LeBouef said. "I don't have a gun, but there's a knife in my belt."

"Keep your right hand out in front of you and with your left, remove it. Put it down by your side. Good. Now, lie down and roll over on your stomach and then hold your hands behind your back."

"Mr. Elkamal—"

"Do it."

With a sound of annoyance, LeBouef did as he was told. Haji kicked the knife away then, shoving the barrel of the gun into the back of LeBouef's head and putting his knee in the middle of his back. Using his free hand, Haji lashed LeBouef's wrists together. Then, trusting neither his rope-tying skills nor LeBouef's seeming passivity, he leapt back.

"Roll over and get up on your knees."

With a venomous glare, LeBouef complied.

Quickly and from behind his captive, Haji bound LeBouef's knees tightly together so that even if he managed to work his hands free, he would be unable to get to his feet. Then, and only then, did he tear open the front of LeBouef's robes and withdraw a small pillow from within. A very heavy pillow, one end tied shut. Keeping his eyes on LeBouef, he opened it and turned it over. A pair of sandals tumbled out.

Solid gold sandals.

They were clearly for funerary purposes only; no one would have been able to walk in such heavy devices. The edges of the soles were lined with carnelian and malachite in cloisonné fashion. On each sandal a huge cabochon ruby was mounted at the terminus of twin straps lined with pearls the size of chickpeas. But what was most intriguing, most exciting for a historian of ancient Egypt, were the figures worked into the inner soles.

Haji had seen pharaonic sandals twice before, and each time the figures depicted on the inner soles had been of Negro and Asiatic captives bound with stems of lotus and papyrus and four arrows. They represented the nine traditional enemies of Egypt whom the pharaoh symbolically trod underfoot. It was a conceit with a history dating back thousands of years. But these figures were neither Negro nor Asiatic, and the arrows were missing. Instead, there were a number of smaller figures in elaborate dress that Haji could not identify.

His heart started to beat faster. Though worth a fortune for the gold they contained alone, these sandals' value as archaeological specimens was incalculable. On the insoles of these sandals might be the undocumented history of central African states.

"Pretty, aren't it?" LeBouef said in the same voice he might have used to admire a simple poppy.

"Magnificent," Haji breathed.

"And now they're yours," LeBouef said.

Haji tore his gaze from the sandals.

"So you might as well let me go," LeBouef continued conversationally. "We both know you aren't going to kill me in cold blood. You just aren't that sort. I can see it in your eyes."

He was right, damn him. Haji loathed violence. "Maybe I'll just take you back to Fort Gordon and let Jim Owens deal with you," he suggested grimly.

"Jim Owens," LeBouef mused thoughtfully. "Yes," he conceded, "given the proper set of circumstance, he is that sort." His eyes grew cold as a desert night. "As am I. I owe that boy. He stole from me, broke one of my ribs, and worst of all, he made a fool out of me. Which is not good for business.

"But we weren't talking about Jim, were we? We were talking about you taking me to the garrison. Speaking subjectively, I don't think that's a good idea. Mostly for you."

"Oh?" Haji asked. No doubt about it, the man made him nervous. There was something reptilian about his lack of fear, his blank eyes.

"Ask yourself this: Do you really want to take me all the way to the fort by yourself as your prisoner?" LeBouef asked. "Do you do well without sleep? I do. Of course, you could always ask Miss Braxton to give up her quest and go back. Twenty men should be plenty to ensure your safety. Should be. But, well, frankly, do you think she'd go?"

He was right, damn him.

"Just let me go," LeBouef said. "I'm not a fool, Mr. Elkamal. Nothing is worth dying for. Not even solid gold sandals. I won't come back."

Haji didn't believe him. If he let him go, he'd bide his time for a likely opportunity to retrieve the sandals. He'd sneak in at night or wait until they were spread out and then possibly take one of the men hostage, or even Ginesse herself. The damnable thing was that Haji couldn't even send the sandals back to the garrison. LeBouef would pick off a courier as easily as shooting a bird in a tree.

"What of Jim?" Haji asked.

LeBouef's smiled thinned. "What of dear James?"

"If I let you go, will you leave him alone?"

"No," he said flatly. "He sold something that was mine to another. If that gets around—and things like that always get around—well, who knows who else might take it into his head to become an independent contractor? No, I'm afraid unless Jim comes up with the pectoral he will become a cautionary tale."

Haji thought, and he hated the course of his thoughts. His stomach roiled at them. His head hurt. But he had no choice.

"What if give you the sandals?"

He'd finally caught the Frenchman by surprise. He frowned, studying Haji closely.

"What if I gave you the sandals and let you go?" Haji repeated.

"Why would you do that?"

"I don't want to die. And I don't want Jim to die, either."

"I'm listening."

"If I give you the sandals, you can tell everyone they came from Jim, that he offered you a choice between the pectoral and the sandals. You know the sandals are more valuable. Those rubies alone are worth a fortune."

LeBouef's eyes narrowed thoughtfully. It was amazing how a man tied and on his knees could still manage to project such an aura of danger. "How do I know that Jim will not contradict me?"

"Jim's a duke now."

LeBouef's eyes narrowed. "I'd heard that rumor from the *fel-lahin*. I didn't give it much stock."

"It's true. He inherited his father's title. He's the Duke of Avandale. If you don't believe me, look into it when you get back to Cairo," he said dryly. "Jim isn't going to want his association with you to come out any more than you want it broadcast that he didn't deliver the pectoral to you. I'd be surprised if you ever crossed paths with him again."

At this, LeBouef burst into laughter. "But how wonderful! My former purveyor is a duke."

Haji could almost see the plans for some future blackmail unrolling in LeBouef's mind. He wished him joy with that. Haji had never met a man less likely to care about others' opinions than Jim Owens.

"All right, Mr. Elkamal," LeBouef said. "You have a deal. The sandals for Jim's life. And," he smiled, "yours."

A chill ran up Haji's spine, but he nodded. Going behind the Frenchman, he quickly cut through the rope binding his hands and leapt back as LeBouef brought them forward and rubbed his wrists. He looked amused.

"Oh, don't worry. I have nothing to gain by harming you now and everything to lose. Before your friends return, I wish to be a long ways from here." He bent and made quick work of untying his legs. "Added to which, Sir Robert seems inordinately fond of you, fond enough to make quite a fuss if something should happen to you. Fusses are bad for business.

"As for Jim, if things are as you say, the same goes for him. Now," he rose to feet and held out his hand, "the sandals."

A part of Haji felt like he was giving away his first child. He might never come close to something as important again. If only he had an hour, he could make copies of the little figures on the insoles, but LeBouef was snapping his fingers imperiously and Haji doubted he would wait for him to draw pictures. Reluctantly, Haji hefted them into LeBouef's waiting hands. They had to weigh twenty pounds each. No wonder LeBouef had been sweating.

"I will, of course, be taking one of the camels."

"Of course," Haji said. "And you will not take it amiss if I hold this gun on you until you've left."

"Of course."

* * *

As it was, Haji carried the gun a long time after LeBouef and the sandals left, heading south. He stuck it in his belt and climbed to the top of the ridge's rocky tip and watched him, the wind whipping his robes about his legs and peppering his face with sand. LeBouef disappeared from sight, and Haji was about to climb down when his gaze was caught by the western horizon.

He frowned. When they'd arrived the horizon had been mauve-stained, a sort of pinkish brown that he'd taken for far-distant hills. But somehow the horizon seemed to have lifted against the blue sky above, like buff-colored cliffs. He wondered if it was a mirage, embarrassed that he didn't know. He'd been raised and had lived in cities all his life. He was no nomad, and his knowledge of the desert was slight, most all of his tomb explorations having been done in the Valley of the Kings, and though the terrain was rough, it was within close proximity to a comfortable bed and meals.

He was still watching the west when he heard someone hail him. He drew his pistol and wheeled around. A gray Arabian horse pawed the ground thirty feet below him with Jim Owens, robed and turbaned like a Bedouin, sitting atop.

"What are you doing with that pistol, Haji?" he asked. "Planning to shoot it?" He nodded toward the west.

Haji grinned, glad to see him. "You just missed saying goodbye to your friend Henri LeBouef."

Jim straightened in the saddle. "What do you mean? Where's Ginesse?"

"She's fine."

"*Where is she?*"

"Nowhere near LeBouef, I assure you. I just watched him disappear to the south. Ginesse is, well, I'm not *exactly* sure, but she's somewhere in that rift." He nodded at the entrance to the *wadi*.

"*Alone?*"

"No. Of course not. She took half a dozen men with her."

"Men? As in unsuspecting, inexperienced, incautious men?"

"Well…yes."

"With a *khamasin* bearing down on us?"

"What?" Haji exclaimed.

Beneath Jim, the gray horse began to dance impatiently. "Good God, Haji. What do you think you've been staring at?" he asked, and without another word he turned his horse into the *wadi*.

CHAPTER

THIRTY-FOUR

But that she might die without ever having told him how much she valued him and how sorry she was she had lied, seemed the gravest missed opportunity of all.

—from the personal diary of Ginesse Braxton

With a groan, Ginesse rose to her feet, coughing and choking on dust while carefully gauging any injuries she might have sustained. She appeared to be all right. Where the hell was she?

The area all around her was steeped in blackness, scented with the mineral tang of an area closed off for a millennium. A dry, underground riverbed? The Sahara was riddled with them. However, few of them were so close to the surface that one could plunge through to them.

She looked up. Fifteen feet overhead the hole she'd made plunging through the desert floor glowed like a bright blue disk.

It provided a spotlight of illumination on the uneven ground on which she'd landed, but not enough to penetrate the gloom.

Fifteen feet. It may as well have been fifty.

She closed her eyes, reining in her fear. Someone would find her. They knew which way she had gone. But they thought she was in the *wadi*. How long before they realized she'd gone down off the escarpment into the desert on the other side? Hopefully, soon enough.

She shrugged off her knapsack and opened it. She breathed a sigh of relief. The canteen was intact. Now if only the torch would still work, she could wait until nightfall and shine it through the hole above. With any luck, someone close enough, and looking in the right direction, and with good sight, would see it. With any luck.

Unfortunately, luck had never been her strong suit.

Maybe there was another way out…

She slid the switch on her tubular torch and played the light into the darkness. Her mouth fell open.

She had found Zerzura.

In disbelief, she shined the light around what appeared to be a low chamber about fifteen by twenty feet across. While the walls were rugged, certain portions had been smoothed by masons and incised by artisans, depicting figures and images she had seen hundreds of times in other tombs and temples, though there were some fundamental differences she could not at once identify. She moved her torch up toward the ceiling. Her first instincts had been correct; it appeared to be the channel of an ancient underground river, long ago dried up and put to later use by an ancient population.

She crossed a floor covered with several millennia of dust, peering about breathlessly. Along the walls were thousands of little bundles stacked shoulder height. Tens of thousands. They were roughly the same size, and cylindrically shaped, about eighteen inches in length and as round as a grapefruit.

Carefully, she picked one up. It was surprisingly light, and brittle. She shined her torch on it, her face clearing with understanding, and tipped it. It was a mummified ibis, the disintegrating linen wrappings revealing the telltale bill and long legs of the sacred bird. She picked up another. It was an ibis, too, and equally as fragile. She shined her light along the wall, nodding. *The Oasis of Little Birds.*

But also, she recalled, "home to a dead king and queen." Most scholars had thought this referred to the antiquity of the city, perhaps its original rulers. Clearly the meaning had been more literal. Zerzura was a burial tomb. She played her light along the walls, expecting to see a doorway leading from the chamber. Sure enough, she found one. Had the tomb been intact, the door would have been sealed. It wasn't. Rubble was piled at the base on either side.

With a quick glance at the still-bright sky, Ginesse passed through the door into a chamber three times larger than the one she'd fallen into. It was empty; not even a stick of broken wood remained, and the walls, where she would have expected to find painted scenes, were naked. Likely, this would have been an antechamber, filled with the larger items necessary to enjoy life in the afterworld: shrines and furniture, horses, servants, beds and lounges, chariots and boats.

She spotted another opening. This, too, had been broken open. On inspection, this one proved empty, too. Had it been a treasury? A burial chamber? It was impossible to tell. Nothing remained to relate its history or give a clue to its purpose. In fact, it was too empty. As though everything had been removed wholesale, with calm calculation and efficiency and plenty of time. It was not like the tombs she'd seen that had pillaged, the contents broken and heaped carelessly as the terrified robbers frantically rifled through the contents for only the most precious and portable items.

She looked around. This room had no other access.

The torch light flickered against the blank wall. Fear shadowing her steps, she returned to the room where she'd fallen through. The blue disc above was not so bright anymore—it looked muddier. Dimmer. She stepped directly under the opening and looked up. Little particles of sand were siphoning down as she realized that more sand was being blown across the opening overhead…

She frowned. A stiff breeze stirring the sand or something more…? A sandstorm? She fought down the prickling of fear that started at the base of her spine. It was too early for sandstorms. But then scholars claimed that a freak sandstorm had swallowed King Cambyses's army of fifty thousand men. To this day, no sign of them had ever been found.

She looked up at the small hole above her. A large enough sandstorm could move entire sand dunes. A sandstorm could fill this chamber or cover it. At the very least it would obliterate her torch's weak beam.

Quickly, she catalogued her options. They were few. She considered and dismissed the idea of stacking the ibis bodies. They would never support her weight; they would crumble beneath her. There was no possible way for her to climb up to that hole.

She sat down beneath the opening. For perhaps the tenth time since she'd left Cairo, she thought, *I might die here.* She almost smiled, the thought had become so familiar, so hackneyed. Though this time it might very well be true. Especially if there was a sandstorm brewing out there.

Because this time, Jim Owens was not lying unconscious in her lap. This time, Jim Owens was not coming for her. This time, Jim Owens wasn't even looking for her.

She was on her own in Zerzura. And except for its flocks of dead birds, it was as empty as her triumph in finding it.

What was she doing here? She looked around and did not see a tomb waiting patiently to reveal its centuries-old secrets to worthy eyes. She did not see the fulfillment of a lifelong dream simply because, she realized, it had never been her dream. It had always been someone else's: her father's, her great-grandfather's, Lord Tynesborough's, Haji's.

Tears began to form, slowly overflowing and trickling down her cheeks. Not because she was going to die, but because she was going to die without ever having truly lived. She was going to die without ever having set her foot on the road she was supposed to follow. Without ever knowing a companion in the journey...

No, that wasn't true.

She had set foot on that road and she had found a companion, but the time had been too short and the journey begun too late. She hugged her knees to her chest, and as she did so something struck the ground beside her. She looked up.

A rope hung down from the hole, strong brown hands attached to the end. As she stared, a *khafiya*-covered head and face appeared in the opening.

"Ginesse!" Jim Owens shouted.

"Yes! I'm here!" she shouted, bolting to her feet. "Yes!"

"Are you hurt?"

"No!"

"Tie the end of the rope around your waist and call out when you're done. Hurry. We don't have much time."

She didn't waste time answering. Quickly, she looped the rope around herself, tied it off tightly, and shouted, "Ready!"

A second later she was jerked clean off her feet. She shot upward, grabbing the rope, and then Jim was seizing her arms and hauling her through the hole. There was no time for words. She looked to the west, and her blood ran cold. A huge wall of billowing, churning sand nearly a mile high was bearing down on them.

He dropped her feet to the ground, leaving her to catch her balance as he undid the rope from the Arabian's saddle. Then he wheeled back, grabbed her around the waist, and tossed her onto the gray's back. He leapt up behind her, his arms coming tight around her to grab the reins.

He bent over her. "Hang on!" he shouted over the increasing din.

And they were in flight, spearing through the raucous, buzzing dust. The storm was fast, but the stallion was faster. He stretched out, his neck almost parallel with the ground, his legs eating up the distance, flecks of foam flying from his wide nostrils. She didn't see or feel Jim do anything to control or direct him, and yet he flew straight and true toward the escarpment, following its length eastward, trying to outrace the storm.

"Look for a place to shelter!" he yelled in her ear.

Frantically, she peered at the ridge's face, seeing no opening, no gully or—

"There!" She stabbed her hand out, pointing at a narrow fissure, barely visible in the rock wall.

By some unspoken transference of intent, the horse broke off his headlong flight and swung back toward the escarpment, slowing as he approached the narrow pass. Jim did not let him hesitate. He dug his heels in, and the horse clattered up the steep defile, loose rock and pebbles spraying beneath his hooves. At the last minute, the defile turned sharply, leading under an enormous rock ledge. Beneath it, time and wind had carved a broad, deep pocket, not quite a cave but just as good a shelter.

Jim jumped from the saddle and led her and the horse inside. He looked up at her. Bright daylight had given over to a murky twilight illumination as the storm covered the sun. Shadows played over his stern features, the taut mouth, the hard jaw and clear gray eyes. She had never seen a more welcome face.

"You came for me," she said, her lips curving tremulously.

He frowned as if her comment somehow offended him. "Yeah," he said brusquely. "Didn't I tell you I would?"

This wasn't the reply she'd hoped for. She'd hoped he would take her in his arms, overcome with the joy of finding her alive and…and kiss her and…and…

He reached up and she leaned down obligingly, putting her hands on his shoulders. Visceral sensation shot through her palms as they molded to the hard muscle beneath. Memory of his body moving over hers flooded her thoughts.

She bent her head to his, her lips parting—

"No," he said flatly, setting her on the ground.

"No?" she echoed, disoriented and disappointed.

"No," he repeated. "I don't want that kind of reward."

And she swung at him again.

CHAPTER THIRTY-FIVE

His eloquence came from the embattled soul.

—from the personal diary of Ginesse Braxton

This time Jim caught her fist a few inches before it hit his face, neatly turning it down and behind her. He spun her around and caught her back hard against his chest. "Would you stop trying to hit me?" he said in a low, calm voice, his lips pressed against her ear.

"I wouldn't have to if you didn't keep saying things that provoke me," she said, trying to sound equally nonchalant and fearing she missed the mark entirely.

He shoved her lightly away from him, brushing past her and going to where the stallion danced nervously, his ears flattening and flickering. Gently, Jim soothed his hand down his arched neck. Then he moved back and dug into his saddlebag, removing a rolled blanket. Working quickly, he flicked it open and secured it over the mouth of the cavern. It didn't entirely cover the opening, but it would deflect a substantial part of any blown-back sand that got caught in the rift. When he'd finished, he tethered the stallion in the far corner, wrapping a shirt over the horse's eyes to keep him from panicking.

And then the storm was on them. It filled the air with the angry hissing of a million wasps, so loud it covered any incidental sound. Ginesse crept close enough to the opening to look upward. The wind-driven sand swept over the ledge and streamed almost parallel in the sky.

"It's mostly going over us," she called out and turned to find Jim already at her side, his gaze fixed on the sky above. He'd pulled the end of his *khafiya* over his mouth and tucked it in at his temple. All that was exposed were his tarnished-nickel eyes, narrowed against the ravaging wind outside.

"Stand still," he said, opening a square of woven silk and wrapping it over her mouth. He tied it at the back of her head. "In case there's dust."

The sand was painful, little needles scoring any exposed flesh, but the dust was worse, filling nostrils and throat, clogging eyes and thickening in the lungs. The heavier sand stayed near the bottom of the *khamasin*, but the higher up in the storm wall you were, the more likely you were to feel the effects of the talc-like powder that could be driven into the smallest seam, the narrowest opening.

For long moments they watched, riveted by the sight of the thick curtain of sand, praying they weren't so high up in the storm that the dust found them. Finally, Jim loosened his *khafiya* and let it fall from his face.

"I think we're lucky," he said. "We're situated at the right angle to keep the sand from blowing back on us and not so high up to be in the dust. As long as the storm doesn't suddenly stop and dump all the sand it's carrying, we should be all right."

"How long will it last?" she asked, untying her veil.

"I don't know. It depends on how big it is. It could blow for days, but it's more how quickly it's moving that concerns me. It's early for this sort of storm, but then…" he looked at her pointedly, "there are extenuating circumstances."

"You can hardly blame me for the sandstorm."

"Can't I?" he asked, sounding exasperated and resigned at the same time.

She started to stalk toward the back of the cavern, but he grabbed her wrist. She turned and looked coldly down at the hand holding her prisoner. It didn't seem to have any effect.

"Oh, no," he said. "You're not going anywhere. Not this time."

"Of course I'm not," she said disgust. "I'm not about to stomp out into the middle of a sandstorm just because I find you offensive. Despite what you and everyone else thinks, I'm not an idiot."

"Oh, yes. You are."

She gasped. "How. Dare. You."

"What were you doing out there?" he demanded. "If I hadn't see that wooden staff…if I hadn't brought field glasses…" A shudder ran through him. Abruptly, he dropped her hand and turned away from her.

"I…I found Zerzura," she said, knowing she sounded apologetic when she wanted to sound victorious.

He looked over his shoulder at her. "Who cares?"

She blinked.

He turned around, facing her. "Who the bleeding hell cares if you found Zerzura? Or Timbuktu? Or the bloody Garden of Eden?" he asked, his voice gaining volume with each word. "You might have died, Ginesse!"

"But I didn't," she pointed out reasonably. "You came for me."

He nodded, at first in agreement, but somewhere along the way it turned into a shake of negation. "Yes. I came for you. I will always come from you. Because I can't seem to help myself. It doesn't matter where you are or if you're officially someone else's problem. I don't even care if you're married to someone else. Where is Jock, anyway? No. Don't answer that." He gave an elaborate shrug. "It doesn't matter. He's not here. I am."

She stared at him in confusion, concerned that somewhere along the way he'd become unhinged.

He held his hand out as if asking her opinion. "And that's the rub, isn't it? *It doesn't matter.* Because who's going to pull you out when the earth swallows you whole or fish you out of the ocean when your ship sinks—"

"Only the *felucca* sank, and it didn't even really sink. It listed," she interjected. "The *Lydonia* was fine. Mostly."

"Don't interrupt me," he said. "Who is going to catch you when the mountain you're standing on explodes? Or the heavens fall?"

He glared at her, waiting.

"You?" she ventured.

"*Me.* I can't help myself any more than you can help being… you. You're a like a magnet for everything disruptive and dangerous in the world. No matter where you go, no matter who you're with, chaos will find you and *I will know.*" He stared at her angrily. "In my heart, in my soul, in my bones, and in my blood, I will know and I'll come because I can't help myself." He raked his hair back with his hand. Looked away. Looked back at her. Looked away again.

She stared at him, dumbfounded. She'd never seen him like this. He looked like a man on the frayed edge of sanity, holding on by only the thinnest strand. His usual composure had cracked— no, it had shattered. He strode back and forth in front of her with a frenetic sort of energy. "Did he ask you?"

"Who? Ask me what?" she asked in confusion.

"Jock. Did he ask you to marry him?"

"Oh. Yes. How did you know?"

"A blind man—" He shook his head. "It doesn't matter. What did you answer?"

"No."

"Why not?"

Now she felt her own anger rising in answer, hot and fierce. "That's none of your business."

"The hell it isn't. I've asked you to marry me three times and you've refused me each time. I thought it was because you were in love with my brother."

"Well, you were wrong."

His hands balled into fists at his side. She noted it, raising her brows haughtily.

"Why did you refuse to marry me then?" he demanded.

She should be quiet; she should just stay mute. But she was angry and hurt. Only moments before he'd been saying such lovely things; now he was being horrible. "Why can't you help yourself?" she countered, shouting back.

"What?"

"*Why* are you compelled to come after me?" she demanded, setting her hands on her hips.

For a moment, he just stared at her as if she was daft.

"Because I love you," he finally said, as if it were the most obvious thing in the world.

"What?" She'd waited to hear him say those words for what seemed like an eternity, and now he'd said them just as casually and unconcernedly as he might have said, "I like that dress" or "Spot is a good name for a dog."

"Because I love you," he repeated. "Why else would I?"

"I don't know. Because you're *mad*?" she suggested. How dare he say he loved her here, in such a manner, with so little fanfare?

He was watching her carefully. "You seem upset."

"Oh. Do I?" she asked sweetly. Behind her, the horse shifted uneasily. Smart horse. "Perhaps it's because *I do not believe you.*"

He drew back as if she'd slapped him. "Why?" he asked, wholly bewildered.

"Because though, as you pointed out, you have proposed three times—although simply agreeing to Pomfrey's suggestion that we marry does not in my mind constitute a proposal—this is the first time you have mentioned the word love to me."

She held up her hand when he opened his mouth, forestalling him. "Added to which, while Pomfrey was defaming me in the worst possible way, saying awful, terrible things to me, you stood by and let him. A man in love would never suffer his beloved to be spoken of in such derogatory terms."

"What did he say? I don't remember him saying anything in particular," he said, frowning. "But then I wasn't really listening."

"Oh! Oh, you…" She sputtered to a stop, unable to come up with nasty enough words. "We are done talking."

He stared at her for a tense few seconds before spinning around and pounding his fist against the cavern walls, sending a spray of gravel shooting out. "Ah, hell, Ginny!" he shouted above the roaring storm outside. "Come on! Give me a break!"

"I don't know what that means," she said primly.

"It means that's not fair," he ground out through clenched teeth. "I'd just found out the woman I'd made love to and was in love with wasn't who she claimed to be. Compounding that was the fact that I'd just discovered she didn't even know the man she'd turned me down for. It was confusing, and I was a little," he pounded the cavern wall again, "*preoccupied.*"

She flinched.

"I didn't *hear* Pomfrey. So if he insulted you, I'm sorry. Do you want me to go back and beat him bloody? Because if that's what it takes for you to believe me, I will. Hell, I'll even enjoy it! Because right now, I really, *really* want to hit someone."

"I suppose by that you mean me," she said haughtily.

He froze, the muscle jumping at the point of his jaw, his eyes glittering. Then, all at once, he sighed.

"Ah," he muttered, "the hell with it." And with that, he grabbed her, bent her over his arm, and kissed her.

He kissed her long and thoroughly and single-mindedly. One arm lashed her against him, and the other snaked between her shoulder blades, cupping the back of her head. He kissed her breathless. He kissed her until her head swam and her heart trip-hammered in her chest, and then he kissed her some more, until her legs wouldn't hold her and silvery lights exploded behind her closed lids. He kissed her until she forgot about any storm but the one he was rousing in her.

Her mouth yielded entirely under his determined assault and her body surrendered. Her breath came shallow and quick, and she knew if he hadn't been holding her, she would have swooned. He finally lifted his head from hers and gazed down into her passion-muzzed eyes and at her lips already parting for more kisses, catching her when her knees threatened to buckle, and steadying her.

"I love you," he said, his breathing rough and his eyes still glittering but with a different fire. "I can't make it any clearer than that. Do you understand?"

"Yes," she said, trying to catch her breath and losing it again when he caught her in his arms to steady her. "Yes."

"And that's all you wanted to hear?"

"Yes," she said, a shade unsteadily. "I wanted the only reason you proposed to me to be because you loved me, because that is the only reason that ever mattered to me." Her gaze slipped away from his. "I suppose you think that's pathetically romantic? To want to hear you say it?"

With one arm around her waist, he used his free hand to tip her chin up so he could look directly into her eyes. "I love you," he said, and this time the words did not sound light or incidental. "I love you, Ginesse. Don't you see? *You* are my Zerzura. You are my undiscovered country, both my heart's destination and journey. Gold and temples, jewels and gems don't hold one bit of your enticement."

With his thumb, he tenderly brushed her lips, then charted a course down her throat. All traces of hardness had left his gray eyes, leaving them smoky and dark.

"You," he whispered, "are my Solomon's mine, my uncharted empire. You are the only home I need to know, the only journey I want to take, the only treasure I would die to claim. You are exotic and familiar, opiate and tonic, hard conscience and sweet temptation."

He smiled then, a touch of self-amusement in his eyes. "And now I have no more words to give you, Ginesse. I only have my heart, and you already own that."

Tears sprang to her eyes. She tried to blink them away. "Good heavens," she sniffled and hated herself for sniffling because a heroine never got a runny nose upon hearing her hero's declaration of love, "that was impressively romantic coming from an unsentimental American cowboy."

A brief grin lit his face, tenderness and humor comingled. "Ah well," he said kindly, "it turns out I'm actually a duke."

She laughed, and his arms clasped around her more tightly. "What more can I offer you, Ginny?" he demanded. "Tell me. It's yours. I'm yours."

In reply, she wrapped her arms around his neck, pressing her face to the hollow of his neck and touching her lips and tongue briefly to his skin. A shiver ran through him. He tasted salty and dusty, an earthy tang to his masculinity. Who would ever think a man would have so many flavors?

She pulled open his robes, and he went very still.

Beneath the Bedouin robes, he wore an open-necked shirt. With quiet efficiency she set about unbuttoning it, seeing out of the corner of her eye the way his lips parted and hearing the sharp intake of his breath. He turned his head, so that his lips were a hairsbreadth from her face.

"What are you doing?" he asked, the breath of his speech caressing her temple.

"Taking what was given to me," she replied unevenly.

"I was hoping as much," he replied as the robes dropped from his shoulders and the shirt came open beneath her hands.

He was gorgeous, a beautiful example of male architecture: clean lines and lean muscle; hard, sculpted chest; strong, finely honed arms. She pressed her palms against his chest where they rode the heavy rise and fall of his breathing. She leaned forward and pressed an open-mouthed kiss over his nipple. He made a rough sound, catching her by the shoulders and holding her away.

For a second she feared he was going to be honorable again, but he only took hold of the edges of her own robe and peeled it from her shoulders, letting it fall and pool around her feet.

His gaze traveled over her, as hot as the sun. "Save me," he muttered thickly, "those are worse than those damn cadet's trousers."

She felt her whole body warm beneath his ardent gaze. She'd forgotten the *shintiyan* she'd donned beneath the robes. Wide, loose trousers of filmy cotton, hitched up with silk threads at the calves and held up by a thicker silk cord low around the hips, they were far more comfortable—and cooler—than either her skirts or the heavy young men's trousers she'd worn on their trip. They were also so sheer as to be transparent.

But she'd never expected anyone to actually see her in them. They were just to be worn underneath the loose robe.

"They're comfortable," she said in a small voice.

He shook his head. "Not for me."

She squirmed self-consciously and he smiled, again sweetly, earnestly, without a trace of bravado, and as she watched, he sank gracefully to his knees in the sand before her. His head came just above her waist, his face inches from her stomach.

"What are you doing?" she asked breathlessly.

"Pressing my suit," he replied a little hoarsely. A tingle ran through her as he spoke; she could feel his breath through the thin fabric, warming and exciting her at the juncture of her legs. She started to step back, unnerved by the heady sensation, but he wouldn't allow it. He clasped her hips, drawing her forward and opening his mouth over that most sensitive area, boldly pressing his tongue against her mons, dampening it through the sheer fabric.

Electricity shot through her body, curling in her belly, tingling in her nipples and lips, her fingertips and the backs of her knees, pulled tight to the center where his mouth covered her. She trembled, her legs growing weak, but he wouldn't let her fall. He pulled the harem trousers down off her hips, wrapping one big arm around her thighs and holding her tight to him.

"Put your hands on my shoulders," he murmured against her, each warm word tapping at the uncomfortable kernel of need blooming beneath his mouth.

She could hardly do otherwise. She steadied herself on his shoulders as she felt his mouth opening against her naked skin and his tongue delving deeply along her body's seam.

She jerked at the shock of it, the intimacy, the pleasure. He found the nub between and with exquisite delicacy, sipped against it. She cried out, sensitized to the point of pain, her body reacting forcibly, melting into liquid gold.

She fell, clutching at his shoulders, and he caught her behind her knees, sweeping her from her feet and laying her gently down on the warm, talc-like sand as the storm raged outside. "Too much, too soon," he whispered. "I'm greedy. Forgive me."

"No," she said, shakily. "It's just...I had no idea."

He laughed softly, sweeping the hair from her face, and his expression sobered. "You are so unearthly beautiful," he whispered.

She started, frowned. She knew he meant to please her, but she was not beautiful and to hear him say so here, now, made her uncomfortable. At once, he discerned some error, some withdrawal. He rolled over, holding himself above her with arms rippling with muscle.

"What's wrong?" he asked quietly. "Did I insult you? Do something that offended you?"

"No."

"Then what?"

He was watching her intently. No one had ever had regarded her so closely, she thought. She had never been so...*seen*. There was nothing she could hide from him. Ever.

"It's silly. It's just that…you called me beautiful, and I know you meant to please me, but I'm not and it made me realize that this is what one says, what you say, when you're…doing this. And it reminded me that…others have heard the same words from you."

For a long moment he simply stared at her, emotions flickering across his face. How had she ever thought him enigmatic? She could read his confusion, his shock, then disappointment, a touch of anger and exasperation, and finally amazement and, yes, love.

"I'm not sure if your assumptions about my sexual experience are insulting or flattering. There have been no others. Not like this. Not remotely like this. A few encounters that provided… release. But I've never 'said things when doing this.' There was very little saying going on, just," he looked away and she could see his discomfiture, his chagrin, "mutual physical satisfaction. Certainly not love." His gaze returned to her face, searching. "Do you understand?"

She nodded.

"And as for your not being beautiful…No," he said as she started to turn her head. "Look at me. You are the most exquisite woman I have ever seen. You are certainly the most beautiful. Hasn't any man ever told you that?" he asked, and for the life her she could hear nothing but stunned amazement in his voice. "Then it could only be because you intimidated them, and you are, God preserve me, intimidating.

"It was your beauty that almost sent me to my knees the first time I saw you, and I hadn't even seen your gorgeous eyes yet, the wit and warmth in them. Your lips haunt my dreams with the memory of their taste, your neck inspires a wicked desire to trace its length with my tongue. And your magnificent nose, imperiously belying all the lush, wanton beauty of your eyes and mouth. Ginesse, your beauty dazzles me."

And she looked into his eyes and realized he was telling her the simple unadorned truth, nothing less and nothing more. He thought she was beautiful. And so, she was.

With a little cry of delight, she pulled him down to her, relishing his weight covering her. Hungrily, she set about exploring him. Her lips skated along the hard column of his neck, across the smooth skin capping his broad shoulders and back to the tender flesh beneath his ear. Her hands flowed down his back, the muscles tensing in his hard buttocks, and back up the velvety ladder of his ribs, to the silky slide of his hair and the beard-rasped angle of his jaw.

Her mouth found his, and a shudder ran through him. He angled an arm beneath her, lifting her, the other hand peeling back her top, exposing her breasts. He cupped one in his hand, lifting and molding it, his thumb rubbing back and forth, teasing it into a taut nub. He broke off the kiss, shifted her beneath him, lowered his head, and took her nipple into his mouth.

She gasped. With exquisite intention he stroked it with his tongue and sucked it into his mouth. She arched back, her fingers flexing deeply into his shoulder muscles. Her hips lifted in an involuntary plea, rocking against the hard thigh pressed between her legs. He murmured against her breast, dropping his head lower and sliding his hand between their bodies. He looked up into her face as he pushed the *shintiyan's* belt down past her hips, his hand following the silk's retreat, caressing the newly uncovered skin beneath.

She moved restlessly against the too tender touch, wanting more, and when he did not acquiesce, she reached between them, jerking open his trousers and shoving her hand down inside them, closing over his erection. He froze, his eyelids slipping closed, his breath ragged. For a long moment he waited, looking more like a man enduring torment than one enjoying his lover's ministrations, and finally, with a rough sound, he grabbed her wrist and pulled her hand away.

He rose up on his knees, stripping off his shirt and jerking his belt free of the loops as she followed his example, working frantically to rid herself of her clothing. Abruptly, finally, they were naked, or mostly so, their bodies coming together, skin sliding against skin, heat stoked by desire, her hands learning his powerful form, the sensation of hard muscle flexing and releasing.

He cupped her buttocks, lifting her, and then he was in her, penetrating slowly and purposefully, an exquisite torment, a fullness that edged toward pain. She spread her knees wider, clasping him between her thighs, lifting up to seat him more deeply. With a groan, he thrust deep inside her. She cried out with the pleasure of it, the torment of it, for each of his thrusts built a sense of carnal anticipation.

Pleasure spiraled inward, molten and powerful, burning ever brighter, ever more focused. He moved more swiftly, his body pushing hers into the deep, silky sand, his breath hoarse in her ear. "Take it," he urged, his voice deep and rough. "Your climax. Move on me."

She did. She shifted, tipping her pelvis. She felt his arm tighten around her waist as he clasped her hips and thrust deeply, his body rock-hard, his face strained with effort...

Passion crescendoed around her, swelling to an unbearable promise. She cried out, impaled at the pinnacle of sensation, her throat arching, her shoulders drawn back. Wave after wave of intense pleasure erupted in her. She sobbed with the beauty of it, the unexpectedness, crying out when it peaked, and she heard him make a harsh, strangled sound deep in his throat, as he thrust and held, pulsing deep inside her.

Seconds or an eternity later, he looked up and brushed the damp hair from her face, feathering kisses on her forehead and along her nose. She stroked his lean cheek, kissed his collarbone, and marveled at how perfectly formed he was until it occurred to her that she'd been sadly negligent in one respect.

"I love you," she whispered, gazing up into his pale gray eyes.

He smiled crookedly, for a moment looking at her with a dazzled air. He had, she realized sadly, no experience hearing those words. He didn't know how to react. "I figured as much."

This time, she didn't hit him.

* * *

Sometime later, Jim pulled Ginesse into the curve of his body and gently shifted her onto his chest. The sand still roared like the surf outside the cavern, and the sun was still blotted from the heavens. He didn't care. For a long time after she fell asleep, he cradled her tenderly and watched her.

His. And she loved him. His wonder was only outstripped by his sense of homecoming, of finally arriving on that distant, longed-for shore. *His.* There was nothing else he needed. Nothing else he wanted. But there was a good deal more she needed and wanted, and he intended to see that she had it. She'd placed her heart in his care, and he would go to the ends of the earth to see that she never regretted it…

"Ginesse! Ginesse! Where are you?" The sound of a man's voice woke him.

He was not too far away.

Jim frowned. The voice was unfamiliar. It wasn't Haji, and it wasn't Jock. He stood up, pulling on his trousers and waking Ginesse in the process. She blinked blearily up at him from her nest of discarded clothing.

"Someone's coming," he said, moving to the front of the cavern so she had time to quickly don some clothing.

His frown turned into a fiercely protective scowl. He glanced at Ginesse. She'd pulled the *habarah* over her head providing more than adequate covering, but her hair hung about her shoulders like a toffee-colored shawl. She looked ripe and flushed and deliciously tumbled.

"Another suitor you failed to mention?" he asked, only half in jest.

Her eyes widened innocently, she started to shake her head—

"Ginesse!"

—and froze.

"Oh, dear," she said, grabbing a handful of her hair and twisting it into a knot. She scrambled to her feet just as a tall, well-built man in a dusty shirt and trousers, a white *khafiya* on his head, appeared in front of the cave, backlit against a now bright sky.

Jim couldn't make out his features, but the direction of his gaze was clear enough. It flew to Ginesse and then came pointedly back to Jim and Jim's bare chest.

"Look, mister," Jim said tiredly. "I don't know who you are, and I don't care. You're too damn old for her—"

"Hi, Daddy."

Jim watched Harry Braxton move back into the light. Yup. Same eyes. Same nose. He nodded curtly toward his daughter, but his eyes, as cold and hard as steel, remained on Jim. "Looks like I made it in time for the wedding," he said. "Doesn't it, son?"

Jim, caught off guard and a little irritated, opened his mouth to reply, "Barely in time, sir," when he caught sight of Ginesse out of the corner of his eye.

She was standing in the shadow near the blanket partition, the hastily donned robe twisted around her slight form, her bare feet peeping from beneath the dragging hem, her hair falling in a tawny river around her shoulder. She caught his eye and smiled. It was a confident smile, full of love. But there was just the smallest hint of wistfulness there. Just a soupcon. She had wanted to hear him say he loved her and then worried that he would find it pathetically romantic. He wasn't going to satisfy anyone's expectations but hers. Even if it hurt, which, he glanced at the lean muscular man in front of him, he imagined it would.

"No, sir," he said.

"What?" thundered Harry Braxton.

Ginesse's eyes widened in surprise. But there was no fear there, no hurt, just curiosity. She trusted him. And that meant more to him than he would ever be able to express.

"No, sir. There is nothing romantic about a shotgun wedding, so that's not the marriage Ginesse is going to have, and when I ask her to marry me, her daddy isn't going to be standing there watching while I try to button my fly in between choking out the words."

"Oh, Jim!" A soul might have thought he'd just given her a piece of heaven instead of telling her father he wasn't going to propose to her.

Harry Braxton wasn't as enthusiastic about it. "You sonofabitch," Harry said, stepping forward.

Jim didn't answer. He didn't even try. He just stepped back as the virago he loved launched herself between Harry and him, sticking her hand square on her father's chest and shoving him back a step.

"No," she said. She shoved him again. "No." She shoved again. "No!"

"No what?" shouted Harry.

"No, you are not going to make him marry me. Or me him!"

"Look, honey, I don't know what this man—"

"Jim. Jim Owens."

"Jim Owens," Harry repeated. His startled gaze shot to Jim. His jaw clenched. So did his fists, and Jim tiredly anticipated that this wasn't going to end well. "Jim Owens is a disreputable, morally questionable, possibly criminal artifacts dealer and gun-for-hire."

"I don't care!" Ginesse shouted gleefully. "I'm still not marrying him!"

Harry, finally seeming to divine that things were not quite as he'd imagined, but just as clearly pretty used to that state of affairs when it came to his daughter, unclenched his fists. "Anyone care to take a stab at explaining things?"

"No," Ginesse said angrily. "It's none of your business. It's no one's business but mine and Jim's, but everyone keeps insisting on interfering. So let me make this perfectly clear. I am not going to marry Jim because he thinks it's the right thing to do. I am not going to marry Jim because Colonel Pomfrey told him proposing was the right thing to do. I am not going to marry Jim because he's a duke—"

"You're a duke?"

"Be quiet," Ginesse snapped. She took a deep breath and continued. "I am not going to marry him because you showed up and told him he had to marry me, and I am not going to marry Jim because of the state of my hymen."

"Merciful Mother of God, Ginesse!" Jim and Harry burst out in unison.

"Ach!" she sputtered in disgust. "What a pair of old ladies." She shot them both a venomous, contemptuous glare. "It's true. Everyone is so concerned with whether I'm a virgin or not, but no one seems too interested in a far more fragile organ: my heart." Her gaze softened. "Except Jim," she said, bestowing on him such a rapturous smile it made the beating he anticipated worth it. "And because he does, we won't be marrying right away."

"Why?" Harry asked, looking bewildered.

"Because," Jim said, "I have five weeks to get to London and make sure that the man who proposes to your daughter is still a duke with a place to take your daughter once we're married. And I'm not going to rush her through some civil union in a borrowed dress. She deserves more than. She deserves my best. And I won't offer her anything less."

She hadn't figured on that. "You're leaving?" she asked, her brow furrowing.

"For a while."

Horrified, Jim watched tears spring to her eyes, turning the blue-green irises into gemstones. He reached out to take her in his arms, but her father stepped between them. Not a wise move. Had it been anyone other than her father it would have been more than unwise; it would have hurt. He forced himself to stay put.

"When will you be back?" Ginesse asked.

"As soon as I get my affairs in order. As soon as I possibly can." He wouldn't leave if it would hurt her. God knew, he didn't want to. "Please, Ginny. Let me do this for you. Please."

Her gaze searched his face a long time before finally, with an air of sad resignation, she nodded.

"Let me see if I understand," Harry said slowly, his gaze moving back to Jim. "You're not going to marry this man?"

"Why, Dad," Ginesse said, the shadow of an impudent smile curving her lips. "The gentleman hasn't even asked me. Recently, anyway."

"Fine," said Harry, nodding with satisfaction. "Then there's no reason I shouldn't do this."

And with a right hook, he laid Jim Owens out cold.

CHAPTER THIRTY-SIX

Together they rode off into the glory of the

setting sun toward the new one rising

swiftly ahead!

—from the personal diary of Ginesse Braxton

FIVE MONTHS LATER
CAIRO, EGYPT, 1906

"Oh, there is no doubt about it, the Duke of Avandale is all the lux!" enthused the fresh-faced young English miss to her equally dewy-skinned companion at the table they shared on Shepheard's famous balcony.

Though still very early in the morning, the balcony was already filling up with tourists and expats taking in the first fine spring days. As it was Saturday, there was little traffic on the broad avenue below. The strains of "Sweet Adeline" playing on a gramophone inside the hotel drifted through the open windows.

"Mum and I saw him yesterday at the consulate's. He looked at me! I do not mind admitting, dear, that I thought I would faint dead away, he was so fierce." She flapped her gloved hand in front of her face, presumably cooling her overheated cheeks. "*And* manly. Oh, my!"

"I saw him last night. He was having drinks with some young man at the Marmeduke. The young man was good looking, but compared to Avandale he seemed but a pup!"

Yesterday, Ginesse Braxton thought grimly. Jim had arrived in Cairo yesterday, and everyone seemed to have seen him except her.

"I wonder what he's doing here?"

"Well, Father says that he is turning his estate in England into a stud farm for Arabian horses. I shouldn't be surprised if he isn't looking for a good brood mare—"

This last proved too much. Ginesse, sitting at a table next to the balcony's rail with old friends, a pair of middle-aged archaeologists and their wives, choked.

"Ginny, my dear, are you all right?" Mrs. Throckmorton asked in concern.

"I'm fine, thank you," she said, hastily taking a swig of tea. If she heard that simpering female extolling the virtues of Jim Owens any longer—no, she thought, Lord Avandale—she would tip said simpering female over the railing onto the street. Though the short three-foot drop from the balcony to the ground would probably not knock very much sense into her head.

Lux. Fierce. Manly. What claptrap.

"I have heard Tynesborough intends to return to the Fort Gordon site this season and try to find Zerzura, Ginny," Mr. Arnout said. "Will you join him?"

"No," she said. "The sandstorm that swept through the area was enormous. Heaven knows how vast an amount of sand was moved."

"Then you think all is lost?" Mrs. Arnout traded a tragic look with her husband. Ah, thought Ginesse, true enthusiasts.

"Not at all," she reassured the stricken couple. "With two such brilliant researchers as Mr. Elkamal and Lord Tynesborough looking for it, it is only matter of time before it is found. It just won't be found by me. I have come to the conclusion that I am not much of an Egyptologist."

This was met by a series of quiet gasps and telling glances, quickly masked and immediately covered with too-effusive denials.

"Not at all!" Mr. Arnout said.

"You are a gifted scholar," Mr. Throckmorton exclaimed.

"A most accomplished researcher!" Mrs. Arnout enthused.

"Another star attached to the illustrious Braxton name," declared Mrs. Throckmorton. "Your parents are most proud."

"Oh, I know," said Ginesse calmly. "Have you seen the review Mr. Coleman of the *London Gazette* gave *The Belle of Montana: True Love's Rough Trail*? It is enough to turn one's head. They said it was the most astonishing portrayal of the American West—"

"Ginny!" a masculine voice bellowed from somewhere out in the street.

Ginesse looked up, half expecting to see one of her brothers now that the entire Braxton clan was once more united in Egypt, especially since the whole lot of them were given to just such undignified bellowing.

Instead, she saw a tall, lean young man dressed in the brilliant white robes of a Bedouin sheik seated upon a magnificent gray stallion. Beneath the open robe he wore an impeccable white shirt and khaki trousers. His hair, neatly trimmed and clean, gleamed like burnished gold, his chiseled jaw was smooth and freshly shaved, and his riding boots gleamed almost as brightly as his hair.

Her heart leapt at the sight of him and began racing wildly.

"Ginesse Braxton!" he called again. Though why he kept insisting on shouting her name was a mystery as clearly she was looking at him and just as clearly he was looking directly at her. Around her, conversation died, the rattle of china and silverware stilled.

"I think that young man is hailing you, Ginny," Mrs. Throckmorton said helpfully.

"Hm." They had corresponded freely over the last five months. His letters had been brief, initially to know if she was pregnant—she wasn't—and then castigating the English legal system for "its ineptitude in regards to inheritance law." Her letters had been more loquacious. And far more genteel.

"Good heavens," she heard one of the young English misses whisper. "It's him. It's Avandale!"

"Are you listening, Ginesse?" Jim shouted.

Mrs. Throckmorton nodded encouragingly.

"Yes," she called back, trying to hold on to her sense of decorum. But he looked magnificent, so imperious and…dukely.

"Excellent," he replied. The stallion danced beneath him. "I love you. Madly, passionately, devotedly, eternally. Marry me."

She should have been satisfied. She should just stay quiet, but that had never been her way, and alas, a part of her sadly recognized even as the words were forming, it never would be.

"If you love me so much, where have you been for the last thirty-six hours?" she demanded, standing up from the table.

Good *Lord* he was handsome. He was grinning like a very devil now, as if her temper not only amused but delighted him. The stallion moved toward the stairs. What was he doing?

"Why are you smiling like that?" she demanded.

"Because for a moment there I thought someone had switched my adored *afreet* for a pallid English gentlewoman."

Ginesse glanced down at Mrs. Throckmorton. "Did he just insult me? I think I have just been insulted," she said.

"No, dear," said Mrs. Throckmorton, "I think I have."

The stallion began mounting the short flight of steps leading into Shepheard's. Alarmed guests flew before the beautiful animal's measured progress. Riyad came rushing out of the front, waving his hands. "You cannot bring that horse up here!"

"What are you doing?" Ginesse demanded. "You are disturbing these good people."

"I am coming to claim my bride," he said calmly. The horse turned at the top of the steps, moving onto the balcony.

Her eyes grew wide. He wouldn't dare. "You didn't answer my question. Where have you been if you are so eager to marry me?"

"Oh. All those things necessary when one marries," he said amiably, edging his horse carefully amongst the linen-covered tables to a choir of muffled shrieks and astonished whispers and Riyad's loud admonitions. "License, the interview with the father—and by the way, my jaw wasn't broken after all, and he seemed genuinely glad of it—letting an apartment, getting the once-over from the future brothers-in-law, and let me tell you, young Thorne drinks like a fish, finding servants. That sort of thing."

He was almost to her now, and she found herself backing up before his advance. "And you could not find any time in which to come and see me?" she asked.

"If I had, I wouldn't have left you," he returned with such obvious meaning that the ladies on the balcony commenced tittering like a flock of little birds and the men cleared their throats uncomfortably.

"I never will again," he said, his easy air abruptly vanishing, replaced by a tone of such ardency, such constancy and devotion that her breath caught in her throat. She stopped backing up.

"I am no good without you, Ginesse," he said. "I spent a lifetime alone, but I never understood loneliness until I was away from you. I never understood happiness until I saw you again."

He looked up into her eyes, his own as warm and soft as fresh ashes. "I love you, Ginesse. God alone knows how much I love you. So put me out of my misery. Say you'll marry me. Because I cannot stand to live another moment without you."

"Oh, Lord, love, if you don't I will," yelped a woman from somewhere behind her.

"Say yes!" whispered one of the English misses.

But Ginesse simply held out her arms, and the next thing she knew she was being swept up onto the stallion's back and into Jim's arms. Where she belonged.

His handsome face broke into a wide grin of triumph and elation and love. He gathered her close and whispered, "Hold on tight; don't let go."

And touching his heels to the stallion, he sent them flying over the balcony rail. The guests on the balcony rushed to the rail, laughing and shouting their approval as James Tynesborough, Duke of Avandale, gathered his bride close against him, turning his stallion's head. "Is that romantic enough, my love?"

"Oh, yes," she breathed, adding with a glint of humor, "but shouldn't we be riding off into the sunset?"

He laughed. "But that only happens at the end of the story, my love," he said, touching his heels to the stallion and sending him forward into the sunrise. "And this, this is just the beginning."

EPILOGUE

"The obvious reason the ibis mummies were the only thing Ginny saw in the tomb was because they had been purposely left behind," Sir Robert said, pressing a finger along his nose and contriving to look mysterious. "The question remains why? Find the answer to that and you will find Zerzura."

He peered over his gold-rimmed spectacles at his captive audience. Lord Geoffrey and Haji Elkamal were seated across the wrought iron table from him on the front terrace of the Avandales' recently renovated farmhouse where the Duke and Duchess of Avandale had decided to reside. They had sold their Mayfair property after the dowager duchess died the previous year, falling down stone steps leading to the Thames. An eyewitness reported the old lady had been trying to kick a stray cat.

And who could blame them for selling it? The Mayfair property had been a cold, unwelcoming place, and the farm was warm and lovely, especially on such a beautiful autumn day. The sun shone in a robin's-egg blue sky, and a soft breeze ruffled late-blooming wildflowers in the meadow, where a pair of Arabian yearlings played a game of tag. The last diadems of morning dew sparkled in the shade of the magnificent beech tree sheltering

357

the old stone farmhouse, and a spotted spaniel lurked hopefully under the table.

It was a beautiful day but, alas, not a quiet one. A half dozen boys ranging in age from eight to twenty-two, all bearing a pronounced resemblance to one another, had been playing a game called baseball that their brother-in-law, the Duke of Avandale, had introduced them to.

A questionable call at the home plate had resulted in a heap of swinging fists and general mayhem that required paternal intervention. With a long-suffering sigh, Harry Braxton rose from the hammock in which he'd been blissfully swinging and went to extricate the smallest combatants from the pile. The older ones he would let suffer the consequences of hot tempers—though there was, to Harry's mind, seldom anywhere near enough suffering to balance the gleeful triumph with which his sons sported black eyes and fat lips.

"Mind you get Edward, too!" Dizzy Braxton called out from where she was sharing a blanket with her daughter, youngest son, and granddaughter. "That's a new shirt he's wearing, and I won't have blood on it!"

"Your wish, my command," Harry said, dutifully plucking twelve-year-old Edward from the heap of wrestling, squirming males.

"Ah, Dad!" protested Edward, his budding masculinity affronted.

"Just take your shirt off," Harry suggested, winning a grin from his son, who at once shed the culpable garment and dove back into the fray. Harry looked down at sons number five and six and advised them to head to the stables to wash up, then went to join his wife.

"Where's Avandale?" he asked, settling his tall, lean frame next to Dizzy.

The Duchess of Avandale looked up from where she had been blowing noisily against the bare, plump tummy of her two-year-old daughter, Poppy. "He'll be up soon. He was hoping to get up on Afreet today."

Afreet was their two-year-old filly, a gorgeous and capricious sorrel, the first of the Avandale Arabian bloodlines.

"I could use some help keeping your brothers from killing one another."

"I say let them have at it. Keep the bloodline strong. Last man standing and all that. Right, Poppy?" Ginny said with a mischievous grin and buried her face into her daughter's tummy again, eliciting gales of laughter.

"I'll be the last one," declared Daniel, Poppy's five-year-old uncle and Harry and Dizzy's youngest.

"Not if I eat you first!" said Ginny, grabbing his leg and hauling him toward her, shrieking with joy.

"Don't eat Danny. He's the only one who Poppy listens to," a male voice called out.

At the sound, Ginny straightened, her eyes lighting up as she caught sight of Jim, bareback atop Afreet. She sprang to her feet, her hair, already loosened in play, tumbling free down her back.

"You've done it!" she exclaimed, her voice rife with admiration, her appreciative gaze traveling over her husband's lean, athletic physique, his white shirt open at the throat, his sleeves rolled up over his forearms, his trousers molding to his long, muscular thighs. "Oh, Jim!"

"Don't misunderstand me, Dizzy," said Harry, sotto voce to Dizzy. "Avandale is a more than adequate rider, but Ginny tends to exaggerate his skills."

"I don't think so, Harry," Dizzy answered with such blithe assurance that her husband frowned. "I believe he is every bit as skilled as she believes him to be. You are simply going to have to accept that the young man is better at something than you."

"No, I don't," replied Harry. "I shall valiantly continue on in my self-delusion. If you truly loved me, you would support me in my fantasy."

"But darling, there are any number of fantasies I'd much rather support you in," Dizzy said, earning a look of such warmth from her husband that her cheeks turned as pink as when she was a girl under his ardent gaze.

"Show off!" Ginny called to her husband with a light laugh. "You know you are dying to!"

With a grin, Jim effortlessly set the filly through her paces, from passage trot to canter to gallop and back. Effortlessly, the youngster switched leads, her gaits as fluid as silk floating on water, her mane streaming back in the soft autumn air, her coat glistening like a starry night, responding instantly to the gentlest pressure of his calf.

When they were done, Jim moved her close to where his wife stood, her expression rapt. His gaze roved ardently over her face, touching her lush lips, her tumbled hair, the bare feet peeking from beneath her light skirt.

"I think your mother wants to go for a ride, my darling," Jim said to Poppy, though his gaze was on Ginesse. He held a hand out toward her.

She had never been able to refuse him. "Will you mind Poppy, Mom?" she asked.

Dizzy smiled knowingly at her husband. "Of course."

Ginesse lifted her arms and was swept into Jim's warm embrace and felt her heart start beating in a wild, untamed response.

"Ready?" he whispered in her ear.

She nodded, the old excitement rising anew as the filly broke into a gallop.

"Hold on tight, Mama!" Poppy shouted gleefully after her parents. "Don't ever let go!"

And she never did.

AUTHOR'S NOTE

I've said it before, I'll say it again: one of the most fun things about being an author is all the stuff you discover while on the hunt. The problem is avoiding "over-sharing" with the reader. As remarkable as it might seem, some people do not care that the first tube flashlight, patented before 1905, was made out of cardboard or that the expression "Give me a break!" was then in common usage.

But for those of you who do and have questions about veracity of the history in this book (or whether a word was anachronistic), I can only assure you that like the *National Inquirer*, I checked, rechecked, and checked again. Which means, of course, there are going to be kerfuffles.

Now some of these mistakes I'm just going to flat out admit to having made consciously and with full volition. To wit: In 1900, the English army would not have considered stationing men at a desert fort in southwestern Egypt, nor is there any oasis in that area which could support one. In fact, the topography I describe doesn't exist there. However, the huge plateau that Ginesse and her explorers find the very terminus end of does exist. It is called the Gilf el Kebir and can be found at the longitude I suggest.

The huge (and I mean huge—it's roughly the size of Puerto Rico) plateau was first seen by a European, W. J. Harding King, in 1910. Its long, flat plains were used as an airbase by British troops in World War II. You can still find traces of them in the navigational arrows laid out in stone.

The Tuaregs, a nomadic tribe found primarily in modern-day Libya, were, in fact, slavers until French occupiers banned the trade in 1910. But the Tuaregs would not have been in Egypt— ergo the device of having them enter the country to buy an Arabian horse.

And speaking of Arabians, in the late 1870s almost the entire population of Arabian horses in Egypt was wiped out by the African horse disease epidemic. Ardent devotees of the breed, from many different countries, united to preserve bloodlines that may well have been lost otherwise.

Another place where I took rampant liberties was with poor old Cambridge. They did not accept female students, nor did they offer degrees in ancient history. But in the best of worlds they would have, and as a romance author, the "best of worlds" is my special jurisdiction.

Language, especially slang, presents its own challenges. Especially when you are dealing with two different cultures. Slang used by Brits was not the same as that employed by Americans. While finding usage for single words is relatively easy, finding the first usage for phrases can prove challenging. Where it was impossible to chase down a date, I made informed choices. But many of the words I employed were in popular use like "puppy love," "floozy," "ramrod," and "take a stab at." If you're an etymologist, you probably already own *English Through the Ages* by William Brohaugh. Even if you're just casually interested, I highly recommend it.

Now, about how Ginesse found Zerzura: I'm sure there will be some readers out there casting a jaundiced eye at my device of having Ginesse drop through the sand into the heart of Zerzura. But that's pretty much how Queen Hetepheres's tomb was found.

In 1925, a photographer setting up to take pictures of the pyramids dinged the ceiling of the staircase leading to the tomb with his tripod.

Finally, Zerzura. A lost city described by the various titles I used in the book has been rumored for centuries. Its location and history are vague, and speculation has ranged from it being simply a caravan outpost to its being a colony of lost crusaders. While there has never been any definitive evidence supporting its existence, many explorers have searched for it, primarily in the location I have described. Which means it's still out there, waiting to be discovered...

ABOUT THE AUTHOR

Photograph by Heidi Ehalt

USA Today and *New York Times* bestselling author Connie Brockway published her first novel, *Promise Me Heaven*, in 1994, and has since written eighteen novels and several anthology stories. Her books have been published in fifteen countries and earned her starred reviews and unqualified recommendations from *Publishers Weekly*, *Library Journal*, and *Booklist*. She is an eight-time finalist and two-time winner of the Romance Writers of America's prestigious RITA award. A regular speaker at both the national and regional level, when she is not traveling, Brockway enjoys reading, gardening, tennis, and cooking. She lives in Minnesota with her husband, David, a family physician, and their two spoiled mutts.